THE GRANDMOTHERS

THE GRANDMOTHERS

FOUR SHORT NOVELS

Doris Lessing

This Large Print book is published by BBC Audiobooks Ltd, Bath, England and by Thorndike Press®, Waterville, Maine, USA.

Published in 2005 in the U.K. by arrangement with HarperCollins Publishers.

Published in 2005 in the U.S. by arrangement with HarperCollins Publishers Inc.

U.K. Hardcover ISBN 1–4056–1088–3 (Windsor Large Print)
U.K. Softcover ISBN 1–4056–2076–5 (Paragon Large Print)
U.S. Softcover ISBN 0–7862–7222–8 (General)

These short novels are entirely works of fiction. The names, characters and incidents portrayed in them are the work of the author's imagination. Any resemblance to actual persons, living or dead, events or localities, is entirely coincidental.

The text of this Large Print edition is unabridged.
Other aspects of the book may vary from the original edition.

Set in 16 pt. New Times Roman.

Printed in Great Britain on acid-free paper.

British Library Cataloguing in Publication Data available

Library of Congress Cataloging-in-Publication Data

Lessing, Doris May, 1919–
[Novels, Selections]
The grandmothers ; Victoria and the Staveneys ; The reason for it ; A love child / Doris Lessing.
p. cm.
ISBN 0–7862–7222–8 (lg. print : sc : alk. paper)
1. Large type books. I. Title.

PR6023.E833G69 2005
823'.914—dc22 2004060614

CONTENTS

THE GRANDMOTHERS

On either side of a little promontory loaded with cafés and restaurants was a frisky but decorous sea, nothing like the real ocean that roared and rumbled outside the gape of the enclosing bay and barrier rocks known by everyone—and it was even on the charts—as Baxter's Teeth. Who was Baxter? A good question, often asked, and answered by a framed sheet of skilfully antiqued paper on the wall of the restaurant at the end of the promontory, the one in the best, highest and most prestigious position. Baxter's, it was called, claiming that the inner room of thin brick and reed had been Bill Baxter's shack, built by his own hands. He had been a restless voyager, a seaman who had chanced on this paradise of a bay with its little tongue of rocky land. Earlier versions of the tale hinted at pacific and welcoming natives. Where did the Teeth come into it? Baxter remained an inveterate explorer of nearby shores and islands, and then, having entrusted himself to a little leaf of a boat built out of driftwood and expertise, he was wrecked one moony night on those seven black rocks, well within the sight of his little house where a storm lantern, as reliable as a lighthouse, welcomed in ships small enough to get into the bay, having negotiated the reef.

Baxter's was now well planted with big trees that sheltered tables and attendant chairs, and on three sides below was the friendly sea.

A path wandered up through shrubs, coming to a stop in Baxter's Gardens, and one afternoon six people were making the gentle ascent, four adults and two little girls, whose shrieks of pleasure echoed the noises of the gulls.

Two handsome men came first, not young, but only malice could call them middle-aged. One limped. Then two as handsome women of about sixty—but no one would dream of calling them elderly. At a table evidently well-known to them, they deposited bags and wraps and toys, sleek and shining people, as they are who know how to use the sun. They arranged themselves, the women's brown and silky legs ending in negligent sandals, their competent hands temporarily at rest. Women on one side, men on the other, the little girls fidgeting: six fair heads? Surely they were related? Those had to be the mothers of the men; they had to be their sons. The little girls, clamouring for the beach, which was down a rocky path, were told by their grandmothers, and then their fathers, to behave and play nicely. They squatted and made patterns with fingers and little sticks in the dust. Pretty little girls: so they should be with such good-looking progenitors.

From a window of Baxter's a girl called to them, 'The usual? Shall I bring your usual?' One of the women waved to her, meaning yes. Soon appeared a tray where fresh fruit juices and wholemeal sandwiches asserted that these were people careful of their health.

Theresa, who had just taken her school-leaving exams, was on her year away from England, where she would be returning to university. This information had been offered months ago, and in return she was kept up to date with the progress of the little girls at their first school. Now she enquired how school was going along, and first one child and then the other piped up to say their school was cool. The pretty waitress ran back to her station inside Baxter's with a smile at the two men which made the women smile at each other and then at their sons, one of whom, Tom, remarked, 'But she'll never make it back to Britain, all the boys are after her to stay.'

'More fool her if she marries and throws all that away,' said one of the women, Roz—in fact Rozeanne, the mother of Tom. But the other woman, Lil (or Liliane), the mother of Ian, said, 'Oh, I don't know,' and she was smiling at Tom. This concession, or compliment, to their, after all, claim to existence, made the men nod to each other, lips compressed, humorously, as at an often-heard exchange, or one like it.

'Well,' said Roz, 'I don't care, nineteen is

too young.'

'But who knows how it might turn out?' enquired Lil, and blushed. Feeling her face hot she made a little grimace, which had the effect of making her seem naughty, or daring, and this was so far from her character that the others exchanged looks not to be explained so easily.

They all sighed, heard each other and now laughed, a full frank laugh that seemed to acknowledge things unsaid. One little girl, Shirley, said, 'What are you laughing at?' and the other, Alice, 'What's so funny? I don't see anything funny,' and copied her grandmother's look of conscious naughtiness, which in fact had not been intended. Lil was uncomfortable and blushed again.

Shirley persisted, wanting attention, 'What's the joke, Daddy?' and at this both daddies began a tussling and buffeting of their daughters, while the girls protested, and ducked, but came back for more, and then fled to their grandmothers' arms and laps for protection. There they stayed, thumbs in their mouths, eyes drooping, yawning. It was a hot afternoon.

A scene of somnolence and satisfaction. At tables all around under the great trees similarly blessed people lazed. The seas all around them, only a few feet below, sighed and hissed and lapped, and the voices were low and lazy.

From the window of Baxter's Theresa stood with a tray of cool drinks momentarily suspended and looked out at the family. Tears slid down her cheeks. She had been in love with Tom and then Ian, and then Tom again, for their looks and their ease, and something, an air of repletion, as if they had been soaking in pleasure all their lives and now gave it out in the form of invisible waves of contentment.

And then the way they handled the little girls, the ease and competence of that. And the way the grandmothers were always available, making the four the six . . . but where were the mothers, children had mothers, and these two little girls had Hannah and Mary, both startlingly unlike the blonde family they had married into, being small and dark, and, while pretty enough, Theresa knew neither of them was good enough for the men. They worked. They owned a business. That is why the grandmothers were so often here. Didn't the grandmothers work, then? Yes, they did but were free to say, 'Let's go to Baxter's'—and up here to Baxter's they came. The mothers too, sometimes, and there were eight.

Theresa was in love with them all. She had at last understood it. The men, yes, her heart ached for them, but not too severely. What made the tears come was seeing them all there, watching them, as she did now. Behind her, at a table near the bar, was Derek, a young farmer who had wished to marry her. She didn't mind him, rather fancied him, but she knew that this, the family, was the real passion.

Over deep layers of tree shadow lanced with sunlight, sun enclosed the tree, the hot blue air, interfused with bliss, happiness, seemed about to exude great drops of something like a golden dew, which only she could see. It was at that moment she decided she would marry her farmer and stay here, on this continent. She could not leave it for the fitful charms of England, of Bradford, though the moors did well enough, when the sun did decide to shine. No, she would stay here, she had to. 'I want it, I want it,' she told herself, allowing the tears at last to run freely. She wanted this physical ease, the calm of it, expressing itself in lazy movements, in long brown legs and arms, and the glint of gold on fair heads where the sun had been.

Just as she claimed her future, she saw one of the mothers coming up the path. Mary—yes, it was. A little dark fidget of a woman, with nothing in her of the poise and style of The Family.

She was coming up slowly. She stopped, stared, went on, stopped, and she was moving with a deliberation that was willed.

'Well, what's got into *her*, I wonder?' mused Theresa, at last leaving her window to take the tray to by now surely impatient customers.

Mary Struthers was hardly moving at all. She stood staring at her family, frowning. Roz Struthers saw her and waved, and then again, and while her hand slowly lowered itself, as if caution had made an announcement, her face was already beginning to lose its gloss and glow. She was looking, but as it were indirectly, at her daughter-in-law, and because of what her face was saying, her son Tom turned to look, then wave. Ian, too, waved. Both men's hands fell, as Roz's had done; there was fatality in it.

Mary had stopped. Near her was a table and she collapsed into a chair. Still she stared at Lil, and then at Tom, her husband. From one face to the other those narrowed accusing eyes moved. Eyes that searched for something. In her hand was a packet. Letters. She sat perhaps ten feet away, staring.

Theresa, having dealt with her other tables, was in her window again, and she was thinking accusing thoughts about Mary, this wife of a son, and she knew it was jealousy. She defended herself thus: But if she was good enough for them, I wouldn't mind her. She's just nothing compared to them.

Only the eye of jealousy could have dismissed Mary, who was a striking, attractive, dark young woman. She wasn't pretty now; her face was small and putty-coloured and her lips were thin. Theresa saw the bundle of letters. She saw the four people at the table. As if they were playing statues, she thought. Light was draining away from them. The splendid afternoon might be brazening it all out but they sat struck, motionless. And still Mary stared, now at Lil, or Liliane, now at Roz or Rozeanne; from them to Tom, and to Ian, and then around again, and again.

From an impulse Theresa did not recognise in herself she poured water from the jug in the fridge into a glass, and ran across with it to Mary. Mary did turn her head slowly to frown into Theresa's face, but did not take the glass. Theresa set it down. Then Mary was attracted by the glitter of the water, reached out her hand for the glass, but withdrew it: her hand was shaking too hard to hold a glass.

Theresa went back to her window. The afternoon had gone dark for her. She was trembling too. What was the matter? What was wrong? Something was horribly, fatally wrong.

At last Mary got up, with difficulty, made the distance to the table where her family sat, and let herself subside into a chair that was away from them: she was not part of them.

Now the four were taking in that bundle of letters in Mary's hand.

They sat quite still, looking at Mary. Waiting.

It was for her to speak. But did she need to? Her lips trembled, she trembled, she appeared to be on the verge of a faint, and those young clear accusing eyes moved still from one face to another. Tom. Lil. Roz. Ian. Her mouth was twisted, as if she had bitten into something sour.

'What's wrong with them, what's wrong?' thought Theresa, staring from her window, and whereas not an hour ago she had decided she could never leave this coast, this scene of pleasantness and plenitude, now she thought, I must get away. I'll tell Derek, no. I want to get out.

Alice, the child on Roz's lap, woke with a cry, saw her mother there, 'Mummy, Mummy,'—and held out her arms. Mary managed to get up, steadied herself around the table on the backs of chairs, and took Alice.

Now it was the other little girl, waking on Lil's lap, 'Where's my mummy?'

Mary held out her hand for Shirley and in a moment both children were on her knees.

The little girls felt Mary's panic, her anger, sensed some kind of fatality, and now tried to get back to their grandmothers. 'Granny, Granny', 'I want granny.'

Mary gripped them both tight.

On Roz's face was a small bitter smile, as if she exchanged confirmation of some bad news with someone deep inside herself.

'Granny, are you coming to fetch me tomorrow for the beach?'

And Alice, 'Granny, you promised we would

go to the beach.'

And now Mary spoke at last, her voice shaking. All she said was, 'No, you will not be going to the beach.' And, direct to the older women, 'You will not be taking Shirley and Alice to the beach.' That was the judgement and the sentence.

Lil said tentatively, even humbly, 'I'll see you soon, Alice!'

'No you won't,' said Mary. She stood up, a child on either hand, the bundle of letters thrust into the pocket of her slacks. 'No,' she said wildly, the emotion that had been poisoning her at last pulsing out. 'No. No, you won't. Not ever. You will not ever see them again.'

She turned to go, pulling the children with her.

Her husband Tom said, 'Wait a minute, Mary.'

'No.' Off she went down the path, as fast as she could, stumbling and pulling the children along.

And now surely these four remaining, the women and their sons, should say something, elucidate, make things clear? Not a word. Pinched, diminished, darkened, they sat on, and then at last one spoke. It was Ian who spoke, direct to Roz, in a passionate intimacy, wild-eyed, his lips stiff and angry.

'It's your fault,' he said. 'Yes, it's your fault. I told you. It's all your fault this has happened.'

Roz met his anger with her own. She laughed. A hard angry bitter laugh, peal after peal. 'My fault,' she said. 'Of course. Who else?' And she laughed. It would have done well on the stage, that laugh, but tears poured down her face.

Out of sight down the path, Mary had reached Hannah, the wife of Ian, who had been unable to face the guilty ones, at least not with Mary, whose rage she could not match. She had let Mary go up by herself and she waited here, full of doubt, misery and reproaches that were beginning to bubble up wanting to overflow. But not in anger, no, she needed explanations. She took Shirley from Mary, and the two young women, their children in their arms, stood together on the path, just outside a plumbago hedge that was the boundary for another café. They did not speak, but looked into each other's faces, Hannah seeking confirmation, which she got. 'It's true, Hannah.'

And now, the laughter. Roz was laughing. The peals of hard laughter, triumphant laughter, was what Mary and Hannah heard, each harsh loud peal lashed them, they shrank away from the cruel sounds. They trembled as the whips of laughter fell.

'Evil,' Mary pronounced at last, through lips that seemed to have become dough or clay. And as Roz's final yells of laughter reached them, the two young women burst into tears and went running away down the path, away from their husbands, and their husbands' mothers.

* * *

Two little girls arrived at the big school on the same day, at the same hour, took each other's measure, and became best friends. Little things, so bravely confronting that great school, as populous and busy as a supermarket, but filled with what they already knew were hierarchies of girls they felt as hostile, but here was an ally, and they stood holding hands, trembling with fear and their efforts to be brave. A great school, standing on its rise, surrounded by parkland in the English manner, but arched over by a most un-English sky, about to absorb these little things, babies really, their four parents thought—enough to bring tears to their eyes!—and they did.

They were doughty, quick with repartee, and soon lived down the bullying that greeted new girls; they stood up for each other, fought their own and each other's battles. 'Like sisters,' people said, and even, 'Like twins.' Fair, they were, with their neat gleaming ponytails, both of them, and blue-eyed, and as quick as fishes, but really, if you looked, not so alike. Lilian—or Lil—was thin, with a hard little body, her features delicate, and

Rozeanne—Roz—was sturdier, and where Lil regarded the world with a pure severe gaze, Roz found jokes in everything. But it is nice to think, and say, 'like sisters', 'they might be twins'; it is agreeable to find resemblances where perhaps none are, and so it went on, through the school terms and the years, two girls, inseparable, which was nice for their families, living in the same street, with parents who had become friends because of them, as so often happens, knowing they were lucky in their girls choosing each other and making lives easy for everyone.

But these lives were easy. Not many people in the world have lives so pleasant, unproblematical, unreflecting: no one on these blessed coasts lay awake and wept for their sins, or for money, let alone for food. What a good-looking lot, smooth and shiny with sun, with sport, with good food. Few people anywhere know of coasts like these, except perhaps for brief holidays, or in travellers' tales like dreams. Sun and sea, sea and sun, and always the sound of waves on beaches.

It was a blue world the little girls grew up in. At the end of every street was the sea, as blue as their eyes—as they were told often enough. Over their heads the blue sky was so seldom louring or grey that such days were enjoyable for their rarity. A rare harsh wind brought the pleasant sting of salt and the air was always salty. The little girls would lick the salt from their own hands and arms and from each other's too, in a game they called, 'Playing puppies'. Bedtime baths were always salty so that they had to shower off the bath water with water coming from deep in the earth and tasting of minerals, not salt. When Roz stayed over at Lil's house, or Lil at Roz's, the parents would stand smiling down at the two pretty imps cuddled together like kittens or puppies, smelling now they were asleep not of salt but of soap. And always, throughout their childhoods, day and night, the sound of the sea, the gentle tamed waves of Baxter's sea, a hushing and a lulling, like breathing.

Sisters, or, for that matter, twins, even best friends, suffer passionate rivalries, often concealed, even from each other. But Roz knew how Lil grieved when her breasts—Roz's—popped forth a good year before Lil's, not to mention other evidences of growing up, and she was generous in assurances and comfort, knowing that her own deep envy of her friend was not going to be cured by time. She wished that her own body could be as hard and thin as Lil's, who wore her clothes with such style and ease, whereas she was already being called—by the unkind—plump. She had to be careful what she ate, whereas Lil could eat what she liked.

So there they were, quite soon, teenagers, Lil the athlete, excelling in every sport, and Roz in the school plays, with big parts, making people laugh, extrovert, large, vital, loud: they complemented each other as once they had been as like as two peas: 'You can hardly tell them apart.'

They both went to university, Lil because of the sport, Roz because of the theatre group, and they remained best friends, sharing news about their conquests, and making light of their rivalries, but their closeness was such that although they starred in such different arenas, their names were always coupled. Neither went in for the great excluding passions, broken hearts, jealousies.

And now that was it, university done with, here was the grown-up world, and this was a culture where girls married young. 'Twenty and still not married!'

Roz began dating Harold Struthers, an academic, and a bit of a poet, too; and Lil met Theo Western, who owned a sports equipment and clothes shop. Rather, shops. He was well off. The men got on—the women were careful that they did, and there was a double wedding.

So far so good.

Those shrimps, the silverfish, the minnows, were now wonderful young women, one in a wedding dress like an arum lily (Liliane) and Roz's like a silver rose. So judged the main fashion page of the big paper.

They lived in two houses in a street running down to the sea, not far from the outspit of land that held Baxter's, unfashionable but artistic, and, by that law that says if you want to know if an area is going up, then look to see if those early swallows, the artists, are moving in, it would not be unfashionable for long. They were on opposite sides of the street.

Lil was a swimming champion known over the whole continent and abroad too, and Roz not only acted and sang, but was putting on plays and began devising shows and spectacles. Both were very busy. Despite all this Liliane and Theo Western announced the birth of Ian, and Rozeanne and Harold Struthers followed within a week with Thomas.

Two little boys, fair-haired and delightful, and people said they could be brothers. In fact Toni was a solid little boy easily embarrassed by the exuberances of his mother, and Ian was fine drawn and nervy and 'difficult' in ways Tom never was. He did not sleep well, and sometimes had nightmares.

The two families spent weekends and holidays together, one big happy family, as Roz sang, defining the situation, and the two men might go off on trips into the mountains or to fish, or backpacking. Boys will be boys, as Roz said.

All this went on, and anything that was not what it should be was kept well out of sight. 'If it ain't broke, don't fix it,' Roz might say. She was concerned for Lil, for reasons that will emerge, but not for herself. Lil might have her problems, but not she, not she and Harold and

Tom. Everything was going along fine.

And then this happened.

The scene: the connubial bedroom, when the boys were about ten. Roz lay sprawling on the bed, Harold sat on the arm of a chair, looking at his wife, smiling, but determined. He had just said he had been offered a professorship, in a university in another state.

Roz said, 'Well, I suppose you can come down for weekends or we can come up!

This was so like her, the dismissal of a threat—surely?—to their marriage, that he gave a short, not unaffectionate laugh, and after a pause said, 'I want you and Tom to come too.'

'Move from *here*?' And Roz sat up shaking her fair and now curly head so that she could see him clearly. *'Move*?'

'Why don't you just say it? Move from Lil, that's the point, isn't it?'

Roz clasped her hands together on her upper chest, all theatrical consternation. But she was genuinely astounded, indignant. 'What are you suggesting?'

'I'm not suggesting. I'm saying. Strange as it may seem . . .'—This phrase usually signals strife—'I'd like a wife. A real one:

'You're mad.'

'No. I want you to watch something.' He produced a canister of film. 'Please, Roz. I mean it. I want you to come next door and watch this.'

Up got Roz, off the bed, all humorous protest.

She was all but nude. With a deep sigh, aimed at the gods, or some impartial viewer, she put on a pink feathered negligee, salvaged from a play's wardrobe: she had felt it was so *her.*

She sat in the next room, opposite a bit of white wall kept clear of clutter. 'And now what are you up to, I wonder?' she said, amiably. 'You big booby, Harold. *Really,* I mean, I ask you!'

Harold began running the film—home movies. It was of the four of them, two husbands, the two women. They had been on the beach, and wore wraps over bikinis. The men were still in their swimming trunks. Roz and Lil sat on the sofa, this sofa, where Roz now was, and the men were in hard upright chairs, sitting forward to watch. The women were talking. What about? Did it matter? They were watching each other's faces, coming in quickly to make a point. The men kept trying to intervene, join in, the women literally did not hear them. Harold, then Theo, was annoyed, and they raised their voices, but the women still did not hear, and when at last the men shouted, insisting, Roz put out a hand to stop them.

Roz remembered the discussion, just. It was not important. The boys were to go to a friend's for a weekend camp. The parents were discussing it, that was all. In fact the mothers were discussing it, the fathers might just as well not have been there.

The men had been silenced, sat watching and even exchanged looks. Harold was annoyed, but Theo's demeanour said only, '*Women, what do you expect*?'

And then, that subject disposed of the boys—Roz said, 'I simply must tell you . . .' and leaned forward to tell Lil, dropping her voice, not knowing she did this, telling her something, nothing important.

The husbands sat and watched, Harold all alert irony, Theo bored.

It went on. The tape ran out.

'Do you mean to say you actually filmed that—to trap me? You set it up, to get at me!'

'No, don't you remember? I had made a film of the boys on the beach. Then you took the camera and filmed me and Theo. And then Theo said, "How about the girls?" '

'Oh,' said Roz.

'Yes. It was only when I played it back later—yesterday, in fact, that I saw . . . Not that I was surprised. That's how it always is. It's you and Lil. Always!'

'What are you suggesting? Are you saying we're lezzies?'

'No. I'm not. And what difference would it make if you were?'

'I simply don't get it.'

'Obviously sex doesn't matter that much.

We have, I think, more than adequate sex, but it's not me you have the relationship with.'

Roz sat, all twisted with emotion, wringing her hands, the tears ready to start.

'And so I want you to come with me up north.'

'You must be mad.'

'Oh, I know you won't, but you could at least pretend to think about it.'

'Are you suggesting we divorce?'

'I wasn't, actually. If I found a woman who put me first then . . .'

'You'd let me know!' she said, all tears at last.

'Oh, Roz,' said her husband. 'Don't think I'm not sorry. I'm fond of you, you know that. I'll miss you like crazy. You're my pal. And you're the best lay I'm ever likely to have and I know that too. But I feel like a sort of shadow here. I don't matter. That's all.'

And now it was his turn to blink away tears and then put his hands up to his eyes. He went back to the bedroom, lay down on the bed, and she joined him. They comforted each other. 'You're mad, Harold, do you know that? I love you.' 'And I love you too Roz, don't think that I don't.'

Then Roz asked Lil to come over, and the two women watched the film, without speaking, to its end.

'And that's why Harold is leaving me,' said Roz, who had told Lil the outlines of the situation.

'I don't see it,' said Lil at last, frowning with the effort of trying.

She was deadly serious, and Roz serious but smiling and angry.

'Harold says my real relationship is with you, not with him.'

'What does he want, then?' asked Lil.

'He says you and I made him feel excluded.'

'*He* feel excluded! I've always felt—left out. All these years I've been watching you and Harold and I've wished . . .' Loyalty had locked her tongue until this moment, but now she came out with it at last: 'I have a lousy marriage. I have a bad time with Theo. I've never . . . but you knew. And you and Harold, always so happy . . . I don't know how often I've left you two here and gone home with Theo and wished . . .'

'I didn't know . . . I mean, I did know, of course, Theo isn't the ideal husband.'

'You can say that again.'

'It seems to me it's you who should be getting a divorce.'

'Oh, no, no,' said Lil, warding off the idea with an agitated hand. 'No; I once said in joke to Ian—testing him out, what he'd think if I got a divorce and he nearly went berserk. He was silent for such a long time—you know how he goes silent, and then he shouted and began crying. "You can't," he said. "You can't. I won't let you." '

'So poor Tom is going to be without a father,' said Roz.

'And Ian doesn't have much of one,' said Lil. And then, when it could seem the conversation was at an end, she enquired, 'Roz, did Harold say that we are lezzies?'

'All but—well no, not exactly.'

'Is that what he meant?'

'I don't know. I don't think so.' Roz was suffering now with the effort of this unusual and unwonted introspection. 'I don't understand, I told him. I don't understand what you're on about.'

'Well, we aren't, are we?' enquired Lil, apparently needing to be told.

'Well, I don't think we are,' said Roz.

'We've always been friends, though.'

'Yes.'

'When did it start? I remember the first day at school.'

'Yes.'

'But before that? How did it happen?'

'I can't remember. Perhaps it was just—luck.'

'You can say that again. The luckiest thing in my life—you.'

'Yes,' said Roz. 'But that doesn't make us . . . Bloody men,' she said, suddenly energetic and brisk with anger.

'Bloody men,' said Lil, with feeling, because of her husband.

This note, obligatory for that time, having

been struck, the conversation was over.

Off went Harold to his university which was surrounded, not by ocean and sea winds and the songs and tales of the sea, but by sand, scrub and thorns. Roz visited him, and then returned there to put on *Oklahoma!*—a great success—and they enjoyed their more than adequate sex. She said, 'I don't see what you're complaining about,' and he said, 'Well, no, you wouldn't, would you?' When he came down to visit her and the boys—who being always together were always referred to in the plural—nothing seemed to have changed. As a family they went about, the amiable Harold and the exuberant Roz, a popular young couple—perhaps not so young now—as described often in the gossip columns. For a marriage that had been given its notice to quit the two seemed no less of a couple. As they jested—jokes had never been in short supply—they were like those trees whose centre has rotted away, or the bushes spreading from the centre, which disappear as its suburbs spring up. It was so hard for this couple to fray apart. Everywhere they went, his old pupils greeted him and people who had been involved in one of her productions greeted her. They were Harold and Roz to hundreds of people. 'Do you remember me—Roz, Harold?' She always did and Harold knew his old pupils. Like Royalty who expect of themselves that they remember faces and names. 'The Struthers are separating? Oh, come on! I don't believe it.'

And now the other couple, no less in the limelight, Lil always judging swimming or running or other sports events, bestowing prizes, making speeches. And there too was the handsome husband, Theo, known for the chain of sports equipment and clothes shops. The two lean, good-looking people, on view, like their friends, the other couple, but so different in style. Nothing excessive or exuberant about them, they were affable. smiling, available, the very essence of good citizenship.

The break-up of Roz and Harold did not disrupt Theo and Lil. The marriage had been a façade for years. Theo had a succession of girls, but, as he complained, he couldn't get into his bed anywhere without finding a girl in it: he travelled a lot, for the firm.

Then Theo was killed in a car crash, and Lil was a well-off widow, with her boy Ian, the moody one, so unlike Tom, and in that seaside town, where the climate and the style of living put people so much on view, there were two women, without men, and their two little boys.

The young couple with their children: interesting that, the turning point, the moment of change. For a time, seen, commented on, a focus, the young parents, by definition sexual beings, and tagging along or running around them the pretty children. 'Oh, what a lovely little boy, what a pretty little girl, What's your name?—what a nice name!'—and then all at once, or so it seems, the parents, no longer quite so young, seem to lose height a little, even to shrink, they certainly lose colour and lustre. 'How old did you say he is, she is . . .' The young ones are shooting up and glamour has shifted its quarters. Eyes are following them, rather than the parents. 'They do grow up so fast these days, don't they?'

The two good-looking women, together again as if men had not entered their equation at all, went about with the two beautiful boys, one rather delicate and poetic with sun-burnished locks falling over his forehead, and the other strong and athletic, friends, as their mothers had been at that age. There was a father in the picture, Harold, up north, but he'd shacked up with a young woman who presumably did not suffer from Roz's deficiencies. He came to visit, and stayed in Roz's house, but not in the bedroom (which had to strike both partners as absurd), and Tom visited him in his university. But the reality was, two women in their mid-thirties, and two lads who were not far off being young men. The houses, so close, opposite each other, seemed to belong to both families. 'We are an extended family,' cried Roz, not one to let a situation remain undefined.

The beauty of young boys—now, that isn't an easy thing. Girls, yes, full of their enticing eggs, the mothers of us all, that makes sense, they should be beautiful and usually are, even if only for a year or a day. But boys—why? What for? There is a time, a short time, at about sixteen, seventeen, when they have a poetic aura. They are like young gods. Their families and their friends may be awed by these beings who seem visitors from a finer air. They are often unaware of it, seeming to themselves more like awkwardly packed parcels they are trying to hold together.

Roz and Lil lolled on the little verandah overlooking the sea, and saw the two boys come walking up the path, frowning a little, dangling swimming things they would put to dry on the verandah wall, and they were so beautiful the two women sat up to look at each other, sharing incredulity. 'Good God!' said Roz. 'Yes,' said Lil. '*We* made that, *we* made them,' said Roz. 'If we didn't, who did?' said Lil. And the boys, having disposed of their towels and trunks, went past with smiles that indicated they were busy on their own affairs: they did not want to be summoned for food or to tidy their beds, or something equally unimportant.

'My God!' said Roz again. 'Wait, Lil . . .' She got up and went inside, and Lil waited, smiling a little to herself, as she often did, at her friend's dramatic ways. Out came Roz with a book in her hand, a photograph album. She pushed her chair against Lil's, and together they turned the pages past babies on rugs, babies in baths—themselves, then 'her first step' and 'the first tooth'—and they were at the page they knew they both sought. Two girls, at about sixteen.

'My God!' said Roz.

'We didn't do too badly, then,' said Lil.

Pretty girls, yes, very, all sugar and spice, but if photographs were taken now of Ian and Tom, would they show the glamour that stopped the breath when one saw them walk across a room or saunter up out of the waves?

They lingered over the pages of themselves, in this album, Roz's; Lil's would have to be the same. Photographs of Roz, with Lil. Two pretty girls.

What they were looking for they did not find. Nowhere could they find the shine of unearthliness that illuminated their two sons, at this time.

And there they were sitting, the album spread out across both their stretched-out brown legs—they were in bikinis—when the boys came out, glasses of fruit juice in their hands.

They sat on the wall of the verandah's edge and contemplated their mothers, Roz and Lil.

'What are they doing?' Ian seriously asked Tom.

'What are they doing?' echoed Tom, owlishly, joking as always. He jumped up, peered down at the open page, half on Roz's, half on Lil's knees, and returned to his place.

'They are admiring their beauty when they were nymphets,' he reported to Ian. 'Aren't you, Ma?' he said to Roz.

'That's right,' said Roz. 'Tempus fugit. It fugits like anything. You have no idea—yet. We wanted to find out what we were like all those years ago.'

'Not so many years,' said Lil.

'Don't bother to count,' said Roz. 'Enough years.'

Now Ian captured the album off the women's thighs, and he and Tom sat staring at the girls, their mothers.

'They weren't bad,' said Tom to Ian.

'Not bad at all,' said Ian to Tom.

The women smiled at each other: more of a grimace.

'But you are better now,' said Ian, and went red.

'Oh, you are charming,' said Roz, accepting the compliment for herself.

'I don't know,' said the clown, Tom, pretending to compare the old photographs with the two women sitting there, in their bikinis. 'I don't know. Now?—' and he screwed up his eyes for the examination. 'And then.' He bent to goggle at the photographs.

'Now has it,' he pronounced. 'Yes, better now.' And at this the two boys fell to foot-and-shoulder wrestling, or jostling, as they often still did, like boys, though what people saw were young gods who couldn't take a step or make a gesture that was not from some archaic vase, or antique dance.

'Our mothers,' said Tom, toasting them in orange juice.

'Our mothers,' said Ian, smiling directly at Roz in a way that made her shift about in her chair and move her legs.

Roz had said to Lil that Ian had a crush on her, Roz, and Lil had said, 'Well, never mind, he'll get over it.'

What Ian was not getting over, had not begun to get over, was his father's death, already a couple of years behind, in time. From the moment he had ceased to have a father he had pined, becoming thinner, almost transparent, so that his mother complained, 'Do eat, Ian, eat something—you must.'

'Oh, leave me alone.'

It was all right for Tom, whose father turned up sometimes, and whom he visited up there in his landlocked university. But Ian had nothing, not even warming memories. Where his father should have been, unsatisfactory as he had been with his affairs and his frequent absences, was nothing, a blank, and Ian tried to put a brave face on it, had bad dreams, and both women's hearts ached for him.

A big boy, his eyes heavy with crying, he would go to his mother, where she sat on a sofa, and collapse beside her, and she would put her arms around him. Or go to Roz, and she embraced him, 'Poor Ian.'

And Tom watched this, seriously, coming to terms with this grief, not his own, but its presence so close in his friend, his almost brother, Ian. 'They are like brothers,' people said. 'Those two, they might as well be brothers.' But in one a calamity was eating away, like a cancer, and not in the other, who tried to imagine the pain of grief and failed.

One night, Roz got up out of her bed to fetch herself a drink from the fridge. Ian was in the house, staying the night with Tom, as so often happened. He would use the second bed in Tom's room, or Harold's room, where he was now. Roz heard him crying and without hesitation went in to put her arms around him, cuddled him like a small boy, as after all she had been doing all his life. He went to sleep in her arms and in the morning his looks at her were demanding, hungry, painful. Roz was silent, contemplating the events of the night. She did not tell Lil what had happened. But what had happened? Nothing that had not a hundred times before. But it was odd. 'She didn't want to worry her!' Really? When had she ever been inhibited from telling Lil everything?

It happened that Tom was over at Lil's house, across the street, with Ian, for a couple of nights. Roz alone, telephoned Harold, and they had an almost connubial chat.

'How's Tom?'

'Oh, he's fine. Tom's always fine. But Ian's

not too good. He really is taking Theo's death hard.'

'Poor kid, he'll get over it.'

'He's taking his time, then. Listen, Harold, next time you come perhaps you could take out Ian by himself?'

'What about Tom?'

'Tom'd understand. He's worried about Ian, I know.'

'Right. I'll do that. Count on me.'

And Harold did come, and did take Ian off for a long walk along the sea's edge, and Ian talked to Harold, whom he had known all his life, more like a second father.

'He's very unhappy,' Harold reported to Roz and to Lil.

'I know he is,' said Lil.

'He thinks he's no good. He thinks he's a failure.'

The adults stared at this fact, as if it were something they could actually see.

'But how can you be a failure at seventeen?' said Lil.

'Did we feel like that?' asked Roz.

'I know I did,' said Harold. 'Don't worry.' And back he went to his desert university. He was thinking of getting married again. 'Okay,' said Roz. 'If you want a divorce.'

'Well, I suppose she'll want kids,' said Harold.

'Don't you know?'

'She's twenty-five,' said Harold. 'Do I have

to ask?'

'Ah,' said Roz, seeing it all. 'You don't want to put the idea into her head?' She laughed at him.

'I suppose so,' said Harold.

Then Ian was again spending the night with Tom. Rather, he was there at bedtime. He went off to Harold's room, and there was a quick glance at Roz, which she hoped Tom had not seen.

When she woke in the night, ready to go off to the fridge for a drink, or just to wander about the house in the dark, as she often did, she did not go, afraid of hearing Ian crying, afraid she would not be able to stop herself going into him. But then she found he had blundered through the dark into her room and was beside her, clutching at her like a lifebelt in a storm. And she actually found herself picturing those seven black rocks like rotten teeth in the black night out there, the waves pouring and dashing around them in white cascades of foam.

Next morning Roz was sitting at the table in the room that was open to the verandah, and the sea air, and the wash and hush and lull of the sea. Tom stumbled in fresh from his bed, the smell on him of youthful sleep. 'Where's Ian?' he asked. Normally he would not have asked: both boys could sleep until midday.

Roz stirred her coffee, around and around, and said, without looking at him, 'He's in my bed.'

This normally would not have merited much notice, since this extended family's casual ways could accommodate mothers and boys, or the women, or either boy with either woman, lying down for a rest or a chat, or the two boys, and, when he was around, Harold with any of them.

Tom stared at her over his still-empty plate.

Roz accepted that look, and her look back might as well have been a nod.

'Jesus!' said Tom.

'Exactly,' said Roz.

And then Tom ignored his plate and possible orange juice, leaped up, grabbed his swimming-trunks from the verandah wall, and he sprinted off down to the sea. Usually he would have yelled at Ian to go too.

Tom was not around that day. It was school holidays, but apparently he was off on some school holiday activity, generally scorned by him.

Lil was away, judging some sports competition, and was not back until evening. She came into Roz's house and said, 'Roz, I'm whacked. Is there anything to eat?'

Ian was at the table, sitting across from Roz but not looking at her. Tom had a plate of food in front of him. And now Tom began talking to Lil as if no one else was there. Lil scarcely noticed this, she was so tired, but the other two did. And he kept it up until the meal was over and Lil said she must go to bed, she was exhausted, and Tom simply got up and went with her into the dark.

Next morning, lateish for them all, Tom walked back across the street and found Roz at the table, in her usual careless, comfortable pose, her wrap loose about her. He did not look at her but all around her, at the room, the ceiling, through a delirium of happy accomplishment. Roz did not have to guess at his condition; she knew it, because Ian's similar state had been enveloping her all night.

Now Tom was prowling around the room, taking swipes as he passed at a chair arm, the table, a wall, returning to aim a punch at the chair next to hers, like a schoolboy unable to contain exuberance, but then standing to stare in front of him, frowning, thinking—like an adult. Then he whirled about and was close to his mother, all schoolboy, an embodied snigger, a leer. And then trepidation—he was not sure of himself, nor of his mother, who blushed scarlet, went white, and then got up and deliberately slapped him hard, this way, that way, across the face.

'Don't you dare,' she whispered, trembling with rage. 'How dare you . . .'

Half crouching, hands to his head, protecting it, he peered up at her, face distorted in what could have been a schoolboy's blubbering, but then he took command of himself, stood and said directly to her, 'I'm sorry,' though neither he nor she could have said exactly what it was he was sorry for, nor what he was not to dare. Not to let words, or his face, say what he had learned of women in the night just passed, with Lil?

He sat down, put his face in his hands, then leaped up, grabbed his swimming things and was off running into the sea, which this morning was a flat blue plate rimmed by the colourful houses of the enclosing arm of the bay opposite.

Tom did not come into his mother's house that day but made a detour back to Lil's. Ian slept late—nothing new in that. He, too, found it hard to look at her, but she knew it was the sight of her, so terribly familiar, so terribly and newly revelatory, it was too much, and so he snatched up his bundle of swimming things and was off. He did not come back until dark. She had done small tasks, made routine telephone calls, cooked, stood soberly scanning the house opposite, which showed no signs of life, and then, when Ian returned, made them both supper and they went back to bed, locking the house front and back—which was something not always remembered.

A week passed. Roz was sitting alone at the table with a cup of tea when there was a knock. She could not ignore it, she knew that, though she would have liked to stay inside this dream or enchantment that had so unexpectedly consumed her. She had dragged on jeans and a shirt, so she was respectable to look at, at least. She opened the door on the friendly, enquiring face of Saul Butler, who lived some doors along from Lil, and was their good neighbour. He was here because he fancied Lil and wanted her to marry him.

When he sat down and accepted tea, she waited.

'Haven't seen much of you lot recently, and I can't get any reply at Lil's.'

'Well, it's the school holidays.'

But usually she and the boys, Lil and the boys, would have been in and out, and often people waved at them from the street, where they all sat around the table.

'That boy, Ian, he needs a father,' he challenged her.

'Yes, he does,' she agreed at once; she had learned in the past week just how much the boy needed a father.

'I'm pretty sure I'd be a father to Ian—as much as he'd let me.'

Saul Butler was a well-set-up man of about fifty, not looking his age. He ran a chain of artists' equipment shops, paints, canvases, frames, all that kind of thing, and he knew Lil from working with her on the town's trade associations. Roz and Lil had agreed he would make a fine husband, if either of them had been looking for one.

She said, as she had before, 'Shouldn't you be saying this to Lil?'

'But I do. She must be sick of me—staking

my claim.'

'And you want me to support—your claim?'

'That's about it. I think I'm a pretty good proposition,' he said, smiling, mocking his own boasting.

'I think you'd be a good proposition too,' said Roz, laughing, enjoying the flirtation, if that was what it was. A week of love-making, and she was falling into the flirtatious mode as if into a bed. 'But that's no use is it, it's Lil you want.'

'Yes. I've had my eye on Lil for—a long time.' This meant, before his wife left him for another man. 'Yes. But she only laughs at me. Now, why is that, I wonder? I'm a very serious sort of chap. And where are the lads this morning?'

'Swimming, I suppose.'

'I only dropped in to make sure you are all getting along all right.' He got up, finished his tea standing, and said, 'See you on the beach.'

Off he went and Roz rang Lil, and said, 'We've got to be seen about a bit more. Saul dropped in.'

'I suppose so,' said Lil, her voice heavy, and low.

'We should be seen on the beach, all four of us.'

A hot morning. The sea shimmered off light. The sky was full of a light that could punish the eyes, without dark defending glasses. Lil and Roz, in loose wraps over their bikinis, slathered with suncream, made their way behind the boys to the beach. It was a well-used beach, but at this hour, on a weekday, there were few people. Two chairs, set close against Roz's fence, were faded and battered by storm and sun, but serviceable, and there the women sat themselves. The boys had gone running into the sea. Tom had scarcely greeted his mother; Ian's look at Lil slid off her and away.

The waves were brisk enough for pleasure, but in here, in the bay, were never big enough for surfing, which went on outside, past the Teeth. For all the years of the boys' childhood they played safe, on this beach, but now they saw it as good enough for a swim, and for the serious dangerous stuff they went out on to the surfers' beaches. The two were swimming well apart, ignoring each other, and the women's eyes were behind the secretive dark glasses, and neither wanted to talk—could not.

They saw a head like a seal's quite far out grow larger, and then it was Saul, and he came out of the sea, waving at them, but went up through the salty sea bushes and past the houses up to the street.

The boys were swimming in. When they reached the shallows they stood up and faced each other. They began to tussle. Thus had they fought all through their growing-up, boy fashion, but soon it was evident that there was nothing childlike about this fight. They were standing waist deep, waves came rushing in, battering them with foam, and streamed away, and then Ian had disappeared and Tom was holding him down. A wave came in, another, and Lil started up in anguish and said, 'Oh, my God, he's going to kill Ian. Tom's going to kill . . .'

Ian reappeared, gasping, clutching Tom's shoulders. Down he went again.

'Be quiet, Lil,' said Roz. 'We mustn't interfere.'

'He's going to kill . . . Tom wants to kill . . .'

Then Ian had been down a long time, surely a minute, more . . . Tom let out a great yell and let go of Ian, who bobbed up. He was hardly able to stand, fell, stood up again, and watched Tom striding through the waves to the beach. As Tom stepped up on to the sand, blood flowed from his calf. Ian had bitten him, deep under the waves, and it was a bad bite. Ian was standing swaying in the water, choking, gasping.

Roz fought with herself, then ran out into the waves and supported Ian in. The boy was pale, vomiting sea water, but he shook off Roz and went to sit by himself on the sand, his head on his knees. Roz returned to her place. 'Our fault,' whispered Lil.

'Stop it, Lil. That's not going to help.'

Tom was standing on one leg, to examine his calf, which was pouring copious blood. He went back into the sea and stood sloshing the sea water on to the bite. He came out again, found his swimming towel, tore it in half, and tied one half tight around his leg. Then he stood, hesitating. He might have gone back into his house and through it to Lil's. He might have stayed in his own house, claiming it from Ian? He could have flopped down where he stood near the fence, not far from the women. Instead he turned and stared hard, it seemed with curiosity, at Ian. Then he limped to where Ian sat, and sat down by him. No one spoke.

The women stared at these two young heroes, their sons, their lovers, these beautiful young men, their bodies glistening with sea water and sun oil, like wrestlers from an older time.

'What are we going to do, Roz?' whispered Lil.

'I know what I am going to do,' said Roz, and stood up. 'Lunch,' she called, exactly as she had been doing for years, and the boys obediently got up and followed the women into Roz's house.

'You'd better get that dressed,' said Roz to her son. It was Ian who fetched the box of bandages and Elastoplast and put disinfectant on the bite, and then tied up the wound.

On the table was the usual spread of sausages and cheese and ham and bread, a big dish of fruit, and the four sat around the table and ate. Not a word. And then Roz spoke calmly, deliberately. 'We all have to behave normally. Remember—everything must be as usual, as it always is.'

The boys looked at each other, for information, it seemed. They looked at Lil. They looked at Roz. They frowned. Lil was smiling, but only just. Roz cut an apple into four, pushed a quarter each at the others, and bit juicily into her segment.

'*Very* funny,' said Ian.

'I think so,' said Roz.

Ian got up, clutching a big sandwich stuffed with salad, the apple quarter in his other hand, and went into Roz's room.

'*Well*,' said Lil, laughing with something like bitterness.

'Exactly,' said Roz.

Tom got up, and went out and across the street to Lil's house. 'What are we going to do?' Lil asked her friend, as if she expected an answer, there and then.

'It seems to me we are doing it,' said Roz. She followed Ian into her bedroom.

Lil collected up the box with the medicaments and bandages, and walked across to her house. On the way she waved to Saul Butler, who was on his verandah.

School began: it was the boys' last year. Both were prefects, and admired. Lil was often in other towns and places, judging, giving prizes, making speeches, a well-known figure, this slim, tall, shy woman, in her pale perfect linens, her fair hair smooth and neat. She was known for her kind smile, her sympathy, her warmth. Girls and boys had crushes on her and wrote letters that often included, 'I know that you would understand me.' Roz was supervising productions of musicals at a couple of schools, and working on a play, a farce, about sex, a magnetic noisy woman who insisted that her bite was much worse than her bark: 'So watch out; don't make me angry!' The four were in and out, together or separately, nothing seemed to have changed, they ate their meals with windows open on the street, they swam, but sometimes were by themselves on the beach because the boys were out surfing, leaving them behind.

Both had changed, Ian more than Tom. Diffident, shy and awkward he had been, but now he was confident, adult. Roz, who remembered the anguished boy when he had first come to her bed, was quietly proud, but she could never of course say a word to anyone, not even Lil. She had made a man of him, all right. Look at him . . . never these days did he clutch and cling and weep, because of his loneliness and his vanished father. He was quietly proprietorial with her, which amused her—and she adored it. Tom, who had never suffered from shyness or self-doubt, had become a strong, thoughtful youth, who was protective of Lil in a way that Roz had not seen. These were no longer boys, but young men, and good-looking, and so the girls were after them, and both Lil's house and Roz's were, they joked—like fortresses against delirious and desirous young women. But inside these houses, open to sun, sea breezes, the sounds of the sea, were rooms where no one went but Ian and Roz, Tom and Lil.

Lil said to Roz she was so happy it made her afraid. 'How could anything possibly be as wonderful?' she whispered, afraid to be overheard—by whom? No one was anywhere near. What she meant was, and Roz knew she did, that such an intense happiness must have its punishment. Roz grew loud and jokey and said that this was a love that dare not speak its name, and sang, 'I love you, yes I do, I love you, it's a sin to tell a lie . . .'

'Oh, Roz,' said Lil, 'sometimes I get so afraid.'

'Nonsense,' said Roz. 'Don't worry. They'll soon get bored with the old women and go after girls their own age.'

Time passed.

Ian went to college and learned business and money and computers, and worked in the sports firms, helping Lil: soon he would take his father's place. Tom decided to go into theatre management. The best course in the whole country was in his father's university, and it seemed obvious that there was where he should go. Harold wrote and rang to say that there was plenty of room in the house he now shared with his new wife, his new daughter.

Harold and Roz had divorced, without acrimony. But Tom said he would stay here, this town was his home, he didn't want to go north. There was a good enough course right here, and besides, his mother was an education in herself. Harold actually made the trip to argue with his son, planning to say that Tom's not wanting to leave home was a sign of his becoming a real mummy's boy, but when he actually confronted Tom, this self-possessed and decided young man, much older than his real age, he could not bring out the evidently unjust accusation. While Harold was staying, several days, Ian had to stay home, and Tom too, in his own house, and none of the four liked this. Harold was conscious they wanted him to leave; he was not wanted. He was uneasy, he was uncomfortable, and said to Roz that surely the two boys were too old to be so often with the older women. 'Well, we haven't got them on leashes,' said Roz. 'They're free to come and go.'

'Well, I don't know,' said Harold, in the end, defeated. And he went back to his new family.

Tom enrolled for theatre management, stage management, stage lighting, costume design, the history of the theatre. The course would take three years.

'We're all working like dogs,' said Roz, loudly to Harold on the telephone. 'I don't know what you're complaining about.'

'You should get married again,' said Roz's

ex-husband.

'Well, if you couldn't stand me, then who could?' demanded Roz.

'Oh, Roz, it's just that I am an old-fashioned family man. And you must admit you don't exactly fit that bill.'

'Look. You ditched me. You've got yourself your ideal wife. Now, leave me alone. Get out of my life, Harold.'

'I hope you don't really mean that.'

Meanwhile, Saul Butler courted Lil.

It became a bit of a joke for all of them, Saul too. He would arrive with flowers and sweets, magazines, a poster, when he had seen Lil go into Roz's, and call out, 'Here comes old faithful.' The women made a play of it all, Roz sometimes pretending the flowers were for her. He also visited Lil in her house, leaving at once if Tom were there, or Ian.

'No,' said Lil, 'I'm sorry, Saul. I just don't see myself married again!

'But you're getting older, Lil. You're getting on. And here is old faithful. You'll be glad of him one day.' Or he said to Roz, 'Lil'll be glad of a man about the place, one of these days.'

One day the boys, or young men, were readying themselves to go out to the big ocean for surfing, when Saul arrived, with flowers for both women. 'Now, you two, sit down,' he said. And the women, smiling, sat and waited.

The boys on the verandah over the sea were collecting surfboards, towels, goggles. 'Hi,

Saul,' said Tom. A long pause before Ian's, 'Hello, Saul.' That meant that Tom had nudged Ian into the greeting.

Ian resented and feared Saul. He had said to Roz, 'He wants to take Lil away from us.' 'You mean, from you?' 'Yes. And he wants to get me too. A ready-made son. Why doesn't he make his own kids?'

'I thought I had got you,' said Roz.

At which Ian leaped at her, or on her, demonstrating who had got whom.

'Charming,' said Roz.

'And Saul can go and screw himself,' had said Ian.

Saul waited until the two had gone off down the path to the sea, and said, 'Now, listen. I want to put it to you both. I want to get married again. As far as I'm concerned, Lil, you're the one. But you've got to decide.'

'It's no good,' said Roz, and Lil only shrugged. 'We can see how it must look. You're just about as good a bargain as any women look for.'

'And you're talking for Lil, again.'

'She's often enough spoken for herself.'

'But you'd both do better with a bloke,' he said. 'The two of you, without men, and the two lads. It's all too much of a good thing.' A moment of shock. What was he saying? Implying?

But he was going on. 'You are two handsome girls,' said this gallant suitor.

'You're both so . . .' and then he seemed to freeze, his face showed he was struggling with emotions, violent ones, and then it set hard. He muttered, 'Oh, my God . . .' he stared at them, Lil to Roz and back again. 'My God,' he said again. 'You must think me a bloody fool.' His voice was toneless: the shock had gone deep.

'I'm an idiot,' he said. 'So, that's it?

'What?' said Lil. 'What are you talking about?' Her voice was timid, because of what he might be talking about. Roz kicked her under the table. Lil actually leaned over to rub her ankle, still staring at Saul.

'A fool,' he said. 'You two must have been having a good laugh at my expense.' He got up and blundered out. He was hardly able to get across the street to his own house.

'Oh, I see,' said Lil. She was about to go after him, but Roz said, 'Stop. It's a good thing, don't you see?'

'And now it's going to get around that we are lezzies,' said Lil.

'So what? Probably it wouldn't be the first time. After all, when you think how people talk.'

'I don't like it,' said Lil.

'Let them say it. The more the better. It keeps us all safe.'

Soon they all went to Saul's wedding with a handsome young woman who looked like Lil.

The two sons were pleased. But the women

said to each other, 'We're neither of us likely to get as good a deal as Saul again.' That was Lil.

'No,' agreed Roz.

'And what are we going to do when the boys get tired of us old women?'

'I shall cry my eyes out. I shall go into a decline.'

'We shall grow old gracefully,' said Lil.

'Like hell,' said Roz. 'I shall fight every inch of the way.'

Not old women yet, nor anywhere near it. Over forty, though, and the boys were definitely not boys, and their time of wild beauty had gone. You'd not think now, seeing the two strong, confident, handsome young men, that once they had drawn eyes struck as much by awe as by lust or love. And the two women, one day reminding themselves how their two had been like young gods, rummaged in old photographs, and could find nothing of what they knew had been there: just as, looking at their old photographs, they saw pretty girls, nothing more.

Ian was already working with his mother in the management of the chain of sports shops, and was an up-and-coming prominent citizen. Harder to make a mark in the theatre: Tom was still working in the foothills when Ian was already near the top. A new position for Tom, who had always been first, Ian looking up to him.

But he persevered. He worked. And as always he was charming with Lil, and as often in her bed as he could, considering the long and erratic hours of the theatre.

'There you are,' said Lil to Roz. 'It's a beginning. He's getting tired of me.'

But Ian showed no signs of relinquishing Roz, on the contrary. He was attentive, demanding, possessive, and when one day he saw her lying on her pillows, love-making just concluded, smoothing down loose ageing skin over her forearms, he let out a cry, clasped her, and shouted, 'No, don't, don't, don't even think of it. I won't let you grow old.'

'Well,' said Roz, 'it is going to happen, for all that.'

'No.' And he wept, just as he had done when he was still the frightened abandoned boy in her arms. 'No, Roz, please, I love you.'

'So I mustn't get old, is that it, Ian? I'm not allowed to? Mad, the boy is mad,' said Roz, addressing invisible listeners, as we do when sanity does not seem to have ears.

And alone, she felt uneasiness, and, indeed, awe. It *was* mad, his demand on her. It really did seem that he had refused to think she might grow old. Mad! But perhaps lunacy is one of the great invisible wheels that keep our world turning.

Meanwhile Tom's father had not given up his aim, to rescue Tom. He made no bones about it. 'I'm going to rescue you from those *femmes fatales*,' he said on the telephone. 'You get up here and let your old father take you in hand.'

'Harold is going to rescue me from you,' said Tom to his mother, on his way to Lil's bed. 'You're a bad influence.'

'A bit late,' said Roz.

Tom spent a fortnight in the university town. In the evenings a short walk took him out into the hot sandy scrub where hawks wheeled and watched. He became friends with Molly, Roz's successor, and with his half-sister, aged eight, and a new baby.

It was a boisterous child-centred house, but Tom told Ian he found it restful.

'Nice to get to know you, at last,' said Molly.

'And now,' said Harold, 'don't leave it so long.'

Tom didn't. He accepted an offer to direct *West Side Story* in the university theatre, and said he would stay in his father's house.

As always, the young women clustered and clung. 'Time you were married, your father thinks,' said Molly.

'Oh, does he?' said Tom. 'I'll marry in my own good time.'

He was in his late twenties. His classmates, his contemporaries, were married or had 'partners'.

There was a girl he did like, perhaps because of her difference from Lil and from Roz. She was a little dark-haired, ruddy-faced girl, pretty enough, and she flirted with him in a way that made no claims on him. For here, so far from home, from his mother and from Lil, he understood how many claims and ties bound him there. He admired his mother, even if she exasperated him, and he loved Lil. He could not imagine himself in bed with anyone else. But they bound him, oh, yes, they did, and Ian, too, a brother in reality if not in fact. Down there—so he apostrophised his city, his home, so much part of the sea that here, when he heard wind in the bushes it was the waves he heard. 'Down there, I'm not free.'

Up here, he was. He decided to accept work on another production. That meant another three months 'up here'. By now it was accepted that he and Mary Lloyd were a unit, 'an item'. Tom was passive, hearing this characterisation of him and Mary. He neither said yes, nor did he say no, he only laughed. But it was Mary who went with him to the cinema or who came home with him to his father for special meals.

'You could do a lot worse,' said Harold to his son.

'But I'm not doing anything, as far as I can see,' said Tom.

'Is that so? I don't think she sees it like that.'

Later Harold said to Tom, 'Mary asked me if you're queer?'

'Gay?' said Tom. 'Not as far as I know.'

It was breakfast time, the family ate at table,

the girl watching what went on, as little girls do, the infant babbling attractively in her high chair. A delightful scene. Part of Tom ached for it, for his future, for himself. His father had wanted ordinary family life and here it was.

'Then, what gives?' asked Harold. 'Is there a girl back home, is that it?'

'You could say that,' said Tom, calmly helping himself to this and that.

'Then you should let Mary go,' said Harold.

'Yes,' said Molly, on behalf of her sex. 'It's not fair.'

'I wasn't aware I had her tied.'

'Tom,' said his father.

'That's not *on,*' said his father's wife.

Tom said nothing. Then he was in bed with Mary. He had slept only with Lil, no one else. This fresh young bouncy body was delightful, he liked it all, and took quiet satisfaction in Mary's, 'I thought you were gay, I really did.' Clearly, she was agreeably surprised.

So there it was. Mary came often to spend the night with Tom in Harold's and Molly's house, all very *en famille* and cosy. If weddings were not actually mentioned, that was because tact had been decided on. And because of something else, still ill-defined. In bed, Mary had exclaimed over the bite mark on Tom's calf. 'God,' said she. 'What was this? A dog?'

'That was a love bite,' he said, after thought. 'Who on earth . . .' And Mary, in play, tried to fit her mouth over the bite, but found Tom's leg, and then Tom, pulling away from her. 'Don't do that,' he said, which was fair enough. But then, in a voice she had certainly never heard from him, nor anything like it: 'Don't you dare ever do that again.'

She stared, and began to cry. He simply got off the bed and went off into the bathroom. He came back clothed, and did not look at her.

There was something here . . . something bad . . . some place where she must not go. Mary understood that. She felt so shocked by the incident that she nearly broke off from Tom, then and there.

Tom thought he might as well go back home. What he loved about being 'up here' was being free, and that delightful condition had evaporated.

This town was imprisoning him. It was not a large one, but that wasn't the point. He liked it, as a place, spreading suburbs of bungalows around a centre of university and business, and all around the scrubby shrubby desert. He could walk from the university theatre after rehearsal and find himself in ten minutes with strong smelling thorny bushes all around, and under his feet coarse yellow sand where the fallen thorns made pale warning gleams: careful, don't tread on us, we can pierce through the thickest soles. At night, after a performance or a rehearsal, he walked straight out into the dark and stood listening to the crickets, and above him the unpolluted sky glittered and sparked off coloured fire. When he got back to his father's, Mary might be waiting for him.

'Where did you get to?'

'I went for a walk.'

'Why didn't you tell me? I like to walk too.'

'I'm a bit of a lone wolf,' said Tom. 'I'm the cat who walks by himself. So, if that's not your style, I'm sorry.'

'Hey' said Mary. 'Don't bite my head off.'

'Well, you'd better know what you're letting yourself in for.'

At this, Harold and Molly exchanged glances: that was a commitment, surely? And Mary, hearing a promise, said 'I like cats. Luckily.'

But she was secretly tearful and fearful.

Tom was restless, he was moody. He was very unhappy but did not know it. He had not been unhappy in his life. He did not recognise the pain for what it was. There are people who are never ill, are unthinkingly healthy, then they get an illness and are so affronted and ashamed and afraid that they may even die of it. Tom was the emotional equivalent of such a person.

'What is it? What's wrong with me?' he groaned, waking with a heavy weight across his chest. 'I'd like to stay right here in bed and pull the covers over my head.'

But what for? There was nothing wrong with him.

Then, one evening, standing out under the stars, feeling sad enough to howl up at them, he said to himself, 'Good Lord, I'm so unhappy. Yes, that's it.'

He told Mary he wasn't well. When she was solicitous he said, 'Leave me alone.'

From the periphery of the little town, roads which soon became tracks ran out into the desert, to places used by students for their picnics and excursions. In between the used ways almost invisible paths made their way between the odoriferous bushes that had butterflies clinging to them in the day, and at night sent out waves of scent to attract bats. Tom walked out on the tarmacked road, turned on to the dusty track, turned off that and found a faint path to a littlc hill that had rocks on it, one a big flat one, which held the sun's heat well into the night. Tom lay on this hot rock and let unhappiness fill him.

'Lil,' he was whispering. 'Lil.'

He knew at last that he was missing Lil, that was the trouble. Why was he surprised? Vaguely, he had all this time thought that one day he'd get a girl his own age and then . . . but it had been so vague. Lil had always been in his life. He lay face down on the rock and sniffed at it, the faint metallic tang, the hot dust, and vegetable aromas from little plants in the cracks. He was thinking of Lil's body that always smelled of salt, of the sea. She was like a sea creature, in and out, the sea water often drying on her and then she was in again. He bit into his forearm, remembering that his earliest memory was of licking salt off Lil's shoulders. It was a game they played, the little boy and his mother's oldest friend. Every inch of his body had been available to Lil's strong hands since he had been born, and Lil's body was as familiar to him as his own. He saw again Lil's breasts, only just covered by the bikini top, and the faint wash of glistening sand in the cleft between her breasts, and the glitter of tiny sand grains on her shoulders.

'I used to lick her for the salt,' he murmured. 'Like an animal at a salt lick.'

When he went back, very late, the house dark, he did not sleep but sat down and wrote to Lil. Writing letters had not ever been his style. Finding his writing illegible, he remembered that an old portable typewriter had been stuffed under his bed, and he pulled it out, and typed, trying to muffle the sharp sound by putting the machine on a towel. But Molly had heard, knocked and said, 'Can't you sleep?' Tom said he was sorry, and stopped.

In the morning he finished the letter and posted it and wrote another. His father, peering to see the inscription, said, 'So, you're not writing to your mother?'

Tom said, 'No. As you see.' Family life had its drawbacks, he decided. Thereafter he wrote letters to Lil at the university, and posted them himself.

Molly asked him what was the matter and he said he wasn't feeling up to scratch, and she said he should see a doctor.

Mary asked what was the matter and he said, 'I'm all right.'

And still he didn't go back 'down there'; he stayed up here, and that meant staying with Mary.

He wrote to Lil daily, answered the letters, or rather notes, she sometimes wrote to him; he telephoned his mother, he went out into the desert as often as he could, and told himself he would get over it. Not to worry. Meanwhile his heart was a lump of cold loneliness, and he dreamed miserably.

'Listen,' said Mary, 'if you want to call this off, then say so.'

He suppressed, 'Call *what* off?' and said, 'Just give me time.'

Then, on an impulse, or perhaps because he soon would have to decide whether to accept another contract, he said to his father, 'I'm off.'

'What about Mary?' asked Molly.

He did not reply. Back home, he was over at Lil's and in her bed in an hour. But it was not the same. He could make comparisons now, and did. It was not that Lil was *old*—she was beautiful, so he kept muttering and whispering, 'You're so beautiful,'—but there was claim on him, Mary, and that wasn't even personal. Mary, another woman, did it matter?

One day soon he must—he had to . . . everyone expected it of him.

Meanwhile Ian seemed to be doing fine with Roz. With his mother, Tom's. Ian didn't seem to be unhappy, or suffering, far from it.

And then Mary arrived, and found the four preparing to go to the sea. Flippers and goggles were found for her, and a surfboard. Within half an hour of her arrival she was ready to embark with the two young men, on the wide, dangerous, bad sea outside this safe bay. A little motorboat would take them out. So this pretty young thing, as smooth and shiny as a fish, larked about and played with Tom and Ian, and the two older women sat on their chairs, watching behind dark glasses and saw the motorboat arrive and take the three off.

'She's come for Tom,' said Tom's mother.

'Yes, I know,' said Tom's lover.

'She's nice enough,' said Roz.

Lil said nothing.

Roz said, 'Lil, I think this is where we bow out.'

Lil said nothing.

'Lil?' Roz peered over at her, and pushed up her dark glasses to see better.

'I don't think I could bear it,' said Lil.

'We've got to!

'Ian doesn't have a girl.'

'No, but he should have. Lil, they're getting on towards thirty.'

'I know.'

Far away, where the sharp black rocks stood in their white foam at the mouth of the bay, three tiny figures were waving at them, before disappearing out of sight to the big beach.

'We have to stand together and end it,' said Roz.

Lil was quietly weeping. Then Roz was, too.

'We have to, Lil.'

'I know we do.'

'Come on, let's swim.'

The women swam hard and fast, out and back and around, and then landed on the beach, and went straight up to Roz's house, to prepare lunch. It was Sunday. Ahead was the long difficult afternoon.

Lil said, 'I've got work,' and went off to one of her shops.

Roz served lunch, making excuses for Lil, and then she too said she had things to do. Ian said he would come with her. That left Tom and Mary alone, and there was a showdown. 'Either on or off,' said Mary. 'Either yes or no.' 'There were plenty of fish in the sea.' 'It was time he grew up.' All that kind of thing, as prescribed for this occasion.

When the others came back, Mary announced that she and Tom were getting married, and there were congratulations and a noisy evening. Roz sang lots of songs, Tom joined in, they all sang. And when it was bedtime Mary stayed with Tom, in his house, and Ian went home with Lil.

Then Mary went back home to plan the wedding.

And now it had to be done. The two women said to the young men that now that was it. 'It's over,' said Roz.

Ian cried out, 'What do you mean? Why? I'm not getting married'

Tom sat quietly, jaw set, drinking. He filled his glass with wine, drained it, filled it again, drank, saying nothing.

At last he said to Ian, 'They're right, don't you see?'

'No,' yelled Ian. He went into Roz's room and called her, and Tom went with Lil to her house. Ian wept and pleaded. 'Why, what for? We're perfectly happy. Why do you want to spoil it?' But Roz stuck it out. She was all heartless determination and only when she and Lil were alone together, the men having gone off to discuss it, they wept and said they could not bear it. Their hearts were breaking they said, how were they going to live, it would be unendurable.

When the men returned, the women were tear-stained but firm.

Lil told Tom that he must not come with her that night and Roz told Ian that he must go home with Lil.

'You've ruined everything,' said Ian to Roz. 'It's all your fault. Why couldn't you leave things as they were?'

Roz jested, 'Cheer up. We are going to

become respectable ladies, yes, your disreputable mothers are going to become pillars of virtue. We shall be perfect mothers-in-law, and then we shall become wonderful grandmothers to your children.'

'I'm not going to forgive you,' said Ian to Roz.

And Tom said to Lil, low, to her only, 'I'll never ever ever forget you.'

Now, that was a valediction, almost conventional. It meant—surely?—that Tom's heart was not likely to suffer permanent damage.

The wedding, needless to say, was a grand affair. Mary had been determined not to be upstaged by her dramatic mother-in-law, but found Roz was being the soul of tact, in a self-effacing outfit. Lil was elegant and pale and smiling, and the very moment the happy pair had driven off for their honeymoon she was down swimming in the bay, where Roz, a good hostess, could not leave her guests to join her. Later Roz crossed the street to find out how Lil was, but her bedroom door was locked and she would not respond to Roz's knocks and enquiries. Ian as best man had made a funny and likeable speech, and, meeting Roz in the street as she was returning from Lil's, said, 'So? Are you pleased with yourself now?' And he too went running down to the sea.

Now Roz was in her empty house, and she lay on her bed and at last was able to weep.

When there were knocks at her door which she knew were Ian's, she rolled in anguish, her fist stuffed into her mouth.

As soon as the honeymoon was over, Mary told Tom, who told his mother, that she thought Roz should move out and leave the house to them. It made sense. It was a big house, right for a family. The trouble was financial. Years ago the house had been affordable, when this whole area had been far from desirable, but now it was smart and only the rich could afford these houses. In an impulsive, reckless, generous gesture, Roz gave the house to the young couple as a wedding present. And so where was she to live? She couldn't afford another house like this. She took up residence in a little hotel down the coast, and this meant that, for the first time ever, since she was born, she was not within a few yards of Lil. She did not understand at first why she was so restless, sad, bereft, put it all down to losing Ian, but then understood it was Lil she missed, almost as much as Ian. She felt she had lost everything, and literally from one week to the next. But she was not reflective, by nature: she was like Tom, who would always be surprised by his emotions, when he was forced to notice them. To deal with her feelings of emptiness and loss, she accepted a job at the university as a full-time teacher of drama, worked hard, swam twice a day, took sleeping pills.

Mary was soon pregnant. Jokes of a traditional kind were aimed at Ian, by Saul, among others. 'You're aren't going to let your mate get ahead of you, are you? When's your wedding?'

Ian was working hard, too. He was trying not to give himself time to think. No stranger to thought, reflection, introspection, he felt that they were enemies, waiting to strike him down. A new shop was opening in the town where Harold was. They were waiting for their child. Ian did not stay at Harold's, but in a hotel, and of course visited Harold, who had been like a father to him—so he said. There he met a friend of Mary's, who had paid attention to him at the wedding. Hannah. It was not that he disliked her, on the contrary, she pleased him, with her comfortable ways, that were easy to see as maternal, but he was inside an empty space full of echoes, and he could not imagine making love with anyone but Roz. He swam every morning from 'their' beach, sometimes seeing Roz there, and he greeted her, but turned away, as if the sight of her hurt him—it did. And he more often took the little motorboat out to the surfing beaches. He and Tom had always gone together, but Tom was so busy with Mary, and the new baby.

One day, seeing Roz drying herself on the sand, the boatman, who had come into the bay especially to find her, stopped his engine, let the boat rock on the gentle waves, and jumped down into the water, tugging the boat behind him like a dog on a leash to say, 'Mrs Struthers, Ian's doing some pretty dangerous stuff out there. He's a picture to watch, but he scares me. If you see his mother—or perhaps you . . .'

Roz said, 'Well, now. To tell a man like Ian to play it safe, that's more than a mother's life is worth. Or mine, for that matter.'

'Someone should warn him. He's asking for it. Those waves out there, you've got to respect them.'

'Have you warned him?'

'I've tried my best.'

'Thanks,' said Roz. 'I'll tell his mother.'

She told Lil, who said to her son that he was playing too close to the safety margins. If the old boatman was worried, then that meant something. Ian said, 'Thanks.'

One evening, at sunset, the boatman came in to find Roz or one of them on the beach, but had to go up to the house, found Mary, told her that Ian was lying smashed up on one of the outer beaches.

Then Ian was in hospital. Told by the doctor, 'You'll live,' his face said plainly he wished he could have heard something else. He had hurt his spine. But that would probably heal. He had hurt his leg, and that would never be normal.

He left hospital and lay in his bed at home, in a room which for years had not been much more than a place where he changed his clothes, before crossing the street to Roz. But in that house were now Tom and Mary. He turned his face to the wall. His mother tried to coax him up and on to his feet, but could not make him take exercise. Lil could not, but Hannah could and did. She came to visit her old friend Mary, slept in that house, and spent most of her time sitting with Ian, holding his hand, often in sympathetic tears.

'For an athlete it must be so hard,' she kept saying to Lil, to Mary, to Tom. 'I can understand why he is so discouraged.'

A good word, an accurate one. She persuaded Ian to turn his face towards her, and then, soon, to get up and take the prescribed steps up and down the room, then on to the verandah, and soon, across the road and down to swim. But he would not ever surf again. He would always limp.

Hannah kissed the poor leg, kissed him, and Ian wept with her: her tears gave him permission to weep. And soon there was another wedding, an even larger one, since Ian and his mother Liliane were so well known, and their sports shops so beneficial to every town they found themselves in, and both were famed for their good causes and their general benevolence.

So there they were, the new young couple, Ian and Hannah, in Lil's house with Lil. Opposite, Roz's old house was now Tom's and

Mary's. Lil was uncomfortable in her role as mother-in-law, and was unhappy every time she saw the house opposite, now so changed. But after all, she was rich, unlike Roz. She bought one of the houses almost on the beach, not a couple of hundred yards from the two young couples, and Roz moved in. The women were together again, and Saul Butler when he met them allowed a special measure of sarcastic comment into his, 'Ah, together again, I see!' 'As you see,' said Roz or Lil. 'Can't fool you, Saul, can we?' said Lil, or Roz.

Then Hannah was pregnant and Ian was appropriately proud.

'It has turned out all right,' said Roz to Lil.

'Yes, I suppose so,' said Lil.

'What more could we expect?'

They were on the beach, in their old chairs, moved to outside the new fence.

'I didn't expect anything,' said Lil.

'But?'

'I didn't expect to feel the way I do,' said Lil. 'I feel . . .'

'All right,' said Roz quickly. 'Let it go. I know. But look at it this way, we've had . . .'

'The best,' said Lil. 'Now all that time seems to me like a dream. I can't believe it, such happiness, Roz,' she whispered, turning her face and leaning forward a little, though there wasn't a soul for fifty yards.

'I know,' said Roz. 'Well—that's it.' And she leaned back, shutting her eyes. From below her dark glasses tears trickled.

Ian went off with his mother a good bit on trips to their shops. He was everywhere greeted with affectionate, respectful generosity. It was known how he had got his limp. As foolhardy as an Everest hero, as brave as—well, as a man outrunning a wave like a mountain—he was so handsome, so courteous, such a gentleman, so kind. He was like his mother.

On one such trip, they were in their hotel suite, before bedtime, and Lil was saying that she was going to take little Alice for the day when she got back to give Mary a chance to go shopping.

Ian said, 'You two women are really pleased with yourselves.'

This was venomous, not like him; she had not—she thought—heard that voice from him before.

Yes,' he said, 'it's all right for you.'

'What do you mean, Ian, what are you saying?'

'I'm not blaming you. I know it was Roz.'

'What do you mean? It was both of us.'

'Roz put the idea into your head. I know that. You'd never have thought of it. Too bad about Tom. Too bad about me.'

At this she began to laugh, a weak defensive laugh. She was thinking of the years with Tom, watching him change from a beautiful boy into a man, seeing the years claim him, knowing how it must end, must end, then should end, she should end it . . . she and Roz . . . but it was so hard, hard . . .'

'Ian, do you realise, you sound demented when you say things like that?'

'Why? I don't see it.'

'What did you think? We'd all just go on, indefinitely, then you and Tom, two middle-aged men, bachelors, and Roz and me, old and then you two, old, without families, and Roz and I, old, old, old . . . we're getting on for old now, can't you see?'

'No, you aren't,' said her son calmly. 'Not at all. You and Roz knock the girls for six any time.'

Did he mean Hannah and Mary? If so . . . the streak here of sheer twisted lunacy frightened her and she got up. 'I'm going to bed.'

'It was Roz put you up to it. I don't forgive you for agreeing. And she needn't think I'll forgive her for spoiling everything. We were all so happy.'

'Good night, I'll see you at breakfast.'

Hannah had her baby, Shirley, and the two young women were much together. The two older women, and the husbands, waited to hear news of second pregnancies: surely the logical step. And then, to their surprise, Mary and Hannah announced that they thought of going into business together. At once it was suggested they should work in the sports shops: they would have flexible hours, could come and go, earn a bit of money . . . And, it was the corollary, fit second babies into a comfortable timetable.

They said no, they wanted to start a new business, the two of them.

'I expect we can help you with the money,' said Ian, and Hannah said, 'No, thanks. Mary's father can help us out. He's loaded.' When Hannah spoke, it was often Mary's thought they were hearing. 'We want to be independent,' said Hannah, a trifle apologetic, herself hearing that she had sounded ungracious, to say the least.

The wives went off to visit their families for a weekend, taking the babies, to show them off.

The four, Lil and Roz, Ian and Tom, sat together at the table in Roz's house—Roz's former house—and the sound of the waves said that nothing had changed, nothing . . . except that the infant Alice's paraphernalia was all over the place, in the way of modern family life.

'It's very odd, what they want,' said Roz. 'Do we understand why? What is it all about?'

'We're too—heavy for them,' said Lil.

'We. They,' said Ian. 'They. We—'

They all looked at him, to take in what he meant.

Then Roz burst out, 'We've tried so hard. Lil and I, we've done our best.'

'I know you have,' said Tom. 'We know that.'

'But here we are,' said Ian. 'Here *we* are.'

And now he leaned forwards towards Roz, passionate, accusing—very far from the urbane and affable man everyone knew: 'And nothing has changed, has it. Roz? Just tell me the truth, tell me, has it?'

Roz's eyes, full of tears, did meet his, and then she got up to save herself with the ritual of supplying cold drinks from the fridge.

Lil said, looking calmly straight across at Tom, 'It's no good, Roz. Just *don't, don't* . . .' For Roz was crying, silently, allowing it to be seen, her dark glasses lying on the table. Then she covered her eyes with the glasses, and directing those dark circles at Ian, she said, 'I don't understand what it is you want, Ian. Why do you go on and on? It's all done. It's finished.'

'So, you don't understand,' said Ian.

'Stop it,' said Lil, beginning to cry too. 'What's the point of this? All we have to do is to decide what to tell them, they want our support.'

'*We* will tell *them* that *we* will support *them*,' said Ian, and added, 'I'm going for a swim.'

And the four ran down into the waves, Ian limping, but not too badly.

Interesting that in the discussion that afternoon, with the four, a certain key question had not been mentioned. If the two young wives were going to start a business, then the grandmothers would have to play a part.

A second discussion, with all six of them, was on this very point. 'Working grandmothers,' said Roz. 'I quite fancy it, what about you, Lil?'

'Working is the word,' said Lil. 'I'm not going to give up the shops. How will we fit in the babies?'

'Easy,' said Roz. 'We'll juggle it. I have long holidays at the university. You have Ian at your beck and call in the shops. There are weekends. And I daresay the girls'll want to see their little angels from time to time.'

'You're not suggesting we're going to neglect them?' said Mary.

'No, darling, no, not at all. Besides, both Lil and I had girls to help us with our little treasures, didn't we, Lil?'

'I suppose so. Not much, though.'

'Oh, well,' said Mary, 'I suppose we can hire an *au pair,* if it's like that.'

'How you do flare up,' said Roz. 'Certainly we can get ourselves *au pairs* when needed. Meanwhile, the grannies are at your service.'

It was a real ritual occasion, the day the babies were to be introduced to the sea. All six adults were there on the beach. Blankets had been spread. The grandmothers, Roz and Lil, in their bikinis, were sitting with the babies between their knees, smoothing them over with suncream. Tiny, delicate creatures, fair-haired, fair-skinned, and around them, tall and large and protective, the big adults.

The mummies took them into the sea, assisted by Tom and Lil. There was much splashing, cries of fear and delight from the little lines, reassurance from the adults—a noisy scene. And sitting on the blankets where the sand had already blown, glistening in little drifts, were Roz and Ian. Ian looked long and intently at Roz and said, 'Take your glasses off.' Roz did so.

He said, 'I don't like it when you hide your eyes from me.'

She snapped the glasses back on and said, 'Stop it, Ian. You've got to stop this. It's simply not *on*.'

He was reaching forward to lift off her glasses. She slapped down his hand. Lil had seen, from where she stood to her waist in the sea. The intensity of it, you could say, even the ferocity . . . had Hannah noticed? Had Mary? A yell from a little girl—Alice. A big wave had leaped up and . . . 'It's bitten me,' she shrieked. 'The sea's bitten me.' Up jumped Ian, reached Shirley who also was making a commotion now. 'Can't you see,' he shouted at Hannah, over the sea noise, 'you're frightening her? They're frightened.' With a tiny child on either shoulder he limped up out of the waves. He began a jiggling and joggling of the little girls in a kind of dance, but he was dipping in each step with the limp and they began to cry harder. 'Granny,' wailed Hannah, 'I want my granny,' sobbed Shirley. The infants were deposited on the rugs, Lil joined Roz, and the grandmothers soothed and petted the children while the other four went off to swim.

'There, my ducky,' sang Roz, to Hannah.

'Poor little pet,' crooned Lil to Shirley.

Not long after this the two young women were in their new office, in the suite which would be the scene of their—they were convinced—future triumphs. 'We are having a little celebration; they had said, making it sound as if there would be associates, sponsors, friends. But they were alone, drinking champagne and already tiddly.

It was the end of their first year. They had worked hard, harder than they had expected. Things had gone so well there was already talk of expanding. That would mean even longer hours, and more work for the grandmothers.

'They wouldn't mind,' said Hannah.

'I think they would,' said Mary.

There was something in her voice, and Hannah looked to see what Mary was wanting her to understand. Then, she said, 'It's not a question of us working our butts off—and their working their butts off—they want us to get pregnant again.'

'Exactly,' said Mary.

'I wouldn't mind,' said Hannah. 'I told Ian, yes, but there's no hurry. We can get our business established and then let's see. But you're right, that's what they want.'

'They,' said Mary. '*They* want. And what *they* want they intend to have.'

Here Hannah showed signs of unrest. Compliant by nature, biddable, she had begun by deferring to Mary, such a strong character, but now she was asserting herself. 'I think they are very kind.'

'They,' said Mary. 'Who the hell are *they* to be kind to *us*.'

'Oh, come on! We wouldn't have been able to start this business at all without the grandmothers helping with everything.'

'Roz is so damned tactful all the time,' said Mary, and it exploded out of her, the champagne aiding and abetting. She poured some more. 'They're both so tactful.'

'You must be short of something to complain about.'

'I feel they are watching us all the time to make sure we come up to the mark.'

'What mark?'

'I don't know,' said Mary, tears imminent. 'I wish I knew. There's something *there.*'

'They don't want to be interfering mothers-in-law.'

'Sometimes I hate them.'

'*Hate*,' Hannah dismissed, with a smile.

'They've got them, don't you see? Sometimes I feel . . .'

'It's because they didn't have fathers—the

boys. Ian's father died and Tom's went off and married someone else. That's why the four of them are so close.'

'I don't care why. Sometimes I feel like a spare part.'

'I think you're being unfair.'

'Tom wouldn't care who he was married to. It could be a seagull or a . . . or a . . . wombat.'

Hannah flung herself back in her chair, laughing.

'I mean it. Oh, he's ever so damned kind. He's so nice. I shout at him and I pick a fight, anything just to make him—see me. And then the next thing we're in bed having a good screw.'

But Hannah didn't feel anything like that. She knew Ian needed her. It was not only the slight dependence because of his gammy leg, he sometimes clung to her, childlike. Yes, there was something of the child in him—a little. One night he had called out to Roz in his sleep, and Hannah had woken him. 'You were dreaming of Roz,' she told him.

At once awake and wary, he said, 'Hardly surprising. I've known her all my life. She was like another mother.' And he buried his face in her breasts. 'Oh, Hannah, I don't know what I'd do without you.'

Now that Hannah was standing up to her, Mary was even more alone. Once she had felt, there's Hannah, at least I've got Hannah.

Thinking over this conversation afterwards,

Mary knew there was something there that eluded her. That was what she always felt. And yet what was she complaining about? Hannah was right. When she looked at their situation from outside, married to these two covetable men, well-known, well-set-up, well-off, generally liked—so what *was* she complaining about? I have everything, she decided. But then, a voice from her depths—I have nothing. She lacked everything. 'I have nothing,' she told herself, as waves of emptiness swept over her. In the deep centre of her life—nothing, an absence.

And yet she could not put her finger on it, what was wrong, what was lacking. So there must be something wrong with her. She, Mary, was at fault. But why? What was it? So she puzzled, sometimes so unhappy she felt she could run away out of the situation for good.

When Mary found the bundle of letters, forgotten in an old bit of luggage, she had at first thought they were all from Lil to Tom, conventional, of the kind you'd expect from an old friend or even a second mother. They began, Dear Tom and ended Love, Lil, with sometimes a cross or two for a kiss. And then there was the other letter, from Tom to Lil, that had not been posted. 'Why shouldn't I write to you, Lil, why not, I have to, I think of you all the time, oh my God, Lil, I love you so much, I dream of you, I can't bear being apart from you, I love you I love you . . .' and so on, pages of it. So, she read Lil's letters again, and saw them differently. And then she understood everything. And when she stood on the path with Hannah, below Baxter's Gardens, and heard Roz's laughter, she knew it was mocking laughter. It mocked her, Mary, and she understood everything at last. It was all clear to her.

VICTORIA AND THE STAVENEYS

Cold dark was already drizzling into the playground; the voices of two groups of children told people arriving at the great gate where they must direct their gaze: it was already hard to make out who was who. By some sort of sympathy, children in the bigger group were able to distinguish their own among the arrivals, and by ones or twos they darted off to be collected and taken home. There were two children by themselves in the centre of the space, which was surrounded by tall walls topped by broken glass. They were noisy. A little boy was kicking out or pummelling the air and shouting, 'He forgot, I told her he'd forget,' while a girl tried to console and soothe. He was a large child, she thin, with spiky pigtails sticking out, the pink ribbons on them dank and limp. She was older than him, but not bigger. Yet it was with the assurance of her two extra years that she admonished, 'Now Thomas, don't do that, don't bawl, they'll be here.' But he wouldn't be quietened. 'Let me go, let me *go*—I *won't,* he's forgotten.' Several people arrived at the same time at the gate, one a tall fair boy of about twelve, who stood peering through the gloom. He spied his charge, his brother Thomas, while others were already reaching out hands and stepping forward. It was a little scene of tumult and confusion. The tall boy, Edward, grabbed Thomas by the hand and stood while the little boy kept up his thrashing about and complaint. 'You forgot me; yes, you did,' and watched while the other children disappeared out into the street. He turned and went off out of sight with Thomas.

It was cold. Victoria's clothes were not enough. She was shivering now that she did not have the recalcitrant child to keep her active. She stood with her arms wrapped about her, quietly crying. The school caretaker emerged from the dark, pulled the gates together, and locked them. He had not seen her either. She wore dark brown trousers and a black jacket and was a darker spot in the swirling gloom of the playground: the wind was getting up.

The awfulness of that day, which had begun with her aunt being rushed off to hospital, and had culminated in her being abandoned, now sank her to her knees, and she rocked there, eyes blank with tears until fears of being alone opened them again, and she stared at the big black locked gates. The bars were set wide. Carefully, as if engaged in some nefarious activity, she went to the gate to see if she could wriggle between the bars. She was thin, and told often enough there wasn't enough flesh on her to feed a cat. That had been her mother's verdict, and the thought of her dead mother made Victoria weep, and then wail. She had a few minutes ago been playing big girl to Thomas's baby boy, but now she felt she was a baby herself, and her nine years were dissolving in tears. And then she was stuck there, in the bars. On the pavement people passed and passed, not seeing her, they were all hunched up under umbrellas; the playground behind was vast, dark and full of threat. Across the street, Mr Pat's sweet and newspaper shop and café was all a soft shine of light. The street lights were making furry yellow splashes, and, just as Victoria decided to make another effort to wriggle free, Mr Patel came on to the pavement to take some oranges from the trays of fruit out there, and he saw her. She was in his shop, but usually with crowds of others, every school day, and she knew he was to be liked because her aunt, and her mother too, before she died, had said, 'He's okay, that Indian man.'

Mr Patel held up his hands to stop the traffic, which was only a car and a bicycle, and hastened over to her. As he arrived her wrigglings freed her and she fell into his hands, large good hands, that held her safe. 'Victoria, is that you I am seeing?'

Saved, she abandoned herself to misery. He hoisted her up and was again holding up his hand—only one, the other held Victoria—to halt another car and a motorbike. Having arrived in the bright warmth of the café,

Mr Patel set her on the high counter and said, 'Now, dear, what are you doing here all by yourself?'

'I don't know,' wept Victoria, and she did not. A message had come to her in class that she was to be picked up in the playground, with Thomas Staveney, whom she hardly knew: he was two classes down from her. There were customers waiting for Mr Patel's attention. He looked around for help and saw a couple of girls sitting at a table. They were seniors from the school refreshing themselves before going home, and he said, 'Here, keep an eye on this poor child for a minute.' He set her down carefully on a chair by them. The big girls certainly did not want to be bothered with a snotty little kid, but gave Victoria bright smiles and said she should stop crying. Victoria sobbed on. Mr Patel did not know what to do. While he served sweets, buns, opening more soft drinks for the girls, as usual doing twenty things at once, he was thinking that he should call the police, when on the pavement opposite the tall boy who had dragged off his fighting little brother, suddenly appeared, like a ghost that has lost its memory. He stared wildly about, and then, holding on to the top bars of the gate with both hands, seemed about to haul himself up to its top. 'Excuse me,' shouted Mr Patel, as he ran to the door. 'Come over here,' he yelled, and Edward turned a woeful countenance to Mr Patel and the welcoming lights of the café and, without looking to see what traffic might be arriving, jumped across the street in a couple of bounds, just missed by a motorbike whose rider sent imprecations after him.

'It's a little girl,' panted Edward. 'I'm looking for a little girl.'

'And here she is, safe and sound,' and Mr Patel went in to stand by the counter where he kept an eye on the tall boy, who had sat himself by Victoria and was wiping her face with paper napkins that stood fanned in a holder. He seemed about to dissolve in tears himself. The two girls, much too old for this boy, nevertheless were making manifestations of femininity for his sake, pushing out their breasts and pouting. He didn't notice. Victoria still wept and he was in an extreme of some emotion himself.

'I'm thirsty,' Victoria burst out, and Mr Patel handed across a glass of orange crush, with a gesture that indicated to Edward he shouldn't dream of thinking of paying for it.

Edward held the glass for Victoria, who was indignant—she, a big girl, being treated like a baby, but she was grateful, for she did badly want to be a baby, just then.

Edward was saying, 'I'm so sorry. I was supposed to pick you up, with my brother.'

'Didn't you see me?' asked Victoria, accusing him.

And now Edward was scarlet, he positively

writhed. This was the burning focus of his self-accusation. He had in fact seen a little black girl, but he had been told to collect a little girl, and for some reason had not thought this black child could be his charge. He could make all kinds of excuses for himself: the confusion as the other children were running off to the gate, the noise, Thomas's bad behaviour, but the fact was, the absolute bottom line, he had not really seen her because Victoria was black. But he had seen her. All this would not have mattered to a good many people who came and went in and out of those big gates, but Edward was the child of a liberal house, and he was in fact in the throes of a passionate identification with all the sorrows of the Third World. At his school, much superior to the one here, though he had attended it, long ago, 'projects' of all kinds enlightened him and his fellow pupils. He collected money for the victims of AIDS and of famine, he wrote essays about these and many others of the world's wrongs, his mother Jessy was 'into' every kind of good cause. There was no excuse for what he had done and he was sick with shame.

'Will you come home with me now?' he enquired, humbly, of the pathetic child, and without a word she stood and put up her hand for him to lead her.

'Poor little kid,' said one of the girls, apparently touched.

'Oh, I don't know, she's doing all right,' said the other.

'It's not that far,' said Edward to the child, who was half his height. He bent down to make this communication. And she was stretching herself up, so sure was she that she ought to be behaving like a big girl, while she whimpered, like catches of her breath, staring up at his face which was contorted with concern for her.

'Goodbye, Victoria,' said Mr Patel, in a stern, admonitory way, that was directed at this white boy, who was reminding him of those summer insects, all flying legs and feelers, called Daddy-Long-Legs. 'I'll see you tomorrow,' he shouted after the couple, for he was remembering he knew nothing about this boy, who should be informed that Victoria was not without friends. But the couple were already in the street, where their feet made sturdy progress through clogs of wet leaves, and puddles.

'Where? Where to?' the child pleaded, but in such a little voice he had not heard: he was bending continually to send her smiles he had no idea were agonised.

Just as Victoria thought they would be trudging until her feet dropped off, they turned in at a gate and were walking up into the face of a house whose windows blazed light, in a cliff of such houses.

Here Edward inserted a key and they were

in a big place that seemed to Victoria like a shop, of the sort she sometimes gaped at in the High Street. Colour, light and warmth: she was cold now, for the wind had cut through her, and in a great mirror on a stand where Edward was, all touzled by the wind, was herself, yes, that was her, Victoria, that frightened thing, with her mouth open, staring, and then Edward was bundling her jacket off her and throwing it over the arm of a red chair. He was going on ahead and she ran after him leaving herself behind in the surface of the mirror. And now they were in a room larger than any she had seen, except for the school hall. Edward reached out for a kettle, which he filled at a sink, and Victoria thought that this part of the room was like a kitchen. Toys lay about. It occurred to her that this was where Thomas lived, so where was he?

'Where is he?' she whispered, and Edward stood still in the midst of his fussing with cups and saucers to work out what she meant. 'Oh, Thomas? He's gone off to sleep over with a friend,' said Edward. 'Now, you just sit down.' When she did not, he lifted her and deposited her in a chair that was like a cuddle, it held her so soft and warm. She looked about cautiously for fear of seeing more than she could take in. This was a room so big all of her aunt's flat would fit into it. And then, as she gaped and wondered, she slumped down, asleep: it had all been too much.

Edward, who was used to a small child—he still thought Victoria was that, she was such a tiny thin little thing—did not do more than lay her back in the cushions, for comfort, and then began searching in a vast refrigerator for something to eat. He did not know where his mother was, but he wished she was here. He had arranged to go out and meet schoolfriends, and here he was stuck with this child, whom he had so shockingly mistreated . . . it had better be said now that he was on the verge of an adolescence so conscience-driven, agonised, accusatory of his own world, passionately admiring of anything not Britain, so devoted to every kind of good cause, so angry with his mother, who in some way he saw as embodying all the forces of reaction, so sick to death with his father, who represented frivolity and indifference to suffering—his good humour could mean nothing less—that, at the end of it, about eight years from this night, Jessy Staveney told him, and everybody else around at the time, 'Your bloody adolescence, my God, my *God,* it's shortened my life by twenty years.'

Edward sat, in his usual way, as if he didn't really have time for this lazing about, and spooned in yoghurt—low-fat yoghurt, with added vitamin D, and frowned over his dilemma about Victoria. Victoria went on sleeping.

If she were dreaming—she was subject to

nightmares and sleep-walking—her dead mother might have appeared, smiling away, but always out of reach, evading Victoria's reaching arms. She had died five years before. Victoria had had uncles but no father, or none that her mother was prepared to identify. No 'uncle' came forward to claim her or acknowledge responsibility. Victoria's aunt, her real aunt, her mother's sister, had no children. She had only recently agreed with herself that she was lucky, kids were such a grind, when she was landed with a four-year-old orphan. She was a social worker. She lived in a council flat—bedroom, lounge, kitchen, shower—in Francis Drake Buildings on a council estate (the other three were Frobisher, Walter Raleigh and Nelson), whose children went to Victoria's school. She had pared her life down to the outlines of her work, which she loved, but then she had to take on Victoria, and she did, showing no reluctance, only a little weariness.

This very morning she had been taken ill. In the ambulance she remembered Victoria, and told the ambulance man that Victoria would be standing waiting in the playground to be picked up after school. He was not unfamiliar with this kind of situation. He telephoned the school, no easy matter, since Victoria's aunt kept passing out with the pain of her illness, which would kill her when she was still not fifty. The ambulance man got the number of the school from the operator, rang the school secretary, explained the crisis. She went to the classroom where Victoria was copying sentences off a blackboard, a good little girl, while apparently oblivious of the noise made by the other children, who had no aspirations to be good. The teacher said, or shouted, No problem, Victoria could go home with Dickie Nicholls and she supposed someone would fetch her. The secretary said, No problem, returned to her office, looked for the Nicholls number, rang, no reply. Working mother, diagnosed the secretary, being one herself. She tried the numbers of various mothers, and at last one said she couldn't help, but how about trying Thomas Steevey in the register: that was how Staveney had been pronounced. The deputy secretary rang the Staveney number and got Jessy Staveney, who told her son to collect a little girl at the same time as he did Thomas. The deputy secretary had not said that Victoria was black, but why should she? There were more black or brown children at the school than white, and she herself was brown, since her parents had come from Uganda, when the Indians were thrown out.

This kind of frantic telephoning and arranging being so common, because of working mothers, the deputy secretary thought no more of it: Victoria would be all right.

When Victoria woke from a short anxious sleep, into this unfamiliar place, Edward was seated at a very big table, and a tall woman, with her blonde hair down all around her face, sat opposite, leaning her arms on the table. Victoria had seen her in the playground coming to pick up Thomas.

Victoria kept quiet for a little, afraid to make her existence known, but then Edward, who had been keeping an eye on her, cried out, 'Oh, Victoria, you're awake, come and have some supper. This is Victoria,' he told his mother, who said, 'Hello, Victoria,' and finished some remark she had been making to her son. That a little girl she didn't know was asleep in her kitchen was nothing that needed comment. Edward's friends, and Thomas's, washed in and out of her house on social or school tides, and she welcomed them all. Thomas's social life, in particular, since he was after all only seven and could not come and go like twelve-year-old Edward, was a bit of a trial, being such a complicated network of visits to this or that attraction, planetarium, museums, river boats, friends, sleep-overs, sleep-ins, eat-overs. Making events match with kids and times was a feat of organisation. She was pleased, rather than not, that the little girl was black because, as she never stopped complaining to Edward, his friends were all much too white, now that we lived in a multicultural society.

Why was Thomas at a very inferior school? Ideology. Mostly his father's, Lionel, who was an old-fashioned socialist. While Thomas would certainly be lifted out and up into one of the good schools, at the right time, he was taking his chances in the lowest depths now. The phrase was Jessy's, when engaged in altercation with her ex-husband, 'Here is news from the lower depths,' she would cry, announcing measles or some contretemps with a bill she could not pay. But she made the most of a situation she deplored, because she was able to look her less principled friends in the eye and say, 'I'm sorry, but he has to know how the other half lives. Lionel insists.'

Victoria was lifted, put into a chair where her chin barely appeared over the edge of the table, and Edward adjusted the situation with big fat cushions. 'And now, what do you feel like eating, Victoria?'

Victoria was not used to being asked and since nothing she saw on the table seemed familiar, looked helpless, and even ready to cry again. Edward understood and simply piled a plate with what he was eating, which happened to be Thai takeaway that Jessy had brought home, stuffed tomatoes from last night's supper, and left-over savoury rice. Victoria was hungry, and she did try, but only the rice seemed to meet with the approval of her stomach. Edward, who watched her—well, like an elder brother, as he would Thomas—found her some cake. That was better and she ate it all.

Jessy silently observed, her plate untouched, the cup of tea between her long hands held below her mouth, so steam went up past her face. Her eyes were large and green and Victoria thought they were witches' eyes. Her mother talked often about witches, and while her aunt never did, it was her mother's sing-song incantory voice that stayed in the child's mind, explaining the bad things that happened. And they so often did.

'Well, what are we going to do with you, Victoria?' at last said Jessy Staveney, carelessly enough, as she might have done with any of the small children who appeared and had to be dealt with.

At this, tears sprang into Victoria's eyes and she wailed. Even worse than the witchy eyes, ever since she could remember, even before her mother died, What shall I, what are we, what should I do with Victoria, was the refrain of her days and nights. She had been so often in the way, with her mother's uncles. She was in the way when her mother had wanted to go to work, but did not know what to do with her, her child Victoria. And she knew her aunt Marion had not really wanted her, though she was always kind.

'Poor little girl, she's tired,' said Jessy. 'Well, I've got to get off. I've got a client's first play at the Comedy and I must be there. Perhaps Victoria should just stay the night?' she said to Edward, whose own eyes were full of tears too, so terribly, so unforgivably guilty, did he feel about everything.

Victoria was sitting straight up, her fists down by her sides, her face turned up to the ceiling from where struck a clear and truthful light illuminating the hopelessness of her despair. She sobbed, eyes tight shut.

'Poor child,' Jessy summed up, and departed.

Edward, who had not yet taken in that this child was not perhaps six, or seven, now came around to her, picked her up, put her on his lap, and sat clutching her tight. Her tears wetted his shoulder and the heat and fret of the taut little body made him feel not much better than a murderer.

'Victoria,' he said, in the intervals of her sobs, 'shouldn't I telephone somebody to say you are here?'

'My auntie's in hospital.'

'Who else do you go to?'—thinking of the networks of people used by him and by Thomas.

'My auntie's friend.'

At last necessity stopped Victoria's sobs. She said her auntie's friend was Mrs Chadwick, yes, there was a telephone.

Edward rang several Chadwicks until he reached a girl who said her mother was out. She was Bessie. Yes, she thought it would be all right if Victoria stayed the night. There was no bed for her here tonight: Bessie had her friends in to watch videos.

'That's all right, then,' said Edward, abandoning his own plans for the evening. This necessitated several more telephone calls.

Meanwhile, Victoria was wandering about the great room, which she had not yet really understood was the kitchen, staring, but not touching, and she was wondering, Where are the beds?

There were no beds.

'Where do you sleep, then?' she asked Edward.

'In my bedroom?

'Isn't this your room?'

'This is the kitchen.'

'Where are all the other people?'

He had no idea what she meant. He sat, telephone silent in front of him, leaning his head on a fist, contemplating the child.

At last he said, hoping that this was what she was on about, 'My mother's room is at the top of the house, and I have a room just up the stairs, and so does Thomas.'

Some monstrous truth seemed trying to get admittance into Victoria's already over-stretched brain. It sounded as if he was saying this room did not comprise all their home. Victoria slept on a pull-out bed in her aunt's lounge. She was not taking it in: she could not. She subsided back into the big chair which was like a hug, and actually put her thumb in her mouth though she was telling herself, You're not a baby, stop it.

Who else lives here, she wanted to ask, but did not dare. Where are all the other people?

Edward was looking steadily at her, hoping for enlightenment. That anguished little face . . . those hot eyes . . . He followed his instincts, went to her, picked her up, cradled her.

'I'll tell you a story,' he said.

And he began on The Three Bears, which Victoria had seen on television. She had not really thought before that you could listen to a story, without seeing it in pictures. A voice, without pictures: she liked this new thing, the kind boy's voice, just above her head, and the way he changed it to fit Big Bear, Middle Bear and Baby Bear, and Goldilocks too, while he rocked her, and she was thinking, But I'm not a baby, he thinks I am. As for him, he knew very well what he was holding: this was what he championed, made speeches about in school debates, and what he had recently announced he would dedicate his whole life to—the suffering of the world.

When he finished the story, he was about to ask if she would like a bath, but was afraid she might misunderstand.

'Have you had enough to eat?'

'Yes, thank you.'

'Then I'll take you up to bed.' It was nowhere near her bedtime: she stayed up late at home because she could not go to sleep until her aunt did. Or she would fall asleep while her aunt watched television and find herself, still in her day clothes, with a blanket over her, on the day-bed. She held on to the tall boy's hand and was pulled fast up the stairs, flight after flight, and then she was in a room crammed with toys. Was this a toy shop?

'This is Thomas's room. But he won't mind if you sleep in his bed, for tonight.'

No one had mentioned a toilet and Victoria was desperate. She stood staring at him, a silent *please*, and then he said, rightly interpreting, 'I'll show you the lavatory.'

She did not know what a lavatory was, but found herself in another room, the size of her bedroom at her mother's, on a toilet seat of smooth, unchipped white. There was a big bath. She would have loved to get into it: she had known only showers. Edward was waiting for her outside the door.

She was led back to the toy-shop room across the landing.

'When I go to bed I'll be upstairs, just one flight,' said Edward. Panic. She was being abandoned. Above and below reached this great empty house.

'I'll be downstairs in the kitchen,' said Edward.

Her face was set into an O of horror. At last Edward understood what was the problem. 'Look. It's all right. You're quite safe. This is our house. No one can come into it but us. You are in Thomas's room—where he sleeps.

Well, when he's not with one of his friends. You kids certainly do have a lot of friends . . .' He stopped, doubtful. He supposed that this child did too? On he blundered. 'I am here. You can give me a shout any time. And when my mother decides to come home she'll be here too.'

Victoria had sunk on to Thomas's bed, wishing she could go down with Edward to the kitchen. But she dare not ask. She had not really taken in that this great house had one family in it. People might easily have a family in two rooms, or sometimes even in one.

'You'd better take off your jersey and your trousers,' said Edward.

She hastily divested herself, and stood in little white knickers and vest.

He thought, how pretty on that dark skin. He didn't know if this was a politically correct thought, or not.

'Here is the light,' he said, switching it on and off, so that the room momentarily became a creepy place full of the shapes of animals, and huge teddies. 'And there's a light by your bed. I'll show you.' He did. 'I'll leave the door open. I'll be listening.'

He didn't know whether to kiss her good night, or not. Seeing her without her bundling clothes, she was a tough wiry little thing, no longer a soft child, and he said, 'How old are you, Victoria?'

'I'm nine,' she said, and added fiercely, 'I

know I'm small but that doesn't mean I'm little.'

'I see,' he said, knowing he had been making mistakes. Once again scarlet with embarrassment, he lingered a while by the door, then said, 'I'll switch this off, then,' did so, and went off down the stairs.

Victoria lay in a half dark, under a duvet that had Mickey Mouse all over it. She liked that, because she had had Mickey Mouse slippers when she was smaller. But this room, in this half-dark—she did let out another wail and then clamped her mouth shut with both hands. All these animals everywhere, she had never seen so many stuffed toys, they were heaped up in the corners, they loaded a table, and there were some teddies on her bed. She pulled a large teddy towards her, as protective shield against the looming lions and tigers and mysterious beasts and people, their eyes glinting from the light that came from outside. She couldn't stay here, she couldn't . . . perhaps she would creep down the stairs and go back to that place they called a kitchen and ask Edward if she might stay. He was kind, she knew. She could feel his arms tight round her, and she set herself to listen to his remembered voice in the story.

There was another fearful thing she had to contend with. Suppose she wet her bed? She did sometimes. Suppose she walked in her sleep and fell down the stairs. Her aunt

Marion told her she did walk in her sleep, and she had been caught, fast asleep, out on the landing standing by the lift. If she wet the bed here, in this place, she would die of shame . . . and with this thought she fell asleep and woke with the light coming through a window she had not seen last night was there. She quickly felt the bed—no, she had not wet it. But now she wanted the toilet again. She crept out of the room, and in her little knickers and vest ran across the landing to the toilet. She felt like a burglar, and kept sending scared glances up the stairs and down. There were lights on everywhere. What time was it? Oh, suppose she was late for school, suppose . . . back inside her trousers and jersey, she went down the stairs and saw beneath her Edward at the table, eating toast. There was no sign of the woman with all that golden hair. Edward smiled nicely, made her toast, offered her tea, put the milk and sugar in the way she liked it, and then said he was going to take her to school.

She ought to have sandwiches or something, but did not like to ask. Perhaps Mr Pat would . . . she knew her lips were going to tremble again, but she made them tight, and smiled, and went off down the steps with Edward, leaving that house which in her mind was full of great rooms like shops. She scuttled along beside Edward through the lumps of wet leaves on the pavement. He took her to the great gate that last night had been so cruelly locked, and from there she ran to the classroom. On the way she saw Thomas.

'I slept in your room.' she announced proudly, superior and calm: she was her real age again and he was just a little kid.

'Why did you?'

'Your brother made me.'

'Then, I hope you didn't break any of my toys. Did you play with my Dangerman?'

She had not seen a Dangerman.

'That's all right, then,' said Thomas, going off to his class.

She was thinking that this little boy, so much younger, had spent the night in a strange place but it hadn't mattered to him. As for her, the night had been like a door opening into prospects and places she had not even known were there. She was thinking, 'I want my own room. I want my own *place*.' She did not dare to think, my own house, my own flat, that was far beyond her, but if she had her own room she could hide in it and be safe. Those wild animals with their gleaming eyes in Thomas's room were dangers that could get to her, find her. If she had her own room she could go to bed any time she liked instead of having to wait for auntie Marion to get tired. She could have a light by her bed and turn it off. '*My own place, my own* . . .' was what she brought into her own life from that night, which had been like a wonderland. But not entirely comfortable or even pleasant. She had behaved like a little girl instead of a big one, and she was ashamed to think what Edward must think of her. She had not missed his surprise when she had told him she was nine.

That afternoon, when the dark came, she stood near the gate to the street, waiting for someone to come and take her home. She was hoping that Edward would come for Thomas, and planned to smile at him, like a big girl, not all crying and stupid, and she'd say, 'Hello Edward,' and he would say, 'Oh, there you are, Victoria, it's you.' But another woman came, who had a couple of older kids with her, and Thomas rushed towards them, shouting. Victoria was so hungry: at lunchtime she had gone over to Mr Pat's, who would give her a big bag of crisps and let her pay tomorrow, but he wasn't there, only a girl she didn't know behind the counter. If her aunt's friend Phyllis came perhaps she would buy her a bit of chocolate or something. But it was Phyllis Chadwick's daughter Bessie, older than she was, and Victoria was ready with apologies for the mix-up others had caused, but Bessie said, 'Shame, poor little thing, your auntie's very sick, you're going to stay with us till she gets home.'

Running along beside the big girl Victoria said, 'Please, please, have you got some chocolate or something?'

'Didn't they give you anything for

lunchtime?'

'They forgot—they didn't know,' Victoria begged, all apology for noble Edward.

Bessie swerved off into a fish and chips, bought chips for both of them, and they ate as they walked along.

*   *   *

Mrs Stevens, auntie Marion, came home from a stay in hospital an invalid, her formerly large body already gaunt. She was always being rushed back for treatments that left her sick and weak. Victoria looked after her. After school she did not go to other children's homes to play, but came straight back to be a nurse. At school she was diligent and often praised. Victoria's evenings were spent doing homework or watching television programmes that told her about the world.

One afternoon, she was sent by her aunt to fetch urgent medicine, and she took a wrong turning and found herself in a street she felt she knew. The house of that evening when the tall kind boy had looked after her was in a part of her mind that corresponded to her dreams of it, floating in another dimension, nothing to do with the quotidian, the ordinary. She remembered warmth and glowing colour, a room piled with toys. Sometimes she stopped in front of shops in the High Street and thought yes, it was like this, the richness, the abundance.

If that house had a geographical location, then it was far off, in a distant part of London. Her legs had ached—hadn't they? Edward had pulled her along—oh, for ages. Yet wasn't this the house, just in front of her, not ten minutes' walk from her aunt's flat? Yes, it was that one, that very one there—was it?—yes; and at that moment a child came running along the pavement towards her but he turned in at a gate and up the steps. Thomas. He was larger than he had been, no longer a little kid. He reached up to a bell and almost at once the door opened and he dashed inside. She had a glimpse of that room she now knew was a hall, from seeing them on films, full of light and colour. After that she often secretly went to the house and stood there, or walked up and down outside it, hoping no one would notice her, as much as she wished that someone would. This was not an area where black people lived, or not in this street. Once she saw Edward, who was even taller. He strode along not seeing her or anyone, passing so close she could have touched him. He bounded up the steps, letting himself in with his own key. Well, she had a key, Victoria did, tied around her neck on ribbon, so that her aunt wouldn't have to get up and struggle to the door. More than once she saw the tall woman whose hair she remembered as being like Goldilocks, but now it was in a heap on top of her head. She was untidy. She was always worried, seeming in a struggle to keep hold of her bag, shopping bags, parcels. Victoria was critical, feeling that from this house only perfection should come. If she had hair like that, she couldn't let it be in a great lump, with wisps falling down. Then, again, she saw Thomas. They did not recognise her. What Victoria told herself was. They don't see me. Once, as Edward came striding along, no longer a boy, to Victoria's eyes, but a man—he was sixteen—she was tempted to call out, Look, I'm Victoria, don't you remember me? Then she told herself that if he and Thomas had grown out of what she remembered, then she must have too, tall for her age, shooting up, no longer in the junior school.

To her the most extraordinary thing was that the house, a dream, so far away she had never expected to see it again, was so close—only a short walk away.

In her aunt Marion's flat she still slept on the day-bed in the lounge. On nights when her aunt was poorly, she pulled it into the bedroom so she could be there when the sick woman woke and called for water, or a cup of tea, or said in her frightened thick voice, 'Are you there, Victoria?' Victoria had broken nights, and was finding it hard to keep up with her lessons. Her aunt's best friend, Phyllis Chadwick, Bessie's mother, came to see how things went along: she was supervising

Victoria, on behalf of the Authorities. Victoria did not resent it. She longed for help, from anyone. Sometimes Bessie came, and sat with aunt Marion while she went shopping or just to get out. In the day when she was at school, home helps or nurses dropped in. But really, Marion Stevens should be in hospital, she needed proper full-time nursing: it was what Phyllis Chadwick said, and what Victoria thought. 'If I wasn't here, they'd have to do something, but I am here and so they don't bother.'

Now four years had passed since that night when the tall boy had been so kind—so the event stayed with Victoria, in her mind and in her dreams—and her aunt was really very ill. Cancer. There was no hope, Marion herself told the girl. The nurse who came from Jamaica too, had said to her, 'There is a time to live, there is a time to die. Your time is coming soon, praise the Lord.'

Marion Stevens had always gone to church, but not to the same one as this nurse. Yet they prayed together often and Victoria had even heard them singing hymns. She was not sure about praising the Lord, with this dreadfully ill woman here in front of her eyes day and night. She enjoyed church, when she had time to go, because she liked singing, but now she had to stay with her aunt. The nurse said to Victoria that she would be rewarded in heaven for what she was doing for her aunt, and Victoria kept silent: the things she wanted to say were too rude.

It was so difficult, all of it, trying to get to school, doing her homework, when she was being interrupted every minute by her aunt's, 'Victoria, are you there?' Sometimes the sick woman could not be left, when it didn't look as if the home help would come: she often didn't, they were overworked, with too many helpless people on their hands. And often the nurses didn't stay, they checked pills or perhaps washed that smelly sick body and then they were off. 'I won't be a nurse, I won't.' Victoria promised herself. At school they suggested she could easily be a nurse, she could manage the exams. She was clever, they said. 'It's time to think what you want to be,' they told her. Bessie was going to be a nurse. Well, let her, Victoria would rather die, so she told herself.

The teachers were proud of her: not so many children at that school were likely to be anything much—on the streets, more probably. When she couldn't get to school at all, they forgave her and made excuses. They knew what her situation was, asked after her aunt and were sorry for her. One teacher offered prayers, and another actually dropped in to visit, to check on her of course, the girl knew, but it meant Victoria could go out to the shops. The home help never seemed to get things exactly right, though Victoria left lists on the kitchen table, in her neat handwriting, headed Food, or Medicines; and what had to be fetched from the chemist was longer than from the supermarket.

'You've got to eat, girl,' said Phyllis Chadwick, bringing her bits of this and that, some soup, some cake, but Victoria felt permanently nauseated from the smell of her aunt's illness. Sometimes she felt she was slowly submerging in the dark dirty water, that was the illness, down and down, but up there, far above her head, was light and air and good clean smells. When she could no longer bear it, she told her aunt she would be back in a minute and she ran through the streets and stood outside the Staveney house and thought about what was inside. Space, room for everyone. She had understood by now what had been so confused in her mind, and for so long: in that house was one family, the fair woman, who was the mother, and Edward, and Thomas. She had never questioned that there hadn't seemed to be a father. None of the families she knew had fathers, that is, real fathers, who stayed.

Her aunt Marion had never had a husband. When she had been well enough to be interested in her own story, she had said to Victoria that she had no man in her life but then she had no grief either. And that was as far as her explanations had gone. But if there had been a man around, Victoria thought, even an uncle, he could have helped her. She had to do everything, remember rates bills and the electric and the gas and the water, staying at home from school so the meters could be read, fetching her aunt's money from the post office. 'You're a good girl,' Phyllis Chadwick told her. 'You are a very good girl.'

But surely she was getting too old to be told she was a good girl? She was nearly fourteen. She had breasts now. She was not a little girl, but she was sleeping on the day-bed, with her possessions, such as they were, in a suitcase that had a cloth over it to make it look like a seat, and her clothes on a rail in a corner of her aunt's room. One day, prayed Victoria, I'll have my own place, my own room. Her aunt would die and then she would move into her aunt's room, and this would be her place.

For the last few weeks of her aunt's dying Victoria did not get to school. She was simply there, by the deathbed, and so much identified with the illness that she even had pains in her stomach: stomach cancer. It was all a long dark bad-smelling bad dream, the nurses coming and going, medicines, making cups of this and that which cooled untouched by her aunt's bed, while she cried with pain and Victoria measured out another dose of painkiller. Victoria said to Phyllis Chadwick, 'Why can't aunt go into hospital?' but it was put to her that this wouldn't happen until the very end, and meanwhile Victoria was being such a good girl. 'And she gave you a bed and a place.

Don't forget that, Victoria. She did that for you.'

At last aunt Marion was in hospital and Victoria visited her, for most of the day, though it was doubtful if her aunt knew she was there. 'But you never know,' said Phyllis Chadwick, and the nurses agreed. 'You never know these days if they are conscious of what is going on or not.' *These days* referred not to a recently acquired capacity of dying patients, but to new ideas about patients, who could be suspected of knowing everything that was going on around them, even if in a coma or half-dead. Or even dead?

Aunt Marion died and it seemed it was Victoria's responsibility to see to the funeral arrangements, supervised by Phyllis, though the actual signing of forms was done by a social worker, because Victoria was too young. She thought, If I'm too young to sign the forms, how is it I wasn't too young to look after her?

Victoria was in the empty flat, and she opened windows to let out the smell of dying and of medicines. When everything was fresh again she would move into her aunt's bedroom . . . there arrived a man who was consoling and respectful about aunt Marion's death, and her being all alone in the world, but asked where she planned to go, and she said, 'I'm staying here. In auntie's flat.'

'But you're only fourteen,' said this man.

'You can't be by yourself.'

Victoria was not really taking it in that she couldn't have this flat, have her own place, until Phyllis Chadwick came to say she had better come home with her. 'We'll make some room,' she said. 'We'll put you in with Bessie.' She had three children already.

'But I want to stay here,' persisted Victoria, and she went on protesting, and then begging and weeping and refusing to leave until one day Phyllis Chadwick, who knew the officials concerned (she too was a social worker) arrived at the flat with a senior official, who was going to put a lock on the door, to keep it empty until someone the right age arrived to live in it.

And now Victoria was dumb. She was numbed by the injustice. She had looked after her aunt for years, had remembered to pay everything, remembered times for medicines, and kept the place clean. No one thought her too young for that. Now, just like that, she was being taken to the door, Phyllis Chadwick on one side, the man with the keys on the other, both holding her by an arm, while Victoria shouted, 'No, no, no,' and then went silent again, her lips tight closed. On the pavement outside the flats—she had to look up ten floors to see her auntie's windows—they let her go, and Phyllis said to her, 'Now, Victoria, that's enough, girl.' But Victoria hadn't said one word all the way down.

She was frightening both these people: she trembled with rage and with the shock of it, it seemed she could explode. Her eyes were mad, were wild. 'Victoria, surely you couldn't have thought you'd be allowed to live by yourself—a girl of fourteen?'

But that is exactly what she had thought and was thinking now.

At last she went home to Phyllis Chadwick, and she was shown another pull-out bed in Bessie's room, who was being nice, but was furious. She had only just achieved this room, a little one, but her own, and now she had to share it. This flat had three rooms, apart from the kitchen and the lounge, all small. The two younger children, noisy boys, slept in with Phyllis Chadwick, in her room. Another room was used by Phyllis's grandfather, who was very old and dying of something or other. Victoria didn't want to know She had had enough of illness and dying. The two boys had been in the little room but Bessie was taking exams and needed quiet. It seemed Phyllis didn't deserve quiet, and had to put up with the boys: it was this thought that persuaded Victoria to be grateful for what she was being offered. She reported back at school, and the teachers said she could stay an extra year, to make up. No more was said about scholarships and university—she was too far behind. She could go to commercial college and take book-keeping. She was good at figures.

Being too old for the class she was in isolated her. She was alone too because of her experience of illness and responsibility. The others in her class seemed like children to her, and the whole school had shrunk, as people and places do. The playground, which on that long-ago night had seemed to her a vast and dangerous place, with shadows full of muggers and knives, she now saw was a pathetic paltry place, so small that at break there wasn't room for the children to play. Victoria knew now how bad a school this was. That playground summed up everything for her. Grey cement and damp old brick walls, you'd think it was where prisoners were let out to exercise. Good enough for us, she thought, bitter, and then, I bet Thomas and Edward don't go to a school where the playground is like a prison yard. Yes, they were taken swimming once a week in the summer, but that was about it. Good enough for class 5 people. Good enough for the under class. That's us. She got this language from Phyllis Chadwick's pamphlets and social-working guides.

She knew she should be grateful to Phyllis Chadwick, who was a good woman. Without her, she would have been taken into Care. 'You must think of us as your family,' said Phyllis. 'You must call me Auntie Phyl.'

Now, coming home from school, Victoria made detours to pass the Staveney house, and one day saw a tall, fair boy coming up the pavement and turn in at the gate. She thought: *Edward,* and yearned for that long ago kindness but saw it was Thomas. He did look very like his brother. He noticed Victoria, frowned, and went in. Victoria did not at all resemble the skinny little black girl, with her sticking-out plaits. She was tall and slender, and Phyllis Chadwick had sent her to a hairdresser, who was a friend, and now Victoria had a neat soft Afro round a pretty face that had a pointed chin and a full mouth that Bessie told her was her best feature, 'Wow, now make the most of that.' But Victoria thought her big eyes were her best feature.

Thomas had not been at their school for three years. He was at the kind of school people like the Staveneys would send their sons to: she knew enough to know that.

Now she buckled down to exams, and sometimes sneaked looks at the Staveney house, but she did not see Thomas.

She passed her exams well enough, but nothing like as well as had been expected of her, before her aunt's illness. She at once found a job. Mr Pat, who had always liked her, said that his brother, who had a little dress shop, needed an assistant, and someone to keep his books. She would earn enough to give something to Phyllis Chadwick for her keep, but very far was she from a place of her own, and this was what she dreamed of, always. She was not the only one. Phyllis herself had two rumbustious boys in her room every night and, while sometimes they were separated for everyone's peace's sake, one sleeping in the lounge, and one beside Phyllis, the two of them could make the little flat sound like a fairground with noise. Bessie, who was going to be a nurse and needed space for her studies, used the table in the kitchen, where the light was good, but was always being interrupted by the boys. She and Victoria were friends, but Bessie knew that without Victoria she could have had a room to herself. The old man, Phyllis's grandfather, occupied a whole room, with his little television and radio and piles of magazines. He had had a stroke and was part paralysed, and just as for Victoria's aunt, nurses and home helps came in and out when Victoria and Phyllis and Bessie were out working. He sat in a big chair, his body dwindling away into cavities and lumps, under a great head that looked like a lion's. Beside him on the floor was a flask always filled with strong-smelling dark yellow pee. There was a commode in a corner. His old thin knobbly legs stuck out in front, on a stool, and there were cracks in the black skin, which seemed to have grey ash in them. Phyllis oiled his feet and legs, but that didn't help. Everyone secretly thought that it would be best if he died and took his miserable and unenjoyed life away, and then there would be a room, a whole room, where the boys could make their mess and noise and shut the door.

Bessie was good to the old man: she saw it as useful for her training. Victoria dutifully did what she had to do, emptying the urine flask, and sometimes the commode, but she hated it. Phyllis, who worked long hours, and had four youngsters and the old man to see to, was sometimes able to sit with him a little. He said that no one cared about him.

Phyllis said to Victoria, ‘We need a serious talk, girl, so when will that be?’

It would have to be Sunday, and on Sunday evening when the boys were getting up to mischief outside in the streets, with their gang, Bessie absenting herself behind a shut door, Victoria and Phyllis closed his door on the old man, who complained. ‘But it will be only for a short minute, Grandad,’ Phyllis told him.

Victoria had decided Phyllis was going to ask her to leave: there was not a reason in the world why Victoria should be here at all, adding to an over-burdened woman’s troubles.

‘Make us both a good strong cup of coffee, and then come and sit down,’ said Phyllis. She fitted her bulk into a sofa corner, and put her feet up. She seemed tempted to drop off to sleep then and there.

‘Victoria,’ she said, ‘I know you took that job in such a haste because you wanted to give me something, but it makes me sad, girl, you’re not doing as well for yourself as you could do.'

Behind this directive, which was delivered in the manner of one who has been planning words, in Phyllis's case for several nights, lay a story which neither Victoria nor Bessie knew anything about. Not even her grandfather knew half of it.

Phyllis Chadwick's grandparents came to London after the Second World War on the wave of immigrants invited to take on the dirty work which English labourers did not want. They came to streets they had imagined paved with gold and found—but all that has been well documented. A hard life, hard times, and the young couple had two children, one Phyllis's mother, a lively rebellious girl who got herself pregnant aged fourteen, and had a botched abortion which left her, she was told, sterile, and she embarked on what she thought would be consequence-free sex, but became pregnant again, with Phyllis. Phyllis's father, for she must have had one, never made himself known, and her mother kept the information to herself. The very young mother and child took shelter with parents who sermonised, but saw them fed. Phyllis did remember her as a shouting screaming mother, in fact a bit demented, who could disappear for days on some binge or spree, returning sullen and silent to lecturing parents, who had had to look after Phyllis. She got herself killed in a brawl. Phyllis was relieved. She was then looked after by her grandfather, who was now there, just behind that door, from where came loud television noises and radio (he often had both on at once) and her grandmother, who was kind but strict, because of the bad example of her mother. 'You have bad blood,' she was told, every day of her life. Phyllis worked hard at school, determined never to be drunken or vagrant or brawling, and was ambitious to get her own roof and her own family. She passed exams and then had a brief lapse from grace, as her grandparents saw it, telling her she was going the way of her mother, because she did not stick with one job, but took many, one after the other, from a feeling of power, of freedom. She was a large sensible girl, pretty enough, and worked at check-outs, sold shoes in an Oxford Street shop, served food at the big trade fairs in Earl's Court, was a waitress in a coffee shop, and was having the time of her life. The money—yes, that was wonderful, it was fairy gold arriving in her hands every week, but what she was earning was the liberty to do as she liked. She stayed in a job just as long as it suited her, and then the best moment of all was the interview for the next: she was liked, chosen out of sometimes dozens of applicants. There was something about her employers trusted. While her grandparents grumbled and prophesied a feckless future and a disgraceful old age, she felt she was dancing on air, owned her self and her future. But then she met her fate, the father of Bessie, though not of the boys, and had to buckle to. She started on the lowest rung of the Social Services ladder, and in due time was given her own flat, this one. Her grandmother, who had in fact been more of a mother, died, and her grandfather became her responsibility. 'He landed on my poor shoulders like the old man of the sea,' she would say. But she was not only bound to be grateful, she was fond of the old man who, when you saw him naked, was like a dangling puppet, thin and loose underneath the big head and face that had all his history in it.

'Victoria, my girl,' says Phyllis. 'What are you doing in that nothing job, and you are such a clever girl?'

'What do you want me to do? What shall I do?'

What Phyllis wanted to say was, For the Lord's sake! Get yourself *out*, make use of this time, because you'll meet a man and then your number's up. But she didn't want to wake in Victoria the bad blood that was bound to be lurking there, and in any case the devil lay in wait for women, disguised in smiles and flattery.

She leaned forward, took the two young hands in her own and threw all thought of being a bad influence over her shoulder. 'You're only young once,' she said. 'You're pretty, though handsome is as handsome does.

You have nothing to weigh you down yet.' Victoria noted that *yet* which was a giveaway about how Phyllis Chadwick saw her own life.

'There are jobs you could do, Victoria. Unless you try for them you'll never know what you can get.' She suppressed: if I could get a nice little job, when I wasn't even pretty, what could you get for yourself, with your face and figure? 'You don't want to limit yourself to what you can get around here, in this neighbourhood. You just get yourself down to Oxford Street and Knightsbridge and up to Brent Cross and pick yourself the fanciest there is, and walk in bold as brass and say you want a job.' She went on to talk of modelling, which is what she would have liked best, but she was not built for it. 'Why not? You've got a well-made body and a face to match.' The best of the things she had done herself, and the ones beyond her, were being presented to Victoria. Phyllis Chadwick, the descendant of slaves, whose name, Chadwick, had been the slave owner's, knew that she had been good enough to work in places that wouldn't have let her parents through the door. All the time she was talking, a little nerve of panic was twitching: am I sending her into danger, am I doing that? But she's so sensible, so cool, she'll not come to harm.

She gave Victoria money, told her to go out and buy herself a bit of style but not be too flash.

Victoria took all this in, not least that she had been given a glimpse into her benefactor's life that she would have to think over.

She fitted herself out, and, taking heart from Phyllis's homilies, began at the top, in Oxford Street, for she did not yet know anything better and smarter. She worked for a while selling perfume and then, having learned that Oxford Street was not the empyrean, became assistant in a very exclusive shop indeed, but left that, when she became irked by it, for encouraged by Phyllis she was able to acknowledge imperfections even at the top. She hated selling beautiful clothes to women too ugly or too old, clothes that would have looked—*did* look—better on herself, and she found herself modelling for a photographer, not pornographic, but sexy enough to embarrass her, and then, proving herself as contradictory as Phyllis, who urged her on while counselling caution, she did nude poses for another photographer. All this time she was putting money aside, her nest egg, the entrance fee to her own place, her own, hers.

The nude poses seemed to have as their natural end sex with the photographer, so she left.

The grandfather died. The young ones saw from Phyllis's grief that this had been much more than just a smelly old half-dead man, with his urine bottle, who had taken up space better used by the living.

Into the room went the two boys, and Phyllis told Bessie and Victoria that she had never in her life before this time had her own room. She was in her own room, and she actually wept tears of gratitude to life, or fate, or God, for it.

Bessie, a good-natured, easy-going young woman, said to Victoria, as they lay in their little room, talking into the dark, that she had thought the old man, the grandfather, her great-grandfather, a rough type: she had been embarrassed by him. 'Yes, I was, Victoria, he used to get me really upset by some of the things he said.'

Victoria did not comment. She had a good idea of what raw materials Phyllis had made her life. She could feel for Phyllis in ways that Bessie didn't. Couldn't, rather: she had had it easy. She, Victoria, was closer to Phyllis than Bessie was.

Victoria had no idea how Phyllis yearned over her, fretted because of her, was afraid for her. She had lived as Victoria did now, dancing on the edge of danger, and while she urged Victoria on, and triumphed in the young woman's successes, the sparkling new job, the compliment from an employer, or from a customer, she thought secretly that there is no more dangerous item in the world than a pretty young woman on the loose. Luckily, the older woman thought, when we are girls we don't know that we are like sticks of dynamite or like fireworks in a box too close to a fire.

Oh, yes, older women understand why some people think young ones should be locked up! Good God, girl, Phyllis Chadwick might think, watching Victoria go off to work, looking a million dollars, you're a walking catastrophe in the making, though you trip along so meek and mild not looking to right or left, you don't sway your little hips and come on fast, you wouldn't let that photographer go too far (Phyllis knew about the first but not the nude-poser), but all the same, girl, you're playing with fire, and so was I, and I had no idea of what I was like. Sometimes I could shake and shudder at the risks I took.

'Don't you worry so much, Ma,' said Bessie to her mother, after they had watched Victoria go off to work as a croupier in a gambling place. 'She's got an old head on her.'

'I hope she has, my dear,' and Phyllis thought how odd it was that this daughter of hers, whom of course she loved, since she was her daughter, was far away across a gulf of incomprehension, that generation gap that is the cruellest of all, between parents who have done it the hard way, to win ease and safety for their children, who then have no understanding of what they have been saved from. 'But Victoria understands me,' Phyllis thought.

Now Victoria was in a job she liked better than anything so far, a big music shop, in the

West End. She had earned more in other places, but this was where she belonged. The music, the people who came in, the other assistants—all perfect, all a pleasure, and she told Phyllis and Bessie that this time she would stick.

One afternoon who should come in but Thomas Staveney: for a moment she again thought she was looking at Edward. She watched him wander about the store, at his ease in it, familiar with everything: he picked up tapes and put them down and finally bought a video of a concert from The Gambia. Then he arrived in front of her, and said, 'You're Victoria.' 'And you're Thomas,' she rejoined smartly. He was eyeing her but not in a way she could object to: of course he must be surprised: she knew what he was remembering. She stood smiling, letting him come to conclusions.

Then he said the last thing she expected: 'Why don't you come home with me and have some supper?'

'I'm not free for another hour.'

'I'll come back for you.' He sloped out. His style was one no one need notice in this place, more Jimmy Dean than Che Guevara; there was a hole at the knee of his jeans, and another in his sweater elbow

When the two left the store, as it closed, they were an incongruous pair, for she was in a sleek black leather jacket, a black leather skirt, heels like shiny black chopsticks. Her hair was straight now, like black patent leather.

They took a bus, another, and were soon outside that house that had been inhabiting her dreams for ten years.

She was now nineteen, he, seventeen. They knew to the month how old each was. He looked much older, and she did too, a smart young woman, no girl, this.

As he went up the steps she lingered, to grasp the moment. She was here with the tall fair boy she had been dreaming of, yet it was like those dreams where a familiar figure comes towards you, but it is not he, this is a stranger; or with what delight you see across a room your lost sweetheart and she turns her head with a smile you don't know. This was Thomas, and not Edward, and the theme of deception continued as she tripped fast up the steps to join him at the opening door: the hall which had stayed in her mind as a place of soft colours and lights was smaller, and the spring afternoon sent a cold light where she remembered a warm diffusing glow. She remembered a reddish-rose softness, and here they were, old rugs, on the floor and on the walls, but she could see white threads where the light highlit worn patches. They were shabby. Yes, pretty, she supposed: could not these rich people afford new ones? At once she put the remembered room, unchanged, into another part of her mind, to keep it there safe, and condemned what she saw as an imposter. Now they were in the enormous room she remembered she had been told was a kitchen. It still was—nothing had changed. A child, she had not taken in all the cupboards and the fridge and the stove, which could easily appear in a magazine that endorsed such things, and here was the table, large, yes, as she remembered, and the chairs around it, and the big chair where she had sat on Edward's knee and he had told her a story.

Thomas had put water into the kettle and switched it on, and reached into a vast refrigerator. He brought out various items which he deposited on the table, and said, 'But if you'd like something else? I'm making coffee.'

At Phyllis's, coffee was drunk, often and copiously, so she said, 'Coffee, please,' and sat down, since he had not thought to suggest it.

If she could not stop herself sending glances of enquiry, and then confirmation, at him, he could not stop looking at her. She thought he was like someone who had bought something special at the supermarket and was pleased with his buy.

'Where's your brother?' she asked, half afraid to hear what he would say, since the answer was bound to confirm that this was not Edward, nor ever could be.

'He's in Sierra Leone, gathering *facts*,' was the reply, and she could not miss the resentment that was supposed to be concealed by indifference. 'Gathering facts as *usual*,' he added. And then, deciding that politeness needed more, 'He's a lawyer, these days. He's with a lawyer's outfit that gathers facts about poverty—that kind of thing.'

'And your ma? Does she still live here?'

'Where else? This is her house. She comes and goes at her own sweet will. But don't worry, she keeps her distance.'

In this way her suspicion was confirmed that there was something clandestine about this escapade. After all, he was seventeen. He must still be at school somewhere. She was the prize got at the supermarket.

For all of Edward's tumultuous decade of growing up, Thomas had been the very pattern of a younger brother. He belittled and he jeered and he mocked, while Edward championed this cause or that, filling the house with pamphlets, brochures, appeals and quarrelling with his mother. Yet Jessy supported Edward, on principle, and Thomas might go off with both of them to a concert of musicians from South Africa or Zanzibar. At one of these shows Thomas, aged eleven, fell in love with a black singer and thereafter went to every black concert or dance group that came to London. The secret torments of teenage lust were all directed towards one black charmer after another. He said openly and often that he thought white skins were insipid, and he wished he had been born black. He collected African music from everywhere, and from his room when he was in it came the sounds of drumming and singing, as loud as he could get it, until Edward shouted at him to give it a rest and his mother complained that her sons did nothing by halves. 'If only I could have had a nice sensible girl,' she mourned: this was very much the note of the women's movement of the time.

Thomas had in a thousand fantasies come up those steps with some delectable black star or starlet and when he saw Victoria in the music shop his dreams in one illuminating moment came close and smiled at him.

Victoria asked if he remembered she had slept in his room that long ago night. He did not, but he grasped at this gift from Fate and said, 'Would you like to see it?'

Up the stairs they went and into a room no longer like a toy shop, but full of posters of black singers and musicians. Never has an old sweet dream of something unobtainable turned so sharply to say: But I was not that, I was this all the time. She knew all the performers from their recordings, and now she sat on the bed to listen to music from Mozambique, staring around at the posters, while Thomas stared at her.

Victoria was not entirely a virgin, because she had only just escaped from the predatory photographer number two. Thomas was not pristine either, because he had managed to persuade a waitress—black, of course—that he was older than he was. But he was inexperienced enough, and nervous enough of this cool black chick, to delay and put off and then put on another tape, and another, until Victoria got up and said, 'I think I should be getting home, it's late.'

But he jumped up and grasped her arms and stammered, 'Oh, no, Victoria, please, oh, do stay.' So he gabbled, and she stood, helpless, because it was not Thomas just then, but Edward who held her. He began kissing her on her neck, her face and then, well, you could say it was inevitable, given that years had gone into the making of the moment.

Since both were so unskilled, they had to confess, and that made conspiring innocents of them, and so she stayed, while he begged her not to leave him, and stayed, and it was hours later that she crept down those steps, with his arm proudly around her, he hoping he would be seen, she hoping she was not. When she got home Phyllis accepted her apologies with a sigh, and she was saying to herself: So, that's it, I suppose I should be glad she's been safe until now.

It was a long summer, a warm good summer, and Thomas, who should have been studying for his final exams, was meeting Victoria at her music shop every day, and going home with her, and up to his room, where they made love to the sounds of music from most of Africa, not to mention the West Indies and the Deep South of America too.

Jessy found them at the big table, drinking strong black coffee.

'Make me some,' she told her son, and sat, falling back into her chair, eyes shut. 'What a day,' she said. When she opened them a large cup of strong black coffee steamed in front of her and she was looking into a face she seemed to know.

'I'm Victoria,' said Victoria. 'You let me stay here one night, when I was little.'

Jessy had had children of all ages in that kitchen for years, and some had been black, particularly more recently, during Edward's Third-World phase. Who was this frighteningly smart black girl? She was feeling a generalised warmth, reminiscent, even nostalgic: she had enjoyed that time of children, who came and went and slept over.

'Well,' she said, 'it's nice to see you again.' And having swallowed the coffee with a grimace—it was much too hot—she jumped up. 'I've got to get to . . .' But she was already gone.

You might be tempted to say that two people whose deepest secret fantasies had been made flesh in each other were in love, had to be, even that they loved. Never has anything been more irrelevant than being in love, or loving. Thomas was not Edward: this was a rougher, coarser-fibred creature—not a man, he was still a boy after all. And Thomas was not finding in Victoria the luscious sexy black charmers of his fantasies. She was a careful correct young woman, who walked as if afraid of taking up too much space, who hung her clothes on the back of the chair, folded nicely, before getting into bed. She was pretty, oh yes; he adored that warm brown skin against the white sheets; she had the nicest little face, but she was no siren, no temptress, and he knew that sex could be different from this—wilder, hotter, wetter, sweeter.

In short, no two people who have spent a summer making love most afternoons could have learned less than they did about each other's minds, lives, needs.

The summer began to dim for autumn, and he would have to go back to school, and Victoria was pregnant.

She at once told Phyllis, who was neither surprised, nor angry. The boys were out, doubtless raising hell, Bessie was at her hospital. The two were alone: they did not have to lower their voices or watch for an opening door.

'And is the father going to stand by you?'

'He's white.'

'Oh, my Lord,' said Phyllis, and her dismay was not so much for the weight of history she was managing to put into those three syllables, but for much nearer trouble.

'Oh, Lordy-Lord,' she said again, with a sigh from her depths. Then she summed up, 'There'll be problems.'

'I don't want him to know.'

Phyllis Chadwick nodded, accepted this, while she sighed and frowned—brows puckering, lips woeful—knowing what Victoria was in for: the girl herself didn't. The end of her butterfly time—well, that had to happen, and it had been too short, but Victoria could have no idea how her horizons were going to tighten around her.

'I can manage,' said Victoria, and now Phyllis's face showed some humour that was meant to be seen: Victoria would manage because Phyllis would help her. But the young woman had got further ahead in hcr thinking than the older woman knew

'As a single mum I'll be entitled to my own place,' said Victoria. She knew all about it because she had heard it from her aunt and from Phyllis: girls got pregnant because they wanted to escape from their families, most often their mothers.

'I hope that is not why you let yourself get careless?'

Careless? Thomas used condoms and she had no idea if he had been careless or not. 'No. But when I knew, that was when I thought I can have my own place.'

'I see.'

'I can work in the music shop till the baby.

They like me there.'

'And so I should think, that they like you. You're such a good girl.'

'And they said I can go back when the baby's old enough.'

Phyllis was smiling, but there was something there that made Victoria slip off her chair and crouch beside the older woman like a child needing to be held. Phyllis held her, and Victoria began to cry. What she was crying for Phyllis could not possibly guess: if Edward, if that tall fair kindly boy, had been the father of this child, then Victoria would have told him.

'We'll start seeing about your own place,' said Phyllis. 'I'll speak to the housing officers.'

There were waiting lists, but when the baby was three months old Victoria moved into a flat in the same building, four floors up. You could say she had a perfect situation. Phyllis, who would help with the baby, was so close. Bessie, a nurse, would be on hand too. The two boys, growing up fast, tearaways and bad lots, were delighted with this baby, 'A penny from heaven,' they said, and promised to babysit and teach her to walk.

When Mary was a year old, Victoria, again a slender pretty young woman, still not quite twenty-one, went back to work. There was a child minder in these buildings, one known to Phyllis. At weekends Victoria took Mary to the park and wheeled her around and played with her and there the two were noticed by a handsome young man, who turned out to be a musician, a singer in a pop group. He thought Victoria with her little girl the prettiest thing he had seen in his life, and said so. Victoria could not resist. Phyllis Chadwick had feared the man who would be Victoria's doom; the unknown white progenitor of little Mary had turned out not to be him, but she had only to take a look at this one to know the future. Phyllis had told Victoria to hold out for a good man, who would stick; yes, there weren't many of them around, but Victoria was pretty and clever enough to be worth one. This man, she told Victoria, would be all spice and sugar, but 'You'll not get much more out of him than that.'

But Victoria got her way and her man, for she married him and became Mrs Bisley. Now there were real difficulties because he moved in to live with her and the little girl, and there wasn't room enough, and besides, Victoria got benefits as a single mother, which she now had to forfeit. Sam Bisley was out every night, playing gigs all over London and other cities, he came and went, and while Mary had a father, which was more than most of the other black kids did, she scarcely saw him. And he didn't see all that much of Victoria either, working at his music seven days a week. Then Victoria was pregnant again and Phyllis mourned. She had not seen the man who had impregnated her with her two boys since the night the deed was done. 'Now you've done it,' she told Victoria. 'Well, we'll have to manage.'

And was this tragic sympathy really necessary? Yes, Sam Bisley was hardly the perfect husband and father, but she loved him, and knew the little girl did too. And when there was his baby, he'd be around more and . . . so she reasoned, trying to calm Phyllis.

Her job in the music shop must end, though they valued her. Two small children—no. She would stay at home for a while and be a mother, and then later . . . she did get money from Sam, if not much. She could manage. Her life had become the juggling act familiar to all young women with small children. She found herself a few hours a week working for Mr Pat and he was pleased to have her: he was getting on. She took one babe to the minder and another to nursery school, looked after other women's children in return for their helping her, and knew that the real theme of her life was waiting: she waited for Sam, who was always coming back from somewhere. Sometimes he brought friends who had to sleep on the sofa and the floor. She cooked for them and put their clothes into the washing machine with Sam's and the kids'. She could scarcely remember the free young woman who was a bit of a pet in the music shop, let alone the girl who had had all those glamorous jobs in the West End. But it all went on well enough, she was holding her own, the babies were fine—only they already were not babies, but small children, and Phyllis Chadwick was there, four floors down, always helpful, kind and ready with advice, most of which Victoria did take. And then Phyllis died, just like that. She had a stroke, a bad one. She didn't linger on, as her grandfather had done. Now Bessie was responsible for the boys, and could not help Victoria as much as she had. Perhaps who missed Phyllis most was Victoria. 'What's wrong with you and your long face?' Sam wanted to know, not unkindly, but he was not a man for the miseries. But he did go to the funeral, and the two little children stood between Victoria and Sam and saw earth thrown down over the woman whom they had called Gran.

Soon after that Sam Bisley was killed in a car crash. He was always on the road to and from somewhere, and he drove—as she had told him often enough—like a madman. She was afraid to drive with him, and when the children were in the car she begged, 'Drive more slowly—for the kids, even if you won't for me.' He was smashed up with a friend, one who had spent the night sometimes, on the sofa, or on the floor, and for whom she had cooked plates of fried eggs and fried bananas and bacon.

Victoria took hold of herself, rather like picking up the pieces of a vase that has fallen, and sticking the bits together. There were the children to consider. They depended on her now, and she knew to the roots of her being what depending on someone could mean: the absence of Phyllis Chadwick was as if behind there had been warm rock, where she had leaned, and now there was space where cold winds wailed and whistled. Victoria had to beat down waves of panic. Bessie told her she would find another man. Victoria did not think so. She had loved Sam. Long ago Edward had marked her for his own, and then there had been Sam. Thomas had not come into it. For better or worse, Sam had been her man.

One afternoon she saw Thomas in the street. He had not much changed. He was with a black girl, and they were laughing, arm in arm. Victoria thought: That was me. If she had bothered to consider Thomas at all, she would have decided that he would go on with black girls. 'I like black best,' he had joked. She remembered how he had brought forth a photograph of her—by the second photographer—nude, posing and pouting, and had said, 'Go on, Victoria, do that pose for me now' She had refused, had been offended. She was not like that. Maybe that girl there across the street . . . ? A smart girl she was, not like Victoria now, who did not have time for doing herself up.

Thomas was walking towards his home with the girl. Victoria followed them, on the other side of the street. If Thomas did look up and see her, he would wave—but would he? He would see a black woman with two kids: he wouldn't really see her at all.

And now she stopped dead on the pavement, and the thought hit her, but really taking her breath away: she stood with her hand pressed into her solar plexus. She was crazy! Thomas's child was here, sitting beside Sam Bisley's son, Dickson. So far and so completely had she shut out any thought of Thomas as a father, it was as if she was in possession of a completely new idea. She had made a good job of that, all right—cutting Thomas out of her mind. Why had she? There was something about that summer that made her uncomfortable. She knew she didn't really like Thomas—but he had been a kid, seventeen: what was he really like? She had no idea. He wasn't Edward; for all of the summer that had been her strongest thought. Now she bent to peer at the little girl who was the result of that summer: she didn't look like Thomas. Mary was a pretty, plump little thing, always smiling and willing. She was a pale brown, lighter than her mother by several shades, and much paler than the little boy, who was darker than Victoria. Sam had been a black black man, and she had liked to match skins with him—in the early days, before they had got used to each other. He used to call her his chocolate rabbit . . . and then he would eat her all up. 'I'll eat you all up,'—but she did not like to think of their lovemaking, it made her want to cry. Not thinking of Sam was part of her holding herself together. But here was little Mary, and there, walking rapidly away down the street towards his home, was Mary's father.

She was so shaken by all this that she went home earlier than usual with the kids, made them sit quietly in front of the television, and thought until she expected her mind to burst. That little girl over there, staring at the telly and licking at a lolly—she was an extension of that house, that big rich house.

Victoria knew the Staveneys were famous. She knew *now.* That was how she categorised them, famous, a word that meant they were far removed from the undistinguished run of ordinary people where Victoria belonged. She had seen Jessy Staveney's name in the papers, and had made enquiries: that woman with her golden hair—so Victoria still thought of her—was famous in the theatre. Victoria thought of a musical, like *Les Misérables,* which the first of the photographers had taken her to see. She remembered that afternoon as she did the Staveney house, a vision into another world, beautiful, but she Victoria did not belong: she had never thought of going to a musical or the theatre by herself or with Bessie. And Edward, the fair kind boy—Victoria could still feel the warmth of those arms around her—he had been in the newspapers because he was a lawyer and had returned from somewhere in

Africa, and had written letters about conditions. Phyllis Chadwick had cut out the letters, and kept them, not because of the connection with Victoria, but because in her social work she dealt with people from there—Ethiopia, was it? Sierra Leone?—and she found what was in the letters useful, to fight some battle she was having with superiors about housing refugees. And there was more. Lionel Staveney was famous because he was an actor, and she had seen him on television. It had taken Phyllis to say, 'Is that the same Staveneys?' The truth was, Phyllis had always been more interested in the Staveneys than she had ever been. Until now.

And that too was so upsetting to think of, like something pricking into her side, or in her shoe, that she positively wriggled as she sat trying to rid herself—*what had been the matter with her?* What had got into her that she had cut the Staveneys so completely out of her mind? When Phyllis mentioned them she felt a sort of revulsion, and it was Thomas she had not wanted to think of. But surely that was unfair? An ordinary seventeen-year-old, pretending to be older, having his first real sex, and she had gone there most evenings for weeks. No one had forced her!

Now Victoria had begun to think, she kept it up. She thought about the Staveneys and looked hard at little Mary. You can't go wrong with Mary, Phyllis had said. You can't go wrong with the Mother of God. She was Mary Staveney Not Mary Bisley.

She had a pretty good idea what the future of the two little children would be. The six-year-old, the two-year-old, would have to go to the same school she had, and she knew now what a bad school it was. Much worse now than when she had gone there. It was a violent school, full of drugs, fights, gangs, and these days the children who went to that kind of school were seen rather like wild animals who had to be kept restrained. It had been rough when she was there, she knew that now, though then she had not questioned anything. A good little girl, a star pupil, doing her homework—that was why they had made a fuss of her: she had liked to learn and do her lessons. Not like most. These days she would probably be wild and fighting, like the other kids now. And soon there would be Mary and Dickson, having to fight battles every minute, and they would come out the other end of it ignorant—worse even than she had been. She did know now how ignorant she had been, that pretty good little girl who owed everything to Phyllis, who had made her do homework, kept her at it. But in spite of the homework and the hard work, she had been ignorant. She was in that Staveney house most evenings for a summer and had not understood a thing. She had not been curious enough to ask questions. She had not known the questions to ask; not known there were questions to ask, and now, six years later, she could measure her ignorance then by what she had not asked or even wondered at. There was a father, Lionel Staveney, and so used was she to families that had mothers and no fathers, or fathers that came and disappeared again, she had taken it for granted there was no man around in the Staveney house. The truth was, she, Victoria, with her man Sam Bisley, had been better off than most of the women her age: he had not only married her but was sometimes there. A father; a father actually taking responsibility.

She did remember Thomas had said his mother and his father did not get on. She seemed to remember that Thomas said his father paid for school fees 'and that kind of thing'.

And Jessy Staveney? She had never asked who Victoria was or what she did, was seldom there, and when she was accepted her presence, without a nasty word or look, though surely she must have sometimes wondered if she and Thomas . . . Retrospectively Victoria was a bit shocked. Surely Jessy Staveney should have said something?

Seventeen: that meant Thomas was now twenty-three or twenty-four. Victoria was twenty-six. Edward who had seemed so unreachably above her in age as in everything else, when he was twelve to her nine, was almost thirty. Edward wrote letters to newspapers, which were published. No one would ever print a letter by her, and nothing she said could be considered important or even interesting.

And these two children, Mary and Dickson, would emerge from school even more ignorant than she had been. Would Mary ever learn enough to be a nurse, like Bessie? And Sam's son, if he didn't have some music in him from his father, what would he be?

Thomas's children, when he had them, and Edward's, they would be writing letters to the papers that would be printed. And they might turn out famous, like Jessy and Lionel and Edward.

All these thoughts that should—surely?—have marched profitably through her mind years ago during that long lovemaking summer, were presenting themselves now. Now she believed that she must have been a bit simple, not merely ignorant, but stupid.

She had never then thought, Thomas has a right to know. Now she was thinking: But it takes two to make a baby, a favourite saying of Phyllis who had often to deal with paternity cases. 'I don't think the idea even knocked at the door,' Victoria thought. 'Why didn't it? And if it had been unfair to Thomas, then what about little Mary who had a father in that part of society where people's names were known, and they had letters printed in newspapers. And children were sent to real schools. Thomas had been at the same school as her, she dimly remembered, because the father—Lionel Staveney—had said his children should know how the other half lived. So Edward and Thomas had both spent some years with the other half's children before being whisked off to real schools where children learned. If she, Victoria, had been at a real school, then . . . but children who go to real schools don't have to nurse sick mothers and fall out of the race—fall off that ladder that goes up—and become girls working in supermarkets or posing for dirty little photographers. If they are pretty enough.

Suppose I didn't have my looks? Fat Bessie could never have had that time in the West End, all those jobs I had, I could pick and choose. It was Phyllis who said to me, you just believe in yourself and just walk in, show you aren't scared, and you'll be surprised . . . and Phyllis had been right. But she, Victoria, was pretty. Luck. Luck—it was everything. Good luck and bad luck. What could you call it, that day, when they had forgotten her and her aunt was sick, and Edward had taken her home? Good luck—was it? She had lived for years in a dream, she knew that now, thinking about that house, all rosy golden lights and warmth and kindness. Edward. And Edward had led to Thomas. What sort of luck had that been? Well, she had got Mary from it, a solemn little girl with beautiful eyes—like her own. Mary was alive because of luck, a series of lucky or unlucky things happening because Edward Staveney had forgotten her that afternoon, leaving her alone and afraid in the school playground. And Thomas walking into the music shop? No, that wasn't anything, he was mad about music from Africa and that was the shop for it. But he could have taken his tapes and stuff to the other girl working there that afternoon, black too, and smart and well-dressed, just as she had been.

Victoria seemed to herself like a little helpless thing that had been buffeted about, by strokes of luck, not knowing what was happening, or why. But now she was not helpless, at last she had her wits about her. What did she want? Simply that Mary should be acknowledged by the Staveneys, and after that—well, they would all have to see.

* * *

Thomas was with a black girl in his room when his telephone rang. He heard, 'I'm Victoria. Do you remember me?' He did, of course he did. These days, when he thought of her, it was with curiosity: he could make comparisons now. The girl he was with had said to him, 'In my country we say, laughing together, for making love.' This made Thomas laugh and they did laugh together. But he would never have said of Victoria, We laughed together.

Now she was saying, 'Thomas, I have to tell you something. Now, listen to me, Thomas, that summer I got pregnant. I had a baby. It was your baby. She's a little girl and her name is Mary.'

'Now, hold on a minute, don't go so fast, what are you saying?' She repeated it. 'Then, why didn't you tell me before?' He didn't sound angry. 'I don't know. I was silly.' She had been expecting anger, or disbelief, but he was saying, 'Well, Victoria, I don't think much of that. You should have told me.' By now she was weeping. 'Don't cry, Victoria. How old is she? Oh, yes, I suppose she must be . . .' And he did rapid calculations, while Victoria sobbed. 'Now here's a thing,' he said. 'She must be six?' 'Yes, she's six.' 'Wow.' And then, since the silence lengthened, she said, 'Why don't you come and see for yourself?'

For a bit, he kept the silence going. She thought, Oh what a pity she doesn't look like him. What is he going to see? A little brown girl called Mary. But she's so sweet . . . 'I go to the park'—she named it—'most afternoons.' 'Okay. I'll see you. Tomorrow?'

She left Dickson with the minder, and took Mary, in a pink frilly dress, with a pink bow in her hair, done into a little fuzzy plait, and met Thomas on a park bench.

He was humorous, he was quizzical, as if holding scepticism in reserve, but he was pleasant. In fact, they were getting on more easily than during that summer when their relations had been defined by the bed. He was easy with little Mary, and actually said to Victoria that she had her grandmother's hands.

Grandmother? He meant Jessy.

He bought Mary a lolly, gave her a kiss and went off, saying, 'I'll be in touch.' He had the telephone number now and the address.

Victoria thought: Perhaps that's the last I'll see of him. Well, I'm not going to court! Either he does or he doesn't.

That evening at supper he told his mother and his brother that he had a daughter and her name was Mary, she was a sort of pale milk-chocolate colour. Did they remember Victoria?

Edward said no, ought he to? His mother said she thought so, but there had been so many in and out.

Edward was now a handsome man, grave, authoritative, and he was tanned and healthy because of just having returned from fact-finding in Mauritius. He was a credit to his family, his school, and his university, not to mention the organisation for which he fact-found. Thomas was still a younger brother at university where he was studying—*reading*—arts and their organisation: he proposed to organise the arts, specifically, to found a pop group. All his choices were because of his being the younger brother of a paragon. How could Thomas ever catch up with Edward, who was married, as well, and with a child?

When Thomas told them, 'I have a daughter and I've seen her and she's a poppet,' it was definitely in the spirit of one catching up in a race.

'I hope you've considered the possible legal consequences,' said Edward.

'Oh, hell, don't be like that,' said Thomas.

Jessy Staveney sat brooding. The yellow, or golden, hair of Victoria's imagination was now a great greying bush, tied back by a black ribbon whose strenuous efforts to cope left it creased and greying too. Her face was bony handsome, with prominent green eyes delicately outlined with very white lids. She was staring out into perspectives bound to be fraught with fate, if not doom. Her emphatic hands were in an attitude of prayer, or contemplation, and on them she rested her chin.

'I have always wanted a black grandchild,' she mused.

'Oh, Christ, *mother*,' said Thomas, affronted not by the sentiment, but perhaps by the fact she could have done well as a ship's figurehead, staring undaunted into a Force Eight—at least—gale.

'What's the matter?' said Jessy. 'Do you want me to throw you out?'

'Well, Jessy,' said Edward, humouring them both with a well practised smile, 'this could be blackmail, have you thought of that?'

'No,' said Thomas. 'Money has not been mentioned.'

'This is a classic blackmail situation.'

'Of course we should give her some money,' said Jessy. 'No, of course we shouldn't, not until we know it's true.'

'I'm sure it's true,' said Thomas. 'You don't know her. She's not the sort of person who'd do that.'

'There's an easy way of finding out,' said Edward. 'Ask for a DNA test.'

'Oh, God, how sordid,' said Thomas.

'It certainly does introduce a belligerent note,' said Jessy.

'It's up to you,' said Edward. 'But this family could be supporting anybody's by-blow, for years!

'No,' said Thomas. 'She's all right.' And then he added, coming out at last with one reason for the pride which shone from him: 'Dad's going to be pleased.'

'If he isn't pleased he's not very consistent,' said Edward.

'You can't expect consistency, not from Lionel,' said Jessy. She never spoke of her ex-husband except with a careless contempt. This was partly because of the manner of their parting, and partly because of the feminist movement which she energetically supported.

Lionel, very handsome, irresistible in fact, had been so unfaithful that at last she had to heave him out. 'Love you, love your infidelities,' she had screamed at him. 'Well, I won't.' 'Fair enough,' he had equably replied.

They met often, and always quarrelled, describing this as an amicable divorce.

Lionel paid the school bills, and, given the precariousness of an actor's life, his payments for clothes, food, travel and so forth had been dependable. The parents had quarrelled violently, about the boys' upbringing, but less now. He was an old-fashioned romantic socialist and insisted on both boys going to ordinary schools, as then was common among his kind. 'Sink or swim.'

'Do or die,' his wife riposted. Although Edward had emerged from the junior school, Beowulf— the same as Victoria's—pale, thin, haunted by the bullying, hardly able to sleep, and stuttering badly, this had not prevented his father from insisting on the same treatment for Thomas. His prescriptions for them had borne fruits, though unequally. Edward had learned a compassion for the underdog, or the other half, that burned in him like a tormented conscience. 'You'd think you were personally responsible for the slave trade,' his mother might shout at him. 'You are not personally responsible for people being hanged for a loaf of bread or stealing a rabbit.' As for Thomas, he had learned to love black girls and black music, in that order. No one could ever fail to admire Edward, but Thomas? And now here he was, in his last year of university, a father, with a child of six.

'I think the best thing to do is to ask her here with the child, to meet us all—Lionel included,' said Jessy.

This being considered too much of an ordeal, Victoria and Mary came one Sunday afternoon, when Edward was there, and Jessy.

It was indeed an ordeal, mostly because Edward was being so grand, so aloof. He cross-examined Victoria as if he did not believe her. He sat at the foot of the table, in the vast room they called the kitchen, Jessy with her sad grey hair at the top, remembering to smile from time to time at Victoria and the child. Thomas, who seemed ready to flirt with her, he was so pleased with himself, sat opposite Victoria. The child, in a white dress this time, with little white boots and white bows, sat on a pile of cushions and behaved with painful care. She had been told she was going to meet her other family, but had not really taken it in.

'Are you my daddy?' she asked Thomas, her great black eyes full of the difficulty of it all.

'Yeah, yeah, man, that's about it.' His American phase was useful to fall back into, at such moments.

'If you are my daddy then you are my granny,' said Mary, turning to Jessy.

'That's exactly right,' said Jessy, encouragingly.

'And what are you?' she asked Edward. She

did not miss the hesitation before Edward brought out, 'I'm your uncle.' He smiled, but not as his mother did.

'Am I going to live with you?' Mary asked.

Edward sent a sharp glance at his mother: was this a clue at last as to what Victoria was after?

'No, Mary,' said Victoria. 'Of course not. You'll be with me.'

'And Dickson too?'

The Staveneys had only just managed to take in that there was another child, from another father.

'Yes, you and me and Dickson,' said Victoria.

Considering the difficulties, it all went off well, and at the end Jessy kissed Victoria. Thomas gave her a brotherly kiss, and Edward, hesitating again, put his arms around the child, and it was a good hug.

'Welcome to the family,' he said, nicely, even though it did sound a bit like a court order.

He had complained that all this was happening before anything had been clarified with the DNA test.

Victoria went home, not knowing what had been achieved, part regretting she had ever rung Thomas, and she wept, thinking of Sam, who had been such a strength when he was alive. It is not only in Rome that saints are created from unlikely material. If Victoria had been able to foresee a couple of years before, how she would be thinking and talking about Sam, after his death, she would have not believed it.

All this was being discussed with Bessie, every twist and turn, usually talking into the dark in Victoria's bedroom. Bessie's own flat—Phyllis's—had become impossible. The two boys, now sixteen, young men, were out of control. Their mother had managed, just, to keep them in check, but they took no notice of Bessie. The flat was just as much theirs as hers, as they kept telling her, but she paid the bills for it. They stole cars and car parts to get money for their needs. Bessie might come into her home and find it full of young men, drunk, or stoned, the place a pigsty. She regularly had to clean it up. Her bedroom she kept locked, to stop her brothers and their friends stealing her money, but these were not youngsters likely to be deterred by a locked door. The police knew these lads and from time to time took one or two of them off. 'They're going to end in prison,' Bessie said to Victoria, who did not contradict her. 'Then perhaps I'll get my flat back one day,' Bessie might be thinking, but did not say. Phyllis's death had left an absence that told them continually that some people are much more than a sum of their parts. Her influence had been enormous, in this building and beyond it. People were always coming up to tell Bessie how much her mother had done for them. 'I wish she was here to do something for me,' Bessie would think, but did not say. There was a laboratory technician from Jamaica she would have invited to share her flat and her life, had it been possible. He was a sane, sensible person of whom Phyllis would have approved—but he did not have a place of his own and neither did Bessie. That was why she and Victoria were sharing a bedroom again.

Bessie said to Victoria that she ought to arrange for a DNA test. Victoria had never heard of it. The two young women made draft after draft of a letter to the Staveneys, thought safe and correct by Bessie, but stiff and unfriendly by Victoria. The letter Thomas eventually did get had been written by trembling and weeping Victoria, surrounded by all the torn-up drafts. She went down to post it, at four in the morning, daring the dangers of the dark estate, thinking that any muggers or thieves she was likely to meet were bound to be Bessie's lay-about boys or their friends.

'Dear Thomas, I am so unhappy thinking that you are thinking I might be trying to put something over on you and your family. I can't sleep worrying. I would like it best if you and Mary could have the DNA test, the one that proves if a child has a real father. Please write or telephone soon and let me know how you feel. I don't want to impose.' This letter too had been torn up more than once, because the first one ended 'Love', No, surely, that was a bit of cheek? Then she thought, But what about that summer, how can I put, With good wishes? Love and good wishes alternated and then, worn out with it all, she wrote, 'With my very best wishes', ran out to post the letter—and fell into bed.

As soon as Thomas read this, he rang Edward and read it to him. 'So what do you have to say now?'

'All right, you win, but I was right to warn you.'

Jessy read the letter and said, 'Good girl. I like that.'

'Do I really have to go and have that bloody test?'

'Yes, you do. We've got to keep Edward happy.'

Thus she allied herself with her erring son. 'A little girl,' she said. 'At last. And she seems such a sensible little thing.'

The test was made, but before the result came, Thomas had telephoned to ask what Victoria's bank account number was. She didn't have one. He then said she must open one at once, it would make things easier. 'Things', it turned out, was an allowance for Mary, of so much monthly, 'and we'll see how we all go along'. The money was from Jessy, but when Lionel was informed, he said he would contribute.

There was another afternoon tea, this time with Lionel. Mary was told she was going to meet her grandfather, and went along without fear, thinking of Jessy's kindly smiles.

Lionel Staveney was a big grand man, in style rather like Jessy, who always seemed to take up the space of two people. He had a mane of silvery hair and wore a shirt of many colours, again like Jessy's. They sat at either end of the big table, reflecting each other.

Lionel took Mary by the hand and said, 'So, you're little Mary. Very nice to meet you at last.' And he bent to kiss that small brown hand, with a solemn face, but then he winked at her, which made her giggle. 'What a delicious child,' he remarked to Victoria. 'Congratulations. Why have you kept this treasure from us for so long?' He held out his arms and Mary went up into them, burying her face in the rainbow shirt.

So that was that afternoon, and soon there was another.

'Here's my little crème caramel, my little chocolate éclair,' was Lionel's greeting to Mary, and Lionel saw Victoria's face, whose nervous look was because she was remembering Sam's culinary endearments. 'If I say I am going to eat you all up,' Lionel said to Mary, 'you must not take it as more than a legitimate expression of my sincere devotion.'

When Victoria and Mary had gone home, Edward said to his father, 'If you can't see why you shouldn't call her a chocolate anything, then you are a bit out of step with the times.'

'Oh, dear,' said Lionel, 'dearie, dearie me. Is that what I am? Well, so be it.'

'Lionel,' said his ex-wife, 'I think you sometimes scare her a bit.'

'But not for long. What a little sweetie. What a little—I'm in heaven. Now, if we had a little girl, do you think we'd have stuck?' he enquired of Jessy.

'God only knows,' said Jessy, giving the Almighty the benefit of the doubt.

'Certainly *not*,' said Edward, but this was as much a warning for the present as a judgement on the past.

'Yeah, yeah, yeah,' said Thomas. 'Happy families.'

'I'm claiming visiting rights, that's all. Aren't grandparents encouraged these days?'

'You're welcome to visit,' said his ex-wife. 'But let's not push our luck.'

Thomas telephoned Victoria to ask if he could take Mary to his swimming pool. Victoria said the child didn't know how to swim, and Thomas said he would teach her.

Then it was the zoo, the planetarium and a trip on the river-boat to Greenwich.

Meanwhile Victoria was thinking, 'But I have two children. What about Dickson?' What was happening was unfair. Yes, Dickson was still tiny, just three, but he knew his sister was getting treats that he didn't.

Jessy had remarked that it was not right, when there were two children, if one got more than the other.

Edward said at once, 'Don't even think of it, Mother.'

'Perhaps we could take him out sometimes with Mary?'

'No. One's enough. I'm sorry, but there are limits.'

Now Mary was in her first year at school and miserable. This made Victoria remember how miserable she had been, though she had managed it by being quiet, and keeping out of trouble and—frankly—sucking up to the big boys and girls. She told Mary to do the same, and suffered herself, knowing that the child cried herself to sleep at nights.

She speculated, amazed, how it was that the Staveneys could willingly submit their precious children to such nastiness, such cruelty—for she believed that the good schools, the ones children like theirs would attend, would be free of all that. In her most secret dreams, not shared even with Bessie, Victoria was hoping the Staveneys would send little Mary to a good school where she could learn and become somebody.

Then Jessy telephoned to ask if Mary would enjoy a matinée? Victoria thought of *Les Misérables* and said Mary would love it. Victoria took Mary to the Staveney house where off went Jessy and Mary in a taxi, to be returned, in a taxi, to the council estate. Mary was in a state of babbling incoherent delight. Victoria never came to grips with what the little girl had seen. But the next time she was whisked off to that other land, the Staveneys, Mary asked Thomas if she could go to another 'matney'. 'A what?' It turned out she thought matney was the name for a theatre. She went to another matney with Jessy and then to the zoo with Edward and Edward's wife, and their three-year-old. And then, having begged, to another matinée, of a show Lionel was in. She returned to say that her grandfather was a funny man but she liked him. 'He likes me, Ma,' she confided in Victoria.

Whenever this grandfather was mentioned grandfathers whirled dolefully in Victoria's mind. She was being reminded that she must have had a grandfather, but as a fact he had simply disappeared. It was Phyllis's grandfather she thought of as grandfather, a generic progenitor, an old man with his smelly urine bottle. But—she could not dispute it—Lionel Staveney was her little girl's grandfather, and when Mary said, 'She told me I was her grandchild and so I must call her grandmother,' Victoria felt the earth shaking under her feet. When she confessed how she felt, Bessie reasonably said, 'But what did you expect, when you told them?'

Well, what had she expected? Nothing like this. It was the thoroughness of the acceptance of Mary that was—well, what? It was all too much! Bessie told her she was ungrateful, she was looking a gift-horse in the mouth. Victoria at last came out with: 'I wouldn't have thought they'd be so pleased to have a black grandchild.'

'She's not black, she's more caramel,' Bessie pronounced. 'If she was my colour I bet they wouldn't be so pleased.'

About a year after she had first telephoned Thomas, Jessy wrote a letter to say the family were taking a house in Dorset in the summer, for a month, and people would come and go. Would Victoria agree to Mary's joining them? Edward's Samantha would be there for the whole month. Victoria was not invited, and she knew it was because of Dickson. Mary was sweet, lovable, biddable and friendly, but Dickson, now nearly four, was a different matter.

The question of colour—no, it couldn't be evaded—though Victoria could be pardoned for thinking that the Staveneys, except for Thomas of course, had never noticed that colour could be a differentiator, often enough a contumacious one, believing that whatever had happened—regrettably—in the past, was no longer a force in human affairs.

Dickson was black, black as boot polish or piano keys. Somewhere long ago in his family tree genes had been nurtured to cope with the suns of tropical Africa. He sweated easily.

Sometimes sweat flew off him as freely as off an over-hot dog's tongue. He roared and fought; at the minder's he was a problem, making trouble, causing tears. Mary was able to calm and charm him, but no one else could, certainly not Victoria, who often found herself weeping with exhaustion over Dickson's brawling and biting. Bessie adored him, called him her little black imp from hell, her hell's angel, and sometimes he would allow himself to be held by her, but not often. By now he knew that he was excessive and impossible and everyone's headache, but that made him worse in behaviour and worse in effect, for he acquired pathos, saying things like, 'But why am I impossible? Why am I a headache, why, why, why, I'm not, I'm not,' and he would kick out around him until he fell sobbing on the floor.

He could not possibly be an easy guest in any family, black or white. The Staveneys had scarcely seen the child. It seemed they had enquired of Mary if she would like Dickson to be invited, but Mary had replied, gravely, in her responsible little way, that Dickson would quarrel with everyone and would scratch and bite Samantha. 'I told her—Jessy—that he would grow out of it,' Mary told Victoria she had said. Quoting Bessie. 'Don't worry, Victoria, he'll grow out of it.'

But here was a real turn of the screw. Little visits here and there, a matinée, a tea party, but to go away by herself, for a month—they were asking her for a month? Yes, they were. The politician a mother has to be—let alone an economist—told Victoria that the Staveneys wanted Mary because of Samantha. Mary was good with small children. At the minder's she was commended for it. Victoria thought—and it was bitter—Mary's going to be a nurse for Samantha. Bitter and unfair and she knew it. Mary loved Samantha. An unanchored bitterness, ready to become suspicion, floated near enough to the surface in Victoria to be dangerous—she pressed it down. Wasn't this what she had wanted for Mary? The little girl was being so lucky, and Victoria should be giving thanks for the blessing of it. This was what Bessie, who was taking to religion, called it. 'It's a blessing, Victoria. That family—they're Mary's blessing from God.'

Now there was the question of clothes. Samantha's were different, and Mary knew exactly what she needed. Victoria found herself being taken to a shop, by her little daughter, and instructed on what to buy. So this was what Samantha wore? Cheeky little clothes, and the colours were gorgeous—and it was all so expensive. But there was money in the bank for Mary's clothes, put there by Thomas, and this was when she must spend it.

Victoria was thinking, I am losing Mary to the Staveneys. She was able to contemplate this calmly. She did not believe Mary would come to despise her mother: she was relying on the child's kind heart. She was thinking, as mothers so often seem to do, How is it possible that these two such different children came out of the same womb? A little angel—the minder's name for Mary—and a little devil. 'Never mind,' said Bessie. 'They'll both grow out of it.' And Victoria found she was thinking about her daughter as Phyllis had thought about her. The terrible dangers that lie in wait for girls . . . the traps, the snares, baited by the devil with a girl's best qualities—Bessie had just had an abortion. She wanted the baby, but she would have liked a father for it, and while she had a flat to put it in, she didn't have a home.

Off went Mary, wild with excitement, with the Staveneys. She rang her mother most days, for Victoria had insisted, and kept saying that it was lovely, oh, it's so lovely, Ma. And then Victoria was asked to go down for a weekend. She arranged for Dickson to stay at the minder's and took the train, two hours, into England's green and pleasant land. But Victoria had hardly ever been out of London. It seemed to her she was being smothered in green, a wet green: it had rained.

She stood on the platform of the station, in her hand her new suitcase full of her best clothes, and waited until appeared Lionel, with Mary on his shoulders. Mary slid down her grandfather to get to Victoria and kiss her, and the three went off, linked hand to hand, to the old car. Lionel's mane of hair had a leaf in it and Mary's new dungarees, bright purple, were patched with mud. She was fatter and sparkling with happiness.

Victoria was in the front seat by Lionel, with Mary on her knee. The child smelled of soap and chocolate. Lionel kept up a banter with Mary, a chant of bits of nursery rhymes, references to things Victoria did not recognise, and Mary giggled, sitting on her mother's lap but watching the big man's mouth, from whence spilled words like spells. 'Contrary Mary, smooth and hairy, the spider beside her big and scary . . . ' 'That's wrong, that's wrong,' the child shrieked. 'You're mixing them all up.' 'But Hairy Mary, did not scream, she ate up the spider with curds and cream.' 'I'm not hairy, I'm not,' the child protested, dying of giggles.

'Mary as smooth as silk, drank up all the milk, none left for her mother, her mongoose and her brother, she . . .'

He kept it up, while Mary squirmed in Victoria's arms, and as for Victoria, she was longing for the thing to end. They were driving fast through lanes where the wet green was heavy overhead, splashing down showers of wet around the car. She felt she could not breathe. Soon, soon, they would reach the house, which she imagined rather like the

Staveneys' town house, but they had stopped outside a little house all by itself with the trees growing close, and a great squash of garden, where a big tree leaned over a patch of lawn. On the lawn chairs and a table stood waiting. The house seemed to Victoria a nasty little place, not worthy of the Staveneys. What were they doing here? But Mary was out of the car, and tugging her mother out, by the hand. It seemed no one was about.

All Victoria wanted was to lie down. Lionel told her to make herself at home: there would be tea in half an hour. Mary tugged her mother up tiny slippy stairs and into a dark little room that had windows broken up all over into patterns, letting in thin light. There was a big high bed with a white cover, and on this Mary was already bouncing, 'Oh, it's lovely, it's a lovely bed.'

Victoria wanted to be sick. Mary showed her the bathroom, which was tiny, with thatch showing through the window, where things were flying about. 'Look at the bees, Ma, look, look.' Victoria was discreetly and tidily sick, and retreated to her room.

'Where's your bed?' she enquired, falling into the big white one.

'I'm with Samantha. We sleep in a room by ourselves!

Told that her mother felt bad—a headache—Mary kissed her, and ran out.

Victoria lay flat on her back, and saw the

ceiling had a crack across it. In the corner of the room was a spider web? *Was* that a spider's web?—Victoria fell asleep, just like that, but perhaps it was more like a swoon. She was shocked deeply, painfully, to her core. How could the Staveneys . . . and when she woke, Jessy was just putting down a cup of tea on the bedside table.

'Sorry you're not feeling too good,' she said. 'Come down when you're better.' And she left, the big tall woman, who had to bend her head at the door.

Victoria lay and watched dusk invade the room. That meant it must be getting late. She should go down, shouldn't she? Cautiously she slid from the bed, careful that her feet would not encounter—well, what? She imagined something soft and squishy that might bite. At the window she stood, careful to touch nothing, and looked down. Under the big tree, which had birds in it, making a noise, an assortment of people, not all of them Staveneys, sat about drinking.

If Victoria went down, she would have to descend those stairs, find her way out, join all those people, who would have to be introduced. She could see Mary sitting on her grandfather's knee.

Just as Victoria had got up courage, she saw the company rise, variously. Some people went off to cars parked outside in the road. And then the Staveneys came in to the house and she heard them just below. The house echoed. It was a noisy house. And it was then that she saw, just beside the window, a great spider, making its way—she knew—towards her. She screamed. In no time Thomas had appeared, identified the trouble, and having taken her towel off a chair he enveloped the beast and shook it out of the window. It would climb back!

'Well, Victoria, how are you, you look great . . .' How could he see? It was dark in here. 'Are you better?' He kissed her cheek, and laughed, a tribute to their past. 'Come down and have some supper.'

Victoria wanted to say she would get into bed, put her head deep under that wonderful white counterpane and not come out until it was time to go back to London. Instead she began opening her case to find something to wear.

'Oh, don't bother about that,' said Thomas. 'No one bothers here.'

And off he went and she heard him bound down the stairs.

She followed. A big table almost filled another smallish room. Around it already sat Jessy and Lionel, facing each other, from the head and the foot, Thomas, with a chair opposite him for Victoria, Edward and a sharp observing young woman who must be Edward's Alice. A chair piled with cushions accommodated Mary, near to her grandfather.

Wine bottles stood about, and plates of cold meat and salad. Friday night, she was told: this picnic had been bought, but tomorrow she would see better things.

Jessy had been here for most of the month, which was nearly up, and Lionel had come every weekend. 'I can't keep away from your daughter,' he announced, 'she's my lady love.'

Thomas had been several times. Edward not at all (this was his first time), because he was too busy. Alice had come to visit Samantha, who was in bed, young for late nights.

Alice was eyeing Victoria, who felt criticised. In fact it was Alice who believed she was at a disadvantage. She had been brought up in a provincial lawyer's family and was sure the Staveneys criticised her. They were so travelled, worldly, liberal and generous, often in ways that shocked Alice. She thought worse of the Staveneys for letting the little dark girl call Jessy and Lionel granny and grandfather. She did believe she was in the wrong to feel like this, but could not change. When Mary attempted uncle for Edward, he had told her, 'No, call me Edward,' and Mary did so; she was already calling her father, Thomas. If Edward was Mary's uncle that meant that Alice must be Mary's aunt, but the little girl had sensed Alice wouldn't like that.

Victoria was not jealous of Alice. Her Edward, the kind boy of long ago, lived in her mind, unchanged, and the Edward of now she did not much like. In fact these days she thought Thomas was nicer than Edward.

It was a slow sleepy meal. Jessy kept yawning and apologising, and that made it easy for Victoria to say she was tired too.

'Normally,' Thomas said to Victoria, 'we spend the evening in healthy parlour games, but tonight we'll skip all that.'

Victoria went with Mary to her room, where Samantha was prettily asleep in a little bed. Mary had a big bed, like Victoria's. Mary put up her arms to kiss her mother and smiled and fell asleep.

Victoria went to her room, looked for the spider, did not see it, dived into bed, and pulled up the white cover. In here, she was safe.

Friday night. Two more nights to go—she couldn't, she wouldn't, she hated it all. She could hear an owl hooting. Didn't that mean death? It was in the big tree. The garden was full of horrors. At supper Lionel had said to Mary that she mustn't forget to take crumbs out for the toad.

'It's dark,' Mary had said, comforting Victoria with this sensible protest. 'Toads can see in the dark,' said Lionel. 'It's a perverse toad,' Jessy had said. 'I don't expect they see many wholemeal crumbs in their usual diet, so why they like ours, I can't think.'

'We'll find him some worms tomorrow,'

Lionel had said.

Victoria did sleep at last and woke early to find Mary had come in the night and was asleep near her, on top of the coverlet. For a long time Victoria lay on her elbow watching her child sleep, rather as she would a ship sailing away over a horizon—if she had ever seen a sea that was not on television or in a film. Behind those tight smooth sealed eyelids was already a world that Victoria did not share.

In the morning Victoria tried to find something in her case that would match Lionel's old sweater that had a hole in its sleeve, or Jessy's slacks and grey tweedy skirt. She did not have the right shoes either. They talked of walks and of Mary and Samantha going off on ponies with some other little girls.

Victoria stood at the door of the house and felt that she was surrounded by jungle. She knew all about jungles, the way we do, from the screens, big and small: they were dangerous, full of wild animals, crocodiles, snakes and insects. This jungle had none of those but nevertheless was filled with hostile creatures. If she could just leave, leave now—but she didn't want Mary to be ashamed of her.

When the long breakfast was over—she drank some tea, and had to listen to Jessy lecture them all on the importance of a proper breakfast—she watched while they all went off to walk in woods that were near, and very wet. She said she would stay sitting under the tree, which was bound to be full of creatures that might drop on her, and tried to find haven in a room they called the sitting-room. She sat in a big chair with her feet drawn up, so that nothing could crawl up on them.

Lunch over, they all piled into cars and drove off some miles to a famous tea-room, where they parked, and everyone went walking again, but Victoria and Mary, who insisted on staying with her mother.

'Poor Ma,' said Mary, acutely, and her eyes were full of tears. 'But I love you always.'

Supper was the same. This time Jessy had cooked stew, which Victoria liked and a big fruit tart had been bought at the tea-room to bring home.

Saturday night. Another night to go. By now Victoria was feeling like a criminal. They knew she was not enjoying herself, though had no idea just how much she was hating it, how she feared it. The spider was back on her wall and it had fled when she stamped her foot at it, into the crack, where it bided its time. She tried to keep her eyes on it, but moths had flown in, before she shut the window tight. A big moth crouched on a wall, making a shadow She had last seen that hooded shape, a frightening shadow on a wall, in a film about Dracula.

Next morning she went down early, with her

suitcase. She did not know how she would get to the station but somehow she would. She found Alice, already up, drinking tea.

'Do you hate it?' Alice asked.

'Yes, I do.'

'I'm sorry.'

'Don't you?'

'No, I wish I could live here for always, never leave.'

'Oh, dear,' said Victoria feebly.

'Yes, it's true. Edward can't leave London yet but we will buy a house in the country and then we'll live in it.'

'A house like *this*?' Victoria looked incredulous.

'No, bigger. More comfortable.' She looked kindly at Victoria and said gently, 'Don't mind them. I know they are a bit overwhelming.'

'It's not them,' said Victoria. 'It's this place.'

Absolute incomprehension: Alice frowned and was perturbed. Victoria seemed about to cry.

'I wish I could go home,' said Victoria, like a child. And then, as an adult, said, 'I would, only I don't want Mary to be ashamed of me.'

'She wouldn't be. She's a nice little girl, if there ever was one. Samantha adores her. I tell you what. I'll drive you to the station and I'll tell them you don't feel well!

'That's not a lie,' said Victoria.

And so Victoria got into Edward and Alice's car and was driven through the early morning countryside to the station.

Victoria had never driven, had never had to, and the skill and speed of Alice was depressing her. She was actually saying to herself, ‘But there are things I am good at.’

At the station, Alice took the bag and went before to the booking office, bought a ticket, said, ‘There’ll be a train in half an hour.’

The two stood together, waiting. Victoria had understood that this young woman, who so intimidated her, meant her well, but—did that matter? What mattered very much was that she liked Mary.

‘I feel a real fool,’ she said humbly. ‘I know what the Staveneys will think. I ought to be grateful—and, well, that’s all.’

‘Poor Victoria. I’m sorry. I’ll explain to them.’ And as the train came in she actually kissed Victoria, as if she meant it. ‘It takes all sorts,’ she added, with a little pleased smile at her attempt at definition. ‘I don’t think they’d ever understand you don’t like the country.’

‘I hate it, hate it,’ Victoria said, violently, and got into the train that would carry her away—for ever, if she had her way.

Mary came home a few days later. Victoria saw the child’s bleak look around the little flat, criticising what Victoria had greeted with such relief: a bare sufficiency, and what there was, in its proper place. And then Mary stood at the window looking down, down, into the concrete vistas and Victoria did not have to ask what it was she missed.

Mary kept saying, rushing to embrace her mother, 'You're my Ma and I'll love you always.' Bessie and Victoria exchanged grim-enough smiles, and then Mary forgot about it.

Thomas took Mary to concerts of African music, twice, but she thought they were too loud. Like her mother, she wanted things to be quiet and seemly.

Then Victoria was invited to an evening meal at the Staveneys, 'preferably without Mary—and anyway it will be too late for her, won't it?' This, from people who had her up to all hours in Dorset. 'Without Dickson' could be taken as read. Victoria put on her nicest outfit, and found herself with a full complement of Staveneys, at the supper table. Undercurrents, some well understood by Victoria, others not at all, flowed about and around Jessy, Lionel, Edward, Alice and Thomas. Lionel at once opened with, 'I wonder what you'd think if we suggested Mary went to a different school?'

This was Lionel, who had insisted on both his sons going through the ordeal of that bad school, Beowulf.

Victoria was not afraid of Lionel—she was of Jessy—and did not find it hard to enquire, 'Then, you've changed your mind about schools, is that it?'

At this Jessy let out a snort, of a connubial kind, meant to be noted, like putting up your hand at a meeting to register *Nay*.

'You could say our father has changed his mind,' said Thomas.

'Yes, you could say that,' said Edward.

'I'm not saying I was wrong about you two,' pronounced Lionel, flinging his silvery mane about while he speared roast potatoes judiciously on to his plate.

'You wouldn't ever admit it,' said Jessy, confronting him, while the concentrated exasperation of years of disputation flared her nostrils.

'When have you ever admitted you were wrong about anything?'

'Isn't it a bit late for this altercation?' enquired Edward.

'For better or worse,' said Thomas. 'But the birds in your nest couldn't agree.'

'Oh, worse, worse,' said Jessy at once, 'of course worse.' But from her look at Thomas it could be seen that what she meant was her bitter acknowledgement that his highest ambition was to manage a pop group. 'As for agreeing, no, we never agreed about that, never, *never.*'

'Okay,' said Thomas, 'I'll accept your verdict. I am the worse and Edward is the better.'

'At least the gap between you two was wide enough for you not to quarrel—that really would have been the last straw.'

This spat ended here, because Edward was

pouring wine for Victoria, which she didn't much like. She put her hand over the glass, and then, since a few drops had splashed, licked the back of her hand.

'There,' said Lionel. 'You do like wine.'

'You should have some, it does you good,' said Jessy. 'The Victorians knew their stuff. At the slightest hint of wasting away or brain fever or any of their ghastly diseases, out came the claret.'

'Port,' said Lionel.

'Best Burgundy,' said Edward. 'Like this. Best is always best. If I had been asked—for after all I wasn't given a choice, was I, father?—I'd have said no. I do not have pleasant memories of that school. It was your school, Victoria, I know . . .'

At this reminder to her that he did not remember the event which was so present and alive in her mind, tears came into Victoria's eyes.

She madc her voice steady, and said, 'Yes, it's not a good place. And it's worse since I was there. Since *we* were there,' she addressed Thomas.

'There was a stabbing there last week,' remarked Jessy, aiming this at her ex.

'Which brings me to my point again,' said Lionel, addressing Victoria. 'Suppose we send Mary to a good school? I have to say that there is disagreement in the ranks . . .'

'When is there not?' said Jessy.

'Some of us think—I, for one—that Mary could go to a boarding school.'

'A boarding school?' And now Victoria was shocked. She knew that people like the Staveneys did send their children, when they were still little, to boarding school. She thought it heartless.

'I told you,' said Thomas. 'Of course Victoria says no to a boarding school.'

'Yes,' Victoria bravely said, smiling gratefully at Thomas, who smiled back, 'I say no to a boarding school.' For a tiny moment the current between them was sweet and deep, and they remembered that for a whole summer they had felt two against the world.

Alice broke in with, 'I was at boarding school and I loved it.'

'Yes, but you were thirteen,' said Edward.

Who then of the Staveneys, would agree to Mary being sent off to the cold exile of boarding school? Alice and Lionel.

'Very well, then,' said Edward. 'No boarding school. Well, not yet. Meanwhile there's a good girls' school, not far, it would be a few stops on the Tube and a short walk.'

Victoria was thinking, She'll have a bad time. She'll be with girls who have money and the things the Staveneys have, and she'll come home to . . . it would certainly ask a lot of Mary's kind heart: two worlds, and she would have to fit in to both of them.

Victoria said to Lionel, who was the author

of this plan, which in fact fulfilled her dreams for Mary, 'I couldn't say no, how could I? It will be such a big thing for Mary.' And now she dared to turn to Thomas, reminding them all that he was after all the child's father. 'What do you say, Thomas? It's for you to say, too.'

'Yeah,' said Thomas. 'Yeah. That's exactly right.' Here his belligerent look at his father, and his brother, told them that he was feeling—as usual—belittled. 'Yeah, it is for me to say too. And I say, Victoria should have the deciding vote. Providing Mary doesn't go to Beowulf, that's the main thing.'

Victoria said, 'If I say no, I could never forgive myself. But I'd like to talk it all over with—she's not my sister, but I think of her as.'

Bessie heard what Victoria had to tell her, nodding and smiling *I told you so*. She said, 'They'll get Mary away from you, but that's not how they'll see it.'

A central fact was there, out in the open, still unvoiced, with its potentialities for pain and gain. Mary had spent a month with the Staveneys, and that experience had made it urgent for her to be rescued from her environment and be sent to a good school.

'Well,' said Bessie, 'she's going to come out the other end educated. Which is more than can be said about Beowulf.'

'You went there and you do well enough,' said Victoria.

'You know what I mean.'

They were back at what was not being said. For one thing, it was Mary's way of speaking, which was very far from the Staveneys'. Thomas might speak badly, his phoney American, or his cockney, as he called it, but she had never heard a cockney—who were they when they were at home?—talk like that. And the Staveneys spoke posh, and Thomas too, most of the time. Mary's voice was ugly compared to theirs.

'She'll have a hard time of it,' said Bessie. 'There's no pretending she won't.'

'I know,' said Victoria, thinking that she had had a long hard time of it, and yet here she was, she had survived it. Bessie had had a better time, because of Phyllis being her mother, but she was having a hard enough time now—and she would survive it too.

She wrote to Thomas, asserting *his* rights, 'Dear Thomas, I agree to your kind suggestion. Please tell your father and your mother thank you for me. It won't be easy for Mary but I'll try and explain it all to her.'

Explain what, exactly? And how?

Mary must be thinking many things already that she might not want to say to her mother. She was kind—that was her best quality: she had a good nature. And she wasn't stupid. Victoria could easily put herself back into herself at Mary's age. Kids always know more than adults think, even if they know it the wrong way around, sometimes.

And Victoria knew more than the Staveneys about the future.

Mary would go to that good school where most girls were white. She would have many battles to fight, of a different sort from the rough-housing of Beowulf. The Staveneys would be Mary's best support. Probably, when the girl was about thirteen, the Staveneys would ask if she, Victoria, could consider Mary going to boarding school. Neither they nor Mary would have to spell out the reasons why Mary must find things easier, for she would no longer have to fit herself into two different worlds, every day. Victoria would say yes, and that would be that.

There was another factor, which Bessie was reminding her of. Victoria was an attractive woman, not yet thirty. She was going now every Sunday to church, because Bessie did, and there she enjoyed the singing. She had been noticed. She took the lead in some hymns, was no longer just one of the congregation. Thc Reverend Amos Johnson had taken a fancy to her. Her dead Sam, who with every year became more of a perfect man in her memory, could not be compared with Amos Johnson, who was twenty years older than she was. The incomparable lustre of Sam made it possible for her to consider Amos. She had visited his home, full of God-fearing and sober people, and while she was not particularly religious, liked the atmosphere.

She had always been a good girl, Victoria had—like Mary now.

If she married Amos she would have more children. Little Dickson, the child from hell, as he was known generally around and about the estate, would calm down, with brothers and sisters.

And Mary? To match the Staveney world with the world of Amos Johnson—she even laughed about it despairingly, with Bessie.

Yet if she married Amos she would be binding the two worlds together, even if both were careful never to get too close. And Mary, poor Mary, in the middle there. Yes, thought Victoria, she will be pleased to get out of it and into boarding school: she'll want to be a Staveney. Yes, I have to face it. That is what will happen.

THE REASON FOR IT

Yesterday we buried Eleven, and now I am the only one left of The Twelve. Between Eleven and One in our burial place is an empty site, waiting for me, Twelve. All gone now, one by one. The night Eleven died I was with him. He said to me, 'While The Twelve have been dying the truth has been dying. When you come to join us no one will be left to tell our story.' He grasped me by the arm, pulling all his strength back into him to do it. 'Tell it. Call The Cities together and tell it. Then it will be in all their minds and cannot disappear.' And with that he fell back into dark and the Silence.

His mind had gone, otherwise he could not have said, 'Call The Cities.' It is a long time since that has been possible. But the substance of his message has been burning inside me. Not that it is a new message. What else have we Twelve been talking about these very many years, always fewer of us. How long is it since we could have said: Let us call The Cities together? Nearly half my lifetime, at least.

When I left Eleven I came home here and sat where the scents and sounds of a warm starry night could come wafting over me from the gardens and splashing waters, and I was challenging the indolence in myself, which I have always known was my worst enemy. You could call it—I *have* called it—many more flattering names, prudence, caution, the judiciousness of experience, even my well-known (once well-known) Wisdom: they call me—they used to call me—The Sage Twelve. The truth is it is hard for me to act, to gather up my energies behind a single focus and simply do. I see too many aspects of a situation. For every Yes there is a No, and so, through the long years, while The Twelve have one by one vanished away, I have thought, Is this the time to do it? *Do what!* I have never known, we, The Twelve have not known. We always ended by sending DeRod, our Ruler, yet another message. I remember right at the very beginning of his rule we jokingly called him by our nickname for him, The Beneficent Whip. Long thought, worry, have always ended in the same thing: a message. This was correct, was protocol, no one could criticise us, criticise me. At first casual, almost insultingly casual, messages came back. And then silence. It has been years since he replied, either to me, who am after all a relative, or to The Twelve.

The Ruler he might be, but he has a Council, and in theory at least it is a collective responsibility. But so much has been theory that was meant to be substance and reality. Many times our cautious approaches to DeRod have seemed to me cowardice, but there was more: to feel the conviction that leads to good action means you must first believe in your efficacy, that good results may come from what you do. As the silence from DeRod persisted, and things went from bad to worse, there was a deadening of hope, of our hopes, which I secretly matched with the darkening mind of The Cities. A paralysis of the Will, I remember we called it in one of our gatherings. But we have met in the ones and twos of special friendship, as well as in the collective, we have met constantly—after all, we have known each other since we were born—and what have we always discussed, if not something which we refer to simply as The Situation. What we have slowly come to see as a kind of poisoning. What has been the constant theme of our talk, our speculation? We have not understood what was happening. Why? I suppose that word sums up our years-long, our decades-long preoccupation. Why? What is the reason for it? Why was it we could never grasp something tangible, get hold of fact, a cause? It is easy to characterise what has been happening. There has been a worsening of everything, and we have seen it as a deliberate, even planned, intention.

That word, analyze . . . one of our sobriquets (The Twelve) was The Analyzers. It is some time since we would have dared use it, for fear of mockery. And so much have I (until so recently I could have said *we)* become infected by the time, that I confess that to me now the word has a ridiculous ring to it.

Yet what have we always done, except try to analyze, understand? And since I wrote the above that is what I have been doing and as always coming up with a blank. My instinct is to send another message to DeRod. What is the use?

Something must be done. And by me . . .

When Koon, or Eleven, spoke last he said soon no one will be left to tell our story. That is how it seemed to him as he died. A story has an end. To him the story was finished. The story: well, our history was something told and retold—when we were still telling our history. And now as the familiar disinclination to do anything invades me I wonder if it is only a symptom of the poisoning. Poison? That was only one of the words we have used. But has our history all been for nothing? The excellence? The high standards? The assumption once shared by everyone in The Cities that the best was what we aimed for?

*   *   *

It is now seven days since Eleven died. I might die in any breath I take. So much I can do: record, at least in outline, our story.

Six lives ago we were conquered by The Roddites, from the East. *We.* But that *we* has changed. Who were *we* before the Roddites? Along this shore were scattered villages, of poor dwellings, each thinking of itself as a town. But they had no proper sanitation, or paved streets, or public amenities, had nothing of what we (we of after The Roddites) take for granted. They were fisherfolk, and the fishing is good, and a great many coveted our fishing shores. The Roddites were desert people, strong, hardy, disciplined, with bodies like whips, and their horses were feared almost as much as the people who rode them. They were taught to trample with their hooves and bite flesh from whatever enemy was before them. Their neighing and roaring and screaming was louder than the shouting of the soldiers or the sound of the trumpets. The Roddites and their horses swept easily over the sea villages, and soon had the fishing and the shore and the boats.

The leader we called Rod, but that was because their system of nomenclature was so convoluted and difficult for us. No one was simply Rod, or Ren, or Blok, or Marr, but to the core name was attached a multitude of suffixes and prefixes: To the Rod, of the Rod, by the Rod, with the Rod, from the Rod; and *Rod* with its start-sounds and endings could mean 'Rod who is the third son of so and so has just arrived and is all powerful and commands . . .' It seems that the first Rod's names, with its history and his situation and the honorifics, took a day to recite—so the old joke went. Whatever else, that Rod was a strategist of genius. Not that it needed much more than strength and will—and the horses—to make short work of the shallow little towns, but then he used his victories to build them into a whole, and call them The Cities. Flattery served him well. He made his wild desert raiders into an army that was feared by all the lands we had heard of, and many that we hadn't, and so, where once we had been at the mercy of every raider or band of thieves, The Cities were safe. This Rod was more than a conqueror. He created a rough but adequate system of laws. An Eye for an Eye and a Tooth for a Tooth was the spirit of it. If The Roddites learned from their defeated enemies how to catch fish, prepare it and eat it, The Cities who before then had owned a few goats, now learned the care and the breeding and uses of sheep, cattle, asses and horses.

So that was the first of the Roddite dynasty, Rod, and his son EnRod succeeded. He lacked his father's wild energies. He was a consolidator, a preserver, one who sees a potential and develops it. He did away with nothing of his father's rule, but he made vital changes. The law became gentler, and women were given the same property rights as men. The Cities, which so recently had been crude and primitive, an assembly of villages, were spreading, joining, and by then it would have been more accurate to call them The City. It was felt a mistake—EnRod did—to abolish the identity of places, when each prided itself on an individuality. The old names were kept and the idea of a multiplicity of cities was preserved. It was learned that the nearest city over the mountains, which we heard tales about from travellers, was smaller in area than our city, The Cities. Which was governed as if it were a whole, single, of a piece. You could walk half a day and never leave our streets, while crossing streets that announced, 'Here begins the village of Ogon.' Or Astrante. Or Ketasos. Whichever fishing village it once had been.

The rule of EnRod was beneficent. Already people were saying, My father, my grandfather, came with the Roddite invasion.

EnRod's son was almost at once called by the populace, The Whip, and that characterised him well. He was cruel, easily enraged, arbitrary, and would have destroyed everything made by his father and grandfather. The Cities were saved by his bride, who came from the East, from a tribe kin to The Roddites, a beautiful girl who it was said had not wanted to leave the life of horses and desert and the songs for which they were famous, but it seemed that it had been put to her that it was her duty to marry a savage, The Whip, and civilise him. But in fact that would have been beyond her. The Whip was mad. He died. How fortuitous. Not really, she had him poisoned. The arts of the desert people in poisons and medicine were and are famous. The populace rejoiced. Of course there were mutters and threats, but as the rumours flew about that this smiling gentle beauty was a murderess, the people applauded. Everybody knew what they had been saved from. There were tyrants in other towns in the peninsula and we heard news of them. Because of the laws introduced by EnRod, she could assume the throne on The Whip's death and she did so. Soon The Whip was remembered only in tales and songs. The rule of Rod was remembered in epic style, thundering verses like horses' hoofbeats, all bravery and fine deeds, while his son's reign, so salubrious, good for everyone and for peace, for progress, was less celebrated. Unfortunately a quiet competence is not as attractive a subject for a story or a song as conquest and heroism. Stories about The Whip gave rise to some uneasiness, for in those wiser days it was known that tales and songs could change minds and hearts.

It is from The Whip's short reign that a whole genre of stories came, and songs too, of cruelty for cruelty's sake, of torture, of the screams of people from pits deep under the earth, the screams of horses, of animals, of demons whose task it is to torment people, of witches and witchcraft.

The new ruler was Destra, and it was she who first tried to ban these cruel and perverted tales and songs which created cults among the populace, who used them as a justification for wrongdoing. So I heard, so I was told: Destra was old by the time I was born. I can testify to the power of storytelling: I could never see her as anything but a young and beautiful and kind princess from the desert, because of the tales about her, in her youth. Destra soon put right what had been made bad by her husband. She reinstituted EnRod's laws. She did not change the management of the army, which The Whip had made strong. She merely gave the soldiers long leaves, very long, she said for the benefit of their families. The army remained a worry to her. She had to have one. Rival citics after all flourished, and wars did go on: The Cities were covetable. But during the reigns of Rod, EnRod, The Whip and then Destra there had been no actual fighting. Marches, manoeuvres, rallies, all kinds of parades and shows of strength, but no actual fighting. There were jokes that if we were invaded our soldiers would scarcely know how to act.

Destra created a College of Storytellers and another of Songmakers.

There were already stories and songs, but she wanted something specific, the story of our people, from the time we became one, under the first Rod, Rod the Progenitor. You can imagine that there was plenty of material, opportunities for every kind of tale, legend, song. Many were, frankly, instructional. Destra wanted what she called an instructed and informed people, and a good part of the songs and tales were for the purpose of teaching. The reign of EnRod, which had been so little of an inspiration, now became a source of all kinds of instructional material about peacetime arts. For instance, the management of herds, or building, of the new practice of crop rotation, and how to control rivers, springs, water generally. From the ruler least used by the tale-makers and the singers, he was the best. EnRod became a synonym for good government, just as The Whip was execrated.

In this short summary of Destra's encouragement of the arts, I can give no idea of the wealth and complexity of our treasury of songs and tales, but I hope to amplify it all, before I die.

Destra was already old when she called us The Guardians of the people. That was our first and primary name, and afterwards came The Analyzers, The Watchers, The Recorders, and so on. I was among them because my mother was a friend of Destra, from one of the families from which Destra chose administrators, governors, generals. There were then twelve or so families. Who knows, now? Then, it was easy to say, Those are the governing people, but now? Families that were famous for their probity and their good sense are now dissolute and their offspring are worthless. The Twelve were at first in fact thirteen, because one of us would succeed Destra. DeRod of course, as Destra's son, was among the thirteen. We used to call him The Beneficent Whip, as a joke, when he showed signs of petulance and wilfulness and might sulk. But we all had nicknames. When my comrades laughed at me, it was The Sage.

But I am getting in advance of my tale. I am telling it as if it is a tale, just that, and the fact I am makes me uneasy as if I were rolling something up into a ball and throwing it from me. Done. Finished. I want to leave a record. I must. How quickly things do change. Anybody would have thought that the Rule Destra set up must last: it seemed so solid, so efficient, so easily built upon and extended. How easily and well things happened. For instance, it was then enough to say to one of our talented storytellers: 'make a good song about the terrible horses of the first Rod', and you would soon hear the song in the inns and the guard houses and the public gardens where the festivals were held. Or Destra would say, 'Some travellers brought this grain to sell us, they knew we don't grow it. Take it out to the gardeners and get them to make a trial plot. We must have it here, too.'

It has all gone. What has? For one thing, the simplicity of it all. Once—then—it was all easy and pleasant. Now, nothing is. Even if I don't know why, I can at least say, This happened.

The events which I described earlier were once known to everybody in The Cities. Each child was taught the core tale, and around that all the tales, repeated them, made his or her version of, let's say, The Terrible Horses, or The Wise Ruler who Changed the Law from Revenge to Kindness. Destra has been dead almost as long as I have been alive, and I have been alive as long as she was. In that stretch of time, two long lifetimes, Destra's creation of storytelling and songmaking as a means of instruction, refinement, something which lifted up our whole population to a height of culture not matched anywhere else that we knew of, this wonderful education began, grew, reached perfection, held it for a while—and then . . . But what happened I do not know. None of The Twelve did. Simply, Destra's adopted son, DeRod, destroyed it. Why did he? How often have we all—all The Twelve that is—tried to understand and failed. And it was not possible simply to ask our old friend and playfellow because he ignored us.

The name DeRod means something wonderful in the language of the desert tribes, but we called him Benny, short for Beneficent Whip. I think we soon forgot how 'Benny' began. He was one of those chosen when we were still infants to be instructed by Destra herself. She was a wonderful teacher. She taught us good behaviour, how to make decisions, how to think, how to put the welfare of The Cities before anything else. All this by means of tales and songs. She had tutors to teach us the art of numbers, weights, measurements. The instruction took place in Destra's house, The Big House, the populace called it. It is the largest of the big houses, but not by very much. The Cruel Whip was going to double it in size but Destra silenced him before he could. If she did.

There is a large room, open on one side, where there is a screen of reeds if there is rain or dust, and there we were educated. Thirteen, who always knew we would be a Council of Twelve. DeRod was taught with us. We were equals. There was never a suggestion that as Destra's child he would be favoured. And there was the girl, Destra's adopted daughter, DeRod's sister, Shusha, later my wife who, if DeRod should die or be killed, would be Destra's only progeny, brought up as if she were in fact Destra's daughter. I think we all forgot those two were adopted. It was never assumed that DeRod would be ruler after his mother. On the contrary, Destra told us, and from our earliest days, that from one of us a ruler would be chosen, and that The Twelve would be advisers.

And so it went on, a time of such happiness, and I am sure this is no flattering memory, for it was shared by all The Twelve and we often spoke of it, saying that this was how every child should be educated. And yet none of our children had anything like as good. Perhaps such an education needs someone like Destra to make it work.

When we were all fifteen years old, or near that age, Destra was ill and was carried into our instruction room, which was usually filled with sunlight and the shadows from the great trees that surrounded The Big House, and so it was that day. Destra told us that she would soon die, and now we must choose her successor. She was sitting up, cushions piled behind her, a tiny old woman with her white hair down around her face, her black eyes burning with urgency—like the urgency I feel now—and with fever. It was a surprise and yet not one. We all knew, had always known, that this day must come. We knew that Destra was very old, and that she was ill. And yet we were taken by surprise and were uneasy and afraid for the future.

I remember we stood about in that room, which was as much our home as our own homes were. We stood about looking at each other, not liking that now we would have to make a choice.

Destra sat up there, with a woman on either side of her, watching us, waiting. And still we did not speak out.

Then she did. 'Just because DeRod is my son, it does not mean he should be chosen. Nor should Shusha, just because she is my daughter. You must choose the best one, the one you all agree would be best. You must have made your choice. You must have discussed it.' Well, we hadn't much. That was the trouble. The trouble was perhaps, we had been discussing it too long, expecting it. We knew our qualities and our deficiencies. Some of us were out of the question as rulers. Shusha was one. This was not because she was a girl—five of us were female. She said herself it wouldn't suit her. She was a smiling, modest, careful girl, who liked looking after the house animals and tending plants. Later she became responsible for agriculture and the welfare of children. Others had long ago judged themselves to be unsuitable, and so we had not considered them. The others had been discussed, DeRod too. We told him that if he could cure his tendency to sulk and to go off in little fits of petulance, he would do well. I think we were all a little bit in love with DeRod. There was nothing much about him to dislike ever. Perhaps he was too eager to please, always, to fall in, to agree. He was such a beautiful child, and then as beautiful a youth. He was tall and slight, with dark eyes that compelled, and brooded, and with a gleam in them that we joked was because of his desert inheritance: Destra had those eyes too. When we discussed him as a possible Ruler we always joked that he would be all right with us to keep an eye on him. I would say now that five or perhaps six of us would have done well as

Ruler. I know that there were those who thought that I would. There was a time, being young and conceited, when I would agree with them—but I know better now. Well I did have some of the qualities. I thought easily in terms of how to govern well, looking at The Cities as a whole; I knew how to manage people, bringing out their good qualities, never demeaning them. I knew the Story of our people better than anyone: that is why later they made me Chief Official Memory. But they didn't choose me. Nor any of the other good ones—and believe me, I have often imagined one or another in DeRod's place, and wondered. We chose DeRod. This was, perhaps, a foregone conclusion. So I think now, looking back. He was after all Destra's heir, in the line Rod, EnRod, Cruel Whip, Destra. There is pleasure in that, a fitness, a pattern, as if you are guarding some inherent order. We chose him though we knew Destra was sincere in saying we must choose the best. We knew absolutely how she would judge the best: she had been telling us for all those years. She had told us tales often about tribes and peoples who, on the death of a ruler chose a successor by vote, sometimes passing over elder sons, more than once choosing a daughter when there were sons. No, we could not blame Destra, for us choosing DeRod. And in fact he was surprised, and we realised he had not expected we would settle for him.

He was so pleased. And we took such pleasure in his pleasure. When we said, almost unanimously, 'DeRod', he seemed to shine and swell, he stretched out his arms in a movement like a bird about to fly. He then made some little dance steps, first because he had to, and then in jest, laughing at himself and at his pleasure. His eyes were full of tears. He embraced us then, one by one, and as it were as a group. For a few moments we were standing in a sort of heap, with our arms around each other, hugging and laughing, and DeRod there in the middle shouting in triumph. Then he pushed his way out, ran to his mother in that quick wonderfully graceful way he had, and kissed her hand. And then it was we remembered Destra, and that she had been waiting for us to choose. We would have gone to kiss her hand but it was too late. She was already being carried off. I remember she was breathing heavily, a harsh and awful noise. She did not make any sign towards us though we were waiting for one.

I remember how we all stood about, waiting, feeling most terribly let down. Feeling perhaps, too, that Destra's refusal to acknowledge us then meant she was disappointed, or even angry. In the end DeRod clapped his hands, jumped about in the way he had, as if he were younger than he was, and said he could command a banquet. A funny way of putting it we thought, not

Destra's style at all. And a big banquet there was, and DeRod announced as Destra's heir. We drank the wine that by now was being grown by us in The Cities, and we all got drunk and—were as happy as I can remember. I would like to be able to say I felt foreboding, or uneasiness. If I had, at the very beginning, by then I had suppressed them. DeRod was so delightful with us that day of the banquet, so simple, and, we could see, grateful. It was a day that marked the end of our instruction: fifteen years of learning and listening and taking in, of preparing ourselves. And now this was it, when Destra died we would begin to use what we had learned.

And now I must wrench myself away from these pleasant memories and decide what I should do. I have at least begun by making a record—an over-simple, very short one, but a record—of the beginnings of The Twelve. I can fill it all out later if there's time . . . and perhaps there isn't: I had not expected Koon, or Eleven, to die. And why not? He was as old as I am. I would like to have the time to write down the wealth of tales and stories that seem to have been lost. How could they have been lost? I have lived now for nearly a hundred years. For at least half that time the tales and songs were on everybody's lips. And yet now only old people—my son can be described as old—remember them.

What am I to do? In the past, when in doubt

I took myself to the house of one of The Twelve, or asked them to visit me here. I have decided to visit the place where only days ago we buried Eleven. 'We'? Mourners who had no knowledge of him, or of us, mourners who weep and wail for money.

* * *

I stood for a long time at the edge of the great Fall of water, where I have been so often, for the pleasure of watching how the water bounded or crept or frolicked from the top of the Fall to the bottom, its antics measured and ordered by our clever Nine—the water engineer. And then, the pleasure of deciding whether to climb up its course to the top where it gushed over natural rocks, and then over the hill and through the buildings and squares of our public life, or down to see how the water fled into channels for the irrigation of the market gardens. This Fall was created early in Destra's Rule, over steps like a giant's stair, so that when I was born the Fall was already a wonder known to everyone and visited by travellers, some of whom had come to The Cities for the purpose. It was much later that The Twelve made a great pool at the foot of the Fall, where the waters crashed down but soon spread out into a great wash always in movement because of the cascade, but so shallow the smallest child could paddle in it. This pool, Shusha's inspiration, was for children, who had to be under six years old; and for small children a more delightful place has never been. The charming ripples from the Fall were of course waves to them, the spray that greened the low bushes around the pool was part of their fun, a mere breath of freshness on the hands and faces of adults, but for the little ones a source of delight because of the way the breezes blew this way and that, unexpectedly dousing them, so that they screamed with delight. This was one of my favourite places. Was.

This morning I stood a long time, remembering that it was on this spot I encountered DeRod for the second time after we had chosen him and celebrated with the banquet. The first was when I married his sister Shusha (Seven). Because Destra was recently dead it was a simple ceremony, and that suited us both. DeRod surprised us. I thought he was in mourning, but perhaps . . . he was all courtesy, formally officiating, kindly, pleasant, but distant. This was our friend DeRod, whom we had known all our lives. Both Shusha and I made excuses for him. We confessed that we could not remember a particular closeness to his mother that could justify a real grief. And this although he was always saying, 'My mother and I . . .', 'We . . . meaning Destra and him, 'I and Destra . . .'. No. The fact was, Shusha said, putting into words what I had only felt until then, he was not a loving person. He was affectionate, yes, in a pretty playful way that suited him, as a child. 'He never loved me.' I remember Shusha saying then. 'What? What do you mean?' 'I think he is a really cold person,' she said, to my discomfort, and I seem to remember I put it down to brother and sister rivalry. What a fool I was.

Destra did not die for a year after the day we chose him. During that time we did not see him. This day, by the Fall, when I came on him standing there watching the waters, it was some four years after his accession. During that time he did not come to the meetings of The Twelve, was pleasant if he met us in the streets, but was always in a hurry, ignored the usual invitations to suppers or family reunions. When we did meet there was always between us the familiarity of our childhood knowledge of each other, and that was why The Twelve were confused when we asked ourselves and each other, Why? What is it?

What was he doing? Reports came from The Big House, mostly from servants. He played with his zither for hours. A girl from the town, not one of us, or from any of the leading families, was his companion. He often visited the army and took part in its exercises.

We simply got on with our job, which was to do as well as we could for The Cities. Those early years after Destra's death, building on what she had created, were as successful as any in our history. None of it was owed to DeRod. He was simply not available to us.

I remember when I caught sight of him on that day, standing by the Fall, the rush of old affection I felt for him. There he was, the old DeRod, as handsome as ever. How potent a spell good looks do impose. I don't think I ever thought of that as a weakness until I was forced to think about DeRod's effect on us. Seeing him there, brooding, moody, apparently deep in thought, I forgot that for four years every thought of him caused me—caused us all—pain.

And it was from the old ease with him that I walked up to him and embraced him, while he, after a moment, frowning with shock, turned and embraced me. 'DeRod,' I complained, 'why do we never see you?' Now I was close I could have a good look. He was a man, no longer a boy.

He nodded and said with a frown, 'But I hear you are all doing very well without me.'

Now that was an odd false note to strike, surely?

I said, 'But DeRod, that sounds as if you are not one of us?

He made an impatient movement, frowned, 'I've got things to do.' He was glancing up at the top of the path, expecting someone.

I felt more and more that this conversation did not—fit. He did not make sense. 'But

DeRod, we miss you. We talk about you. We wonder why you never . . .'

At this he shrugged me off, us off, brusque, rude, but he felt the rudeness himself, and having already walked off a few paces he stopped and said, half-turning, 'I'll see you. Yes . . . soon.' At the top of the path a woman had appeared. Presumably his town girl. Nothing much to say about her: she was a nice enough looking woman. But she stood there waiting for him, not looking at me at all. He was hurrying up to her, and the noise of the Fall made it useless to call after him.

And we did not hear one word from him. Not for years. Then it was always messages putting us off. And, always, there was about this communication, if you could call it that, something unexpected, discordant. We couldn't make sense of it. What was he doing? He had become obsessed with his army. Instead of an institution that we saw as a useful way of keeping young men out of mischief, and discouraging greedy people who might be tempted by the riches of The Cities, it had become a major part of our economy. It glittered and excelled, it was marched and drilled and exercised out of its wits—the soldiers actually complained. He invented new clothes for them, using extravagant colours, scarlet, blue, gold. To stand on one of our little hills watching our army at their exercising down there on the plain—what a spectacle.

And for what? He did not go to war, he did not threaten or even use it for his own prestige. He was nominally Commander-in-Chief—a title we knew had not been used before with us—but he did not interfere in the actual exercises and manoeuvres. And this went on. And it went on. We began to be alarmed at the way our wealth was being drained off into the army. And then there was a change, which we would have thought impossible.

But I am describing my visit to the burial place, and here I am still standing on the edge of the Fall, remembering. I walked down the path beside the Fall, hardening myself for what I would see. The pool for infants and small children was now a playground for the youth. It had become the fashion for them to assemble there, day and night, sitting around the edge, lolling in the shallow water, eating, drinking, smoking and—much else. For longer than most of the time these young ones had been alive, small children had not used this pool. It was now the property of The Young Hawks. Their name for themselves.

I walked by, at a small distance, because the noise was horrible, remembering the happy cries and shrieks of the little children's play. The Hawks took no notice of me. What they were seeing was a very old man, in the brown garment of The Twelve. Whom they had forgotten, and their parents had too. Sitting on the edge close to me were some girls and boys, about the age I think of when we became The Guardians, as always eating and throwing food about. A girl shouted at me, 'Hey, old thing, what's that you've got on?' I went a bit closer, and said, 'This is what The Twelve wear.' I heard, as I knew I would, 'The Twelve? What's that?' Then another girl said, 'Hey, let me look. Would it suit me, do you think?' Then she laughed and said, 'I'm only joking, don't worry.' 'You could easily make it,' I said, knowing that none of them knew how to use a needle. And she boasted, 'I wouldn't know one end of a needle from the other.' Her companions were all laughing and applauding. Clearly, she was some kind of leader.

'You take a length of cloth,' I said. 'You cut a hole for the head. You sew up the sides, leaving room for the arms. You can wear it as it is in hot weather, as I am now, or put it over others if it is cold. She was straining to listen, to understand. They know no crafts, have no skills now. They arc dependent on the Barbarians. Because she was interested I went on. 'When Destra chose The Twelve it was thought best that we should wear the simplest garb available. In cotton.' I omitted to say that this was partly to encourage the use of cotton, which we had just begun to develop.

'Who's Destra?' she asked smartly: she had decided to entertain her comrades by baiting me. 'And who are The Twelve? I thought you were all dead long ago.' Well, she had at least heard of us, if not of Destra.

She began turning it into a song. 'Twelve old men, they keep it—neat. They wear old sandals on their feet.'

'Men and women,' I said.

But she only grimaced, prettily, and began splashing the boy next to her with water.

I said to a youth near her, 'Did you know this pool was once only for small children?'

He frowned. 'Really? Oh—shame.' He began clowning, 'The Young Hawks have taken the little kids' pool.'

Much laughter and then some horseplay. These were bored youngsters looking for an excuse to have some fun, as they would put it. The violence in The Cities is growing, and I had no intention of becoming a victim.

They saw themselves as hawks: now that was painful. They were a good-looking crowd, true enough, but they were soft and fatty.

'Goodbye,' I said, and walked on, thinking that the girl had been prompt in making up rhymes and singing them: not all of Destra's legacy had gone.

I walked along the irrigation ditches that run out from the pool, and along the edges of the fields which grow our vegetables. There were people at work, men and women, all Barbarians. Our young despise this work, bending and tending, their hands in earth.

What do they do, then? A good question.

Nothing much. They like to dress each other's hair, tend each other's bodies, create new kinds of food, new clothes. We are still so rich, though these days it is what we loot from others. We are rich because we don't make war. We raid and steal and our victims are afraid of us, and do not fight back. Over the mountains that are like a barrier between us and the cities on the opposite edge of the peninsula, they fight each other and are poor. I wondered if their young people call themselves Young Eagles. Panthers, perhaps? Mountain Lions? These sour thoughts took me part of the way up the hill, approaching the burial ground. When I reached the big trees which I saw planted as saplings, I began walking cautiously: there were young people there, among the graves.

It is a beautiful place, surrounded by a triple ring of trees, mostly oaks. In the centre the eleven graves ray out from an empty space, long mounds of yellow earth, each covered with a slab of our dark grey stone. Eleven's grave, a few days old, still does not have its stone lid. Inside the ring of trees, the soft yellow earth of this hillside is allowed to grow the sparse grass of the region, a mat that keeps the soil from blowing. There are always birds in the trees. The tree shadows move, mass, thicken, grow thin, as the sun moves. A young couple leaned against a tree, embracing. A youth was digging soil from the heap over

Eleven. I stood where my grave would be, and said to him, 'Just a minute, young man, show some respect.'

He was a burly, unappetising youth, wearing an outfit that seemed wrong on him.

He stopped, looked up, and said, 'Whadyewmean?'

'That is where an old friend of mine is buried.'

There was a knife in his belt, and his hand went to it. But he was frowning, apparently thinking: I reminded myself that these days they need some time to take in facts.

I repeated, 'A friend of mine was buried there a few days ago.' He looked down at the now damaged mound. I saw that he was imagining how just beneath him . . . he jumped away from the grave, brushed his hands free of soil, and said, 'Right, then.'

'What do you want the earth for?'

'My house is letting in water. This makes good clay, this soil up here, mixed with a little of the fine chalk near the shore.'

'Why don't you make yourself a stone house?'

'My house does well enough. It needs some patching.'

He yawned, stretched, sat down on a grave. Nine's. The water engineer who had created the Fall. He pulled some dried meat from his garment and began eating. Over in the trees, the couple were copulating. These days they couple any place they feel like it. The youth sitting on the grave saw them and shouted: 'Go to it!' He laughed. Then he said to me, sobering, 'Oh, go on, it's only a bit of fun.'

I had remembered what his clothes were. The desert people under the first Rod had worn tunics belted over loose trousers in sandy colours, and these had become a fashion, which must have looked well on those lithe quick people. On this hulk of a youth, with his bulging stomach, they were wrong.

'So, you're one of Rod's warriors?' I teased him.

'What?'

I explained. He was interested. 'That's green,' he said. 'Did you know Rod?'

'It was getting on for four hundred years ago.'

Again the frown of incomprehension. He shook his head, dismissing it all, stood up. The two copulators, having finished, strolled over, dishevelled but not discomposed.

'Got your earth?' asked the young woman.

'Go on, take some.' I said. 'When they come to fit on the slab they'll have to tidy it all up anyway.'

'No . . . no . . . actually we just came up for a laugh, and then I saw this soil just lying here.'

The three turned, to go off down the hill.

I said, 'One day I shall be put here, just here, where I am standing.'

This embarrassed them. 'Is this a special

place?' asked the youth who had his arms around the girl.

'You could say that, I think,' I said.

'Green,' said the girl.

I saw that green was the new in-word.

The two young men gave a kind of salute, but it was a joke, the girl made a joke curtsey, and off they went, running down the hill.

I sat myself down on the stone that covered Shusha and looked at the graves, one after another, thinking of my friends. Then at the lacing of vigorous grass over the yellow soil. Then at the enormous trees around this circle. Here was my life. All my friends, my wife, all gone under the earth.

How much I wished I could just lie down in my place and be done with it. I did not want to stand up, with the creaking effort it costs me these days, walk slowly down the hill, carrying such a load of doubts, fears, sorrow. Everything I had worked for had vanished. There had been that wonderful time, that excellence, which seemed like a dream, it was so far away, so done with. And the future was not anything I cared to think about.

I lay down on my place, on the rough grass, and folded my arms, as they will be, soon. The sun was striking low through the tree trunks, and black spokes marked the grass, the graves. Straight above me the blue air dazzled. I closed my eyes and dreamed.

Twelve youngsters were dancing in a ring

that matched the encircling trees, and the almost complete circle of graves. They tripped and stepped and sang, cram-full of the energies and hopes of the very young. There we all were, The Twelve, not much more than children, just about the age we were when Destra died. There I was, too. The sun shone on our hair, on our bare brown limbs, and the happy shouts and singing rose up into the air like birds. I was both one of them and sitting on the grass, supporting my old weight with my hands. I wanted to call out to my younger self, but could not. And then, it seemed, the light dimmed, the sun darkened, and one by one my young companions turned to smile at me over their shoulders as they ran off into the trees, going out like sparks or like fireflies. Each one, the quick flash of a smile, teasing, mocking, affectionate, and then he or she was gone, Shusha too, and I among them. Twelve. But where was DeRod?—and then there he was, strolling along near the trees, not a boy, or even a youth, but a grown man, as he had been long ago that day near the Fall. He was not looking about him, was self-absorbed. Or absent—yes: as if he did not know where he was. He stopped, urinated near one of the graves. This was done so casually, almost absently. He was thinking of something else. He walked off down the hill as the spray of urine came on the breeze to my face. I woke; the dew was falling; and night was falling too.

The great clearing was filled with the blueish dark of twilight.

I stood up, trying to loosen my limbs from the stiffness of lying still for what must have been quite a time. I wanted so much to weep. My throat was sore from the tears that choked it. Oh, how brilliant is the Dreamer that lives in us all, how witty, and how well it uses the events of a day for its purposes. What an apt depiction of my situation. Standing there in the half-dark I saw again how each of my old comrades and my young self turned to send me the fleeting, half-mocking goodbye smile and then—out, gone. And DeRod. There was something in that dream of him that said to me: Pay attention. I am telling you something. It was not contempt that he was using, when he urinated almost on the grave of an old friend, no, it was carelessness. You could say indifference. It did not matter to him, that was the point. *That* was the point. And what a contrast between how we all had been seeing him, talking of him, wondering, speculating: he had come to assume in our eyes the demeanour, the stature, of something not far from that old fabled Whip, who had been so cruel. We had spoken of him more and more as a tyrant, a monster of a ruler, deliberately destroying everything that was good. But the DeRod of my dream was not like that, commonplace, he was; someone you'd not look at twice. A pleasant fellow. Matching him with our years-long deliberations—such complicated and sometimes far-fetched explanations we had found for his behaviour—we had even laughed at ourselves. They nearly always focused on arrogance, on the distortions of sense that come from the loneliness of power. And there was always something that did not fit our thoughts of him. We knew that he lived as simply as his mother had done, that his children were not more privileged than anyone else's, and that he occupied himself with . . . and that is what I must now record.

When I was able to move comfortably, I found my clothes too damp for comfort, and imagined I must have wet them with my tears. Though I had not wept, I had been thinking too hard about DeRod. I kept seeing him, indifferent, careless: and now to my memory of the dream I added something else, his smile at me as he turned to go, almost embarrassed, almost irritated, as if at someone importunate, demanding too much. How painful, and how informative that dream had been, and my thoughts about it afterwards.

I walked through the trees and down the hill into the thinly scattered lights of the city which stopped on the edge of the dark of the ocean. I went past the pool, which was still full of youngsters. All around it flared the torches which we, The Twelve, had ordered to be kept always burning. We had imagined, when the infants and the little children and the women who attended to them had gone off to bed, how the flames from the torches would move and shine on the water that was never still, or would sometimes drip fire on a windy night, so that it would be hard to tell if the little waves on the pool were fire or water. Now it was a noisy drunken scene, and it was easy to walk past in the half dark, unnoticed. The girl who had asked about my garment was lying half in, half out of the water, one of a group who it seemed were all copulating together like a tangle of snakes in spring.

A youth on the other side of the pool was trying to grab a girl: she was very young, not more than a child. He was shouting at her, half-singing it, 'New girl in the pool, fears the push and fears the shove, Come to me, I'll give you love . . .' I was able to recognise this as a debased version of

New lamb on the hill
Fears the snow and fears the storm,
Bring it down and keep it warm,
Mend the cracks in barn and shed,
The lamb will pine without the ewe
The ewe without its lamb pine too,
Keep them warm and keep them fed . . .

These days when the wind blows cold across our hills no one brings the lambs and ewes down for safety, and the white patches that are dead lambs look like the last shreds of snow on the grass, or like white flowers spattered everywhere.

I came into my house in the dark and sat in the dark, alone. *My* house? It is a long time since I could think of this spreading house as mine. In the middle of my life, half a century—almost—ago, my son Bora came to me and said that he had a wife and three children and needed more space than he had, in a smallish house in one of the cities from the old time, which meant, in a rough area. There was much more to this than simple practicality. I would not say we were estranged, but for a long time wc had not had much to say to cach othcr. My house—poor Shusha had died—is in the part of The Cities where the elite live. I put it like that, simply, without evasions or the usual justifications, because, well, I am too old for all that. I, The Twelve, were a governing elite, but for a long time we have not been. People like my son went in for a lot of vilification and even when The Cities were doing very well indeed. 'The powerful oligarchy which rules us.' That kind of thing. But young people vociferous in this way usually end up standing where the vilified elders stood. For him to move up here, to this house, was a statement to all concerned and we both knew it. A wing of four rooms was built on, and here I moved, the house servants easily accommodating themselves to balancing my meagre wants with the family's. Our relations were cordial enough. We didn't see each other sometimes for weeks. And then in his turn my son Bora found he was being faced with—in his case—a daughter-in-law, saying, You don't need all that room. And he built a wing on the other side of the house, to let my grandson and his wife and children move in. They were prominent in DeRod's circles and I would have liked to joke with someone about this new elite—but these days I have no one to enjoy jokes with.

And now I must record the worst thing that happened to us, the most unexpected, and still the most puzzling. A message came from DeRod that he was abolishing The College of Storytellers and The College of Songmakers. It was not possible to console ourselves by saying it must be a mistake. DeRod's agents had requisitioned the two buildings. This was not long before Shusha died and my son moved in. Shusha was beside herself. She was responsible for the education of the young and the two colleges were what she relied on. For a while we sat together, doing what so often resulted from an order from DeRod: we were trying to understand how he was thinking, why he did what he did.

For a good while after Destra's death and DeRod's accession The Cities were at a height of brilliance. A golden age. Our festivals of storytelling, our song festivals, our entertainments, followed each other through that cycle of the sun from a grand climax on the day when it is coldest, but we know it will get warmer, until the generous blaze of the day when we know that from now it will get colder, and that was the other big festival. Mid-Light. People were coming from far-away cities all over the peninsula. People still do come, but they are different people and bring with them strife and disturbance, and their enjoyment is expressed in a raw jeering laughter that was never heard in our time.

DeRod did not take part in these festivities, or not much. Always affable and obliging, he might appear at a festival, but it was as if what was after all the pulse and beat of our communal life did not touch him, had nothing to do with him. He preferred his armies. He had even made up a song for them, catchy, full of a patriotic fervour we had not associated with The Cities until then. It was popular, and sung not only by the soldiers. Just how far this army song was in spirit from our music was shown when it was sung by a young aspirant at a song competition. The audience laughed at it—at the song, not the singer; in those days to mock a performer would have been thought unkind.

The festivals were held not in one place, but in several, in public places everywhere: we were still trying to make sure ancient rivalries were not being fostered. For several days, at these times, you could not walk down a street or enter a garden without finding yourself part of singing, dancing, or some enactment, which might be the joining of the old towns at the time of the birth of The Cities, or perhaps the short reign of The Cruel Whip. But we discouraged the kind of music he introduced, the violence and the crudity of it, though we could not deny it attracted crowds. From small seeds big trees may grow. As we often say but perhaps we do not think often enough about the meaning. The Cruel Whip's effusions and effluences, discouraged by Destra and then by us, have grown into a nasty poisonous flood.

The message from DeRod, ending our prosperity—though at the time we had no idea how thoroughly and soon the end would come—arrived at the height of our happy festival culture.

Shusha said she would go and see him, and went off then and there. After all, her brother, whom she had scarcely seen for years, lived a short walk away. She returned looking as if someone had hit her. Shusha was always a sensitive soul, too much so, for her own good, as she knew, and as I often warned her. And the story, when at last she was able to tell it, did not seem at once to justify such pain. DeRod at first did not recognise her, and then apologised by saying it was a long time since she had visited. She had to swallow indignation: she had once made every kind of attempt to see him. But he did not seem to see that she was angry. It was a family occasion, the room full of people. His children were like my son, with families of their own. Shusha was only just able to put names to the men and women who must be DeRod's progeny, and there were a lot of children. A long table was loaded with food. Plentiful, reported Shusha, but not very elegant. And this was the note or tone of what she saw: she was puzzled by it and surprised. She said they were a crude and ordinary lot, and you'd never think they were anything more than a gathering of the kind of people you might find in a low-class eating house or inn. 'I kept thinking, *This* is Destra's son, he was brought up by Destra,' she said, sorrowful, and with that unfailing note of bewilderment that had to accompany our discussions of DeRod. She was introduced as an aunt, to some, who said it was nice to meet her and as a great-aunt to others. They offered her food but she said to DeRod that she wanted to talk to him, even for a minute. 'Well, talk away,' he said, as if it did not occur to him that she might have a special reason for needing to talk. 'It's about the festivals,' she said. 'Why are you abolishing them?' She said she felt like some idiot, the way they all looked at her. 'What makes you think I am abolishing anything?' DeRod enquired, impatient with her. 'You've just taken over the colleges, you've taken our buildings.' 'Oh, have we?' said he, not impudently, but as if hearing the news for the first time. 'Well, never mind, I'm sure you can fix up your festivals.'

Soon she excused herself and came home, weeping.

The Twelve sent him messages of all kinds, and visited him in delegations of twos and threes at his house. He greeted us with his usual affability, making it clear by his manner that we were an irrelevance; he might offer us a cup of wine, but the most we could get out of him was, 'I'm working on something, I'm sure you'll like it.'

On my visit to him, with Eleven and Nine, I said to him, 'You are destroying the very essence of what we are, the soul of The Cities. We are admired for it by everyone. Why are you doing this?' I remember his look—I'm not likely to forget it! How often I have recalled that look, to see if there was something there I had missed. His look at me, at us, was not angry. Not discommoded. It showed nothing of the discomfort of one who feels inferior. There was a little embarrassment, not on his own account, but on ours. 'I didn't say I am doing away with music,' he repeated. 'There are plenty of different kinds of songs and music.'

'And the tales? Our story? The history of The Cities?'

Did he shrug? Well, as good as.

'We teach our children,' I said. 'It is how they learn their skills. They learn from them an enquiring habit of mind, how to think, how to make comparisons. How are our children going to be taught?'

How well I remember his long preoccupied stare, at this. He frowned, he fidgeted, his eyes wandered and then returned, he leaned forward to stare at my face, into our faces, and then sat back. He sighed. He must know what he was destroying: he must. And yet he did not seem to.

The festivals were cancelled, and The Cities began to fall into disorder. There was a sullen, angry mood, and that was when began the outbreaks of public violence. As for us, The Twelve, we were as if he had hit us in the heart region: the way fighters do, to disable an opponent. Some of us became ill. Quite soon Shusha died. I knew it was because of shock, of grief.

Then the new thing began. A Festival was announced, and it would be organised by the armies. When it took place, people who were used to the old ways were uncomfortable. It was all military, to do with army exercises, marching, army life, and even fighting, though that was a rather abstract affair, more like games, and it would be hard to associate blood and death with them. Above all, the spirit had gone, the old spirit. Everything was trivial and unimportant. Hard to imagine the ceremonies of our festivals, which insisted on the deep seriousness of our lives, our responsibilities for each other and for The Cities. The choirs of

DeRod's armies sang wonderfully: after all, many had been trained at our schools. But what were they singing! You could imagine that not very clever children had written these songs, children who had no idea that anything better was possible. They were pompous, or bombastic; they were silly and jokey—the kind of jokes small children like. The audience showed their disappointment. This did not last. A new generation arrives quickly on any scene, and soon the children were youngsters who became adults, and when they said Festivals they meant DeRod's and ours were not much more than a memory insisted on by their parents.

The nastiness of The Cruel Whip came back. Some of the new songs I could hardly bear to listen to, they were so vulgar, so crude, so full of incipient violence.

We, The Twelve, were not surprised that DeRod was threatening the nearest city to ours, over the mountains, with invasion. The strength and reputation of The Cities saved us: the endangered city succumbed at once to DeRod and sent a tribute of slaves.

So, with the next city he decided to master. Soon half the peninsula owed tribute to us, and not a real battle had been fought.

That was the picture not long after Shusha's death, at about the time of my son's coming to live in my house. He was employed by the armies as an administrator, and while of course he had been brought up by myself and by Shusha in the old days, it was as if all that had slipped away from him, gone. I used to marvel that a young man who had had such an upbringing could now see nothing of value in it. His look at me when I tried to remind him that there had been better times was like DeRod's: it was I, it was we, who were out of place, out of step. And so it was with all the children of The Twelve. The new spirit in The Cities had wiped their memories clean.

When that rich feast of tales and music had so suddenly been silenced, all kinds of superstitions sprang up, and new gods flourished. Our tales and songs had not celebrated Deity, not more than the basic truth of our interconnectedness, under the Sun, our Creator. Now there was a moon cult, and with that ceremonies of a bloody kind which even now I don't know much about. My son Bora doesn't either, but my grandson is an initiate. Bora told me, 'He's into some weird stuff, I can tell you. Better not be out at night with that lot around or you'll find yourself with your throat cut and stretched out on a stone to please the moon.' He laughed. You could think he admired that sort of thing. It was the violence he admired. That he does admire.

At the inns and drinking houses the songs were like wails or howlings or battle cries, and where the gentle tones, the subtleties, of our songs had been, was now, louder than anything, a loud drumming, like the heartbeat of a criminal. When I walk past such a place I hurry, because I can feel my whole self being roused to anger, threat, even murder. And yet our people can now spend all evening in such places, with that loud thumping in their ears, drinking, sometimes dancing. It is hard to believe that some of them must remember a different, gentler time.

I missed and miss more and more, the sounds of the games and songs that once you could hear everywhere, as you went about.

There was a skipping song that went like this:

Make a hole
As deep will go
The long wing feather
Of an old black crow.
Water and grain
Go in together.
Cover it well.
Watch the weather.

Now make new holes,
Two feathers span
Four points around
The first, and so
The field is covered
With a net of grain.

The seeds will sprout,

Their roots in mud.
But if there's drought,
Reluctant rain
The sprouts will die.

Begin again.
Make a hole . . .

All the little children used this song in their games, and then, a little older, found themselves in the fields, knowing exactly how to plant. It was wonderful to see their delight, as they realised they had so quickly and simply become part of the world of work, contributing their share. There were hundreds of such songs, some simple like this planting song, increasingly deep and more difficult, to match the growing into understanding of the child.

And always The Twelve met and asked ourselves and each other Why? Why? How many ingenious reasons we did find. We imagined far-reaching policies, sometimes benevolent, sometimes malevolent. We credited him with amazing powers of foresight, but this was when we were seeing him as Destra's son. But he was also The Cruel Whip's offspring—and perhaps he had inherited his father's qualities? Why, why, why? What did he want to achieve? What was his aim? Surely not to dominate the whole of the peninsula, become despot over all its cities? Why destroy something as perfect, as harmonious, as The Cities? What was, what could be, the reason?

Somewhere along the dolorous road we did consider the possibility that Destra had hoped we would not choose her son. We did not like this conclusion. We had chosen the monster who was destroying everything his mother had created. It was our fault . . . but it was too painful to think like this. Because it was painful we refused to see the obvious.

I do not want to give the impression that from the moment DeRod became Ruler everything went wrong. On the contrary. For a while everything got better, on a momentum of success. And The Cities were so beautiful then, so prosperous. I remember walking up from the shore one evening with a flaring sunset behind me and thinking I could imagine I was approaching trees and gardens. But I was approaching the most populous part: the dark grey stone from our quarries that made our heavy and solid houses—made them strong against earth-shakes—was absorbed into the green and the colours of the flowers. You walked up thinking that a garden would open in front of you but as you turned a cunningly-placed bend in the path you saw a house or a group of houses. And all this is still true, even if the houses and gardens are not so well-maintained. Suppose—fancifully—we were able to sweep like birds low over The Cities surely what we must see would be the heavy crowns of trees, massed bushes, flowers, and then, half-concealed, our houses.

It was in that period when in fact everything was going wrong, something like fifty years ago, that we, The Twelve, made the great pool at the foot of the Fall for the small children. We were making new farms and forests, and ponds for fresh-water fish. We built silos for the safekeeping of grain, or rather grains, for we were always acquiring new kinds: when DeRod sent off his raiding parties we quietly approached some soldiers and ordered them to bring back any seeds of crops we did not already grow. We created a lake from a river that ran into the sea near The Cities. We imagined Destra was watching us and approving. DeRod did not seem to care what we did. He never commented, whether to approve or not.

About the time my son took my place as head of our household, we, The Twelve—by then eleven, and soon to be ten—decided to undertake the biggest challenge yet. We were going to transform the oldest part of The Cities, where the first villages had been along the shore. It was the poorest area. There were still some shabby buildings—huts, really—of wood and reeds. Some people, believing themselves to be more sensitive than the rest, find them attractive. But it was—and is—squalid. When there are bad storms the seas rise and the whole area can flood. We planned to build a sea wall of our wonderful and accommodating stone, to keep out the sea, and to straighten the streets, make good sewers and a new public park. It would take years. We were all elated, delighted with the plans, and then, at the height of our achievement, when we sent down overseers to arrange for the labour we found they had already been contracted. There was no labour. Who was to blame? DeRod. We sent messengers, asking him why, for by now we were unwilling to face him ourselves, for he had assumed such an intensity of arbitrary destructiveness for us. Never before had we faced a situation where we could not carry out a plan for lack of labour. His reply was, 'he had use for the labour force'. We sent another messenger asking for explanations, and he said he had plans. We should not worry, he said, he was thinking of raiding the cities across the mountains for slaves. That confounded us. We could not believe it. Never had The Cities made captives of free people. Even The Cruel Whip had not done this.

The lower suburbs on the seashore remained at risk from flooding, stayed in their squalor, and we heard that DeRod was building a wall. He planned a long strong tall wall that would run from one arm of the sea to another, several days' walking long, cutting off The Cities from the outside and accessible only through armed gates. He had made his raids, and his captives were in camps guarded by soldiers, and they had begun working in the hills to fetch boulders to break up for the wall. This force was not badly treated. They were prisoners but adequately fed and not overworked. Some, we heard, were pleased to be here, part of the most powerful state in the peninsula, no longer subject to the extortions of The Cities, no longer liable to be snatched from their families to become part of DeRod's work force. Already there was a strong movement among them to get DeRod to bring their families. And DeRod was listening. After all, the young women could work, if they were not breeding. And there were all kinds of skills we, The Cities, did not yet have. We wondered if he had thought of the problems of feeding all these new people? If he had considered that there must be overcrowding, with space limited by his wall?

And soon there were shortages of food. So many of our workers on the fields and with the animals had been conscripted either for his armies or for the wall our food supplies were suffering. Our silos, for the first time, were half empty. Again we sent messengers, and his reply was to send us women, the wives of the new captives, to work at growing food and with animals. They were mostly pregnant and had families. DeRod was encouraging them to have children. These new people had no skills for agriculture, and it was hard to teach them, because our old ways of teaching by tales and songs and narrative poems were being forgotten. It hurt to compare the standards of husbandry to be seen in our fields now, with the past. These were comparatively barbarous people, coarser, clumsier, ignorant compared with—well, with our people in the past. We had to say that, at least to each other: compared with us, but in the past.

This was the moment of evident, apparently irreversible, change, when DeRod decided to build his wall. After that, the falling off was swift and in every possible way.

About that time there was a confrontation between me and my son Bora. That is how I remember it, but I am sure he would not particularly remember it, or think it important. I wanted him to comment on the pleasure garden we had made on the river that escaped from the dam into the sea. How absurd it is, this need of the old for approval from their children. I noticed it among my friends—I used to, when they were alive. Bora had never mentioned the Fall, the pool, the silos, the gardens—nothing of the things we had done, and I am sure I was always hoping for him to say something.

The day of the encounter I saw him walking up the path and hurried to fall in beside him. I came straight out with, 'Have you seen the new river gardens yet?' When he only nodded, I persisted, 'What did you think?'

'Oh, we always do things well.' This took me so aback I actually stopped, but hurried after him. 'Bora, come into my quarters, I want to talk.' He agreed. Amiably enough. I felt it as a kind of indifference. And while we walked to my verandah that I had built to overlook the gardens and the sea, I thought what that 'we' could mean.

We sat, I clapped my hands for refreshments and I looked for signs of impatience in my son and thought that I saw them. It was some time since we had talked. Years, I think. This was because when we did talk I always felt I was knocking on a locked door.

'Bora,' I said, 'there will be no more gardens, or projects for buildings, or anything at all. You must know we have been denied labour, except for field work.'

At this he turned on me eyes which seemed puzzled. He even scratched his head, an oafish gesture he had certainly never learned from us, his parents.

'But we are building the wall. That will be a fine sight, when it's done.'

'But the wall won't make fields and gardens and dams. There is need for labour for maintenance. The silos are dilapidating. The roads are too.'

'Well, we'll attend to it.'

That we again.

'Bora, DeRod has never repaired anything,

mended anything, planted so much as a tree.'

Again he seemed to be working something out. 'But Father, everyone admires DeRod. When we had the Feast of Praise for him all the armies were singing about the new garden and the new silos too.'

I understood. It was such a blow to my sense of probability: Bora believed—they all believed—that DeRod was the originator of wonderful accomplishments.

'Why didn't you come to the ceremony? It was noticed. You and the old gang never do come.'

'Were we sent invitations?'

And now he was openly irritated. 'Since when did the old ones need invitations.'

'The Twelve,' I said. 'The Council of Twelve. The ones that look after The Cities.'

'But you are family,' he said. 'You are part of The Family?

I had not heard that term.

'Now, listen to me.' I said. 'It's important that you should understand.' And I listed our achievements over the past few cycles. 'This is what we did. The Twelve. Not DeRod. And now we cannot get on with the work we should be doing.'

Well, it's all part of the same show,' he said at last.

I did not know how to counter this, how to explain. Instead I saw the heart, the very heartbeat, of our complaint. The festivals of songs and tales. Bora would remember all that. He would have to. He was brought up with it. I did not often talk to his wife, who was a decent enough woman, though without any depth to her, because when talking about anything but the children or practical things I met with incomprehension. Bora did not meet me with the perfect understanding of shared experience. But it was not with her ignorance, her blankness.

'When DeRod abolished the old festivals,' I said, knowing my voice was full of bitterness, 'he killed the heart and soul of The Cities.'

'But we have festivals,' he said. 'There was a big army rally and there were some fine songs.' And on his face appeared a grin, as if he were laughing with some accomplice I could not see. 'We've got some great new songs.'

'Bora,' I said, 'don't do this. You must remember. It was different then—wasn't it?'

He screwed his face up, he leaned forward, his forearms on his thighs, as if about to jump up and go off. He gave me glances he was not trying to conceal. He knew what I was talking about. I could see that at some time, probably when offered a job in DeRod's armies, he had come to some accommodation with his conscience, if not his memory.

'I don't see the point of that,' he said. 'But that was then. And the old gang did it well. I'm not denying it.'

'The old gang—your grandmother, the

great Destra, and the Council of Twelve!

'But DeRod was part of all that, wasn't he?'

He did not know just how painful a question this was. How often had I tried to remember just how much DeRod had been part of it. I could remember him singing. Not the storytelling, though: he had no aptitude for that. To what extent had he been part of it?

Bora got up, ending it.

'I don't see what you are worrying about,' he said.

It was shortly after that he too built himself a wing to retire into and my grandson, his son, became head of the household. This young man brought disgrace on the family, which was after all DeRod's too, because he chose a wife his father, Bora, told him he would not acknowledge. She was a Barbarian from one of the cities over the mountains, captured as loot. She was beautiful in their wild immodest way, and had been a dancer in one of the taverns. My grandson was wild, mocked his father and mother, and earned his living buying and selling the unwanted babies of the new immigrants, the Barbarians. He did until DeRod heard of the marriage, and that his father had disowned him. DeRod gave him a job as supplier to the armies, where he makes his living still just on the edge of legality. Bora does not speak to either his son or his daughter-in-law.

This new woman, Raned, has achieved what

every Barbarian girl wants, marriage with a citizen, and, in her case, into the leading family. If my grandson had not been such a poor type of fellow he would have aimed higher, perhaps at one of DeRod's descendants. When challenged—by me—he babbled and boasted about love. In my experience love doesn't come so cheap, though I have to say she is a beautiful thing. And there is more. She had none of the manners used by us—I should say, once used by us—and is free and easy with everyone, and thinks nothing of running up to me as I wander in the gardens to show me some garment she had acquired or made for her children—my great-grandchildren—or to tell me in her pretty voice that seems to sing some of the gossip from the lower town. I knew I could easily be in love with her myself. I thought her too good for my grandson. One day she came laughing into my wing of the house, her arms full of branches, and began setting them about in vases, saying it was the Festival of the Wall.

She said there were some fine songs but she thought that they—her city—had better. And she told me a story which had originated from us, from The Cities. I could recognise it though it had become distorted and lost its humour and its subtlety. Its humanity, too. It was the tale of a beautiful princess, captured to marry a barbarous ruler, but she had killed him to secure succession for her son. This was how the story of Destra had changed. I asked if this princess had become a good ruler, but Raned only laughed and said she was beautiful, wasn't that enough? I said to her, complimenting her, that Beauty is always enough. She liked that, though I meant something different from what she thought I did.

I asked for other tales and heard more of ours, similarly transformed and debased, but recognisable. The Cruel Whip had become a magician who filled his coffers by selling magic tales, wicked tales, of power. And they certainly were wicked and cruel: she told me some.

I asked if she would like to hear some of our old tales, and she brought in her oldest child to listen. She enjoyed them, and so did he, but I thought the kinder aspects disappointed her. She liked the brutality of the magician's stories. She had not learned to *hear* anything but the simple and obvious.

She asked me how I knew all these tales, and I said that they were in my mind, but a few had been written: by then I had begun to record them, afraid they would be lost when I died.

The idea of writing excited her: she had never heard that one could make letters, then words, then whole stories. She asked to be shown. And I had the pleasure of taking out the scrolls of reed with their smoothed inner skins ready to take the ink. I set out the sharpened reed, for writing, and the bowl of ink. She was awed. I have never seen such an admiring young woman. She wanted to know how I had learned. I said that in the old days a few of us had been taught to write, to keep the skill alive, but now there were only three still alive, myself and two of The Twelve who were then still living.

Would she like to learn? I asked, for not the least of my anxieties was that soon no one would be left to teach youngsters the art. DeRod, like all our commercial managers, used notches on sticks to measure and count.

She was tempted, I could see, but laughed, and said she was too stupid, she was just an ignorant woman. I told her that if she wanted to fit in to The Cities she would not talk about women as inferior. I saw from the look on her face that she did not understand me, or thought I was ill-informed. The women of The Cities are not as free as once they were. The change had been slow, and at first not noticed. It was the armies, you see: a military state is all hierarchies and ranks and steps of achievement, jealously guarded, and where did women fit into all this? Not only ordinary women, but the singers and the storytellers were not the independent, graceful, skilled women of the old days, under EnRod and then Destra. They do not impose or expect respect or admiration.

I asked Raned if she would like one of her children to be taught to write. 'Or all of them,' I said. She liked that idea, very much. She said they were too young but she would think about it, and look for signs of aptitude in that direction. That made me laugh: what would one look for in a small child to indicate an innate gift for the art of writing? She rebuked me, politely, saying that if one of her children—she already had three—seemed to be quieter and more noticing than the others, then she would bring this paragon to me. 'Surely,' she said, 'you wouldn't expect a child who is good at running about and fighting to have the patience for this.' And she picked up one of my pens, as if it were a snake or a lizard that could bite.

This was not so long ago. And now I am the only one left who has the skill of writing and I am more than ever anxious because soon there will be no one. After all, while we know that north there lives a people with a whole class of scribes who have their history, their transactions and their tales kept on their reed-rolls there is no reason why we should expect another wanderer from their mountains to come our way. That is—was—one of our tales, how this ragged starving man appeared and taught us the art of writing in return for protecting him. He had run away to avoid some punishment for a crime we were careful not to ask him about.

I again asked Raned to let one of her children study with me, and she said she thought two might be suitable. They will start with me soon. They had to be prepared to accept the idea of writing. When I was young, under Destra, the men and women who could write were admired. It was a great day for me when I was chosen. Some people used to say that there was no need for the new skill, writing, because we had all our knowledge, our history, our tales, in our memories, and every child knew it all. Writing was a clumsy and cumbersome thing compared to that. I am sure no one then could have believed that our heritage of songs and tales could be lost, could disappear, and in such a short time. Now only old people remember.

If I still had the power to do it I would call all The Cities together and ask the old people who did remember to come forward and tell everything to young people enough interested: surely there must be some left?

What a weight it all is, this anxiety, this sorrow. I do sometimes wonder why old people bother to keep alive, it is such an effort. Being old is a tedious business. How I love watching Raned's young ones skip and dance about, the ease of it: above all, that is what one loses, the pleasure in simple movement.

And yet I mean to make sit down at least two of them, immobilising them long enough to learn their signs, that will open the world of

The Word to them.

I sent out to find people who know the old skills of preparing reeds for writing, and a very old woman came up the hill to me, and I gave her money to teach others to do it, before she dies. She was so pleased to hear of anyone who needed her skills that she wept. She at least remembers how things once were.

'It is so ugly now,' she whispered, glancing about for fear of unfriendly listeners—and that, too, is a new thing. 'Why is everything so loud and so ugly? Sometimes I sit and sing the old songs to myself, but I find a time when the youngsters are not about because they laugh at me. They say the old songs are insipid.'

'I understand very well.' I said, and so we went on, as the old do, remembering, until the servant came in, and we stopped talking. I know that my son asks his servants what I am doing and who I am seeing. He sends doctors to me when I am quite well. It is all meant kindly, I expect, but it makes me feel imprisoned.

And now I have reached the present. I wrote the word 'imprisoned' last night.

Bora remarked yesterday that DeRod was not well: people were speculating who would succeed. This took me aback. I know it will seem ridiculous and even impossible, but I had not been thinking of him as an old man—my age, in fact. My mental image of him has been for a long time of something not far off. The

Cruel Whip, supplanting memories of a charming handsome fellow—one of those people who, when you think of them, make you smile. An old man. Well, of course he must be . . . I sent him a message that I would like to see him, exactly as if nothing of the sort has happened for such a long time—getting on for half a century. Is that really possible? Well, yes, it must be nearly that. No reply. Did I expect one? Yes. This is because since the death of Eleven my mind has been filled so much with memories of us all, mostly of us as young things. I was so full of affection for the past, for us all, DeRod too, as he was.

I waited. And then, today, I simply took my stick from its place where it leans in the corner, and set off. Not far. Walking distance, even for me. I have never used the new chairs that are lifted and carried by porters. Partly because I don't need them and partly because among the young they have become a sport: they race each other, as if the porters are animals, whipping them along. I think this shameful, but know that in this new spirit that reigns in The Cities my objections would seem merely another example of an old man's whimsy.

It was a fine afternoon. My way went up to the top of the hill, by the Fall, and then through the public squares and places, and then through a wood, which we, The Twelve, had planned and planted. Fine trees now, and spacious shady places where in summer you can find coolness and shade.

I had been walking in my now slow careful way for as long as it took the sun to drop a level in the sky, striking direct through the trees, when I heard the loud laughter and jeering that these days means the youth are near. A gang of seven young men appeared, running up through the trees towards me; they saw me, and then with cries of excitement, as if they had glimpsed a running animal, came towards me. I stopped and faced them. They stopped, a few paces away. Each face was distorted into that sneer which is obligatory now

'What have we got here?' said the leader.

I knew him, I was sure, right from that first moment.

'Look, an old beggar,' said another boy. Beggars, once impossible with us, are now common.

'I like his fwock,' said the first. This is the new fad among them: they lisp, and put on effeminate airs.

They were wearing a fashion derived from the Barbarians: leather trousers and jerkin, showing their shoulders and chests. I was wearing, as always, my old brown robe.

'Give me your fwock,' said the leader.

I stared. I could not help it. Those faces, they were familiar to me anyway, because they were not the now so familiar Barbarian face, which is sharper, bolder, strongly incised, often beautiful, or handsome, where our generic face is broad, frank, open, honest, the face of a perhaps not over-subtle people, but one you trusted. On this face, one so likeable, the sneers and jeers were like a mask which did not fit, and the raucous derision of their style of speaking did not suit their voices either.

Who was he? Who could he be, this boy?

He snatched my stick away, so that I stumbled and nearly fell, and then used it to lift up the bottom of my robe far enough so they could admire my ancient sex: what they were seeing, what I saw every day in the bath, was something like a lump of dried mushrooms. They pointed and sneered and sniggered.

Then I remembered: I knew that face so well. It was part of my oldest, dearest memories: I said, 'Are you Rollard's son . . . grandson . . . great-grandson?' I amended.

That face, born to be pleasant and agreeable, returned to this condition for just a moment, then he went deep scarlet, and dropped the stick.

'Green,' he muttered. 'Good green, he's got the Sight.'

They clustered around me, mouths open, awed, staring.

'I knew your great-grandfather well.' I said, and my voice was unsteady, and my eyes wet, seeing that loved face there, before me. He,

Rollard, had been one of The Twelve.

They turned and sped off, on one impulse, like birds or fishes. I stood alone in that glade in the wood, and wept, thinking of Rollard, thinking of us all. I picked up my stick, and went on, carefully, through the leaf litter, to DeRod's gate. There two armed men stood forward, to stop me. I said to them, 'Stand aside, this is one of The Twelve.' My emotion had given me an impatience with them, and the unfamiliar words did seem to link up with some chord of memory. They stepped aside, and watched me toil up the path, to the house where appeared to stand watching me a tall striking woman, obviously a Barbarian, who as I arrived in front of her said, 'I know who you are.'

'Tell DeRod I am here,' I said, understanding that he had not received my message. She hesitated, then went inside. I followed her. She did turn to stop me, but there across the room, staring at me, was a very old man, who lifted his stick to point at me and said, 'Oh, it's you at last. Why did it take you so long?'

This knocked the stuffing out of me.

He is a jolly old thing, with puffs of white hair at his ears, a bald pate, and his eyes were full of tears, like mine.

I sat, without being asked.

'I sent you a message,' I said. The woman was standing close, hands folded in front of her, watching me.

'I didn't get it,' he said, glancing at her. 'They take very good care of me, you see.'

He did not seem to be particularly feeble, let alone ill.

'What's this about your being ill?'

'I did have a bit of a turn.'

'He must not get over-tired,' she said.

I said to her, 'I am sure he is capable of deciding when he is tired.'

I don't think anyone had spoken to her like that for some time. She seemed to gather herself in a movement like a snake about to strike, then resumed her watchful pose.

I said, 'I would like to talk to DeRod alone.'

Touch and go . . . Then, 'Yes, leave us.'

I could see this was not a tone he used to her. Her look at me was pure enmity. But she turned and went.

Who was she? I knew that his wife, 'the town girl', had died long ago.

'That is my new woman,' he said. 'She is good to me.' And he giggled.

This was the fearsome, feared DeRod; he was a giggling old man, an old buffer, naughty, like a child.

'I've come on serious business,' I said.

'Of course you have, dear boy. You wouldn't come just for fun, dear old Sage.'

'DeRod, as I walked here I saw the Fall is running low. That means the water channels are silting up. There are big cracks in the silos and the rats are getting in. The irrigation ditches need attention. The roads are going into potholes.'

He could easily have giggled, become a child, called for that woman, but he looked harassed, even annoyed, and said, 'You know how labour is now. They are lazy and irresponsible and incompetent!

'But DeRod, what do you expect? They get no training, they haven't done for a long time.'

'That's why we use the Barbarians, they are used to work.'

Again it seemed as if he simply wanted me to keep quiet . . . go away . . . stop bothering him. Yes, that was it, he was like someone irritated with an importunate or pestering person.

I went on. 'DeRod, when you put an end to the instruction, to the teaching, when you ended the storytelling and the songs—obviously this was going to happen?'

'What do you mean?'

'When your mother died she left behind her a system of education, of training . . . you ended it.'

Again, he stared, and, there was no doubt of it, was surprised. 'Don't you remember, DeRod?'

And that was the moment I understood. Oh, all kinds of enlightenment came flooding, rather late, but there it was, right in front of me. It was not that he had forgotten. Not that he had deliberately destroyed what was good. He had never known it was good. He had never understood. He had seemed to be part of it all, but he, Destra's son, the graceful and charming and delightful DeRod, whom we had all admired, had been a blind person among us. From some spirit of emulation he had gone along with it all, as children do, but he had understood nothing at all.

Oh, yes, the scales were indeed falling from my eyes.

I sat there looking back over my long life, and thinking how we, The Twelve, had not seen the first most obvious thing. We had deluded ourselves with all kinds of imaginings and resentments and suspicions: we had seen this man here, DeRod, as a villain, a scheming, ambitious, unscrupulous scoundrel. The truth, had always been—he was stupid. That's all. We had never seen it. But clearly, his mother had . . . and that was something I had to think out.

When that formidable woman, his jailor, came in, I got up and said to her, 'Thank you. You must take good care of him.' And to DeRod, 'Did you know I am the last of The Twelve?'

'Are you? No, I didn't know. No one told me.'

'Who are The Twelve?' she asked, suspicious.

'It doesn't matter.' And to him, 'Eleven died

a few days ago!

'I'm sorry,' he said, and it sounded as if he really was. 'We had good times, didn't we?' he said, the tears starting. 'Do you remember our games in the teaching room?'

'Yes, I do remember.'

'It was such fun.'

'Yes, it was.' And as I turned to go, 'I have arranged with some youngsters to teach them how to write and read. They are my great-grandchildren.'

'Oh, are you?' He seemed puzzled and I saw he had forgotten about writing. Then he said, and I remember he said it in the old days, 'What use is it, when we've got Memories who keep records of the past, and all that?'

'I don't think many people now know about our history. Or only in a distorted kind of way.' And then I could not help adding, 'Your mother, Destra, is remembered as a sort of clever courtesan.'

At this the woman came in with, 'She was a bar girl. She was a singer in the bars. What's wrong with that?'

So, I knew what *her* past had been.

'Nothing wrong. But she would have been very surprised to hear that she was a bar girl. Destra was a great woman,' I said, knowing this woman would have no conception of greatness. Then to DeRod, 'She was a great woman and a fine ruler and there is nothing left of what she created.'

I turned and left, not wanting to see his face, though I expect it didn't show any real comprehension.

And I walked home slowly through the wood, almost dark now, and dangerous, but I did not see anyone there.

That was last night. I did not sleep. The old are familiar with how memories can shift and change their meanings. A scene from childhood that you have often visited can suddenly say to you, 'No, you've been wrong. *This* is what was going on.' But now it is not a question of a scene, a day, but a lifetime, and it will need more than a night or two of sleeplessness to understand it all.

It is Destra, first of all, who commands my attention. When she first came to us all those years ago we knew no more about her people than a few rumours could tell us, so far away did everything seem that was not The Cities. But since then the other cities of the peninsula have come close to us, because of DeRod's raids, and we know a great deal about peoples and places, and Destra's story is well known. Her father was a minor chieftain of the Roddite tribe, with several wives. Destra did not marry as the other daughters did, obedient to custom, going to a husband's clan as early as ten or eleven. Destra was eighteen when she came to us, old, according to her people's ideas. She refused many suitors. She was headstrong, wilful, and very beautiful. Why did she at last agree to marry? She must have known something of The Cruel Whip's reputation, but the fame of EnRod's reforms had travelled everywhere: Destra wanted to live where women were as free as men. Not everyone admired these reforms! Through all the cities of the peninsula and further, where the Roddite tribes live, people were saying that women given their own way must bring ruin on everyone. Or perhaps it was that she saw The Cruel Whip as a last chance for a husband. Whatever she expected, what she got was a drunken, brutal man who beat her—and worse. Free she was not. And then—fortuitously, he died. Let us give her the benefit of the doubt. I know what I believe; and The Cities were well rid of him.

From being a nuisance of a girl in a minor tribe, she had become ruler of a powerful state. I think that we all of us know, even if it is only an inkling, what we could be capable of: I am sure Destra exulted. She knew her capacities. She at once set about putting right what The Cruel Whip had done wrong and making plans for prosperity, success, achievement. She planned not only for her time but for the future. And here she found her difficulty and it was one that could ruin everything. She had had no children. To whom could she entrust what she was creating? She adopted two children from among the Cruel Whip's illegitimate progeny. There was plenty of choice: DeRod was a delightful baby: he was always a charmer: that was his quality. And my Shusha was always sweet, kind, loving, smiling at everyone. I think I fell in love with Susha when we were both not much more than infants. Destra watched the two, watched and waited. Remember that Destra had been brought up surrounded by children and infants, had learned early to judge, knew that a child shows its nature from the first breath. Shusha could never be a ruler, she did not have the iron that it takes. And DeRod—well, Destra must have watched, and waited, and hoped—he was the most attractive little child: I remember him. He did not have the sweetness of his sister, her warmth, but he did have a brilliance of good looks. One year, two years, three, four . . . An empty brilliance. One had only to compare him with his sister. Well then, Destra must have hoped, if not lovable and kind, then clever, quick, intelligent.

She must have seen pretty early that DeRod was—he was feeble-minded. I have come out with it though it hurts even to think it. We have many words for this condition and most are unkind. He was an idiot. But there are degrees of the condition. Put him in the army as a soldier, obeying orders, it would not matter. He reminds me of a certain idiot to be seen around the streets, good-looking, and smiling, so that you do not at once realise he has little intelligence.

The poor idiot often sits near a little pool fed from a crack in the dilapidating wall of the Fall. He plays with leaves and bits of rubbish. He puts a leaf on a stick, or a stick through a leaf, until he has a little army of—to him—people, and he makes speeches at them, his audience. He sounds like DeRod, and that means he is at two removes from Destra who would begin a speech, 'I am going to explain what we are doing . . .' DeRod, sounding like Destra (though people who never heard her wouldn't know this) will begin, 'I am going to tell you . . .' He does not continue as you might expect, but goes off with, 'Have you seen the new army? Have you seen the new bit of wall . . . they say five thousand bits of stone, now that's a fine thing, five thousand, Wow. Oh, yes, we are something to be proud of, I can tell you, there isn't a city in the peninsula that doesn't fear DeRod . . .' And so he rambles on, sometimes for half a day, to anyone who will listen. And they do listen, that is the astonishing thing. Yet he doesn't make any more sense than the poor idiot playing with his bits of straw and sticks and leaves. 'I'm going to explain to you, yes, hear me, it is Fenga talking. I'm going to make an army out of you and we'll go across the mountain and capture some slaves . . .'

I am seeing again something from that long ago meeting with DeRod by the Fall. How he kept looking up to the top as we walked, and how his face went slack with relief when the woman appeared, and how he ran up to her—exactly as a child runs to its mother, for safety.

Somebody has been advising DeRod, guiding him. His town girl? Other women, when she died? His present one is his jailor. It is possible that all these years he had not been getting our messages.

Imagine that poor idiot who amuses himself in the puddle made by the leak from the Fall, in DeRod's place. He would play with his armies, make up simple songs, and speeches beginning, 'And now I am going to tell you . . .'

We have been getting information for some time now from the other peninsular cities, and very eagerly did The Twelve listen to accounts of their rulers. I would say that the word for most of them is—incompetent. We have the comparison with Destra: we know what competence is. You would easily think some of them were idiots, so stupid are their decisions. A stupid person, or an idiot, in a place of power provided he (*she* only in The Cities, no one else has our laws honouring women) has an attractive personality, can compel eyes, make people smile, may easily not be seen for what he is. DeRod has always had that. There were times when you simply had to watch DeRod, the child, the boy, the youth, so winsome, up to a hundred charming tricks, charming us—and knowing that he did. But not his mother, no.

The idiot by the pool is nice-looking, and a lot of people don't seem to see that he is simple. 'He's a bit eccentric, you know.'

Destra must have been frantic with despair. She would not marry again, not after her experience with her first husband. Of course not. She might have considered adopting another cleverer child. But we have all seen what a chancy thing that can turn out to be. She quietly made her plan: the Council of Twelve. She would choose children from the ruling families, which could be expected to try and oust her if she ever showed weakness. This would disarm them. She made it known from the first that these children would administer The Cities, and one of them, not necessarily her daughter, or son, would become Ruler. It was Destra who introduced the word, and the idea, of Democracy, building on what her father-in-law EnRod had done. There would be thirteen children, brought up and taught by her, in her home, and at the right time they would choose the one most suited to be Ruler. Who better than those who had known each other all their lives, to choose right? She must have thought her plan foolproof, but it was not. I look back now on those days, in Destra's house, and at us all there. What a delightful lot of children we were. And among them two, both so pretty, Destra's children. I remember DeRod, a bit of a show-off, but so charmingly eager to please, to be liked: yes, and even then it was easy to contrast him with his sister. Well, we did, of course. But the fact was we were always a bit dazzled by DeRod. Beauty is a terrible thing. When it is matched with a fine nature, a mind, then certainly it is something to bow before, to hold out one's hands to, in supplication. But that beautiful empty boy, so pleased with himself, his charm was a poison. And surely Destra must have laid awake at nights, fearful for him and for us. But among us, as it were supported by us, his emptiness did not show. I remember we were hurt on his behalf if he did not do well in some lesson, or did not understand: we all rushed to help him, explain, make him one of us. I remember so well that smile of his, wondering, a little embarrassed, his always-on-the-watch eyes, trying to understand, to be as good as we were. And so it went on, that charmed childhood of ours, which was presided over by Destra, whom we loved. We did not ever see her as anything but something like our Sun, unfailingly bathing us with light and warmth. We took that effulgence for granted, never questioning, or making judgements for ourselves. In a sense, we were Destra, as we do become what we admire.

In some of the cities across the peninsula they pay allegiance to a female deity, so we hear; she goes under various names. We in The Cities have always scorned such backwardness, worshipping, as we do, The

Sun, our progenitor. We know that our view of things is the true one. But were we so different, with our uncritical love for Destra?

Beauty is a terrible thing: but it is dangerous too for a person to be seen as the sum of his or her admirable qualities. What is left out, the shadow, has to be understood. But there rises a question, not without relevance here: if Destra had been too good, too noble, to get rid of The Cruel Whip, our affliction, the result would have been her continuing wretchedness and our misery as The Cities fell into ruin under him. Well, they have fallen into ruin, under his son, who is stupid. But The Cities enjoyed more than a hundred and fifty years of prosperity, high public morality and culture. Of course, a lot of people are satisfied with the crude raucous violent times we have now, because we eat well—most do—and enjoy the plunder from the Barbarian cities. And we have all our dirty work done for us, by the captured Barbarians. Good times: 'We are having a good time,' you often hear people say.

So, which of us would Destra have liked us to choose? Looking back now, it is easy. She was always gently, tactfully, drawing attention to one of us, citing his good qualities, but not in a way that would make us look bad in comparison. It is easy to see now: I think we spent our childhood in a state of unconditional love: we were dazzled, eyes blinded. She would have liked the one who became our water engineer. Nine. And she was right: he would have made a fine ruler. Why did she not ever say, This is my choice? She did, as openly as she could. But if she had said, I want this one to succeed me, then the other families would have complained, made an alliance against her. Then they would have fought among each other to make sure their own offspring succeeded. A civil war—that is what would have happened. But to arrange things so that all of us were chosen to choose, meant that our families would be responsible with us. I cannot now remember what was being said in my family: the truth is, memories of my family life are dim and dull compared with Destra's home and her lessons. I am sure my family were excellent people, but they did not matter to me. Destra was my mother. She was our mother.

I wonder if she was anxious about our affection for her son, about how we always supported and helped him? It was natural to behave like that, with kindness; she had taught us kindness.

When she was ill, at the very end, and was carried in on the day that we had to choose, how she must have suffered. I do remember her face, though I see it now differently from how I have all these years. She was ill—that was all I saw. But she was also ill with anxiety. She lay there, held up on her pillows, and watched us choose, thoughtlessly, gaily, her silly son, her charming, delightful silly son—and now I see her face, that old grim face, set hard. She knew what was to come.

And now it is easy to see why we, The Twelve, never did like to call things by their proper names. We complained of DeRod, feared him, speculated *Why*, but we never said, 'We, The Twelve, are responsible for everything that has happened because we chose him, and we didn't have to.' Any one of us would have done better than DeRod. None of us was wicked, all of us revered Destra, and would have done what we thought she would have wanted. Even I, slow and lacking in resolution, would have done better.

We let her down. It was our fault. We are responsible. The famous Twelve, so busy with our efforts on behalf of The Cities, proud of our accomplishments, we, and no one else, were the cause of The Cities' downfall. And, very likely, of breaking Destra's heart, before she died.

*   *   *

Before sealing this away I have to record one more thing, a strange thing. There have been rumours from across the mountains of strong earth shakings, that have brought down whole cities. We know that rumours always exaggerate, and so we await confirmation. And at the same time, came news that workmen, building a new section of DeRod's wall, found the ruins of a buried city. We do not yet know how extensive these are. They are at the depth of about two ordinary pickaxe handles. The construction of the buildings is different from ours, more elaborate, and they used very small stones in different colours as pavements and floors and ceilings. This is a craft we know nothing of. We hear that DeRod is wild with excitement and has ordered all other work to cease, so as to dig out the city. 'All of it,' he ordered. 'It will be a wonder people will come to see.' Meanwhile our people have reacted with forebodings. They are remembering that among the tales from the old part of The Cities are some that speak of earth vomiting, rivers swallowing mountains and changing their courses, the sea inundating coasts. Strange to see the old tales, scorned by this sensation-loving people who want only the new and the exciting, coming back into favour, but only because they match with new anxieties. 'Once there was a fine city here, under where we are now,' they say. 'And what is to stop it all happening again? Look what is going on on the other side of the mountain.'

Note to the published manuscript, by the Archaeologist

The site we are excavating is certainly

not less than seven thousand years old. Over it is a layer of pumice and ash. We have not yet unearthed anything similar anywhere in the world. This is a civilisation of a type new to us. The manuscript is of inestimable value in reconstructing the ordinary life of that time. We have taken due note of the fact that under this city, which is still only part exposed, is another. In due course we shall reach that too.

This manuscript was found in a recess in a thick wall, which had been partly toppled. The script was unknown before a group of experts found that there are in some places analogies with cuneiform—enough to unlock the rest. The translation has been made for our easy reading. Words such as 'time' would translate as 'that which is passing and which carries us from birth to death on the rays of the sun'. A year: 'a cycle of changes in the colours of the vegetation, matching the sun's movement from hot to cold'. A stupidity: 'that which is missing from the nobler parts of the mind'.

Our usages, less picturesque, are at least speedier.

We have been labouring over this excavation for four years now. What we see, what we work with, is rock, rocks, hard grey stone, a type of granite. Rock and stones. But what is described by the author in this manuscript are gardens, trees, water, and above all the Fall of water over great blocks of stone which we at first, before the finding of the manuscript, described as a great ceremonial ascent of steps to—we expected a temple or something on those lines.

A LOVE CHILD

A young man descended from a train at Reading and his awkwardness swung the suitcase in his hand so that it nearly clipped the face of a youth who turned, putting a hand to his head to add force to a protest, but then his scowl vanished and he shouted, 'James Reid, it's Jimmy Reid,' and the two were shaking hands and clapping each other about the shoulders in a cloud of steam from the shrieking engine.

Two years ago they had been schoolboys together. Since then James had been taking a course in office management and accountancy, greeting news that Donald was 'doing politics' with 'Fair enough, they've got money'. For Donald had always been able to take advantage of treats and trips and opportunities, whereas, he, James, was kept watching pennies.

'I'm afraid we have to watch the pennies,' was what he heard at home, far too often, and, he now believed, often unnecessarily.

Donald had shone in debates and the dramatic society, and started a magazine called *New Socialist Thought.* James had had no idea what he wanted to do, provided it wasn't sitting from nine to five at a desk. His mother had said, just get the certificates, dear, they'll come in useful.' His father said, 'Don't waste time at university, you'll learn more in the school of life.' But they couldn't have afforded university.

Now Donald said, 'Where are you off to?'

'I'm off home.'

'You do look glum. What's up?'

With Donald, this affable person whose round and smiling face invited frankness, with the guarantee of understanding, it was easy to say what he could not remember even hinting to anyone else, 'Isn't that reason enough?'

Donald laughed out loud, and at once said, 'Then, come along with me. I'm off to the Young Socialist Summer School!

'But I'm expected at home.'

'Ring them. Come on.' And he was already on his way to the tea-room where there would be a phone.

James remembered that Donald always assumed everything was easy, and so for him it was. To ring home and say, I'll not be home this weekend, was for himself a big deal, something to think about, plan, steel himself for, consider the ifs and buts, but here he was at the telephone, while a waitress smiled at the two youths, Donald grinning encouragement. He said to his mother, 'Will it be all right if you don't see me till Monday evening?'

'Yes, of course, dear.'

He knew she thought he should get about more, make friends, but it had needed Donald.

The two got on a train returning to where James had just come from, but now, instead of the dismalness of, Oh God, another day pen-pushing, they were off on an adventure.

So began the wondrous summer of 1938 that changed everything for James. That weekend summer school for which Donald wangled his attendance—it was booked out, but James knew the organisers—was about the war in Spain, but as far as James was concerned it could have been about the conditions of tin-miners in South America (a later lecture). He was dazzled by this largesse of new ideas, faces, friends. He slept in a dormitory of a college that catered for summer courses and schools, and ate in the dining-room, with young men and women from all over the country, in a cheerful argumentative atmosphere that accommodated every conceivable shade of left-wing opinion. Defining one's exact nuance on everything from Spain to vegetarianism was an essential duty to oneself. The weekend after it was the pacifists, where Donald was speaking to provide opposition. For Donald was a communist. 'But I'm not a joiner, I'm with them in spirit.' He felt it his responsibility to combat wrong-thinking everywhere. His duty was politics, but his pleasure was literature, particularly poetry, so James found himself at a weekend of 'Poetry as a Weapon in the Struggle', and another of 'Modern Poetry', then 'The Romantic Poets as Precursors of Revolution!' He heard Stephen Spender speak in London and recite his own poetry in Cheltenham. And so the summer went on, 'The Communist Party for Freedom!' 'American Literature', which meant Dos Passos, Steinbeck, Lillian Hellman, meant *Waiting for Lefty,* and *Studs Lonigan.* 'Whither the British Empire?' 'India's Right to Self-Government'. And it was not just weekends. After his day at the business college he would join Donald somewhere for an evening's lecture or debate, or study group. He was going home to pick up clean clothes, have a bath and tell his mother where he had been. She listened all interest, and there was no end to her questions. A year ago he would have been irritated and evaded her, but he was beginning to understand the indigence of her emotional life and was learning patience. His father listened—James had to suppose—but did not comment more than a grunt or a snort at what he disagreed with.

James seemed to be meeting only vivid personalities who made him feel lack-lustre and timid, and the girls were unlike any he had known, talkative, free with their often alarming opinions, and with their kisses too: he was at first surprised they did not mind his approaches to them and even teased him for his hesitations. Easy with kisses, but parsimonious with everything else: this reassured him for he certainly did not believe in Free Love, the subject of one of the debates. He was not only living in a dream of companionship and quick friendships, but above all he was seeing himself in ways that surprised, shocked or shamed him. Chance remarks, overheard, a sentence or two from a lecture on 'The Fascist Threat to Europe' or 'The Working Conditions of Miners' left him with ears throbbing with what he had heard: for they seemed sensitised to hear words that might have been designed for him personally.

At a pacifist weekend he had his childhood put into perspective as neatly as in a cartoon: 'The soldiers from the Great War, they either can't stop talking about it, they're obsessed . . .' 'Like my Dad' came from the floor, ' . . . or they won't talk about it at all'—'Like my father,' contributed another.

James's father, a survivor of the Trenches, wounded at the Somme, was one who never opened his mouth. Not about the war, and not much about anything. A large man, a rock, with shoulders and hands surely too powerful for what he did—he was in the office of an engineering firm—he could sit silent from the beginning of a meal to its end. Most evenings he went to the pub, to meet his mates, and James had often seen them, all old soldiers, sitting in a group around the fire, not saying much. James had grown up with silence. His mother could not talk if his father didn't, but once, going home for a weekend for the sake of good feeling, he saw her at a social that followed the summer fete, animated, flushed, a glass of sherry being generously replenished by Mr Butler, the local vet, and . . . was she flirting? *Actually* flirting with him? Surely not; it was just that James had not really noticed her as a woman that could talk ten to the dozen and laugh. 'I'm a bit tipsy,' she remarked, walking home, her flush of social animation already gone.

He did remember through his childhood sometimes being secretly ashamed of his mother's animation at public occasions, so unlike was she to her self at home. But now he thought, My God, being married to my father, to be married to a man who never speaks unless you put a question direct, and not even then! And she's not like him, she's good fun, she's . . . but this was his mother, and an impulse of violent pity suppressed thoughts that were unbecoming about one's mother. What she must have suffered all these years: for that matter, what had he suffered, the silent child of a man who had known such horrors in the Trenches that he could be himself only with other soldiers from that old war.

This uncomfortable view of himself and his family was only a beginning. He learned at 'The English Class Structure' that Donald was middle class and he lower middle class. What had he been doing at the same school as Donald, then? He had got a scholarship, that was it, though he hadn't thought about it much before. His mother had wangled the scholarship, writing letters and then pulling strings, wearing her best dress. He knew now his mother had good taste, in simple dark dresses and her little string of real pearls, where other women were in loud florals and too much jewellery. She had impressed—well, who?—with the urgency of her son going to a good school. His mother was a cut above his father, so he could see now. He had been in a daze and a dream about all this sort of thing until Donald had woken him up.

He went home with Donald for a weekend and found a large house crammed with family and friends. Two brothers, older; two sisters, younger; a noisy fun-loving lot. The mother and the father argued—in his home it would be called quarrelling—about everything. The father was a member of the Labour Party, the mother a pacifist, the children called themselves communists. Long loud abundant meals: James thought of the frugal decent meals his mother cooked, with the Sunday joint as high point of the week; but it was a small joint, for it wasn't right to waste money. In Donald's home a large ham stood always ready on the sideboard, with a fruit cake, and bread, and a slab of cheese and a pile of yellow butter. They played games in the evenings.

The two girls had boyfriends and were teased, not very nicely, thought James, but his ideas were changing and he wondered if it was right to be shocked. Surely he was shocked too often?

'Good to have you home, son,' said his father, on the weekend when James attended the Sunday joint (two potatoes each and a spoon of peas), and this so surprised both son and mother they exchanged glances. What could have got into the old man? (His father was not yet fifty.)

'And so you're getting into politics, are you?'

'Well, I'm listening, mostly.'

The big man, with his large red face, moustache cut close (trimmed every day), short grey hair neatly parted (cut weekly by his wife), his big blue eyes that were usually abstracted, as if concentrated on keeping his thoughts in their place, now focused fully on his son, and he was certainly taking him in, judging.

'Politics is a mug's game. You'll find that out for yourself.' And he returned to the business of loading his fork with beef.

'James is only finding things out for himself, dear,' said Mrs Reid, as always conciliatory, surely too much so, as much as would justify a secret fear her husband would one of these days explode and demolish her and everything in their life.

'That's what I said, wasn't it?' said Mr Reid,

presenting an angry face to her, and then to James, chin forward: he might have been expecting a punch on it. 'Crooks and thieves and liars.'

This was a fierce choking cry, in a voice the son did not remember ever hearing. Had his mother? He saw her lower her eyes, play with a bit of bread on the tablecloth, then knead it with her knuckles.

James thought: this has been going on all my childhood, and I never noticed. And now it was the pain he felt for both of them that took him out of the house, as much as his fascination with this brave new world of politics and literature.

Donald was lending him books which he was reading as if literature were food and he was starving. The books were in a pile on the hall table. He would take one up to his room to read, then return it to its place and choose another. He saw his mother stand by the books, then open one. Spender.

" 'I think continually of those who were truly great",' he said, sharing with her something of the richness he had discovered; and he thought that this was the first time he had let her in to his private self. She nodded, smiling. 'I like that,' she said. There were books in a bookshelf, but he did not remember her reading them. They were mostly war books, and that was the reason he had not touched them. They were his father's and shared with him the aura of *Don't Touch.*

Now his mother said, '"I saw a host of golden daffodils, fluttering and dancing in the breeze." I learned that at school.'

He said, lowering his voice—his father was in the room next door—'It seemed that out of battle I escaped".' And she looked over her shoulder, and said, in a whisper, 'No, don't, don't, he wouldn't . . .' And she walked quickly away.

When his father had gone to the pub and his mother was upstairs, James knelt by the bookcase and pulled out the books one by one. *All Quiet on the Western Front. And Quiet Flows the Don. The Battle of the Somme. Passchendaele. Goodbye to All That. An Old Soldier Remembers. If They Should Die . . . If They Should Ask Us* . . . Three shelves full.

In spring 1939 James was called up, with the young men in the age group 20 to 21. His father said, 'That's right, that's what young men are for.' And he got to his feet with emphasis and went to the pub.

Donald had been called up, and when James went to visit he found that boisterous house clamorous with argument, even more than usual. The two older brothers assumed they would be next. The girls were in tears because their boyfriends were in the same age group as Donald and James.

'There can't possibly be a war, it would be too terrible,' said the pacifist mother, and one daughter. 'We have to stop Hitler,' said the father and sons and the other daughter. These were the points of view to be heard on the wireless, in the newspapers, exchanged everywhere. 'With the weapons there are now, no one could be stupid enough to go to war.'

The two young men actually about to be shovelled into the army, smiled a lot and went off together to a debate in the nearby town: 'Is It too Late for Peace?' Donald spoke passionately from the floor that Hitler must be stopped now, otherwise we would all be slaves. A woman in the audience stood up to say that her fiancé and two brothers had been killed in the last war, and if the young ones present knew what war was like they would be pacifists like her. A man of her age, that is to say one presumably schooled in war, asked her sarcastically if she believed her fiancé and brothers would have liked the idea of living like slaves under Hitler, and she shouted at him, 'Yes, yes. Better alive than dead.' An old woman said that it was time they remembered the white feathers that were handed out to cowards in the last war: that was how she felt. The arguments grew so loud and bitter the platform had to call for order, and then ask the ushers to escort out a youth who said the white-feather woman should be shot, she was disgusting.

His father told James, 'They're going to lick you into shape. That's what they call it. They'll make a man of you. You get yourself made an officer. You'll have it easier that way. You'll be officer material, with your education.'

James and Donald went together to the call-up centre in Reading. James had run and played cricket and football for the school, and expected to be told that he was a hundred per cent fit. He was, with the proviso that he must watch out for an old football injury, a torn ligament in his knee, which now could be seen as a thin white scar. Donald was told he was overweight, but the army would cure him of that. All day they were in a large hall, in a mill of sweaty, smelly young men, many from homes that had no bathroom. All the same age: Donald joked that they had reached the age for the slaughterhouse, like lambs or calves. He sounded cheerful about it. The same age, but far from the same shape. Many were thin, and most were short: Donald and James were taller, and their bones were well-covered. Their assiduous attention to the facts of British life had taught them that the working classes subsisted on bread and margarine sprinkled with sugar, and bread and dripping, with cups of very strong tea, full of sugar. 'Sugar is food.' Here were the results, these pallid, undersized men. Some were being discarded because they had rickets, many sent to the dentist because of rotting teeth.

Plans were made for another visit to Donald's, but the summons came first. The war was boiling up while people still talked pacifism, it heated debates and the contents of the News, it seethed in people's veins and in their minds, and it ejected James and Donald out from ordinary life into camp.

James spread his uniform on his bed, and fitted bits of it to himself. His room, usually a quiet, unassertive place, was littered with martial reminders in khaki.

James was a tall, slim young man, quick and alert, everything about him fine and nervy. He had a thin nose, a long curved beautiful mouth, too often made narrow with the tension of determination. His eyes were long, a luminous blue, and his hair was a pale shining brown. His brows were delicate, glistening. He had about him the sleekness of a healthy animal. But when he at last had got the uniform on himself, he was made dull and awkward. He looked at himself in the long mirror on the landing and thought that the girl at the Socialists for Justice Summer School who had said, 'But you're lovely, you're like a film star,' would not say that to him now. He went downstairs, saw his mother sitting under the lamp, with a magazine, the radio jiggling dance music. She glanced up, and her hand flew to her mouth and she said in a gasp, 'Oh, *no*.' Then she stood up, all apology, and said, 'Darling, you look very nice, it was the shock, that's all.' And she tried to embrace this soldier, but the thickness of the cloth he was inside absorbed the embrace, negated it.

His neck was already being chafed and his boots were too large. They were blocks on his feet. She said she would try to soften them, and she warmed them in the steam from the kettle, and rubbed fat into them, while he stood in his socks, his long feet curled towards each other like creatures trying to escape their fate. She warmed and rubbed for an hour or more, and he tried the boots on and said they were better. His feet were narrow, that was the trouble.

Next day he put the uniform on 'for the duration', joking with the new phrase that made people who used it feel full of fortitude and modest courage.

'But perhaps there won't be a war,' said his mother.

'Yes, perhaps it'll all come to nothing.'

His father said goodbye, barking at him that he mustn't believe them if they said it would be over by Christmas. 'They're full of their own nonsense.' Meaning? The War Office? The Government? His eyes were mad with the anguish of the old war.

'Bye, Dad,' said James, gently, and went to the gate and turned to see the parents standing together, his mother's arm through the old soldier's, patting it. Like a postcard, he thought, defiantly refusing pathos. 'Off to War.' He was thinking, as he had done pretty often during the last year of ferment and discovery that it would have been better if his dad had been killed in the Trenches. Well, wouldn't it? What a misery his life had been . . . wouldn't he himself say so? But at least his mother had got a husband, which was more than could be said for many women. No one can imagine themselves not born. With his father dead in the last war, then James would not be marching along the pavement in his painful boots. His derisive mind was commenting, *Cannon fodder for the next war.* Funny how many phrases out of stock he had used all his life, but never thought about them.

He met Donald at the train and they travelled together in a carriage full of young men in new uniforms, and then in two buses, soldiers with civilians, whose faces told them they were now in a category apart. Feared? Disliked? Pitied? Wary faces, and some eyes reminded James of his father's. Twenty years: some of these people had been through the last war. Then they were at the gates of a camp where a couple of corporals stood, to wave them on. The youngsters walked in ones and twos, straggling along to a large hut, where they gave their names, and new numbers, and were directed again through lines of Nissen huts, set out as regularly as the squares on a chess board. At a junction in lanes between huts, Donald had to go in one direction and he in another. This was a blow to James, but he knew not so much to Donald, who went off with a bunch of young men he had never seen before as if they were all old friends. It seemed that the alphabet was dividing them, 'An R and an E—never the twain shall meet,' James tried to jest. He went alone to a hut that would hold twenty men. Ten beds on one side and ten on the other, with a kind of cubicle or cubby-hole for the supervising corporal. Like school. The young men were moving about, standing about, constantly looking around, like animals in a new place who do not yet know from what quarter danger will come. Corporal Jones was giving them time to settle in, with only mild instructions about kit and the proper maintenance of their bunks, when a sergeant arrived and behaved exactly as expected, shouting directions at them which might just as well have been given in an ordinary voice. Then supper, in a big shed: too large to be called a hut. The first shift, a couple of hundred young men, the food not to their liking, or too much of it for anxious stomachs: a lot was left on the plates, and a sergeant, standing with his hands on his hips, yelled at them that he would personally see to it that soon they would be so hungry they'd not be leaving anything on their plates.

In the hut twenty young men tried to combat the dismay of unfamiliarity, their equipment and clothes all over the place, while the corporal threatened them with the imminent appearance of the sergeant.

The youths were complaining they were not used to sleeping so early, when the sergeant arrived to say he would overlook their crimes tonight, but from now on if he saw such a scene as this they'd all be for the high jump. That was his first message to them: the second was that they were not so much as to think about asking for sleeping pills if they slept badly, because it would be his happy duty to see to it that they would be so tired from this day on they would sleep as their heads hit their pillows.

All this was as expected, for most of these young men had fathers or relatives from the last war, who had instructed them in the ways of the army. 'Their bark is worse than their bite,' most of them had heard.

Now the corporal retired to his kennel and the men talked in low voices, grumbling about the hard bunks and pillows, and James knew that, never mind about the school of life, the school of school was turning out to be a blessing. One youth, Private Jenkins, said that anything would be a picnic after boarding school: in this way James located the other person in his hut who might turn out to be officer material. They took each other's measure in some facetious remarks, and the silence that followed told James that this scene might be put into a lecture on Class Structure. Most of these young men could never have dreamed of the amenities of boarding school.

'Nice work if you can get it,' summed up the youth, Paul Bryant, in the bunk next to James, but without hostility. It turned out that James and Private Jenkins had little to say to each other: whereas this Paul, whose father delivered coal to the cellars of Sheffield, became his friend.

Next day the men from this hut and four others, one hundred of them, met in a building that had been a village hall and took lessons in equipment and how to look after it. From the windows they saw the spreading camp, whose severity of regularity nevertheless gave an impression of the improvised, the impermanent. It was raining so hard in gleaming rods that water was jumping up white and frothy to knee height: the knees of a platoon marching through it on their way to somewhere. All that day instruction went on, and when James confessed his boots hurt, hardening himself for blows of contempt from the sergeant's tongue, he was ready to hear that he had better get the right flicking boots this time because he wasn't going to hear any fucking excuses about sore feet tomorrow, when drilling would begin.

The equipment corporal took trouble over him, lifting down from shelves boots and more boots, saying, 'You'd better get your feet right, because if feet are not right then nothing is.' James's feet were difficult, all the boots were too wide. He was going to have to wear two pairs of socks. He felt like a penguin he had watched walking with its feet apart along the edge of a pool, as if its crotch were sore, as his was. Everywhere the thick uniform rubbed and chafed.

Then the drilling began, two platoons from this hut, and the young men were made one because of the intensity of their exhaustion, their anger against the sergeant; and James's discomfort in his uniform and his unhappy feet became absorbed into a general torment. But, deeper than that, he was sustained by a pride that he was sticking it out. As were they all.

Ten weeks. He drilled with his platoon, then with the company. He ran at straw sacks representing human beings with his bayonet, and came to know his equipment so well his rifle was—as the sergeant told them it would be—his best friend. All this, while a quietly derisive private commentary ran in his head, which he could not share, because it was in the language of his education, and he could not match the half-inarticulate communications of his fellow soldiers, all obscenities and the ritualised angers of the common soldier.

Twice he offended, once by not cleaning his boots properly, and once by not standing quickly enough to attention, which crimes he expiated by peeling potatoes for a day, and doing guard duty at night.

Towards the end of this endurance test his knee played up, and it was strapped tight, like a mummy's. A bloody ligament was not going to get in the way of Sergeant Baxter's intention to turn him into a soldier. And so they emerged, a camp full of young men, several hundreds of them, licked into shape, made men of, made one, and they were informed they were off to another camp, west, while their training camp accepted another batch of recruits whom James's lot looked on with compassion and ritualised jeering for form's sake. 'They don't know what they're in for, poor sods,' etc, while they were marched off to buses and trains.

Before that there was a weekend leave at home, which James hated. He knew his father did, and suspected his mother did too. He tried to imagine what it could be like, seeing your precious young that you've fussed over for twenty odd years sent off to war as cannon fodder; but like many thoughts about his mother, he could not persist with them. They did not fall into the category of the mockeries that accompanied his days and nights at the way things were managed, the jeers at Authority—the soldier's necessary offset to obedience. His mother's life—oh, no, he didn't want to think about it. He saw her on those evenings at home, sitting under the lamp, the radio jiggling or crooning away at her elbow, knitting a sweater. For him, he wouldn't be surprised. Her eyes were lowered to her work: she didn't knit automatically, as some women do, their hands apparently able to read patterns by themselves while their owners chat or even read. Or perhaps his mother kept her eyes hidden so people couldn't see what she was thinking. What thoughts? And she looked defenceless, sitting there alone, her husband in the pub with his war pals, waiting up for him. It made James angry, but angry with what? This was not like being angry at the army or the sergeant. For twenty years his mother had sat there under the lamp knitting, alone. Then his father would come in, smelling of beer, go and wash his face and brush his teeth, because she hated the smell, and the two went off to bed. Being angry with his father was hardly the point. But he could have taken a bayonet and stuck it into someone—who? Gone shouting about the streets, No, no, no, *no*.

Instead he kissed his mother goodbye, gave his father's obdurate shoulder a friendly and filial clout, and went off to the West Country.

There, several hundred young men exercised and drilled, but not as obsessively as in the first camp. It was boring. In between the drills and exercises he lay on his bed and read poetry, and so did Paul Bryant. He had become for Paul what Donald had been for him. This man, who had left school at fourteen, took to poetry as James had done. He had more difficulty, though: long words were a problem. But James relived his own final intoxications with words when he saw

Paul Bryant's eyes shine, thanking him for the loan of a volume.

'I like this one,' he would say. 'I do like this one . . .' What the coalman's son who had scarcely been out of a town liked was poems about the country

Loveliest of trees, the cherry now
Is hung with bloom along the bough

or

I went out to the hazel wood
Because a fire was in my head . . .

'Have you got any more like that?' he would ask, shy, but determined, in a way that reminded James of his younger self, of a couple of years back.

They and a few others were luckier than the majority, who were bored, bored. There was nothing to amuse them. Not enough girls, and beer ran out in the pubs, when there were evening passes. Bored and frustrated young men, hundreds of them, but then began the war, which at first dawdled and delayed, but at last there was the first invasion of France, and off they went, to end on the beaches of Dunkirk. James missed it all. His knee had swelled up and he was in hospital, having it drained.

Of his platoon five were killed and two

wounded. His platoon was merged with another, similarly diminished. His unit—his family—gone. And Paul, his friend, was in hospital with a head wound. James heard that Donald was wounded while in a boat coming back from Dunkirk. He got weekend leave to visit Donald, whose head was bandaged, and so was his arm. He looked pretty bad, but before James had even entered the ward the nurses told him that Donald was the life and soul of the place. 'He keeps us all cheerful.' People came in to Donald's room to joke, to have a laugh, and a youth was there when James arrived, and was there when he took his leave, sitting on a visitor's chair watching Donald, bemused with admiration. James thought: that was me. Donald needs his acolyte, he needs someone to educate, well, fair enough.

He stayed as long as visiting hours permitted, watching his younger self, and admiring Donald, to whom he owed everything—so he reflected, while admitting that probably Donald never thought of him at all. But as James left, Donald did give him books and pamphlets.

The Battle of Britain began, Churchill made his stirring speeches, but things were not much improved in the camps of the West Country: the fighting was going on in the skies further over towards Europe. James could have gone into the airforce. Why hadn't he? It was because his father had been a soldier, and it hadn't occurred to him. If it had, he would probably be dead by now, or would be soon. Those fliers in the RAF were his age. By now he would have bought it over the sea, and been lost in the drink; he might have pranged over land and burned in a pyre of flesh and Spitfire. The RAF slang was now pervading language: a form of homage to dead heroes.

Because his father had been a soldier, he had become one. Because his father had not been an officer, he had refused to go to Andover to take the War Office Selection Board examination to find out if he was officer material. He had not wanted to leave his platoon, his mates, particularly Paul. It occurred to him that he must have been lonely, to feel that if he left his platoon he would be leaving his family.

James's company, much changed from since before Dunkirk, heard a rumour they were to be sent off out of Britain into action, and home leave was announced and then cancelled. Instead of North Africa—not that they knew then North Africa was where the fighting was to be—they were despatched to a camp in Northumberland. The trouble was, too many men had been called up. Not knowing how the war was going to shape 'They' had overdone it. Hundreds of thousands of young men were in camps ready for action. The sergeants and corporals shouted that they didn't know their luck: they could have been sent down coal mines. Would they have liked that better, perhaps? Had they fancied a career at the coalface? Well, then, count your blessings. Boredom. They were so bored that some believed they were ill. Boredom in some undefined and undiagnosed way undermines, slows minds, and skews thinking. Rumours, even the most stupid, flourish like newly evolved viruses.

Concert parties came to cheer them up. Vera Lynn's voice solaced them from the radios in every hut. An Education Officer organised all kinds of useful lectures and everybody went because it was something to do. Again, there wasn't much for them in the local town, when they were issued passes. In the half-a-dozen pubs, the beer was always running out. The cafés offered dubious sausages and scrambled eggs made out of dried egg from America. Some food was better, because of vegetables and fruit from the local towns: the countryside was close here. Paul would have liked that, but he had been posted to another company. Meat and eggs went to London, where rich people danced and ate in restaurants in which rationing was unknown. So they all believed. There were few girls. James's first sexual experience was standing up with a landgirl against a wall in an alley. He hated it, the girl and himself, but this nasty little event made him dream more than ever of the real girl, his girl, who was waiting for him. He silenced his ever-ready mocking voice when it threatened his dreams of tenderness, and of a love that could not be anything like his parents'. Nor like the noisy combative marriage of Donald's parents. No, like every soldier in that great camp of hungry young men, his girl was going to be different.

James had sometimes drunk a beer with his father or a sherry with his mother, but now he tried to drink to get drunk, and hated that too. 'Not everyone is cut out to be a soldier,' jeered his inner interlocutor, while he observed his mates drinking themselves sodden, and taking anything they could get from the too few girls.

There was a pleasant interruption in the boredom. From the camp, soldiers who volunteered went to the local farms to help with farm work at harvest time. James always volunteered and wondered if his destiny was to be a farmer. He actually managed a few hours' love-making with a farmer's daughter who was sighing with remorse all the time because her fiancé was in North Africa, fighting. 'I love him, I do!' The harvest ended. Germany invaded Russia and Japan attacked the States. Things were looking up, so the pundits said, though one could be excused for thinking they were at their worst.

'You're being saved for the best,' jested the sergeants, more matey now, perhaps because they were as bored as their charges. James spent any spare hour on his bed reading. He read the books Donald had given him, the usual mix of poetry and real literature with pamphlets. 'The Second Front—*Now!*' 'Let India Go!' Through these he merely leafed, feeling guilty, his mind freezing with boredom, but livening to

When our two souls have left this mortal clay,
And seeking mine, you think that mine is lost—
Look for me first in that Elysian glade . . .

Beautiful, bleak Northumberland: perhaps this would be their final resting place, perhaps they would die here forgotten by humanity and the War Office. Why should they ever leave it, if they hadn't yet? Such are the slowed mad thoughts of people who have had to be patient too long.

And then, for no apparent reason, it was over. They all believed thcy were off to yet another camp, because of the law that what is seems as if it must always be. Their regiment had been forgotten. 'Someone had blundered,' is the soldier's perennial thought.

But no, they were going to India. Not that they were told it was India: careless talk costs lives, but they could figure it out. The Japs were coming closer to India, and the Indian army was set to fight them. Anything, anywhere, just get us out of this place, waiting, drilling for hours every day to keep fit.

James put his things in his kitbag, with his precious books of poetry. He knew that if he hadn't had poetry and books during the last months—no, years, now—he would have found himself in the bin. And he had Donald to thank for it, thank for everything. That summer, just before the war, it shone there in his memory, as strong a dream as his dreams for a future of love and peace, peace and love. He thought, 'After the war, it will be like that.' Meaning, like the happy months of summer schools, friendly debates, unbitter argument, the frank and fair exchange, all hope and excitement and promise. What was this war for, if not to create that, a world of generous friendship and comradeship and generous girls, among whom would be his girl, the one girl.

He went to say goodbye to his parents. His father asked if he had had the chance of being an officer, and he replied yes, but he hadn't wanted it. 'Then more fool, you,' said his father. His mother, weeping, told him to take care of himself.

* * *

The great ship in its camouflage dress, designed to make it look from a distance like a blur or a cloud or perhaps a school of flying fishes, at any rate something ephemeral, now seemed solid, sinister, even furtive, standing there in the dock, and those who had known it as a luxury ship of the famous Union-Castle Line, in peacetime always decked in bright holiday colours, would not now have owned it. '*That* the *Bristol Castle*!'

Five thousand soldiers, with their attendant officers crammed the dockside and backed up into the surrounding streets, waiting to board. Of these it is safe to say the majority had scarcely seen the sea, except perhaps for a day's outing (the Thirties did not run much to holidays for the poor) nor had they seen ships and shipping. Luxury ships had not occupied their imaginations as even remote possibilities for themselves, seen only on newsrccls or as headlines in newspapers. 'The *Queen Mary* arrived in New York this morning, bands playing to welcome the Duke of . . .' a film star . . . an opera singer . . . a boxer.

Five thousand soldiers and their officers would fit into a spacc designed for 780 passengers and crew, and they were embarking on a seven-thousand-mile journey to Cape Town and then on, thousands of miles, to—where else?—India.

The *Bristol Castle* had no name now, just as their destinations had none.

She stood in her tiers, or decks, a neat symbol of the society they were defending, the two top layers, the best, where their officers would go, with the ship's officers, then down, down, down, deck after deck, until a mass of soldiers would fill the worst parts of the ship. Just like the world, if it comes to that—to be tedious.

Up the gangways they stepped, while their sergeants and corporals stood above, watching, barking directions, which they had been given by the ship's officers, for they knew as little about the geography of a ship as their charges.

James Reid was at the tail end of the embarking, with his platoon, their corporal beside them, as dismayed as they were. Corporal 'Nobby' Clark (soldiers called Clark are always Nobby), eyes on the watch for error, a fleshy man often in a perspiration with anxiety, was one of those who find organisation difficult, and have to overdo it. His men put up with him: they had had plenty of time for patience in those months and months of waiting. Beside James was Rupert Fitch, a farmer's son from Kent. He was a lean flat-bodied young man, a horseman, with bold fine features, lightly freckled, and pale hair already receding from a high forehead. James, still dreaming sometimes of perhaps finding himself (how?) a farmer, felt towards Rupert something of the wistful admiration that Paul Bryant had felt for himself, and he, long ago (three years), for Donald. Rupert Fitch never had to be told the why or how of anything: it was as if the army was an extension of his young life planting and reaping. 'Permission to speak, Corporal,' he would say to a corporal or a sergeant as an equal, familiar—at ease. 'Wouldn't it be better, Sergeant, if we . . .' took that direction, instead of the one ordered; suggested to Supplies that such and such a dubbin—for boots—would be better than what they had. Certainly officer material, but like James, he had refused. 'Not my style,' he had said. On the farm he had mucked in with the men, and that was what he liked.

A tall stooping dark youth, with hot defensive eyes and a way of clenching his fists like a boxer expecting attack, was Harold Murray, who worked in his father's shop, selling men's cut-price clothes. Johnnie Payne sold vegetables with his father from a stall in Bermondsey. He had been taking lessons from James in book-keeping, which would come in useful after the war. These five men knew each other well, but the other five of B Platoon were new, moved in some reshuffle ordained from above that the soldiers could see no reason for.

Corporal Clark at last shouted the order to march, to his platoon, and on to the ship they went, low down, E Deck, just above the water line. Then down a ladder, and they were in their quarters, a space that had a table wedged between bulkheads, and a cupboard with china, and another where their hammocks were. The space not filled with the table accommodated the ten of them standing up with a few inches between them, as it would when they would be lying down horizontal in their hammocks. Their gear piled up against a wall seemed to take half of what room there was. 'Up on deck' came the order, and B Platoon, with hundreds, thousands of men, watched England slide away, white cliffs and all, while the gulls squawked around the ship. Waves were already sending up spray. The light was going. An obscured sunset stained a brownish sky red. On E Deck a minute flicker of light showed the steps going down. And down they went again, into stuffy darkness smelling of paint and new wood. Dark. In peacetime this ship blazed light as it moved, gilding and silvering the sea. Once these ships had taken a month for a voyage, but the time shortened to three weeks, and then the aim of two weeks was in sight—but why not dawdle, take your time, in a ship designed for pleasure? Now no light was supposed to show, the ship was blacked out, like the homes in England, like England, and down in their quarters B Platoon took in the fact that there was a single dull yellow bulb.

The holds were stocked with the food of wartime England, worse than they had been eating in camp. Supper was bread and a stew, mostly potatoes. Already the strong tea was slopping about in their mugs, which were sliding despite the little ledges designed to keep them from sliding. Not one of these men had ever suffered seasickness, and now they wondered if they had caught something, and Johnnie Payne said he wanted to get his head down. 'You're queasy,' said Corporal Clark, who wasn't feeling too good himself. 'Better sling your hammocks.' Jokes and jollying traditionally accompany the first time anyone slings a hammock, but the ship was beginning to swing. The lavatories, they already knew, were insufficient: queues were forming. Corporal Clark, who had never known defiance from his men, now, having told them to get into their hammocks, saw them bolting up to the deck, to lean over the rail. Since they were there, he joined them. All along the railings were men being sick.

Up here with the wind on them they felt better, but they were staring out into the dark unknown. They could hear the waves hissing but see nothing. They knew how much danger they were in. This was not a convoy, which has to travel at the pace of the slowest vessel. Troopships, fill of precious soldiers, enormous, must dominate the convoy, presenting themselves as targets. This ship was travelling with two destroyers to guard it from U-boats, but it was a long way to Cape Town, and they must stop at Freetown to refuel and restock, and submarines haunted both ports, and roamed about the Atlantic. Ships had been sunk recently. All this they knew. No one had told them, no one could have told them, yet they all knew. And to stand here at the dark rail, on a dark deck, looking into blackness—no, better downstairs, better below deck, and up and down the tiers of that enormous edifice men were making that decision: below deck was the illusion of safety, with the walls of the ship around them.

So they were thinking, that first night.

To sleep in a hammock takes practice. It was not a comfortable night. On the table where they would have their meals stood basins where, having tumbled out of their hammocks again, some were being sick; they scrambled back into hammocks, falling, cursing, bruising themselves.

The morning was grey and cold; they were in the Bay of Biscay. Corporal Clark, fussy with worry and indecision, and because he was feeling sick, told them to have breakfast. He did not know if this was the right thing: the sergeants were on the deck above, with some of the lieutenants, and he knew, having gone up to see, that many were in their bunks.

James and the farmer's son ate some porridge and wished they hadn't.

Orders came for attendance on deck, for inspection, but Corporal Clark went up again to the sergeants. Most were ill, but Sergeant Perkins, feeling fine, came down, and saw that the men were not up to it.

The Bay of Biscay was doing its worst. From

top to bottom of the great ship, the men were ill, and the smell anywhere below decks, or in the cabins, was foul.

In their hammocks the constant swaying, so bad that the hammock of one man knocking another could set off the five in that row, was unendurable. Out of their hammocks, trying to sit at the table, there was no relief. Up on deck, surrounded by a grey tumult of water, was as bad. By the evening of the second day it was evident this was a ship of the sick, except for a minority who were apparently immune, and who volunteered for mess duty, where they could eat as much as they liked, but were ordered for cleaning duty, which meant swabbing fouled cabins and fouler decks.

Below the layer where B Platoon was, which they had felt must be the ultimate hell-hole, was a deeper layer of crammed humanity. When the ship had been fitted to take troops, attempts had been made at ventilating these depths, but in those commodious spaces, which had once housed the luggage of the rich, or foodstuffs designed for peacetime menus, the air was bad, and everyone was sick down there. On the third night, men on E Deck heard screaming from below them: this was how they became aware they were not the lowest depths of suffering. Claustrophobia, they knew at once; for they themselves were in danger of breaking and screaming. It was not only the press of the ship's walls about them, but knowing how the great dark outside went on to a horizon they knew must be there, but could not see: no moon, no stars, thick cloud, dark above and dark below.

On the fourth night, ignoring the corporal, who followed them, not even expostulating, they were on deck, where at least the air blew cold. They lay along the walls of a deck, keeping their eyes shut, and endured. Rupert Fitch, the farmer's son, was better off than most. He sat with his back against a wall, his head on his knees, and hummed dance tunes and hymns. The great ship ploughed on into the dark, with a deep steady swaying motion. In the morning nothing had changed, but the deck was crowded with men, some from the lower depths. Corporal Clark, the shepherd of B Platoon, was lying like them, rolling a little as the ship did, face down, head on his arms.

There came tripping down the companionway Sergeant 'Ginger' Perkins, a short compact-bodied man, with bristly carroty hair, and a belligerent stance cultivated for his role. He might have intended to impose order on a shocking scene, but while he did not suffer himself, he had spent days now surrounded by the suffering. His nature was such that his impulse had to be a bellow of 'Pull yourselves together!' but he was silent. Some of the men were in pools of vomit, and diarrhoea had made its appearance.

'Corporal Clark!' he shouted, and the

corporal tried to sit up, but the change of position made him retch. This sergeant was famed for his strictness. 'Hard but just', was what he aimed at, but the formula did not apply today. He went down into B Platoon's sleeping quarters—the nearest. Crockery from the cupboard was lying smashed in the vomit on the floor. The smell was horrible. He stood hesitating: his responsibilities were on E Deck, were here; he had no charges in the ship's depths. But up on D Deck, where the sergeants had their being, reports had arrived about what was going on in the ship's dark bowels. The corporals, those who were still functioning, had come up to say something should be done. Sergeant Perkins decided to take a look for himself. Down several ladders he tripped, and stood in a large space, so dimly lit he couldn't see the further walls, and heard moans coming from some hammocks, though most were empty: the sufferers had taken themselves up to D Deck. Against orders! Against anything permissable! This was pure anarchy, and he felt licensed to make a decision. He himself would go up to C Deck and tell any officer on his feet and responsible that if anarchy was to end, then orders should go forth that the wretches still down there in that stinking dark must go up into the air.

Sergeant Perkins returned to E Deck and his level of duty: a hundred men, but who could say which of these poor wretches lying everywhere on deck, most face down, heads in their arms, were his? He turned his back on the scene and stood at the rails, and regarded the heaving grey sea. Sergeant Perkins had paddled in rock pools as a child, taken a crab in his pail to the boarding house, been told by his father to go and put it back. That had been his sea. As a child he had not taken in the desolation of the ocean's vastness, not seen much more than a pool in rocks, a beach where waves ran in over his feet while he jumped and screamed with laughter. Now he looked out, hardly seeing where the sea ended and the sky began, and he thought of the submarines somewhere down there, and he was afraid. A peacetime sergeant, he had not before this voyage had occasion to feel fear.

He turned, slowly, giving thanks for sound stomach muscles—under strain, today—and announced to anyone capable of listening that the weather would improve. He had heard that it would from an officer descending to D Deck from C Deck. 'It can't go on like this,' he mused, in his private voice, which was an all-purpose cockney, modified or strengthened according to the person he was speaking to. In his sergeant's voice he said, 'Corporal, when you're feeling better, report to me.' No reply. Along the deck one of the bodies in a knot of them—A Platoon, he believed—was moaning, 'God, God, God.'

'God is about it,' thought Sergeant Perkins,

smartly ascending the ladder to D Deck, and then up again to C Deck where, having asked permission to speak, he said that what was going on in the bottom of the ship was a crying shame. 'We'd be prosecuted if we kept animals in those conditions, sir.'

When badly seasick, as most of us may remember, death seems preferable to even another ten minutes of this misery—death even by U-boat, some of these men might have agreed. And then, just as Sergeant Perkins had promised, the sea was calm, and men were slowly coming to themselves, sitting up, trying to stand, staggering to the rails and seeing the sea properly, possibly for the first time since they embarked. It was now a quiet grey-silk sea, flecked occasionally with white, and under a blue sky frilled with white cloud.

Corporal Clark sat up. Sergeant Perkins appeared; a squad detailed to restore order was hosing down the decks, and if soldiers' legs were in the way, that was too bad.

Water was certainly what they needed. They and their uniforms were filthy. Off with their clothes, and lines of naked men moved up to where they were issued with soap that would lather in sea water, were told to put on their hot weather uniforms, and deposit their dirty ones in a heap to be washed. Soon piles, each many yards high, rose on the deck, and another squad was bearing them off, to be washed.

On every deck lines of barbers—which is what they had been in civvy street—stood behind chairs where the men came to be shaved and have their hair trimmed.

On decks newly scrubbed men who a few hours ago could hardly sit up, were put through their drills by sergeants who, most of them, had been as sick. Well, almost: their ventilation was better. Then, back to their quarters which had been hosed, swabbed, and now smelled of soap. There was food. Tender stomachs sulked at the hunks of bread, margarine-smeared, the stew, the rice pudding. James ate a little; the farmer's son more; no one did well. They were all tired.

Up on the higher decks similar ablutions and tidyings went on. The highest deck had a swimming pool, and there the officers—so they knew, Sergeant Perkins had told them—in relays of twenty were in the water—salt—and then out at once to let in the next twenty.

The Captain and the senior officers went to bed every night fully dressed, with their boots ready beside them.

The sergeants and some lieutenants were in cabins designed for two but fitted for eight, four bunks on each side.

Some senior officers were four or six in cabins meant for two. But of course the cabins up there were bigger.

'And before you say it I'll say it for you,' said Sergeant Perkins. 'Life's a bugger. But no one on this ship is on a luxury cruise. Right? Right. Now, form fours.'

Well out of the Bay of Biscay, they were on their way to Freetown, that ancient slave-trading port, now prospering out of the ships that went to refuel, restock. But Rupert Fitch told James they were not heading south, but west. 'Look at the sun.' Other farmers' boys were telling town boys 'Look at the sun.' This spread unease throughout the ship. Were they not going to Cape Town, then? Or Freetown?

And then, it was hot. Men who had known only English summers, with their rare really hot days, were sweating and ill with heat. Not enough shade on E Deck for the hundreds of men, lying, sitting, or even standing, and there were already cases of sunstroke. Sergeant 'Ginger' Perkins, with his fair skin, was scarlet when he addressed them, his neck and arms mottled with heat rash, 'Too hot to drill, lads. Just take it easy. And don't get carried away with your water ration—it's running short.'

Fresh water, short; but all that sea water lapping and rippling down there. A few men, ignorant, tempted, let down their mess tins and brought up sea water, and while admonished by Corporal Clark, drank. They were sick. The staterooms set aside for sick rooms were filling. It was known that some of the officers on the second level of the ship, B Deck, had had to double up again.

When the men changed their uniforms for

those washed in sea water, they found that their sweat, enhanced by the salt in the cloth, stung, and the stuff of their shorts and shirts chafed them.

The ship was still going west. Rupert Fitch stood at the rail. He watched how the sun moved, as he had done all his life, how its path on the glittering sea changed, and said that now they were headed south-west.

It was too hot to eat. They wanted only to drink, but a second warning came from above, about using restraint until they reached port.

'Cheer up, lads,' said Sergeant Perkins. 'There'll be water a-plenty in Freetown. And fruit. There'll be fruit. We could do with a bit of that, we'll be eating like kings. What do you say?'

They were saying very little.

Awnings were fitted up all along E Deck and there was a thin hot shade, where men with sun-reddened skins sat or lay dreaming of water gushing from taps, of pools, ponds, streams, rivers; looking, when the dazzle allowed, with eyes used to gentler light, on to the ocean that was calm and seemed to oil and slide, beaten flat by the sun. Shoals of porpoises and dolphins could have entertained them were they not so hot and thinking of U-boats. Flying fishes leaped, and hit the sides of the ship and slid back down into the sea, dead or not, or a high-flier assisted by a breeze landed on the deck among the men, who threw it back.

Harold Murray, the cut-price clothes salesman, rose from the deck, and stalked unsteadily to the ladder going up. He climbed, while Corporal Clark, shouting at him, clambered after him; then another ladder, while the stout man (not quite so stout now) puffed and strained to keep up. Harold Murray reached B Deck, where he saluted a surprised Commander Birch, and said politely, 'I'm fed up, I am. I've 'ad it up to 'ere. I'm going 'ome.' He was taken to join the madmen.

Every day the men lined up for their salt-water douches, which now fell stinging on reddened skins, some of which were breaking into blisters. Newly shaved faces burned.

The heavy food, bowls of stew, reconstituted soup, scrambled eggs from dried egg powder, the milk puddings, was hardly touched, at mealtime after mealtime.

James sat with his back to the wall of the ship, Rupert Fitch beside him, looked at the sea and believed that each porpoise or dolphin was a U-boat. Every man on the ship well enough stared at the sea and saw U-boats. In those days, submarines had to come up into the air: now they may circle the globe with their load of weapons and never surface. Then . . . 'Look,' a man would shout, 'look there—a periscope, sir.' 'No, that's a fish.' Fish there were, the ship was moving through a sea of fish. The ship spewed out its rubbish and the unconsumed food, and the waters behind rioted with competing fish of all sizes, while above seabirds screamed and squawked and mewed, diving to snatch booty from the leaping and mouthing fish. A spectacle. All the decks at the stern were crowded with men well enough to enjoy it, mostly the ship's officers, whose apparent immunity to the sufferings by sun and sea was to the men an affront.

The destroyers that were protecting them seemed to be everywhere, in a different position every time they looked, in front, behind, alongside, their guns slanting down, their searchlights ready to switch on if a submarine were spotted. On their own ship there were guns on the top deck, and anti-submarine guns and waiting searchlights.

Rupert Fitch said they were going east now; they were back on course for Freetown. And for danger, for subs lurked at the entrances to Freetown harbour. James sat with his eyes closed, imagining how the U-boats were moving about down there. He was thinking, If they get us now, if we sink, if I die, then I'll not have found my girl, the one meant for me. I'll never have known real love. He remembered the farmer's daughter in Northumberland and tried to persuade himself that had been love, and that she was dreaming of him. But, if the U-boat got them, it was love that would be extinguished. His love. 'Do you have a girl?' he asked Rupert Fitch, who replied, yes, he was engaged to marry, and showed photographs of his girl: he knew she would wait for him.

Then, at last, the ship that was blistering with heat, its camouflage paint fading, was sliding towards Freetown, and every soul on board listened for the thud of a torpedo. But they made it, they got safely in. The soldiers were not granted shore leave but they watched batches of officers going ashore, and then containers of food, and above all, of water, coming aboard, borne by bare-footed blacks in clothes not far off rags. Water. Inexhaustible water from the taps and in barrels standing on the deck. They drank, could not stop drinking, and some, trying not to be seen, poured this fresh water over their heads, or their sore and blistering bodies, and, particularly, hot and inflamed crotches that did not like sea water at all. Two days in Freetown. The food was at once lighter, better, with chicken and fish; and fruit arrived with every meal. They ate this fruit they had not heard of, many of them, let alone seen, as if they had been craving pawpaws and pineapples and melons and plantains, and not pears and apples. Some bad stomachs resulted.

And now they would run the gauntlet again: they were leaving Freetown and would be on their last leg, the thousands of miles still to go, to Cape Town.

The former *Bristol Castle,* in her coat of

blights and blotches, slid out with a destroyer in front and one behind. Now the soldiers could see the crowds of white-clad men—'They're navy types, they're used to it,'—on the decks under the guns. Salutes back and forth, and melancholy hoots of greeting. Then the destroyers were on either side. Not to anyone's surprise, the ship was going west again. This was to fool the U-boats who would expect them on a southerly route. 'But,' said the soldiers, 'wouldn't they expect a double bluff—us going south?' 'There are probably U-boats in both sea lanes.' If you could call this tossing and tumbling grey-blue waste of water that was empty in front of them, all the way to South America, with rapidly-retreating Africa at their backs, something able to accommodate even the idea of sea ways, sea paths, sea lanes, routes.

So they jested, these soldiers, up and down the ship, in their many voices and accents, staring out, ready to spot a periscope, the emerging dark shape of a U-boat, the dark running shape of a torpedo coming towards them. They joked because the plenitudes and safety of Freetown were still in them, but it was hot, it was so very hot, and soon they were in the same state as before, filling the decks that were sun-lanced under awnings that went up everywhere, reed matting taken aboard at Freetown. And then it was night, their saviour. Through the long angry hot hours they thought of the night to come, moonlit or dark, it was the same to them, just the beneficent cool of it. Or rather, cooler, not the chill they longed for, but at least not the misery of the day. They still went west. The soldiers felt better going south, their proper direction, faster, they would get there sooner. Heading west it was into the unknown, to Rio de Janeiro, was it? Buenos Aires? They tried to joke, but then joking was over, because the sea rose up again, not heaving and rolling but rearing in explosions of foam, battering the ship's sides. At once Rupert Fitch succumbed. His fair skin, well flecked with freckles, disappeared under blisters, and his temperature shot up. He was escorted up to the doctors. James was left lonely, as well as sick and hot. 'That's it, I won't see him again, I suppose.'

No soldiers were left in hell-holds now. They were on deck. The sergeants, those who could stand, Sergeant Perkins among them, had made their way to the top of the ship, found their officers, made urgent requests. A couple of officers came down, saw the deck so crammed with hundreds of men that it was not possible to step between them; the order went forth that a suitable number—it would have to be hundreds, to make the difference—would go up to the deck above, which housed the sergeants and some junior officers. James was one who moved up, with his platoon. There they saw the sergeants' cramped conditions, eight in the space for two, but they had bunks, at least they could lie on something hard that wasn't the deck: they didn't have to fight with hammocks, and they had open portholes.

To preserve proper order, and niceties of the hierarchy, the starboard side was for the sergeants and young officers, port was for Other Ranks. In the mornings port got the sun, in the afternoons, starboard. Not that it made such difference. Still they sailed west, the destroyers moving around them, but hardly visible now because of the waves. And then there was a storm. The soldiers were informed this was a storm, but they could not have said there was a difference between the pounding roughness of before and now. Sergeant Perkins came down to tell them, 'Cheer up, a ship this size has never been sunk by the weather.' So that left U-boats.

Hundreds of men lay on the decks, burning up with heat, and heaved, and retched, needing to be sick, but they were not eating. In the mornings they were ordered to their feet, and crowded to the rails, holding on to them and to each other, while a unit of the lucky ones who were not sick hosed down the decks, and they shrank back from the stinging sea water. And at once they lay down or, rather, collapsed.

Water was short again. From this they deduced that it had not been planned that they should take such a long detour west. And that meant they were taking a detour to avoid something. So they were being dogged by a U-boat or by more than one. They were thirsty. Oddly, though it was so hot, some shivered, while they burned: heat stroke, and up they went to the sickbays.

To endure the unendurable, what that needs is to cling to time, which must pass: another hour, another, another, no I can't, no I won't, I simply cannot bear it, no one could, the pounding knocking headache, as if a load of dirty water were loose in your skull, the nausea, the aching bones, the stinging skin. Some men bled from raw skins and bursting blisters—up they went. Squads appeared twice a day, to locate the worst sufferers, but the ship was swinging so that they could hardly keep on their feet, but staggered among the men cramming the decks, or held to a rail, trying to see from there who was bad. Bruises and blisters were easy to see, but there were broken bones.

Day after day; night after night. And then they noticed—someone did, and the word went around—that they were going south-east. Long ago—so it seemed—the misery had been absorbed into the hopelessness of the long suffering. Why should this end? If it has gone on as long as this, then it may go on for ever. Going east, were they? Then what was to stop the boat turning again to go west? No, they didn't trust good news.

It was becoming noticeable that the sun did not strike down so hard and direct. It was not so hot. The storm was past, so they were told, but they still swung and rolled. And then, while they could hardly stand, they were ordered on to their feet. Drilling was out of the question, but they were going to present themselves in Cape Town at least shaved and in clean clothes. The barbers again sat in rows on the lower decks, deep cans of fresh water sloshing between their knees, and they shaved whoever came forward. Some refused: their faces were too raw. There was no man who did not wince as the steel touched burned skin.

The order was that the rationing of fresh water for drinking was over. Clearly, a longer time of dodging about the Atlantic had been envisaged, and the water had been saved for that. Nothing that these men had heard for weeks heartened them more than the ending of water rationing. Yet, only for drinking, mind you, there was not enough for washing themselves, let alone their clothes.

They must put on their clean, salt-water-washed uniforms, and all other clothing must be piled again to be washed in Cape Town. Again the heaps of dirty, sweaty, sick-soaked, urine-soaked uniforms mounted high.

The order came that now the sea was calm—was it? Really! Was this what they called calm!—to eat what they could of a light supper. Fresh eggs taken on at Freetown had mostly succumbed to the storm, but there was chicken and bread, which they tried to eat.

That last night on board, except for those in the sickbays, except for the poor madmen who were being kept doped in what was once the Second Class Writing Room, everyone was on deck, watching for the first sight of land, blessed land, as sailors and sea travellers have done for centuries after a bad voyage, longing for the fair Cape of Good Hope.

It was dangerous, all knew, approaching port, for where else would U-boats be lurking if not here? The two destroyers were everywhere, behind, in front, taking off apparently at random, and back again, and then it was light, and the seas around them were tumbling and running but not heaving up into the monstrous mountains that had seemed ready to engulf the ship. They were ordered to eat breakfast. 'Get to it, lads,' ordered Sergeant Perkins who remained solid flesh, unlike his thin and haggard charges. Tea and bread and jam was not what shrunken stomachs wanted.

Back on deck, they saw that a low line of cloud on the horizon marked land: that was Table Mountain they were seeing. So it really was over . . . no, not yet, the rumour went around that a U-boat was known to be in the area.

Sergeant Perkins stood in front of his hundred men with their corporals, and said to them, 'Right, lads. It's over. Time and the hour runs through the roughest day. Yes. Nothing was ever better said than that, eh, lads?'

Of the men there looking at him perhaps two or three knew how to attribute the quotation, but every face showed how the words described what they had been through. As for Sergeant Perkins, he had seen them on a calendar, long ago, and they had so perfectly said what he needed at a bad time in an unsafe adolescence that he had used the philosophy offered to him, and indeed, on many occasions since.

Now, as they watched, he reflated himself with the stuff of command and shouted, 'Right, that's it. Playtime over. No more fun and games. Private Payne, your belt's askew. God, what a load of shirkers. Attention. Now, take your turn behind A Platoon for disembarkation.'

* * *

Two young women reclined on deck-chairs on a verandah high on a slope of Table Mountain where they could overlook that part of the sea where the troopship would arrive, today or tomorrow. They were positioned so that the pillars of the stoep did not obstruct their view: ships when they appeared could be mistaken for a mote in the eye, a whale, even a seabird. They knew the troopship was coming because their husbands, both at the base in Simonstown, had told them. They had not been told the name of the ship or its destination. They had not passed on the enticing information. But surely the maids and the men who looked after their gardens would have noticed food arriving, not to mention the wine and the beer?

Both women were hostesses, known for their parties and their largesse. This would not be their first troopship, nor, it was certain, the last. Cape Town, for the period the troops were on leave while the ship was refuelled and restocked with food and clean water, was not itself, was transformed into a city of soldiery in search of food, drink, and girls. Of course black or brown flesh was out of bounds, but this is not to say that the rules were kept.

The women, Daphne Wright and Betty Stubbs, had plans for festive days, at the very least two, with luck four or even five.

Under a tree in the garden the Coloured nanny sat with a pretty child of about eighteen months, who began to grizzle. 'Okay, bring her to me,' called Betty, and the nanny, a big brown girl in a pink dress and a white apron, came to deposit the child on her mother's body, where she lay sprawled, and at once fell asleep. The nanny returned to her place under the tree, where she could watch for when she would next be needed. She began to knit.

Daphne watched the scene from under the

hand that shielded her eyes from the glare, and said, 'I'm getting as broody as hell, Bets.' She stroked her flat stomach. She was wearing a scarlet skirt and white shirt and with her yellow hair looked like a girl on an advertising poster for a happy holiday.

'Hell, give me a break, eighteen months is too soon. We'll start together and keep each other company.'

'Joe doesn't want us to start until after the war.'

'That could be years.'

'He says he doesn't want me to be a widow with a kid. I say I'd like something to remember him by.'

Both husbands went off on hush-hush trips to various bits of Africa, and the wives suffered till they got back.

'Bertie told me that Henry . . .'—her husband—'had to make a forced landing in the bush last month. They nearly pranged. It was a close thing,' remarked Betty.

'Henry didn't tell you?' Daphne knew, because her husband had told her, but not knowing if Betty had been told, was careful not to mention it.

'No, he didn't. I always say it's a lot worse, when he doesn't tell me.'

'There's a lot they don't tell us.'

Betty was stoking her little child's soft back, exposed by a scrap of white shirt, and Daphne said again, 'But I am broody, I'm broody as hell. I think I'll get pregnant and then he'll have to like it.'

'Of course he'll like it.'

They resumed their watch on the innocent-seeming sea, where submarines might be lurking at that moment. No sign of the troop-ship, not a ship in sight, only the blue plains of the sea.

'If it's three nights, we'll be broke for months,' said Betty.

'And if there's a fourth we'll run out of food and everything.'

'We can drive out and see what we can get from the farms.'

'And the petrol?'

'I've got a little stashed away.'

This exchange, on a comfortable grumbling note, had sent Betty to sleep. She lay, her infant on top of her, her long brown arms, long brown legs, extended, her dark hair loose across her face.

Daphne raised herself on an elbow and looked at the charming scene. Tears were not far off. She did want a baby. She had lost one in a miscarriage and now greeted the regular appearance of her monthlies with a feeling that she was a failure: yet they took precautions, or, rather, Joe did: yet they both wanted a baby.

She thought that Betty was the only person among a pretty large circle of acquaintances she could 'really' talk to. They knew everything about each other. This happy state of affairs had begun from the moment she, Daphne, had arrived in Cape Town to marry Joe.

Daphne had been an English girl, in an English country town, when handsome Joe Wright arrived to visit a school friend. He was on leave from Simonstown in South Africa. It was 1937. They had danced all night at the Summer Ball, and he had swept her off her feet. 'He swept you off your feet.' Well, he had. 'Marry me,' he said, or commanded, and she followed him on the next Union Castle ship to Cape Town. The *Stirling Castle.* (Perhaps the same ship that they were expecting now.) There was a fancy wedding. Joe was one of an old Cape family. Daphne, with her narrow experience, could have been overwhelmed, but she was not. The girl who arrived in Cape Town was not the Daphne who had embarked. On board were a group of South African girls returning from good times and trips around Europe. At first she had been shocked, and then envious. They were different in style from English girls, free and easy, loud, assertive, and wearing clothes she had at first thought showy. She had overheard one say to another, about herself, 'She's English, you know, baby-blue English. Little Miss Muffet.'

Daphne, a blonde, with blue eyes and a pearly complexion, did wear baby blue a lot. 'It is your colour.' She wore charming dresses in crêpe de chine with lace collars and little buttons down the front; she wore hats and little white gloves. 'A lady is known by her gloves.' Now she knew herself to be insipid and timid.

No sooner had she arrived in Cape Town, than she jettisoned her trousseau and wore strong colours, and her pale gold hair with its little puffs and tendrils became a heavy yellow chignon; her voice loudened and she lost the shy soft ways she had been taught. She bloomed into a Cape Town hostess, gave parties that were written up in the gossip columns and was generally a credit to her husband.

And what did he think about all this? He had fallen for her because of those qualities she had discarded. A refreshing change from the South African girls, he had said, playing with those girlish pale gold wisps, commending her English skin and her rosebud mouth which she now kept slashed with red lipstick. In fact she out-did the South African girls who had despised her; she was more daring than they. Joe protested once or twice during the transformation, 'Come on Daff. Isn't that overdoing it a bit?'

Did he mourn that timid girl-bride? But they were good pals, that's what he told her and everyone. How could he not be proud of her, overtopping the wives of his fellow officers, for dash, style; and, too, she was funny and brave in everything.

Betty, the South African wife of Captain Henry Stubbs, lived in a house similar to this one, next door, was the same age, twenty-four; the two husbands were the same rank: they were Simonstown wives. That they should have 'known' each other had been inevitable, but they became friends. Real friends. Only friends. Best friends.

Daphne lay propped on her elbow watching that friend of hers, lovely Betty Stubbs, lost to the world with her infant spread on top of her, both mysterious in sleep, and she thought, feeling cold and frightened, that she had her good pal Joe and her good pal Betty beside her in this alarming continent, but apart from them she was alone, without them she would be adrift. Alone, far from home and with a war on. 'There's a war on.' 'Don't forget, there's a war on.' Funny how people liked saying that; no one was likely to forget, were they?

If I had a baby I'd have something of my own, she thought, forlorn and vulnerable and as if she were a bit of flotsam washed up at Cape Town all the way from England. A 'baby-blue' English girl with a bold front who had learned to enjoy shocking people. Just a little, just enough.

'I'm in a mood,' she thought, lying back, but turning her head so she could see the two faces, the woman's and the babe's. She did get moods. When she had her first, and wept and shivered, Betty told her she was homesick and the housegirl made her strong coffee and said, 'Poor medem, you are far from home.' Yet she thanked her luck daily that she was not in Britain, where they were having such a bad time. Yes, she did miss her mummy and her dada and her little brother but she was now so different from that Daphne who had been a daughter and an elder sister. A young man who had been besotted with her had told her she was like a trembling flower. She had laughed at him, but now she thought, well, trembling flower will do for me today.

'But I do want a baby, yes, I do, I do,' and she allowed tears to trickle down and lose themselves in the mass of her chignon. 'I'm going to talk to Joe again.' And she, too, fell aslccp. When the two young women woke, because the infant had let out a yell, the nanny was bending to take the child, and indicating that a big ship was coming fast towards the shore.

'There's the ship, medem,' said she. 'So now we can have a nice party.'

As the ship docked, alien in its camouflage, lines of cars were already creeping down the hilly streets towards it. All had been issued with an extra petrol ration, because this cause, giving the British troops a good time, overrode the need to save petrol. Daphne was in her car, and behind her Betty was in hers. Both women were known to the welcoming committees, who trusted them to entertain as many men as hospitality would stretch to. The sad truth was, there were too many men, not enough hostesses, and a lot of women whom normally these Cape Town matrons would not look at were being smiled at today. Somewhere a little band was playing but the bustle and sounds from the ship and the shouting of orders were too much for it.

Joe had telephoned Daphne to say, 'They've had a rotten time, I'm afraid. And a sub nearly got them but they don't know that. They deserve everything we can give them. Tell Betty her old man's down with the Welcome Committee. And we've got to get a couple of hundred of them into hospital—see what we can do in four days.' 'Oh, so it'll be four days? Yes, but don't spread it abroad. And don't you get sick, because the hospitals'll be full. Every spare hospital bed for miles . . . Don't expect us home tonight.'

When the soldiers began to descend the gangplank, it was evident they had had a bad time. They were more like invalids than soldiers. They held on to handrails, they stared about, they were gaunt and unwell. The first of them had their hands shaken and had to stand unsteadily at ease while speeches of welcome were made. On they came towards the waiting cars, hesitated, and then, invited by welcoming waves and opening car doors, piled in, as many as could cram. Officers first. Last troopship Daphne had entertained officers, and had told

Joe that this time she would take what came. And on they did come, no end to the lines of soldiers, and the ground was clearly unsteady under them; one man actually fell and had to be helped up. Daphne opened her car door to non-commissioned officers, who got in the back, five of them, and then she saw a tall lanky, awkwardly moving soldier who was reaching out his hand as if he wished there was something to hold on to. She opened the door to the seat beside hers, and he turned and blundered towards the car, held on to the door's edge to steady himself, and collapsed into the seat. He was sweating and pale.

'It's been a bit of a rough voyage,' she heard in a familiar accent from the back seat. That was a West Country voice.

'So we've heard,' said Daphne, feeling that her clean and sweet-smelling self must be dismaying these men who stank, that was the only word for it. If she wasn't careful, she'd be sick. From this young man beside her—he seemed a boy, no more—came wave after wave of smell.

'If there's a chance of a wash?' came from the back seat.

'Or even a bath?' came a voice from Scotland.

'Can do,' said Daphne, driving smartly up towards her home. On the steps stood her two maids, and the man who did the garden, and on Betty's stood her maids and gardener.

From their faces could be seen what they felt, looking at these ghosts of men.

The boy beside her woke, stumbled out of the car and up the steps and fell on to the deck-chair she had been sitting in that morning, where he crouched, his head on his knees, his arms enfolding his head.

'Baths,' she commanded. 'And a lot of towels.'

On Betty's steps was the same scene.

'We haven't anything to change into,' said one of the men.

'Get all the dressing-gowns you can find—anything you can find,' Daphne told the maids.

She looked through Joe's clothes for something they could wear, these survivors, and one after another they emerged clean from baths and the shower, in her husband's dressing-gowns and one in an old wrapper of hers. Normally there would have been jokes about the big man in a Japanese kimono of pink and mauve flowers. They were served tea and cakes and coffee, it being teatime. Meanwhile the young man who seemed worse off than any of them lay in a deck-chair and seemed disinclined to move.

A big party was planned for tonight, here. These men were not in any state for a party. She asked them and they said they would be happy to sit still and let the earth stop swaying. Besides, there would be four days.

She left them while she telephoned to stop

events going forward and went to the sick youth. He seemed in a daze or a trance. She knelt beside him and asked his name.

'I'm James,' he said.

'Well, James, how about a bath and we'll get your clothes washed.' He tried to sit up, and she put her arm behind him and felt the pressure of thin bones.

'You need to put a bit of flesh on you,' she said, trying to heave him up.

'We were sick most of the way,' he said, in a normal voice, smiling. She had got him up, and now stood holding him. She progressed with him to the bathroom. There it was evident he was not up to a bath.

'Your mates seem to be in a better state than you.'

'They're sergeants,' he said.

This meant nothing to her yet. She ran the bath and asked the housegirl, Sarah, to help him into the bath and wash him. She could have done it herself; but for some reason was reluctant. While he was being washed, she thought about how to get clothes that would fit this starved young man. She telephoned her husband's brother's house and asked if there were any clothes for a tall thin man. The brother, who was in North Africa fighting Rommel, was thin, and tall.

A maid brought over an armful of clothes.

She handed them in through the bathroom door, and after a few minutes the youth came out, supported by Sarah, in clothes that fitted, more or less.

Now Daphne had to get these piles of stinking uniforms clean. She set the maids to work: on the lawns in front of Daphne's house and Betty's the four maids knelt on sacks to scrub the uniforms with scrubbing brushes on wash boards. Foam flew everywhere.

Beds were then made up all over the house. Supper was served with wine and beer, but the men were nervous of the alcohol. The frail boy, James, sat at the table with the four sergeants. Rank was abolished for the duration of this stay, the sergeant from Devon said. They were looking at roast pork and vegetables. 'Come on, lads,' said the Scottish sergeant, 'we've got to build ourselves up.' They did try, but the big bowl of fruit salad went down better.

It was still early. The men sat about the living-room listening to a radio news made anodyne by censorship. There was a troopship in, was allowed, but nothing was said about for how long. Did she mind if they went to bed? Off they went to their various beds, but James sat on.

Joe telephoned to find out how things were going on. She told him and he said she should ask their doctor to come up and look over the lads.

James was staring at her.

'You're like a vision. You can't imagine . . .

you forget there are lovely women, when you're with all those men, on the ship.'

'And so it was very bad?'

'Yes. It was.' The impossibility of communicating it to her kept him silent, and then he put out his long thin hand, in the sleeve of Joe's brother's blue shirt, and touched her hand. 'You're real,' he said, frowning. 'I'm not imagining you.' He peered into her face, serious, then smiled. 'You're so beautiful,' he concluded.

The maids were standing around, ready to serve coffee. Daphne said to them, 'Okay, that's it, no coffee tonight.'

She went to help him up, but he managed by himself and without holding on to anything followed her to the stoep, where a bed had been made, with plenty of blankets. He sat on it and said, 'What's your name?'

'Daphne,' she said.

'Of course, a goddess's name for a goddess.'

'Not a goddess, just a little ordinary nymph.'

'Don't go changing into a laurel tree,' he said.

She was impressed, though she had been hearing jokes about the laurel tree all her life.

'No pyjamas,' she said. 'Sorry.' He slowly took off his trousers and blue shirt, and stood in Joe's underpants, which hung on him like a loincloth. He slid into bed where he lay, looking at her with the same smile, as at a marvel.

'You're English,' he said.

'Yes, like you.'

'Yes.'

'Are you going to be all right?'

'I'm in a dream,' he said, and reached up with both arms and pulled her down. He held her. He was strong, after all. He turned his head so his face was in her neck and her hair, and said, 'Your hair smells so wonderful.'

'You're going to have to let me go,' she said.

'Why?' he said.

This absurdity made her laugh, and she freed herself, but he found her hand and held it to his cheek.

'Heaven,' he said. 'I'm in heaven.'

And then he fell asleep and she went in, shaken, oh, yes, badly shaken, though she could not have said why. A poor half-starved waif of a boy, but smelling now of his proper smell, of man—and her heart was pumping. She sat by herself in her living-room, smoked a cigarette, another, and then rang Betty.

'My lot are all asleep,' she said.

'So are mine. They are in a bad way.'

'We'll feed them up.'

'Then back on the ship again. It's a shame.'

'What price the party tomorrow night?'

'We'll have it, and they can join in or not as they like.'

Next morning she was up early as usual, and wandered in her wrap through the house where her charges were all lost to the world.

Tom, Dick and Harry, she was calling them in her mind, for she was tending to confuse this lot with the last, of a few weeks before. She went around the garden, which tonight would be festive—it was already decked with lanterns and lights. Festive and crowded. She rang the base and got her husband and said the party would be tonight and tomorrow too, and he said he was sorry, 'Things aren't too . . . no, I'll tell you when I see you.'

She ate her breakfast, fruit and coffee, alone. Then she was in the kitchen planning for tonight with the maids and the gardener. This was their third troopship, and the four were like old campaigners.

Not till mid-morning were there signs of life, but at last Tom, Dick and Harry—Sergeants Jerry, Ted and John—emerged yawning. She sat with them as bacon and eggs and fried tomatoes disappeared: they had their appetites back. Because of what Joe had said, she noticed they all had rough and reddened skins, in patches. They exposed torsos and thighs to her, red and rashy, and in some places beginning to suppurate.

'I've called our doctor.'

Next she went to where James was still asleep. He woke with a cry, then sat leaning on his elbow and smiling. She was sitting at a safe distance.

'How's your skin? The doctor's coming.'

Again she was looking at patches that were

like measles or a heat rash. And his knee: it was swollen, with a scar in a puff of white flesh. And his feet were swollen and red.

'We didn't get our boots off much.'

He took her hand and held it to his cheek, eyes closed, his face grave, lips trembling.

'James,' she said, as grave as he, 'I have a husband.'

'Don't be silly,' he said.

This was certainly not the jest of the seducer, but a fair statement of the position.

'But you do have to see the doctor.'

He kissed her hand and let it go.

One after another, the doctor examined the young men, and pronounced them all in poor shape. Libations of cold water would cure their skins: but soon they would be on the ship again. One had a cough. One had swollen glands. All had bad feet, and bruises where they had knocked themselves as the ship bucked and swung. 'I take it you didn't keep much down, from the look of you?'

And he ordered them to walk a couple of streets to his surgery, for various treatments.

Meanwhile Betty arrived and said to Daphne, 'What's up with you?'

'What do you mean?'

'You don't look yourself.'

'I'm not myself.'

A confession from one and a warning from the other were pre-empted by Sarah in the kitchen calling, 'Mary, Mary, where have you put the chickens, hey?' And Mary answering, 'Where have I put them—when they haven't been delivered yet?'

'There isn't going to be enough food,' said Daphne and they got into Betty's car and drove out into the countryside to any shop or butcher or bakery they could find. But others had had the same idea: shop after shop had been cleaned out. At last they found shelves still stacked with bread and a butcher with a sheep's carcass. They returned, with this booty, to find their charges, all ten of them, under the tree in Betty's garden, sprawling on rugs, being fed ham and chicken and salad by the maids.

'We could drive you to see the sights,' said Betty.

'We could take you up Table Mountain,' said Daphne.

The young men agreed that nothing could be better than sitting here, looking down on their enemy, the sea, which today spread out glimmering like a peacock's tail, looking like anything but what it was, a submarine-haunted killer.

The two women and the baby sat near them on the grass, both with that maternal smile which is as good as a chastity belt. But this lot, unlike previous invasions off the troopships, looked too beaten up to be a threat. Daphne felt the gaze of the young man on her, saw his haunted hungry eyes, and then glanced at

Betty, who of course would notice. He was already better, they all were: these young men were recovering as they breathed, and ate, and ate, and demolished piles of grapes. The air was heavy with the smell of liniments and ointments, there were dressings here and there on sore skins, but you would not think these were the scarecrows who had come off the boat yesterday.

Then they confessed for a need to sleep, and all went off to their beds. It was early afternoon. All over the two gardens that were being made one by that night's party, trestles were being set out, with piles of cutlery and plates and glasses, and smells of cooking meat came from the kitchens. Not only here, everywhere through the city, went on preparations and already men in uniforms were roaming these upper streets. There would be hundreds of them, hoping to be lucky, hoping for a welcome.

The organisations that dealt with incursions from the troopships asked for volunteers for these parties, knowing that only the incapacitated would hold back. The lucky ones were chosen by lot: names taken from a pail. For days and weeks to come slips of paper with the names of Captain E.R. Baker, Sgt. 'Red' Smith, Corporal Berners, Rifleman Barry, Private Jones, hundreds of them, were all over the city, in gutters, clogged on windowsills, fluttering about as the winds blew, Tom, Dick and Harry's names were everywhere, while they were on their way to—but it had to be India.

Betty and Daphne had each put down for four hundred, knowing that the unlucky and the uninvited would be wandering up to stand like poor children at a shop window, looking in at festive gardens. And then they would be invited in: who could turn them away?

The young men woke at five or so, and sleep had taken them another step towards their healthy selves. Their uniforms were clean and ironed now, and they were shaved and brushed.

At six o'clock Betty went off to her house to dress and Daphne looked over the evening dresses in her long crammed wardrobe; she and her Joe had gone in for dancing, when she first came, the two couples had gone dancing often, and here were evening dresses pressed and ready for action.

She took out the one she thought of as her cleverest, though it could be described, simply, as a white dress. It was of white silk pique, stiff and glossy, but a world away from the white dress she would have worn as her English self she could see it, limp white chiffon, with pink embroidery. She put on her white armour, described on the pattern as 'a gown of classical simplicity'. She smiled at herself in the long mirror. She shone, gleaming shoulders, the glisten of the white stuff, her hair, her eyes.

She snapped on shiny jet necklace and bracelets, her grandmother's, a mourning set; jet for mourning but just look how it set her off! And now her hair, down it fell, her yellow triumphant hair, achieved by perms, not to wave it, but to make it heavy and straight. And she peered close into her face that was enclosed in the yellow frame, and then she was saying, 'No, no, no, no, no.' She was trembling. 'I've gone mad,' she said to her reflection, but probably addressing her friend Betty. 'Yes, I have.' She pinned the hair up into the chignon, ageing herself by ten years into a young matron. Nothing like Ginger Rogers now (they said she was like Ginger Rogers, with her hair swinging about). Now she was the hostess, nothing more. Beside her was the English rose in her white chiffon, her invisible alter ego, the chrysalis she had discarded. A rosebud mouth smiled mistily: Daphne took her scarlet lipstick and obliterated it. Well defended, she went out, meeting Betty coming over. The two of them made a picture, and they knew it. 'You do make a picture!' And, 'The dark and the light of it.' Betty wore her dark brown silk dress. They had made their evening dresses from Vogue patterns, running them up on Singer sewing machines, side by side at a table in either house, as they felt. They were proud of their creations. 'Dior, out of my way,' 'Norman Hartnell, here we come,' they would sing to their own and each other's reflections.

Betty's dress had lacked its finish, at first. They tried on it diamante or 'cluster' brooches in strong colours. 'Vulgar,' they pronounced. 'No, that's not it . . .' Daphne remembered that her English-rose self had a little necklace and bracelets of white daisies, that could have been made to go—or rather, go against—the formality, of that stiff brown gown, so apt that the two had fallen about laughing, pleased with themselves.

Two young women, so recently girls in their fathers' houses, had found themselves in their own houses, with indulgent husbands and servants. Time and space to spread themselves, then to discover that what was strongest in them was an appetite for accomplishment. They transformed rooms with colour and texture, changed their gardens, came upon new talents every day, were like conquerors in new lands, but what they liked best was transforming themselves, with the aid of their sewing machines. Often as they flung lengths of material about, or draped themselves, they broke into fits of laughter and collapsed into chairs, helpless. 'Just as well no one can see us, Bets. They'd think us lunatics.' 'Perhaps we are.' And the giggles broke out again. These exuberances of healthy vitality, these festivals of self-discovery, innocent because of the flagrant enjoyment of their vanities, ended with Daphne's miscarriage and Betty's getting pregnant. The zest had gone and two sober young matrons looked back on giddy girls. Now they made baby clothes and shirts for their husbands. But in their cupboard hung the results of their early intoxications, and when they arrayed themselves in this dress or that, the other would signal: 'Oh, Bets, that was a morning, wasn't it!' 'Daphne, we were inspired that day.'

Now they gave each other the swiftest of once-overs and got on to the serious business of the night. Already cars were delivering soldiers to the two houses, and to the others in the street, and groups of soldiers wandered up, clutching bits of paper with addresses. The gramophone, with its stacks of records, was on the stoep and beside it was the gardener, ready to wind it up and change the records. Dance music came from every house, music and voices.

Daphne checked that the furniture in the living-room had been pushed back, leaving a clear floor, and that the drink was flowing. Betty went back to her house, and both women stood on their steps waving up men and girls: all the girls in the city were available tonight, for dancing at least, each worth her weight in gold. 'You girls are worth your weight in gold.' 'Call your friends, everyone, we must have girls.'

As she stood there, James came, put his arm around her, and they set off, on the stoep, cheek to cheek.

‘It’s all very well,’ she protested, trying to pull herself free.

‘Yes, yes, yes,’ he crooned, to the music, pulling her to him. And on and on they danced, and when she was interrupted, to be hostess, he came after her, and led her back again to the dance. Everyone was dancing: all that is, who had partners.

The gardener had positioned himself and angled the gramophone so that he could stand and look over to where on Betty’s stoep Lynda, her maid, was in a parallel situation by the gramophone. He had been pursuing Lynda, without success, and found ‘The Night is Young and You’re So Beautiful’ a perfect expression of his feelings. He put it on again, again, ‘The Moon is High and You’re so Glamorous’, and when some dancer complained there were other tunes, he did put on something else, but returned as soon as he could to ‘The Night is Young . . .’ Lynda, who told him she didn’t trust him (‘You say that to all the girls,’), played as often as she could get away with it,’ ‘Boohoo, you’ve got me crying for you, and everything that you do . . .’ He might riposte with ‘Oh, sweet and lovely, lady be good, oh, lady be good to me . . .’ And she ‘You left me in the lurch, you left me crying at the church . . .’

This flirtation went on all evening.

The evening was a triumph, as it was bound to be. Eight hundred? The two gardens between them and the street outside had held a good thousand. The drink held out, if the food didn't. It was two or later before the cars that were taking some men back to their billets stopped swinging their lights up into the trees, and the shouts and the singing of soldiers died as they descended towards the sea.

In the Wrights' house the soldiers went off to their beds and Daphne to her room. The white dress had done her proud she told herself, full of the vainglory of an imagined victory. 'My God, it's as good as armour'—stripping off jetty baubles and stepping out of the skirt which collapsed in white puffs and puckers around her legs. She went naked to bed, turned off the light, and then James arrived beside her, which she had known he would, while persuading herself he wouldn't dare.

In the very early morning she told him to go back to his room, and he said, 'I won't. I can't.'

'The maids will be here soon.'

He did leave, and went to his bed on the stoep where already the sun was warming the glass of the bottles rolling about there. He woke to the sound of clinking glass, as the maids cleaned around him.

Down in the garden, under the tree, Daphne was standing with Betty. They were wearing flowery wraps, and James thought he had never seen such lovely women. He told himself that after that voyage, that hell, he'd think any woman an angel, but he was not in the mood for common sense. Those two women in their gowns, in the greenery of the garden, they were a vision. And he stared, as long as they stood there, consciously storing it up in his mind, a picture he could look at later, keep, and hold.

Betty was saying to Daphne, 'For God's sake, watch it.'

'Is it really that obvious?'

'Yes, it is. Of course, people were noticing.'

'I can't help it.'

'But Daphne . . .'

'Yes, I know.'

'What are you going to do?'

'Is there going to be another bloody party tonight?'

'Of course there is. You know that. And tomorrow night too—if it's four days.'

'That's what Joe said.'

They looked down to where the great ship, ominous because of its associations, stood offshore, waiting.

'Why don't you take him off to the pondokkie?'

'I had wondered if I should.'

'You've got to get yourself out of sight.'

'Yes.'

The pondokkie was a little house, not much more than a shed, a couple of hours drive away, by the shore. Daphne went there with Joe, for weekends; Betty and her husband used it.

'Where am I going to get petrol?'

'I've still got a bit.'

'And then there's the party, these men, what shall I say?'

'I'll tell them you heard someone was sick. We'll all manage. Don't worry.'

'I'll get James up.'

'Is that his name?' said Betty, bitterly. 'Suddenly, there's a James. Who *is* James? If Joe finds out? Someone will tell him, you know.'

'I can't help it,' said Daphne again.

'I'll say James has gone into a clinic for a couple of days. Well, he looks as if he could do with one. For God's sake, Daphne, he looks like the walking wounded.'

'Yes, I know.'

The gardens were already being tidied for that night's festivities. Soon, the stage would be set, again; the trestles scrubbed, the mounds of plates and cutlery gleaming. The skeins of paper lanterns in the trees were being re-hung and the scorched ones taken down.

The soldiers, both Daphne's lot and Betty's, were asleep, but James was sitting on his bed when Daphne came to say: 'Get on your civvies, leave your uniform, come with me. Yes, now, before anyone wakes.' He did not argue, but obediently put on Daphne's husband's brother's trousers and shirt. She put on slacks and a shirt and let her hair fall on her shoulders: this was like a statement of defiance, but to whom, she could not have said. In the kitchen they drank hasty cups of coffee, ignoring the maids. Daphne put some things into a box, and they set off in her car along the coast.

Betty watched them go, from her windows. She was in a seethe of conflicting feelings but most of all she felt as if her friend had been struck by lightning. Black lightning—if there was such a thing.

The streets ran smooth and citified through the suburbs, then they were on a rough road, the sea on their right hand, and what looked like farmland on their left. Vines and oak trees, a fair and smiling scene, but soon the land was unworked, with only a few scattered sheep. But James looked only at Daphne, until she put out a hand and touched his face with her knuckles. 'Stop it, you're making me nervous.'

'I can't help it,' he said, as she had earlier. She smiled and he said bitterly, 'It's not just an amusement for me.' And then, 'Stop the car, stop it now.'

She drove until they were on the edge of a little bay where waves frisked among low black rocks. He moved up to put his arm round her. His face . . . it frightened her, and he was trembling. Not many cars came along this road, but now she saw one approaching.

'James, wait. Let's just get there.'

'Where?'

'You'll see.'

She put the car in motion again. She saw his face staring down past her at a postcard sea, gulls swooping, sea noise, bird noise, and the sunlight a moving glitter to the horizon. No ships.

'I hate the sea,' he said. 'I hate it. It's out to get us. And it will.'

'Don't look at it.'

So he looked at her, shifting his head a little, but past her head was the glare of the sea.

They turned inland. There was a broken gate. Scrubby unkept land: you'd never guess the sea was a couple of hundred yards off. Then a turn towards it, through low bushes, and ahead a shack or shed, with the bushes growing close all round it.

The car stopped. She lifted out the box of provisions, gathered from the party leftovers, and a big enamel can of water, which he took from her. She went ahead along a faint path, the bushes seeming to want to clutch and bring her down, to a door which she opened with a large key. Inside was dark, till she pulled down shutters. Light showed, first, a wide high bed, piled with all kinds of covers, then shelves around wooden walls, with dishes and plates, and a small wooden table in the middle on a plank floor, with two wooden chairs.

'Our holiday home,' she said. 'Do you like it?'

James might have said that he seemed to spend his life now in sheds or huts—this one was called a pondokkie. What's in a name? A little house, like one in a fairytale, in the woods. But they were scrubby bushes, smelling of salt.

The sea was a murmur, not too far away, with an occasional splash as a wave broke on a rock. The two stood looking at each other. The feverish state that had enclosed them since his arrival in the setting of fine house and gardens might have dissolved here and now, but it didn't. They sank on to the two wooden chairs, and, holding each other's hands across the table, stared, serious, quiet—and oddly, with bitterness, directed, not at each other, but at Fate, the war, something not themselves. She stroked his face with a hand that had pearly pink nails. He thought, those nails wouldn't survive long if she really lived in this pondokkie, a rough hut. This clean and shiny sweetly-smelling woman, this was just where she played . . . and was he what she was playing with?

'Wipe that bloody lipstick off.'

She opened her bag, found a handkerchief and he took it from her and carefully but thoroughly removed the scarlet lips.

'There now,' he said.

She said, 'Let's go and look at the sea. The

tide's out.'

'Why?'

'I don't know.'

Gravely, he took her hand and led her to the bed. Through the open window, came the smell of salt-stung vegetation. Silence except for the murmur of the sea. Their lovemaking, trembling and hungry, seemed to celebrate not love but tragedy. They fell asleep and she woke to find him screaming, his hands over his ears.

'What is it?' he shouted.

'The tide's in.'

It seemed that the ocean was rolling in to focus on just that stretch of shore so close to their shelter that the next wave would rear and crash down on it, dragging them out to sea. The little house shook, the earth shook, crash crash and then a thundering withdrawal: it was as if they were deep under the sea, buried in it.

His face was in her breasts and he was crying, not like a child, oh, no, a deep choking sobbing, and he was clutching to her as if they were helplessly rolling in deep surf.

'It's like this when it's high tide—this must be an unusually high one.' Her voice was like a hush within the pounding tumult. 'I shouldn't have brought you here. I didn't think.'

'But I'm with you,' she heard, as another wave crescendoed and crashed.

'We'll get up and go and look at it. You'll see, it's quite a way off, fifty yards at least.'

'No, no, no.'

'All right, then, get up and we'll have some supper.'

'I don't want to eat. I don't want to waste the time.'

She slid out, standing naked to smile at him, gravely, for this was the note that had been struck from their first moment, but there was something there, what?—melancholy? Well, that was in order, but surely not this edge of bitterness?

'What is it?' he asked, a too-ready suspicion flaring.

'I don't know,' she said, defeated, turning to set out bread and butter and ham. 'I don't know. Perhaps I am trying to laugh at us.'

'At me!'

'Never you,' she said. 'Two days. Two. And I feel . . .'

'Well, tell me, yes, tell me. I want to know . . . am I the first bloody soldier you brought here?'

'Well, thank you. If that's what you think. I think we should leave.' She was crying; he sat on the edge of the bed, and was about to get up and go to her but then he crouched down with his hands over his ears as a wave crashed, seemingly just above them.

'Why me? Yes, why me? But I don't care. You're wonderful—and that's enough.' And he ducked down as the little house shook.

'I care,' and she sat down, laid her head on

her arms on the table and wept.

He left the bed and sat opposite, stroking her hair, watching her cry.

Then he put out his hand, got up, took her hand and said, 'This is ridiculous. Let's get back to bed.' And he led her weeping on to the bed, and lay down beside her.

'This little house, this pondokkie of yours, I won't go back on the ship, I'll just hide here, and you can come and visit me.'

After the wedding of Joe Wright, bachelor, and Daphne Brent, spinster, they had taken a week of conventional honeymoon in a smart hotel up country, famous as a haven for newlyweds, and then he had brought her here. It was not likely that she failed to think, 'I bet he brought his girls here when he was a bachelor.' This did not make her jealous. She rather liked the idea of this frail shelter, that seemed always about to dissolve into the sea, as a place for lovers. In this very room she and Joe, naked and happy, had made love and eaten picnic food and then run exultantly shouting down to the sea at low tide. And now she was here with this man, but she was in a different dimension with him. If Joe walked in now he would come from a sane and healthy world and she would look at him from this dream she was in—a nightmare, was it?—and then disappear, with a shriek, and he'd think he had seen an apparition from a nether world. Such pain, in this young man and in her, and she did not know where hers had come from: she had never envisaged unhappiness in her blueprints for the future. She had not experienced it. She did not know this youth: he was a stranger and this element where she found herself with him was alien. And yet, knowing that soon she would lose him, made her want to do something primitive and brutal, like pulling out her hair, beating her breasts with her fists, sit swaying, sick with grief, a black cloth over her head.

Soon she was lying with a sleeping man in her arms—if he were asleep, and not in some kind of trance: he trembled, or came to himself in little shuddering spasms. She lay with her eyes shut, holding him, and lived through a memory of something that happened soon after she came to South Africa. She and Joe, Betty and Henry and another couple had driven off into the mountains, following little roads known to the South Africans from boyhood rambles. They stopped the cars, not in a campers' site, but where baboons had made a cliff their own. All up the face of the cliff, from rocks and holes that were the openings to ancient caves, the baboons perched and clung and barked at them. The humans took no notice. A few yards from the cliff, in the middle of a little plateau formed by slabs of rock split by heat and cold was a little tree. It was dead, a pale spectral thing growing from between the rocks. Dead.

It was midday and strong light made the dry leaves hang whiteish, sketched in air, with heat waves shimmering around them like the volatile oils made visible. Bread and wine and fruit were set out, and the women cubed some meat. The men set light to the dead tree. The idea was, it would fall and they would use it as fire for their meat. The tree flared up, it was at once a torch of white-hot flames. The baboons on their cliff barked their fear, the humans fell back, the tree was a river of flame, a rush of white sparks. Daphne was standing too close. The quick flare took her by surprise; she could feel the hairs on her arms frizzle. She was struck by the intensity of the fire into an immobility. She cried out, and Joe leaped to her and pulled her back out of the heat that was now shimmering and oiling for yards around the tree.

That was how she felt now.

'Too close,' she was murmuring, eyes closed, holding a naked man lost in his dream. 'It's too close.'

When the light came, the waves began to come close again, and roar and pound, and they held each other, and listened, until the noise abated, and she said, 'Now, I want you to come out and look.'

'I told you I wish I need never see the ocean again.'

'I know, but come on!'

It was late morning. The sea was in retreat.

She took him through the push and clutch of the salty bushes to a little patch of sand, still wet, but drying pale on its surface, and beyond were tall black rocks, where seaweed clung. The sea was rough today, jumping and leaping about among the rocks.

'Do you ever swim here?' he asked.

'Over there is a pool in the rocks. It's safe, when the tide's out.' She stopped herself asking if he'd like to go in, just in time.

They stood with their arms about each other allowing themselves to be hypnotised by the sea's noise, but she could feel him tense, discouraged.

'It's only sea,' she said, though she knew he was rejecting the moment, and probably, her. 'There it is, kept in its place, it can't get us.' And wished she could unsay it; she had forgotten he would be back on the ship.

'When the war's over I'll never go near a ship again.'

She began to cry. She was forlorn and rejected. Why was she? She did not know herself. Her emotional extremes, sorrow, exultation, grief, passion, were leaving her rather like that fish she could see, flapping in the sand. That James should hate the sea so much: she could not bear it. She had often thought that when she came to marry Joe, it was to the sea she had come, the ocean surrounding her always, never out of sight, or out of mind. Joe's gift to her had been the sea, so she had told him she felt.

He said, 'I'm not going back on that ship, I won't.'

'Oh, God,' she said, 'you don't love me.'

'What?'

Why had she said that? She felt as if she had tripped a switch, moved a gear, was in an uncoordinated helpless condition, and anything she said must come out inept, tactless, even brutal.

She clutched him by the shoulders and saw him wince: she let him go. His singlet, which he had put on to leave the hut, was stuck here and there in ruddy patches.

'Oh, God,' she said.

'The sea spray,' he said, 'it's getting to me.'

She should not have brought him out here, she should have thought, everything had gone wrong.

'Come on, let's go in,' he said.

The tide was turning, beginning to thunder and crash; she felt he was estranged from her; he felt he had failed her.

She took his hand and led him back to the hut. As they went through the bushes, a Coloured lad came with a note in his hand. He was from the local shop a mile away where there was a telephone.

The note said: 'Daphne, he's got to be back on board by tomorrow, midday. Betty!

She said to the youth, whom she knew, from previous trips here, with her husband, 'Come to the hut, I'll give you some money.' This was done. He was giving her odd looks, as well he might: would he think this money a bribe?

Then she said to James, 'Deadline for you—twelve tomorrow.'

'I'm not going.'

'We've got another afternoon and night.'

'We've got all our lives.'

Back inside the hut, they were together again in feeling: the emptiness that had claimed them by the sea had gone.

'I'll come for you, after the war.'

She held him close, her head on his shoulder, and felt the rough skin under her cheek.

'You don't believe me,' he said gently, tenderly, as to a child, 'but it's true.'

The afternoon and then the night went past, while the tide came in, and thundered over them, and went out, came in. It was low tide when she got off the bed and began packing up. She was afraid he was not going to move, but at last he did.

'We should have something to eat.'

'I suppose so.'

They sat with some bread and jam between them and looked at each other.

'I'll think of you like this. You're like a little girl, your hair all over the place. And your face needs washing.'

When they walked back through the bushes to the car, clumps of white spume were flying in on a cold wind, and spattered the bushes.

She drove in silence. He watched her all the way; she received that long look like a prolonged embrace.

At the house, Betty came running. 'Our lads have gone. I took them down. They're already on the ship.'

Her two maids, and her gardener, Daphne's maids and her gardener, stood on the respective steps, watching, as the soldier went in to Daphne's house, Daphne staying outside, by the car. He came out in his uniform.

'I'll take you,' said Betty. 'No, you stay, Daphne.' Daphne was not fit to drive down to the docks: she was trembling, and had to hold on to the car.

Betty ran back to her house, drove her car to outside Daphne's, hooted and sat waiting.

Daphne and the soldier stood face to face, not touching, looking. Betty hooted again. The soldier broke away, and ran, pulling his kitbag bumping along behind him. From the car he sent one look back and then, oddly, saluted. He got in. Betty's car shot off down into the town.

The scene broke. Daphne moved slowly up to the stoep and sat on the end of a wicker lounger as if she might fall through it.

The four maids went back to their duties, the gardeners to their plants.

Mid-afternoon. The great ship stood in its nest of white frills. From here would be seen the activity of embarking; ants crawled everywhere over the ship.

Daphne did not move. Sarah came from inside the house with a tray of tea, which she had not ordered. When her mistress took no notice, Sarah poured a cup of tea, sugared it, held it out to Daphne and said, 'Your tea, medem.' Daphne shook her head. The black woman lifted Daphne's limp arm, and put the cup in her hand.

'You must have some tea, medem.'

Daphne sat still, her eyes on the docks, and then at last she did drink.

'That's right, medem.'

The maid left the tray and went in.

Late afternoon. Betty's car was nosing up the street, and then she was beside Daphne. 'He made it. Just.'

Daphne motioned *leave me* with her hand.

Was the distance between the ship and the dock widening?

'Joe rang. I told him you were ill.'

No reply.

'He said the ship was leaving so as to get out of Cape Town while it is light—in case there's a sub about.'

Daphne let out a cry and then slammed her fist against her mouth. She said, 'I'm a very wicked woman, do you know that? I don't love Joe. I never did. I married him under false pretences. I should be punished for that.'

'You had better lie down.'

Daphne began to cry. She stared down after the ship, her hands tugging at her hair tangled with salt spray and wind. Her face had forgotten make-up: her husband would recognise that English girl with her baby mouth, now woeful; as she looked now she would not easily be recognised by her admiring guests. Dreadful, deep sobs, and she was swaying as she sat.

'Do you have any sedatives? Daphne?'

Daphne did not move or respond.

Betty went to call Sarah, who was in the room just behind, keeping an eye on what went on. 'Help me get Mrs Wright to her bed. Then I'm going to the chemist for medicine.'

It took the two of them to lift Daphne: she did not want to go in till the ship had disappeared. The three women stood, the maid and Betty holding Daphne, while the ship dwindled over the horizon. They walked her to her bed, laid her down and Betty said, 'Hold the fort, I'll be quick.' And in a few minutes she was back. Daphne lay on her bed, staring. Betty put an arm around her, lifted her, and made her swallow two tablets.

Daphne collapsed: her eyes closed.

And now Betty and Sarah stood together: slowly, carefully, their eyes met, and held.

When Daphne had arrived in South Africa she had criticised Betty, the South African born and bred, for behaving in front of her staff as if they did not exist. One day Betty had come out of her bathroom naked and walked across her bedroom in full sight of the gardener who was at work just outside the french windows. She had stood there and talked, brushing her hair, and turned about, as if the man were not there, and when Daphne told her off, she realised for the first time that her servants had become as invisible as mechanical servitors. They were paid well—for this was liberal Cape Town ('We pay our people much better than they do in Joburg'), fed, taken to the doctor, given generous hours off. But they were not there for Betty, as human beings. Remorse, if that was the word, had adjusted her behaviour and her thoughts, and she became noticing and on guard, watching what she did and what she said. But she could not think of anything apt for this situation. The four maids, hers and Daphne's, were friends and knew the other maids along the street: this went for the gardeners. By now all of them would be discussing Daphne and the soldier. Any one of them might tell Joe.

'Mrs Wright is very sick,' said Betty at last, knowing she was blushing because of the feebleness of it. And it had sounded like a plea, which she didn't like.

Sarah said, 'Yes, medem.' Compassionate, yes: but no doubt there was derision there, a forgivable allowance, in the circumstances.

'Yes,' said Betty. She was in the grip of the oddest compulsion. Like Daphne, she could have tugged at her locks with both hands; instead she passed her hands across her face, wiping away whatever expression might be there—she didn't want to know. And now, she couldn't help herself, she let out a short barking laugh and clapped a hand across her mouth.

'Yes, medem,' said Sarah, sighing. She turned and went off.

'Oh, my God,' said Betty. She took a last hopeless look at her friend who was lying there, struck down. Somewhere over the horizon, that soldier was on his way north into the dark of the Indian Ocean.

Betty went to her house, sat on her dark steps, and in her mind's eye persisted the sight of Daphne, lying white-faced and hardly breathing.

'Oh, no, no, no, no, no,' said Betty wildly, aloud, and sank her face into her hands. 'No. I don't want it. Never.'

Sometime later Joe's car came up, Betty went to intercept him. At once he began talking. 'Betty, Henry won't be back tonight, he asked me to tell you, it's been a real dingdong these last few days, you've no idea, getting in enough supplies and everything, it's not been easy—for the ship, you know, the one that's just left.' He was talking too loudly, and walked past her up his steps, and turned. And stood talking into the garden, where she stood. 'We lost a ship—the *Queen of Liverpool*—no, forget I said that, I didn't say it. Five hundred men gone. Five hundred. It was the same sub that was chasing the—the ship that's just left. But we got her. Before she sank she got the sub. Five hundred men.' He was now walking about, gesticulating, not seeing her, talking, in an extreme of exhaustion. 'Yes, and the ship that's gone, they left us twenty-five. They're in a bad way. They're mad. Claustrophobia, you know, stress. I don't blame them, below the water line, well, they're in hospital. They're crazy. Henry saw them. When he gets home, he'll need looking after himself. Five hundred men—that's not something you can take in. Henry hasn't really slept since the ship got in.'

'Yes, I see.'

'So, you must make allowances. He won't be himself. A pretty poor show all around, these last four days. And I'm not myself either.' And he went striding towards the bedroom.

'Daphne's not well. She's taken a sedative.'

'If there's any left, I'll take one too.'

Betty went with him into the bedroom.

The sight of his wife stopped him dead.

'Good Lord,' he said. 'What is it?'

'Probably some bug. Don't worry. She'll be all right tomorrow I expect.'

'Good Lord,' he said again. She took pills from the bottle by the bed, gave them to him, and he downed them with a gulp from Daphne's glass.

He sank down to sit on the bed. 'Betty,' he

said, 'five hundred men. Makes you think, doesn't it?' He stood up, pulled off his boots, first one, thump, then the other, thump; walked around to the other side of Daphne, lay down and was asleep.

Betty went to tell the maids that no supper would be needed. 'Go off home. That's right.'

'Thank you, medem.'

Betty returned to stand near the bed. Daphne had not moved.

Joe lay there, beside his wife, Good-fellow Joe, everybody's friend, rubicund and jovial, but there he lay, and Betty would not have known him. He kept grimacing in his sleep, and grinding his teeth, and then, when he was still, his mouth was dragged down with exhaustion.

Betty switched off the light. She returned to her house over dark lawns and sat for a long time, in the dark. Four days. There had been so much noise; soldiers with their English voices, telephones, cars coming and going, dance music, the same tunes played over and over again on the gramophone, while feet in army boots scraped and slid, but now the noise was subsiding, another voice that had been speaking all the time was becoming audible, in an eloquence of loss, and endurance. Four days the troopship had been in. A long way off, on the other side of a chasm, of an abyss, smiled life, dear kind ordinary life.

* * *

Down the gangways they came, between the guns that had been ready to defend them all the way from Cape Town, lines of men, hundreds, to form up in their platoons and companies on the quays, where James was already standing at ease, though at ease he was not, for his feet hurt like, it is safe to say, the feet of most of those young men, some of whom had been there for over an hour, under an unwelcoming sun. These soldiers were not in as bad a way as getting on for a month ago, in Cape Town. Beneficent Cape of Good Hope had loaded the ship with food, and above all fruit. Poor boys who had scarcely tasted a grape in their lives had consumed luscious bunches until the bounty ran out. Three weeks this time, not a month, and the Indian Ocean had been kind except for a four-day storm halfway across, when conditions had been similar to those in the Atlantic. James stood narrowing his eyes against the glare, holding himself so as not to faint; and he watched the great ship and, if hatred could kill, then it would have sunk there and then and be gone forever.

It was very hot. The air was stale and clammy. Thin dark men in loincloths hurried about being told what to do by dark men in uniform, who were being supervised by white men in uniform. No smell of sea now, though it was so near, only oil and traffic fumes. At last the endless lines did end, while men were still forming into their companies. Some had already moved off, to the accompaniment of the barking sounds of the sergeants, which James now found soothing, being reminders of order and regularity. James's company were marched to a barracks, where they were fed, and showered off the seawater which on some skins still festered. Hundreds of naked young men, but while they were in nothing like as bad shape as in Cape Town they were still the walking wounded, patched with red rough skin and fading bruises. They would be sent to the train tomorrow, which would take them to their destination: unnamed. The name, its harsh alien syllables was whispered about through the hundreds of soldiers who were already thinking of it as a haven where they would at last keep still, lose the sway of the ship. Camp X was what they had to call it. The smell in the barracks was enough to make them sick, despite the showers.

Authority on this second stage of the voyage, remembering the twenty-five madmen they had left behind in Cape Town, the dozens that had gone into hospital to be patched up, and the shocking physical state of the disembarking men, had chosen not to notice that more and more slept on the decks, and, disregarding regulations, simply did not turn up for the ritual of the sea-water douches. All that voyage had been very hot. The sickroom was full of cases of diarrhoea, and again officers had to double up so as to provide accommodation for another sickbay. There were always queues for the ship's doctors. That fruit in unaccustomed stomachs, the feasting and drunkenness at Cape Town, added to the queues for the latrines. If an epidemic broke out—and why not?—what was to be done? Five thousand men, most already run down, many coughing: it was a poor show, and no ship's officers had ever been more relieved to see a port appear at last.

In the barracks that night the soldiers lay on top of their bedding and cursed, and sweated. The attendant corporals and sergeants, as sick as their men, dismayed and homesick, advised patience, in raucous voices. 'If you know what's good for you, you'll fucking well be patient,' shouts Sergeant Perkins.

As for James, he did not divide the voyage into two stages, England-Cape Town, Cape Town-Bombay. It had been one long suffering, consuming him, body and soul, interrupted by four days of heaven.

Through the three weeks of the Indian Ocean James, sick and sore, sat with his back against a cabin wall and dreamed . . . It was a dream, that place, with its mountain spilling cloud like a blessing over its lucky inhabitants. A dream of big cool houses in gardens. He held in his mind that scene of two young women, one dark, one fair, in their flowery wraps under a big tree, that scene; and the nights with Daphne, and one memory in particular, Daphne seeming to shine in the lamplight, her yellow hair spreading on white shoulders, holding out her arms to him. And dancing cheek to cheek. And how the sea had thundered over them, deep in love, crashed and banged and sucked, but then retreated, harmless.

A dream of happiness. He would hold it in his mind and not think of anything at all, only that, until this bloody war ended.

Meanwhile he was in a barracks with fifty men, cursing and scratching and calling out in their sleep, if you could call that sleep, and in the morning he marched with the others to the trains that would take them to Camp X, which it turned out was two days' travelling away. The conditions on the train matched those on the ship for discomfort but at least a train goes straight, more or less, it doesn't sway and lurch about. James watched the landscape of middle India go past and hated it. The Cape wasn't alien, with its oaks and its vineyards and its fruit, he had felt at home in a landscape where nothing said: You don't belong.

When they at last reached Camp X, somewhere in the middle of India, and marched in their companies on to the parade ground—the maidan—half the camp was of new shiny huts, or sheds. In other words,

Nissen huts, and white tents covered the rest of the ground. There was a race, everyone knew, though no one had told them, to get the huts up before the monsoon started. Under their feet as they marched or stood at ease was a powdery dark dust, that puffed up and fell in drifts. The smell, what was the smell, wood smoke and pungency and much else, and the soldiers sniffed and tasted the air, this dusty foreign air, while a sun like a brass band blared down on them.

In lines and in queues the men waited at Medical. Rashes and bad feet, eye infections, stomach disorders, coughs, these soldiers were more fit for an infirmary than for fighting, and James's knee was up again, like a lump of uncooked dough, with a scar stretched across it. His feet were swollen.

A couple of hundred men were taken to hospitals in the region and the rest were told they would be given two weeks' leave. If they had nowhere to go—and most would not—they would stay in camp and provision would be made for their relaxation. It seemed there were clubs and bars in town that were prepared to entertain Other Ranks. James was told he was among those invited to stay with a certain Colonel Grant and his wife, to recuperate. That is, he was in a category not bad enough for hospital, but not fit enough for drilling and exercising.

He and nine others were driven off to a big

bungalow in a garden full of heavy dark trees that were spattered here and there with pink, red and white flowers. The smell, the smell, what was it?—a heavy flower smell but the other, pungent, hanging in their nostrils like a reminder of their foreignness. Unknown birds emitted unfamiliar noises. In a garden a black man in a white shirt squatted doing something to a bush. This one had a twist of cloth on his head, but in Cape Town the gardeners in the young women's gardens wore cast-off good clothes, and old canvas shoes.

Colonel Grant was Indian Army Retired, and a friend of the colonel in James's regiment, and was now waiting for the war to let him go Home to England. The Grants' war effort was to entertain soldiers needing a respite. The men did not know each other, though some faces were familiar because of the weeks on the ship. These were all soldiers, Other Ranks, and this was because of a decision by Colonel Grant, since it was always officers who were asked out. James who had been Other Ranks now in various places for two years, had ceased to notice that his way of speaking marked him apart. The sergeants had sometimes picked him out for sarcasm but there was something about how he took this attention that took the fun out of it for them. Here was this quiet, obedient young man, obviously straining to keep up, to hear what was said, to do his best, but not too painfully:

James was not victim material. He did not notice now that he was the odd man among these ten soldiers but the Grants did. And he had brought books in his kitbag. The supper was at a long table, once used for formal and probably grand occasions, but now accommodating men not used to them. The food was English, heavy and plentiful.

Mrs Grant was gracious, she was trying hard. A large, red-faced woman, she was uncomfortable in her skin, for she was sweating, and kept holding her face up to the draughts of warm air—not cool but at least moving—from the punkahs. She had patches of dark under her arms, and her pleasant, or at least trying-to-please face smiled conscientiously as she made conversation.

'And what part of Home do you come from?'

'Bristol . . .' in a strong West Country voice. 'I'm a plumber by trade.'

'How nice. How very *useful.* And do you—I'm afraid I didn't get your namc . . .?'

Then it came to James, who sat preoccupied, apart from the others in spirit, which showed on his abstracted face that was frowning with the effort to be here, to be part of things, to behave well, 'And you, forgive me for not remembering . . . where are you from?'

'Near Reading. I was still at college when the war started.'

'How nice. And what were you studying?'

'Office management and secretarial.'

Here, Colonel Grant, who had exchanged glances with his wife, because of this more refined voice among the other rougher ones, said, 'You'll all have a full day tomorrow. The Medicals will be here early. We start things early here—because of the heat, you know . .

'It doesn't matter how early we start, you can never get the better of the heat,' fretted Mrs Grant.

'So, I suggest you all get your heads down early and tomorrow we'll see.'

'I am sure you would all like some coffee?' Mrs Grant said.

Now the men hung about, exchanging looks. James said he would like coffee, but Colonel Grant said, 'Probably you'd prefer a good cup of tea. Yes, well, that's easy. When you are in your billets just clap your hands and ask for chai.'

The men were disposed in cottages in the gardens: except for two. One was James: he found that his name, down for a cottage, had been without explanation changed for a guest room in this house.

No explanation needed, when you thought about it, and now he did. He was uncomfortable, but consoled himself that his fellow house guest was an electrician from Bermondsey, who said he fancied a cup of tea if they didn't mind and shot off into the dark towards the cottages. That left James, drinking coffee with the Grants, who told him to make himself at home, borrow what books he liked, and play the gramophone.

James lay on his bed in the dark, too hot between covers, and saw bats swoop past the window gauze. The smell, had there been a characteristic smell in Cape Town? He didn't think so. Only the scent of Daphne's skin and hair . . . and so he drifted off to sleep and if he woke and cried out there was no one there to hear.

Next morning a couple of young women in the uniform of some nurses' voluntary service arrived to check them over. Again James's knee was strapped. All ten soldiers sat about in the cottages with their feet in strong-smelling potions, all had their sore skins medicated: all were on their way to recovery.

Now, a problem: nine men already half-mad with boredom, and here they were in this refined and subdued household and what they wanted was some fun—precisely, to get drunk.

But the Grants had thought of that. In the town was a club which would welcome them, and a short walk would take them there. Better wait until evening until it cools down a bit.

That left James, who didn't want any club, other soldiers, distractions from his private thoughts. He wanted to sit on this verandah and watch the birds and think about Cape Town. That meant Daphne, but not exclusively. He was thinking, 'Imagine, we could have been stationed there—couldn't we? But instead we are here.' The enormity of Chance, or Fate, preoccupied him, and he sat for hours, a book open on his knee, thinking so deeply that the Colonel's approach was not noticed until the old man coughed and sat down.

'I hope I am not disturbing you?'

'No, no,—of course not, sir.'

On James's knee was Kipling's *Collected Verses.* Kipling had not been offered in the summer schools of that year which now seemed so long ago. Kipling! What would Donald have said?

The bookshelves of the Grants' living-room were full of red leather volumes tooled in gold—and many of them were Kipling. The Colonel leaned forward, took in the title, leaned back. He said, 'A good lad, Kipling. Though he's out of favour now.'

'I haven't read him before, sir.'

'I'd be interested to hear what you make of it. Your generation . . . you see things differently.'

Outside this bungalow, beyond the tree-shaded garden, on the dusty road, groups of Indians went past in their many colours.

'What's that bird, sir?'

'Crows. Indian crows. Not like ours, are they?'

'They sound as if they've got sore throats.

Like mine.'

The Colonel laughed: clearly, he was relieved to laugh. James's pale intensity disturbed him.

'We've got all kinds of germs. It's the dust. Filthy. But you'll get immune, with luck.'

'And do you get immune to the heat, sir?'

The Colonel looked at the patches of dressing on James's arms and legs, below the uniform shorts; he knew there were more dressings, where they were invisible. The redness on James's neck was prickly heat. 'No, you don't get used to that, I'm afraid.' A pause. 'I'm afraid my wife takes it hard, after all these years. She spends as much time as she can in the hills but at the moment she wants to do her bit, so she's here, and she's not made for it. You must have noticed.'

'Yes, I did.'

'And where are your comrades?'

'They're exploring the town.'

'Poor lads, not much for them to do.'

'We're all pleased to be off the ship, sir.'

'Yes, I heard you had a bad time.'

He got up, nodded, and went off. But he took to dropping in to join James on the verandah, for chats that were brief, but as James saw, not without purpose.

'Didn't they offer you a commission?'

'Yes, I turned it down. Now, I wonder why?'

'You might have had things a bit easier.'

'I thought so on the troopship, yes.'

'Yes.'

And another time, looking at the red volume on James's knee.

The tumult and the shouting dies,
The Captains and the Kings depart.

'They don't seem to be departing, sir. Far from it.'

'That's what they want us to do. The Indians. Depart. You might have noticed.'

James had now been in India for a week and he had not done more than glance at a newspaper.

'Riots.' 'Free India.' 'India for the Indians.' 'The British Tyranny.'

Months of socialist indoctrination, which of course had to include 'Free India', had slid off James. He thought, Well, India for the Indians: that makes sense.

'The lot before you. The previous regiment. They've gone to Burma.'

'Yes, we know.'

'Before they left they were suppressing riots in . . . pretty close to here. They put down quite a nasty spot of bother. What do you think about that?'

James thought that if you were a soldier you did what you were told, bad luck.

'Mine is not to reason why, sir.'

The Colonel laughed. 'Very wise!'

'Are we going to Burma, sir?' James dared.

'I don't know. No, I really don't.'

'And if you did you wouldn't tell me!

'And if I did I couldn't tell you. But as you know, the Japs are threatening to invade India and free it from our tyranny. And they're getting closer all the time.'

'Yes, I suppose so.'

'And some troops will be kept here, in case of that.'

'I see.'

'Yes, it looks like that.'

And another conversation, towards the end of that visit, which James was hardly to remember later, so little impression did it make on him, compared with the vividness of Cape Town.

The Colonel had come on to the verandah, his boots loud on the wooden floor, and he stood looking at the soldier, who was lost to the present and staring, his mouth a little open.

'James . . .'

James did hear, after a pause, then smiled, stood as the Colonel sat down. He sat down again himself.

The Colonel said, 'You know, this isn't an easy country for some of us—well, some do seem to flourish like the green bay tree. Not many. It takes it out of you.' Now he hesitated, trying to think of the right thing to say. He shifted his lengthy legs about in the cream linen trousers which had a shine on them from someone's iron. With one thin sunburned hand he rubbed his chin, while he stared thoughtfully, not at James, but into the garden.

'Are you sleeping—may I ask?'

'Not too well. It is so hot.'

'Yes, it is, things'll get better when the monsoon comes. Not long now.'

'The monsoon, everyone talks about it as if it's some kind of magic wand.'

'Well, it is. Yes, that's what it is. James—if I'm talking out of turn, then forget it. But I want to say . . . you mustn't take things too hard. Bad idea anywhere, but in this country . . . it tips people over the edge, India does, if you don't get a grip of yourself. We aren't made for this climate. It does us in. I've seen it . . . I've been here forty years. Too long. I'd be Home now if it wasn't for the war.'

If James had taken this in, it didn't show on his face; he didn't move, or look at the Colonel.

'Think about what I'm saying, will you? Try and take things a little easier.'

'Yes, sir. Yes . . . it's that ship, you see. I don't think you can have any idea . . .' One does not say to an old man that he hasn't an idea, not about anything. 'I mean . . . I'm sorry, sir. I didn't mean . . .' And then, angry, white-faced: 'It was terrible. It was . . .' And he brought two clenched fists frustratedly down on his chair arms. His book fell, and the Colonel picked it up, sat turning pages. He read aloud.'

'Cities and Thrones and Powers
Stand in Time's eye,
Almost as long as flowers,
Which daily die:
But, as new buds put forth
To glad new men,
Out of the spent and unconsidered Earth
The Cities rise again.

I often recite that to myself when things get rough.'

'Yes, sir.'

'A sense of proportion, one must keep that.'

'Yes, sir.'

'And you do forget, you know, one does forget.'

'I will never forget, sir, never, never.'

'I see. I'm sorry.' And the Colonel moved off.

On the day the cars came to take the Grants' guests back to their camp, the air seemed full of rubbish. A wind was busy in the trees, whirling leaves and even small branches out into the roads where people scurried into doorways and holes in a jumble of shops and little houses, and shopkeepers struggled to put up their shutters to save their goods being whisked into the air. Mouths were dry. Eyes stung from the dust.

The cars passed a platoon, accompanied by

their corporal, returning from some jaunt associated with the two weeks' leave. Their eyes were screwed up, their mouths clenched tight, against the sun and the dust. This made them look indignant. Ten expostulating men with the dirt running off them as they marched, and the dust in clouds as high as their knees. The two cars passing raised the dust even more and looking back, the passengers saw a ghostly platoon vanish in a dirty cloud.

The men went to report their return, and James was told that 'it had been suggested' he should take a commission and then join Administration. Who had suggested? It could only be Colonel Grant, who was a friend, he had said, of Colonel Chase. 'Nine to Five,' thought James. 'It's my fate.'

'Get to Medical tomorrow and then report back.'

James was in a long hut that housed twenty, rather like the hut which was his first home as a soldier getting on for three years ago. None of the men he had been with in Britain were here, but some were fellow sufferers from the ship. On twenty beds, ten to a side, young men sat, listening to the wind fling dust at their shelter.

'Christ, what a country.'

No one disagreed.

They began exchanging news about their two weeks' leave. All grumbled: nothing to do, a couple of 'clubs, so called' making a favour of admitting Other Ranks, a few Eurasian girls, anyone flicking those bints was asking for it, again a shortage of beer, the heat, the heat, the heat.

Then one said to James, 'We hear we're going to have to salute you, sir.'

This was unfriendly. James who had listened to routine criticisms, amounting to hatred, of the officers, realised he was now on the other side.

'So it seems,' he said.

A soldier gave him a mock salute from where he sat. 'Enough of that,' said the corporal.

'Yes, Corporal.'

'Administration,' said James. 'Pen-pushing.'

'Better than square bashing.'

'Oh, I don't know,' said James.

'And how was it at your Colonel's?'

One of the men in the hut had been among the ten, and now James said, 'Ask Ted, he'll tell you.'

'Fucking awful,' said Ted, 'And she's . . .' he screwed his forefinger at his forehead.

'Suited me,' said James, annoyed at the ingratitude. 'I needed a bit of quiet after that voyage.'

'Quiet,' said Ted. 'I'd like a bit of action.'

'Perhaps they'll move us on,' said someone.

'And perhaps not,' said James. And he told them what Colonel Grant had said: some regiments were to be kept in India in case of a Jap invasion.

Groans and curses.

'Roll on the bloody peace.'

In the night, the monsoon arrived and rain battered so loud on their roof that few slept. In the morning the dust of yesterday was in deep chocolate pools where foam scudded as the wind blew The men got to breakfast wet and hot. They went to Medical—hot and wet.

'How's that knee?'

'Better,' said James. It was a lean healthy knee again.

'I see you play cricket. I'll get your name put down.'

The doctor prodded James here and there, and said, 'And now your feet.'

James took off his boots. Liberal applications of a strong-smelling liquid.

'And your sore throat?'

James had mentioned his sore throat to no one but the Colonel.

'It's not too good.'

'Let's take a look . . . yes, I see. It's the dust. But now the rains have come, it'll clear up.'

And how did he know? All the personnel, from the Colonel down, were new to India. All were dismayed by it. 'You'll acclimatise,' said this young man, who had read in his textbooks that one did.

The rain stopped. A clean and well-sponged sun appeared.

Hundreds of young men marched and drilled, drilled and marched, the sweat running under the khaki while the sergeants shouted at them that they had gone soft and useless, but don't worry, we'll see to that.

James was sent that day to Supplies to get a Second Lieutenant's uniform, spent time on new boots, and then was in a hut with one other Second Lieutenant, Jack Reeves, who was fitting books into a shelf when he arrived—so, that boded well.

James now said to his new comrade that he had no idea how to behave as an officer.

'Don't fret,' said Jack Reeves. 'I told the corporal the same and he said, "Just repose on the bosom of your sergeant-major and he'll see you right".'

'Some bosom,' the rejoinder had to be.

And now both young men were in Administration, with fifteen others, under a Captain Hargreaves who in peacetime had been trying to beat the Slump with a chicken farm in Somerset. The war had saved him from bankruptcy. He was a rather loud, blustering sort of fellow, but competent enough. Every morning he arrived in Administration, took salutes, saluted, and then allotted tasks like someone dealing cards. They dealt with supplies of food, of uniforms, of medical supplies; with the movement of men and with transport. Admin knew everything about the camp and its dispositions, and there was in this an agreeable feeling of power, if James's temperament had permitted. But his real life, his secret energies, went into waiting for a letter from Daphne. Almost the last thing he had said to her was, 'You will write, won't you? Promise.'

But had he actually given her his number? Even his full name? Had she ever called him anything but James?

The measure of his disassociation from reality was that it had taken him weeks to realise that he didn't have her full name, and certainly not her address. He could not write to her, but she would somehow find out where he was and write. He trusted her to find a way. It had taken the ship three weeks to get from Cape Town to Bombay. Allow a week—well then, two weeks—for delays; he could expect a letter any day now.

No letter. Nothing.

So he had to write to her. But all he remembered of that four days of paradise was stumbling off the ship into Daphne's arms—that is how it had seemed: a radiance of bliss. A wonderful spreading house on a hillside in a street of such houses, and a garden. A little verandah from where you looked down at the sea, the murdering sea, and where he had danced with her, all night, cheek to cheek. Then that little house in the bushes that smelled of salt, and the waves crashing and thundering all around them.

But no address. Not a number, not the name of the street. The women who organised the hospitality when the troopships arrived, they didn't take account of the name of this or that soldier: they simply despatched soldiers to willing hostesses. How could he find out her surname? The base at Simonstown? Write and ask for the names of the hostesses who had been so kind when the Troopship X was in? . . . Careless talk costs lives. He could not put it in a letter. The censor would have it out.

What was he to do? Never mind, she would write and then there would be an address. Meanwhile he wrote long letters to her, saving them carefully, numbered and dated.

He dreamed of her with an intensity that was like an illness. What he remembered of Cape Town—and with every day the scenes he dwelt on became sharper as he polished them, re-lived them—was clearer to him than this ugly place full of bored young men. This camp!—what a cock-up (so the men grumbled)—even now not all the huts had been built. Some men were still in tents that had been glaring white but now were stained and brownish, where watery mud lapped around the bases and seeped in through ground sheets. Even now gangs of thin little brown men in loincloths—surely cooler at least than thick khaki?—were hoisting up sheets of roofing or running around with hods of bricks. Everything had a look of impermanence, of improvisation. Everything was difficult: food and water, and basic medicines which had to be rushed, if that was the word, by train from Delhi.

There was grumbling over the food. Curries were making their appearance, but what the men wanted was the roast beef of old England, and that made all kinds of problems. The Hindus didn't eat beef, and their cows wandered about, skinny and pitiful but sacrosanct, and beef came from the Moslems. Water was the worst: every drop had to be boiled, or otherwise was supposed to have purification tablets, but sometimes the men forgot. There had already been an outbreak of dysentery and the little hospital was full.

In the intervals between storms of rain the dust dried, but what dust . . . James took up handfuls of it, sifted it between his fingers, a powder as fine as flour. 'The spent and unconsidered earth,' he murmured: that is where Kipling got his line, from the lifeless, fine-blowing soil of India. This soil wouldn't be able to grow the tiniest weed, it was so spent.

He passed requisite time in the Officers' Mess, and its rituals, he was not negligent. He was determined not to be thought an oddity.

And yet he knew he must be, because he sometimes didn't hear when people spoke to him. He was happiest with Jack Reeves, in their hut, reading, or talking about England.

Jack was homesick and said so; James was sick with love, but did not confide in his friend. No one could understand, he knew that.

No letter came from Daphne. Letters from his mother, yes, with messages from his father, heavily censored, but Daphne was silent.

In his position in Administration he learned that another troopship was arriving, not destined to discharge its load at Camp X but at Camps Y or Z; fifty men would arrive here, to replace the twenty-five taken off at Cape Town and the casualties since. There had already been funerals; the Last Post had sounded over Camp X. Some sick men would never be fit for duty and would have to wait until the end of the war to get home. As Colonel Grant had said, India took it out of you.

This camp was so charged with homesickness and longings that it could have lifted up into the air and got home to England without the benefit of ships, or even of aeroplanes—which were for the VIPs. So Jack jested with James: it was a fantasy that was enlivening the camp for a while.

The new arrivals off the unnamed troopship had spent three days in Cape Town: bad luck would have taken them to Durban, but it was Cape Town. James spoke to one, and then another, until he found one who had been a guest, but did not describe anything like the houses and gardens James remembered. Then at last James did, by diligent pursuit, hear that yes, he had got lucky. The man had been whisked off to a house on a hill, with a garden and . . .

'What was her name?'

'Betty, she was called Betty. And what a party, the food, the drink . . .'

'And was there another woman there? A girl with fair hair?'

'There were a lot of girls, yes. What was her name?'

'Daphne, her name was Daphne.'

And now at last James heard: 'Yes, I think there was. Yes. Yellow hair. But she wasn't there much. She was pregnant. Must have popped by now.'

And no matter how James pressed and urged, that was all he could find out.

Pregnant. Nine months. It fitted. The baby was his. It had to be. Funny, he had not once thought of a baby, though now he felt ridiculous that he hadn't. Babies resulted from lovemaking. But that was a bit of an abstract preposition. His lovemaking, with Daphne, what did it have to do with the progenitive? With baby-making? No, it had not crossed his mind. Now he could think of nothing else. Over there, across all that sea, beyond the appalling Indian Ocean, was that fair city on its hills, and there in that house was his only love with his baby.

He tried again with his informant. 'What was the address? Where was the party?'

'No idea. Sorry.'

'What was the fair woman's name?'

'I thought you said Daphne.'

'No, her surname.'

'No idea.'

'Did you get the name of your hostess, the dark one, Betty?'

'I think it was Stubbs!

'No address?'

'Sorry; I never thought to keep it—you know, they just drove us up there and then back again.'

'Is she going to write to you?'

'Who?'

'Betty, Betty Stubbs, is she going to write you letters?'

'No, why should she? There were dozens of us, she isn't going to write letters to every poor sod she invited to a party.'

But James was better off by one name. He had had Betty, and now he had Stubbs. Her husband was a captain at Simonstown and a friend of Daphne's husband.

Bringing himself back from his world of dreams to reality ('what they call reality'—he knew how his state would be criticised, if anyone guessed it) he decided that he could not write to this husband of Daphne's friend Betty and say, 'Please give the enclosed to your friend and neighbour Daphne.' After all, Daphne did have a husband. She had said so. But she could have had two or three husbands and they would not affect the secret life he shared with Daphne and which he knew—she must—share too. No one could have lived through that time and not for ever be changed—that he knew. But he did not wish to harm her.

He wrote: 'Dear Captain Stubbs, I was one of the lucky men who disembarked for four days at Cape Town some months ago. I was the guest of Daphne, who lives next door to you. I would be grateful if you could drop me a line with her address. Sincerely. Second Lieutenant James Reid.'

This innocuous letter, giving nothing away—he was certain—was sent off, through the usual monitored channels. The very earliest he could expect a reply, even if everything went perfectly, was a month, let's say six weeks.

The six weeks passed.

In the intensity of concentration of his dream James hardly noticed that the rains had stopped, the earth was parching, the heat was beating. Outside his hut someone had thrown down a mango pip which had rooted and was already a vigorous six inches of growth. So the soil of India might be unconsidered but it certainly wasn't spent.

James sent another letter to Simonstown. After all, letters went astray, ships sank, his first letter to Simonstown had been like a paper dart with a message on it thrown into the dark.

Months passed. A letter came. It read:

Dear James,

Daphne has asked me to write. She says please don't write again. She is very well and happy. She is having another baby, which will be born by the time you get this, I expect. So she will soon have two children. Joe is named after his father, and if it is a little girl—Daphne is sure it will be—her name will be Jill.

She sends greetings.

With our best wishes,

Betty Stubbs. Daphne Wright

Greetings! She sent greetings! James dismissed the greetings—that is not what she meant, it is what she had to say.

To his intimate memories, little pictures, the two lovely women in their flowery wrappers under a tree, Daphne in a hundred different guises, all of them smiling, he now added Daphne with a little boy, a fair pretty child, absolutely unlike the dark babies with their golden bangles on chubby wrists that he saw on their mothers' hips, on the roads, in the shops, in doorways. When the war was over he would go to Cape Town and claim Daphne, claim his son. He knew he rejected all these pleasant Indian babies because their mothers weren't Daphne.

War is not a continuum, but long periods of inaction and boredom interrupted by fits of intensive activity; that is to say, fighting, danger, death, and then boredom and quiescence again. So the news has always come from the fronts. 'How was the war for you?' 'God, the boredom, that was the worst.' 'But I thought you were at Dunkirk . . . Borodino . . . in Crete . . . in Burma . . . the Siege of Mafeking?' 'Yes, but the bits in between, my God, the boredom, I wouldn't wish that on my worst enemy.' In Camp X boredom was like an illness, one of those diseases where a virus lays your immune system low. Boredom alleviated by a fever of rumour-mongering.

Rumours in wartime: now that's a theme. Prognostications that have the sheen of dreams, bred of terror and loneliness and hope from unlikely places in the human mind, seethe and simmer and then spill out in words from the mouth of some careless talker in a pub or barracks, and then they fly, fly from mouth to mouth, until in no time, a day, a week, the truth is out: 'We are being posted to Y Camp, no, to Z camp, to be nearer when the Japs attack.' 'They're going to attack next week, that's why the 9th Empire Rifles are going up there.' 'We are being sent to Burma—the Adjutant told Sergeant Benton.' 'This camp is too unhealthy, it's going to be closed down and we'll be sent to the hills.' 'They've hushed up an outbreak of cholera.

Keep that under your hat or we'll have a riot. 'They're putting sedatives in our food to keep us quiet.'

Boredom and rumours.

The Japs were closer: they swarmed over Asia, but it was not James's regiment sent to fight them. James's regiment in Camp X, where James dreamed and had his being, was sent nowhere. Life went on, day by uncomfortable day, the hot winds blew about, saliva tasted of dust and the eyes stung and then the monsoon rain . . . the third. 1943. The soldiers saw how Indians came running from their houses and shops and held up their arms to the rain and turned themselves about, singing. No soldiers ran from their huts to stand in the rain; it was their job to give an example, to behave properly, preserve decorum.

Colonel Grant and his lady had invited James to the odd weekend. The Colonel had taken a shine to James, whose diffidence diagnosed things thus: I suppose he likes having someone to talk to about Kipling.

A conversation had taken place. Mrs Grant said to her husband, 'I don't want any more of these Other Ranks. They don't behave. Last time there was vomit all over the place.'

'You exaggerate, my dear.'

'No. They're not of our class, and they don't really enjoy coming to us.'

Colonel Grant suspected this was true, but

he said, 'They're having a thin time of it out here. We should do what we can.'

'I'm putting my foot down, only officers, I'm simply not having it.'

There were hinterlands here. Long ago Colonel Grant had been a clever poor boy who got a rare scholarship to Sandhurst, which, as he progressed up the hierarchy, was proved amply justified. His had been a fine career. But he had not been of his lady wife Mildred's class, not to start with. That is why the Grants had always invited Other Ranks. Not any longer. Mrs Grant was putting her foot down.

'I don't mind that boy, what's his name, James something, he knows how to behave.'

'He's an officer now, my dear.'

'Well, there you are.'

Ten young officers, James one of them, had spent a long weekend with the Grants and behaved well enough, though they, like the earlier guests, took themselves off into the town's clubs.

James did not.

Colonel Grant said to James, while they sat companionably on the verandah, a tray of tea between them, 'James, tell me, what is the talk in camp, about things in general?'

'You mean, being kept here in India, doing nothing?' This was direct, and it was bitter, and not only on his own account.

'Yes, what are they saying?'

Now the Colonel must know what 'they'

were saying, since his friend Colonel Chase heard it all, in the Officers' Mess. Had he forgotten James was no longer with the ordinary soldiers?

'When I was in with the men, there was a lot of grumbling. They don't like it. But you know, the men grumble about everything.' Yes, the Colonel did know, he hadn't forgotten. 'It seems to me, sir, that the men dislike officers as a matter of form . . . but is that what you were asking?'

What Colonel Grant was asking came from many levels and motives in him. He and Colonel Chase had sat together, talking intemperately—for them—about disaffection, and feeling that they were out of touch.

'In the Officers' Mess—is there bad feeling? Dangerous bad feeling?'

Since Colonel Chase heard the kind of thing said, this must be a question of interpretation: and James was startled.

'I don't like politics, sir, I never did.'

To say that, straight out, wasn't something he would have done in the mess.

He had, at the beginning, said, 'I'm not interested in politics,' as he might have said, 'I don't take sugar in my tea.'

He could have said he was Conservative, or—daringly—that he intended to vote Labour, but not, that he was uninterested, any more than in the time of, let's say, Luther's Theses, someone might have said, I'm not interested in religion.

To be not interested in politics: that meant he was callously indifferent to the fate of humanity, at the very least misinformed. On that early evening a dozen young men set themselves to inform him. And so he had evolved some polite ways of indicating interest without committing himself.

But this explosion of interest in his lack of proper feeling had made him think back to the glorious days of 1938. Now he knew that the intense political feeling of that time had not been the nation's usual condition. Mostly left-wing feeling. There had been a boiling up of political thought, because of the Spanish Civil War, because of the Slump and the poverty, because of the threat of the coming war and so there had been all those politics, mostly left-wing. He had gone through it listening, but reading poetry.

In the Officers' Mess most of the young men were left-wing, in various ways, but the talk was—loudly—about India. The young officers, not the older ones. The whole sub-continent was effervescing with talk of freedom, freedom from Britain, and here, in Camp X, their main task was to suppress it.

What had Colonel Chase said to Colonel Grant? He would have talked of troublemakers, Bolshies, even communists. About the Fifth Column, and possibly there might even have been talk of courts-martial.

'You may not like politics, James, but I don't imagine you can avoid them.'

James said truthfully, 'I never think about it.'

Now the Colonel protested, in an old man's aggrieved voice, 'Does what we've done here in India mean nothing to you? We've built all these fine railways, we've built roads, we've kept order . . .' He had to stop. Order was not the word for what was happening now: agitators everywhere, the Congress, people in prison. Then, 'Does the British Empire mean nothing to you, James?'

'The Captains and Kings are going to have to depart, sir, that's what I think.'

'I see, and you don't care.'

James might have said that if he were in Daphne's arms the whole bloody British Empire could sink into the sea.

He said, 'Well, sir, I don't imagine what we think about it will make much difference to what happens.'

And now his voice was full of trouble. One reason why he didn't like to think about politics was that if he did he had to think about the war, and that meant being engulfed in horror, an incredulous, unbelieving, protest that this war was happening at all. He knew that he dreamed about it, the enormity, the weight of it.

Colonel Grant looked sharply at the young man, whom he had been ready to convict of unfeeling. But no, that was not it, there was real pain there, and those blue eyes, which the Colonel thought of as English, were unhappy.

The Grants asked James and some others, one of them Second Lieutenant Jack Reeves, at the height of the hot season, for a week in the hills. They took the long slow train up into the hills and found themselves in a little cottage, that had English flowers in the garden. The winds blew cool and fresh and there was no dust. The villas and houses were called Elm Place, Wisteria Lodge, Kent Cottage, Hollyhock Close. Mrs Grant, no longer flushed with heat, though the neck of her dress showed a raddled red vee, revealed herself as an unremarkable, non-complaining hostess, but with a tendency to fuss, perhaps because she was feeling guilty. 'James, you really must take care, I heard you coughing again last night. And you too Jack, here's some linctus.' The Colonel, evidently and touchingly relieved by his wife's return to normality, could be seen looking at her with—was that actually affection? Concern? *Love?* The young observe their elders' marriages with politeness and a secret resolve never to marry; or, 'If I do it won't be to anybody like that old bag'.

The walks up here were pleasant. There was riding. James didn't ride but the others did. Simply to sit and breathe clean air was a treat. Down in the plains, in the heat, at Camp X, they were sweating as they stood, and it was impossible to sleep. Soon, too soon, these four soldiers would be back down in it, but in the meantime . . .

James sat on the little verandah with a book and sometimes the Colonel sat with him. There was a wistfulness about him now that James, schooled by long observation of his father, had to recognise as regret. 'It is a sad thing,' the Colonel observed, more than once, 'to have spent your life doing a job you thought was worthwhile and then you find you're not valued.'

Colonel Grant was lonely: that was James's discovery on this holiday. But he had a wife, didn't he? Well, yes, he did, but . . . Presumably he had cronies? Now James thought of his father and knew he was lonely: he came to his father's loneliness by way of Colonel Grant's. Yet there were the old soldiers' evenings in the pub, and he did come home to a wife—with whom he did not talk. What would Colonel Grant like to say, if he could, and to whom? Was his troublc only a need to grumble about not being appreciated? No, there was something deeper there and James knew how to respond, in his thoughts at least: after all, he could never speak to anyone about his real self. And his father: what thoughts was he holding safe, in his silences?

Even when the Colonel was not there, James was not alone. In the bungalow ('Butler's Lawn') was a young English couple with a child, a little boy, just walking, or rather, staggering, with his ayah always on the watch. This little creature had taken a fancy to James, perhaps because of the young man's interest in him, and from the verandah of his house he watched James, who was standing watching him on the verandah of the next house. The ayah took to bringing the infant over, to play his new games of crawling, and sitting, clambering up and sitting, while James, tucking his long legs well aside so as not to impede the child's efforts, was as ready as the nanny to prevent harm. The child did not like sitting on laps, but he did like standing in front of James, legs apart, and then sitting, *thud*, on his padded bottom, and laughing, and getting up, assisted by James. All this the Colonel watched and so did Mrs Grant. Not usual for a young man to bother with an infant.

'Do you have brothers and sisters?' enquired the Colonel.

'No, I was an only child.'

'Perhaps that accounts for it . . . that child really does like you—look, Mildred.'

And Mrs Grant stood in the door, briefly, to commend the young man, who could have done without the attention. He would have liked to be alone with this little creature, roughly the same age as his child, far away in South Africa. He wanted to persuade the little boy to sit on his knee, so he could look close into those blue bright eyes and perhaps hug him, feel the warm energetic body—hold this child and think of his own. But the ayah never let him out of her sight.

The Colonel sat with his old legs stretched out, his old hands trembling a little, a glass of whisky beside him, watching the young man and the child. His sons were grown up and were about the world, soldiers, one in danger in Burma. The Colonel was perhaps remembering his own children as attractive imps of promise, contrasting them with what they were now, as the old tend to do, when he saw this little lump of love, clutching at James's knees as he fell back, to save himself, laughing and crowing with delight. On the Colonel's face the tenderest smile. And on James's face too.

'When the war is over it will be your turn,' said the Colonel to the young man.

It is my turn already, exulted James privately, while he said, 'Yes, sir, I hope so.'

Time passes . . . well, it does, one has to acknowledge that, but it does not pass evenly, and that quite apart from the everyday phenomenon of the different pace of time at three years, thirteen, thirty, sixty, ninety, which we all experience. Time moves differently in different places: in Camp X it crawled.

Colonel Grant, appealed to (tactfully) by James as to whether there would ever be a prospect of being sent somewhere more interesting, replied only that 'They had to be always ready for trouble wherever it appears.'

'Trouble' was already not only evident, but increasing, even if you didn't read the papers or listen to the wireless. 'Troublemakers', as the Colonel put it, were increasingly at their work, and 'disaffection' was everywhere like a heat rash.

Companies from Camp X were sent to 'deal with it'. James, too, more than once. He did sympathise with the soldiers grumbling openly that they were expected to fight an enemy, not to 'put down' Indians. Jack Reeves, too, said he was a bit of a Red, but was even more so now he was seeing the Raj at work.

A song was being sung everywhere in Camp X, not only by the Other Ranks.'

What did you do in the war, Dad?
I kept the Indians down,
Yes, we kept the Indians down . . .

Complaints and grumbling at Camp X were alleviated in one way by the arrival of an Entertainment Officer—Donald Enright, now Adjutant Enright—but exacerbated in another because Donald was an open and proselytising Red.

That these hundreds of bored young men needed entertainment no one could deny.

Donald was pleased to see James, but surely not as much as deserved a year of companionship? Well, he had had acolytes since. He was now a large, assertive, extrovert young man, full of bonhomie and goodwill. Wherever he went he was in the centre of a loud group. He moved about the camp collecting admirers like—well, like a politician.

He at once organised a concert party using an impressive number of the troops, but the audience was bound to outnumber performers by many times to one. James was roped in: he was a girl, but this did not bother him at all: not for him the protests and bad jests obligatory at such moments. In his mind he often embraced the loveliest woman in the world, and he was the father of a delightful boy child. He surprised himself and the audience with his vigorous interpretation of a coy maiden. Jack showed a talent for this kind of thing and was soon writing sketches for Donald. Then Donald put on Priestley's *They Came to a City,* that play which during the war more than any other embodied idealistic and perfervid dreams for a better life. He ventured on Shakespeare and *Twelfth Night.* The soldiers went to see it because there was nothing better to do, but were persuaded that they enjoyed it. Some did.

They Came to a City sparked a demand for debates. The first was: 'A Socialist Britain'. A noisy success. Soon Donald had lectures and debates going as well as concert parties. He organised a library—how, no one seemed to know. He begged and borrowed books, failing to return them; he went into the town's clubs and posted up notices begging for books. When there was a demand for a book on a socialist economy, and no such book was in the camp library, he actually wrote a thick pamphlet himself and got it cyclostyled in fifty copies—there was a paper shortage, so he scrounged and probably stole paper.

At all debates and lectures a Political Officer was present, taking notes. The debate, 'Quit India *Now*' (Now being somewhat hypothetical: 'There's a War On—didn't you know?') was the theme of a letter to the camp newspaper, which Donald seemed to have taken over. When people complained that he was running a one-man show, he said, 'Right, then, why don't you muck in? Come on—start a camp newsletter, we could do with one.' The complainer did start a newsletter, the gossip of the camp, but it languished and soon Donald was running that.

Donald was summoned by Authority and told that there were limits and he was testing them. No more lectures on the political situation in India—understood?

'How about a series on the history of India?'

'Fair enough,' Authority agreed.

But did not history include the British contribution, he argued, blandly, when taxed about the titles of the last three lectures: 'Clive of India: The Flag Follows Trade.' 'The East India Company.' The British Empire: Gain or

Loss.' Once again, standing to attention in front of a bench of senior officers, he argued that he had been given permission for history, hadn't he? He was sure he had. Captain Hargreaves, who had said in Administration that he thought the India lectures were just the ticket, he could do with more of that, supported Donald, who asked why was it not in order for British soldiers who were fighting for democracy to hear the arguments on both sides? So he argued, pleasantly, the model of earnest willingness to serve.

The lectures went ahead, the Other Ranks making an issue of it, attending them in force: it turned out that two of the lectures were being given by senior officers who were experts on this very subject. And at the question and answer sessions Donald stood up to say that it was not for them to reason why (the poem had appeared in his newspaper): they might listen but on no account could they express their thoughts.

This was an impertinence so fincly honed that Authority was at a loss what to do, but around the camp flew the rumour that severe punishment was being planned, using the extreme penalty for sedition.

Real rebellion, if not sedition, did simmer. Years of boredom and the appalling heat were raising everyone's moral temperature, and even without Donald's inflammatory presence, all through the soldiers' huts, Other Ranks were arguing about their own role in all this, the role of the British Army.

Donald put on *As You Like It.* Who would have recognised in this flirtatious not to say winsome Rosalind the serious unsmiling young man whom everyone tended for some reason to leave alone. He didn't drink much; he didn't shine at the Officers' Mess; he did play cricket well enough; when it was his turn to be camp librarian he was helpful, full of information. He was friendly with Other Ranks, who seemed actually to like him. And here he was, being applauded as Rosalind.

From the Sergeants' Mess came a little bouquet of flowers with a card, 'To Fair Rosalind'. And the obligatory obscenities. If the sergeants played their traditional barking punishing role on the parade ground, they were tending toward good humour and even behaviour that could be described as avuncular, off it. The long ordeal of Camp X was wearing them down: 'Like a mother to us,' jested some young officers, for, no longer under the rule of the sergeants, but their nominal superiors while obeying their advice in everything, they could afford to jest. This jest reached the ears of Sergeant Perkins, who came into the hut occupied by James and Jack, saluted, and said, 'Right, then, if I'm your mother, then I have to say the condition of this hut is a crying shame. Better clean it up before Captain Hargreaves gets to hear about it.'

And, saluting, he went out.

The senior officers were in a dilemma. They knew all about the sedition that was brewing, even if it was sporadic and disorganised, and they knew that Donald was a focus. But boredom was the parent of this mischief and Donald combated boredom. Without him things would be worse. It was a question of balance. When the senior officers attended debates and lectures, it was not—as the paranoid soldiers believed—to spy on them but because the officers were as bored as they were. 'The Atlantic Charter Unmasked', 'Whither Egypt'. 'Imperialism Past and Present'.

In James's desk was a calendar where a big red cross marked the birthdate of his son, Jimmy Reid. He had worked out the babe's probable entrance to the world. He secretly celebrated the child's first birthday and then his second. Another visit to the hills, with the Grants, allowed him to see the two-year-old, an explosion of charm and mischief. He adored that little boy and when he left the hills he had to hide tears. It is not possible to feel the pain of loss unchanged for ever. James's grief had mellowed; it was there, but no longer was able to lay him low at a sound, a voice, the colour of the evening sky, a line of poetry, a bird's call. He had not realised how much this cherished love, or grief, had diminished, but leaving that child it all came back, and Colonel

Grant was reminded to say again, 'Easy does it, James. Take it easy.' And Mrs Grant, 'How nice it is to see a young man taking an interest in children. Well done.'

Those of us who have lived through such a time, the interminable time that need have no end—so it seems—know that what is left behind of the three, four years of endlessness is fear of being trapped again. But what is to be done about war?—tangling people in nets of circumstances. Nothing. Soldiers in India—who would have thought it, let's say in 1939, as the war was being adumbrated in rousing speeches, that one of the results would be hundreds of thousands of young men, stuck like flies on a flypaper in India—not to mention Rhodesia, South Africa, Canada, Kenya, defending the bad against the worse. No one in 1939 wrote a poem beginning, 'Now, God be thanked Who has matched us with His hour'. Donald Enright actually managed a lecture, 'Defending the Bad Against the Worse', and was reprimanded. 'But we're fighting for democracy!' he beamed at his superior officers, who frowned at him, uneasy, as unwilling to grasp this problem as they would be to take up a fistful of hot coals. He was a wonder, this Donald Enright, with his concert parties and his Shakespeare and his lectures. Who could deny it? 'We told you before, you're sailing too close to the wind.' 'Yes, sir, I'm sorry, sir. I was rather thinking of a debate on "Problems of the Peace, Socialism or Capitalism?" Would that be in order, sir?'

You could look at Camp X, stuck there in the middle of India—looking with a non-military, un-imperial eye—as an arbitrary aggregation of hundreds of young men, united only by a uniform. Which is how at times they saw themselves. Take this ditty, emerging somewhere from the collective unconscious of the camp:

There's a war on,
You tell us they say there's a war on,
But where's the war, the bloody bloody war,
Clean your boots,
Check your kit,
Stand to attention,
Stand at ease,
Mind your Q's, mind your P's,
There's a bloody war on.

Several hundreds of young men kept together by the uniform and the merest framework of discipline, the prescribed measures of saluting, the Yes Sirs, the No Sirs, the drills, and meanwhile months—no, years, now—of the upper ranks and the Other Ranks too made equal (almost) by a hundred non-military occasions, the concert parties, the theatre shows, the lectures: surely this must have frayed the fabric of discipline into ineffectiveness? Not so. First, the rumour:

We're being sent north-east to fight the bloody Japs. At once it was as if the whole camp snapped to attention. Then, the hard fact. It was true. Camp X fizzed with elation, they might be going off to a festival, not certain danger and possible death. At last, they would justify themselves, the whole bloody lunacy of their being here at all would make sense. James, too, as excited as the rest, but then, brought down: his name was not on the lists: he was not going.

He sat in Administration behind his desk, all other desks but one deserted. At each desk a typewriter, folders, loose papers stirring in sluggish air from a dozen ceiling fans that chug-chugged like motors, and James's mouth was a hard ugly line and he looked as if he hadn't slept. Captain Hargreaves was here to calm and to defuse, because it was in Administration that faces like James's were to be expected.

Second Lieutenant Reid and Captain Hargreaves were on Jimmy and Tommy terms except for sometimes, like now.

'Tommy,' began James, still sitting, but saw his superior officer's monitoring frown and he stood up. 'Sir,' he said, 'it isn't fair!

Captain Hargreaves merely smiled, but James persisted. 'It simply isn't fair, it isn't good enough—sir.'

Why me? could have come next, but shame suppressed it.

‘Someone has to stay and keep things going, you know that, Second Lieutenant. We can’t just march off and leave the place empty.’

James was quivering with the arbitrary injustice of it all.

His senior officer went on, ‘There will be ten of us left in Administration, and some for Other Duties.’

James remained at attention.

‘They also serve who only stand and wait,’ offered the captain but went red because of the bathos. He stood up.

‘Are you going with the rest, sir?’

‘Yes. As it happens. I am.’ And he escaped.

Later, walking across to the Officers’ Mess, James encountered Major Briggs, who saw from the young man’s state that he must stop, so he stopped.

James saluted.

‘I know what you are going to say, Lieutenant. But someone has to stay. And you are good at it. You can blame yourself if you like.’

This joke fell well short of its target. James knew he was good at it. Pen-pushing and Admin: that’s what he was good at.

‘They also serve who only stand and wait . . . but you won’t be doing much of that. You’ll be working pretty hard, I’d say.’

‘But perhaps they don’t serve so much, sir?’

‘No, I wouldn’t say that.’ And the major put an end to this miserable conversation, because he knew how he'd feel, left behind in Camp X. James saluted. He saluted. That was that.

Off went the division, in long trains and many lorries. Camp X was nearly empty. Those left behind to hold the fort drank bitterly in the various messes, and talked bitterly about their luck.

James sat alone in Admin, with all the fans going and dust swirling about outside.

'Darling. My darling Daphne. If you only knew how I rely on you. If I didn't have you to think of now, with what has happened to me, then . . .' And he described his situation. 'And so I'm stuck here and the division has gone off, and my regiment. I often wonder, what was the point, all that time training in England, and then I missed the first Normandy invasion and Dunkirk, and we weren't sent to Africa, and I might just as well have faked an excuse, my knee would have done, or gone down the coal mines. I sometimes think that would have been better. But then I wouldn't have met you and that is what matters, the only thing that matters.' And he repeated the refrain of his love for a page or two. Then, as always, he told her what he had been reading. 'I found a lovely poem. Of course you must know it. It is called "Deirdre". By James Stephens? It makes me think of you. "But there has been again no woman born/Who was so beautiful; not one so beautiful/Of all the women born." Deirdre and Daphne. And you are a queen. My Queen

Daphne.' And so he raved on for a page, then another, until it was time to go to the Officers' Mess for dinner and the News.

Their regiment was in the thick of it, up in Manipur and Kohima. There had been casualties.

Weeks passed and back came the soldiers, not elated now, all that had left them, but they had been through it and looking at each other's faces could see how they had all changed.

Jack Reeves was wounded and in hospital. Again James lost his friend. Sergeant Perkins would be decorated for conspicuous gallantry. A few killed. 'Reasonable casualties for what was achieved; we threw the Japs out of India.'

But it did look as if the war was coming to a close, in Europe, at least. There would be an end. Soon. In Northern Europe it is when spring is on the horizon in the shape of longer days and earlier dawns that people subside into depression or think of suicide. Similarly now, with peace actually coming nearer every day, Camp X seethed and boiled with discontent. 'So near and yet so far' was the tide of a poem in the camp newsletter. With the refrain, 'So near to them, so far to us'—*them* being the senior officers, who so often were to be observed taking off in Dakotas for Home. Officers and VIPs.

Donald put on *Romeo and Juliet,* and James was Romeo, a male part at last, astonishing everyone, and added several letters to his pile of them to Daphne, which he would post when censorship was over.

He also gave a lecture on Modern Poetry, while Donald sat proudly listening, for he was remembering how much James was his creation. And James said so: 'I owe you a good deal,' he said, 'don't think I'm ever going to forget it.'

'Oh, jolly good show,' said Donald.

The end of the war in Europe, so now they could go home—but when? Oh, no, not now, don't think it, the ships will be full for a long time yet, you must take your turn, it's not only you, but the RAF boys from all the far-flung parts of Empire, so many impatient young men, not enough ships, wait, wait, you've stuck it out for nearly four years, haven't you? Just be patient a bit longer.

Not all could, or did. In two other camps, where they had been told they would be kept here, in India, to 'maintain order' to 'contain unrest' to 'combat sedition' to 'preserve the British Empire', disaffection broke out.

'We didn't join up to do the dirty work of the British Empire.' 'We joined up to fight Hitler.' 'You were called up and you will do as you are told.'

Speeches, real riots, and the camps were a-boil.

A couple of soldiers, 'hot heads', 'incendiaries', were court-martialled, but the

Authority had listened, had taken heed. In Parliament at Home, questions were asked and speeches being made. And so the soldiers were going home.

Some, who remembered the bad time they had had on the ship coming to India did not look forward to the sea voyage home. But this time it would not be around the Cape, the long long journey, but through the Suez Canal.

But James had dreamed of making landfall at the Cape (though luck might just as well have taken him to Durban), and finding Daphne and his son and . . . there his thoughts became hazy. Yes, of course she had a husband, but she loved him, James, and there was such a thing as divorce, wasn't there? The main thing, what he had to hold on to, was his child. His son—there could be no doubt about it, a love child, there could never have been more of a child of love than his and Daphne's. Jimmy Reid, now four years old.

Hundreds of young men who had seen no more of India and the Indians than what they observed of life on the roads, in the bazaars, or the networks of amenities that surrounded the army—servants, Eurasian girls who were spoken of by the sahibs and memsahibs as if they were so much dirt, or the Indian soldiers in the army who intermeshed hardly at all with the white army, or the cleaners at the camp—these young men left India without regrets, at best thinking that the war had given them a glimpse of what travel might be. They filed on to the ship that was to take them away from a continent they saw as thoroughly unwholesome and unsavoury. But this voyage could not be as terrible as that other; only half the length, and they were going home, Home, which shortened the distance. It was rough, and hot, particularly through the Suez Canal, and in the Bay of Biscay, as was to be expected, the waves chopped and churned and tossed them about and they were sick, but home was in sight—and there they were, at last, the white cliffs, as Vera Lynn had promised.

'How was your voyage?' asked his mother, and James, 'Oh, not so bad, could have been worse.'

On a dirty and rattling train James travelled through a land without light, so it seemed, a thin drizzly dark and faint blurs of light, and then in his home town, the street lights were dim and the windows, if not blacked out, showed parsimonious glimmers, and he was watching his feet as he walked. When he switched on the light on the stairs his mother said, 'Please, only when you have to; and on the landing a faded notice said, 'Save Electricity—Don't Switch It On'. His old room, where he dropped his kitbag unopened, to get down faster to his parents, was small, well, it always had been, but it was so dingy. The supper was in the kitchen because leaving the oven door open heated the room; once his mother had made a point of eating 'properly' in the dining-room. The three sat around the table which had a vase of autumn leaves on it, and Mrs Reid boasted that she had got 'under the counter' liver from the butcher, in honour of his coming home. She served three thin lengths of brown meat like leather straps, with onions and potatoes. James had told himself, having grown up, that his father was not an old man, but though he was not much over fifty Bill Reid was an old man now, with a fuzz of white hair around a red face. James's mother was polite to him and smiled all the time. Her embrace when he arrived seemed embarrassed rather than warm. 'You have filled out,' she said. But she could not stop smiling and tried to blink away tears when he noticed them. His father, silent as ever, kept pushing the dishes of vegetables at him, nodding Help yourself, but while his eyes were moist too, he could not talk, even say, 'Thank God you're home,' so the dishes of vegetables had to do instead. 'Have some potatoes,' said Mrs Reid. 'At least we've got plenty of those.' In the dim kitchen the three sat eating and smiling, and felt so powerfully for themselves and for each other that it was a relief when James said he was tired. He left his mother sitting under the light, the radio switched on, crocheting something, and his father went to the pub.

'He's got to tell his mates you are home,'

she said.

James stood at his bedroom window and looked down at the darkened town. In India lights glared and blared, shadows moved blackly as the sun did, defining the hours. He had returned to a lightless land.

He at once got a job at the Town Hall, but not starting at the bottom, because of his years administrating Camp X. It was a good job. He stayed in his room a lot, reading, ate the meals that were less even than the meagreness he had been brought up with: rationing suited his mother's nature; she enjoyed eking out the bacon ration and making the meat ration stretch. The drear and dark of post-war England—well, he was home, and that was all that mattered. He thought of India and did not like his memories. Except for Jack Reeves, with whom he had exchanged addresses, and Donald, and Colonel Grant—and of course, the little child of those two visits—he did not care to remember India, which was not so much a place as an emotion of holding on, sticking it out.

Alone in his room, the door locked, he read his letters to Daphne. It took hours. He did not see how he could send them: suppose they were intercepted? Suppose her husband . . . no, he would give them to her himself. When? Just as soon as the war's enormous damage had been absorbed and everything had settled down.

He met Donald, who was already well up the ladder that would take him into politics. He visited Jack Reeves, and Jack came to him for a weekend. He joined a club and played some modest and likeable cricket. And he married Helen Gage, who had been a land-girl and enjoyed it: he could see, when he told her how he had longed for the end of the war, she did not understand, though she said she had too. She was a pretty, healthy young woman, tough and strong after her years of hard labour, and his mother was delighted. She had been afraid he would not marry, or marry late, she had not known why, but that had been her secret dread. She had been afraid of another silent man thrown out by war, a man who could not speak of what he had known. James was not communicative: he did not have much to say about India. But in the ordinary affairs of life he was easy enough—normal. His wife would not have to wake in the night beside a man thrashing about in a nightmare.

He told Helen that he had had a fling in Cape Town and that a child had resulted. She was married. When travelling was easier, he was going out to see. In fact, he had gone up to London to ask about travelling within a week of getting home. There wouldn't be air travel for ordinary people for some time, or only for people who could pull strings: did he have strings to pull? No, so he would have to wait. It was not only the soldiers and airmen who were still coming home as the ships became available but everybody was on the move or wanted to be, after years of being stuck because of the war, or because of new jobs abroad. He could reckon on a good wait. Months, no: years, more like it.

It had already been years. He had learned how to wait. Love like theirs would keep, existing as it did out of time. There would be Daphne's white arms welcoming him and the years in between would be forgotten.

Helen asked him how old his love child would be by now. Generous of her to use the word, and he kissed her for it, before telling her the exact age: years, months, days. Helen had had no cause until now for so much as a moment's doubt: this was her first shock and it was a bad one. She had touched something deep and dangerous, and she knew it: this was like one of those doors you carelessly open in a dream and find a house, a world, a landscape, wider, larger, brighter or darker than the one you know. Almost, she broke off the engagement then and there. His face as he told her was one she had not seen before, set, inward-looking, into a world she was not going to share. This moment put in high relief other feelings she had had about James, not easily articulated. She did not try now. She thought, But I've got him, haven't I? *She* hasn't. He says he loves me. And she certainly was very fond of him. She had had her adventures too.

Wartime is productive of 'flings', not to mention broken hearts. Her heart had not been broken, or anything like it, but one of the men she had loved, if briefly, had been killed in Normandy. She knew she had got over it, but while she confessed to James, she broke down, much to her surprise, and wept, finding herself enclosed in his arms. She was weeping not so much for a man but for lost men, her lover, her brother (lost at sea), a cousin (at Tobruk), and then there was a friend, a fireman, killed in the Blitz—unlived lives.

He comforted her, she him, but she knew that something was biting at his heart she was not going to know about. How old? 'Nearly six—five years, eleven months, ten days.'

A wedding, restricted by post-war shortages.

They did everything right. Every Sunday they went to lunch with James's parents, and they visited her parents, who lived far away, in Scotland, for holidays. They had a child, a girl, named Deirdre, because of James Stephens' poem about the Irish queen. Helen liked this poem but joked that it was asking a lot for their little girl to be as beautiful as that. But Deirdre was pretty enough.

Eight years after the war ended James told Helen he was going to South Africa. He could have gone before, but that would have meant a ship, and he would never set foot on a ship again—never. It had to be the air, and when they could afford it. She knew there was no point in minding. He never mentioned his other child unless she asked, but then he promptly told her, 'He is seven years, three months, ten days,' or whatever it was. Sometimes she checked just to see if that invisible calendar was still running there, in him, marking . . . but she did not know what. This was not merely a question of a child's exact age.

James's plane descended at Khartoum, Lake Victoria, Johannesburg, with leisurely time at each for refuelling, restocking. This cumbersome trip seemed to him miraculous, when he remembered that other voyage. Then Cape Town, spread out over its hills, surrounded by sea. He found a modest hotel from where he could look down at the sea, the now innocent sea, full of ships, one being a passenger liner sparkling with new paint. Then he put a thick paper parcel under his arm and walked up through streets he remembered not at all to what he did remember, the two ample houses side by side in a street of gardened houses. On the gate where there should have been the name *Wright*, was the unknown *Williams.* The gate post for next door was still *Stubbs.* He retreated across the street to stand under an oak, and he looked for a long time at Daphne's house, which in his memory lived as zones of intensity, the little room he had been given, Daphne's bedroom, and the stoep, all else being dark. On to the verandah—the stoep—came an old woman, with a book. She sat in a grass chair, put on dark glasses, and gazed down at the sea. There was no sign of other life. Then he as carefully examined Betty's house, of which he remembered only the garden. He could see movement through the windows that opened off the verandah. A maid? A black woman with a white headscarf. But he couldn't see her properly. He moved across the street, cautiously pushed open the gate, and stood under the tree which he remembered spreading over trestles, full of food and drink, and a crush of people—soldiers. The companion tree in the other garden would live in his mind for ever because of the two beautiful young women, one dark, one fair, standing in grass, under it, wearing flowery wrappers.

Someone had come on to the Stubbs's verandah. A tall woman. She shaded her eyes to peer at him and came slowly down the steps towards him. He did not know her. She stopped a few paces off, let her hand fall, and looked forward to have a good look. Then she straightened and stood, arms loose by her side, in a pose it did seem he remembered. A tall thin woman. She wore a short well-fitting blue and yellow dress in small geometrical patterns, with a narrow gold-edged belt, and some little gold beads. Her face was thin and sunburned and her dark hair was waved in neat ridges. On one thin wrist hung a gold bangle. Yes, now he knew—it was the bangle—this was Betty. She spoke: 'What are you doing here?'

This question seemed to him so absurd he only smiled. He thought that the stern face—she was like a headmistress, or the manager of something—almost smiled in response, but then she frowned.

'James—it *is* James?—then you must go away.'

'Where is Daphne?'

At this there was a pause, and then a quick expulsion of breath—the sigh of someone who has been holding it. 'She's not here.'

'Where is she?'

She came a step closer. He was thinking, already afflicted with anguish, that this tall dry uncharming woman had been that lovely creature he remembered as all dark flowing hair and loose soft gowns.

'I must see Daphne.'

'I told you, she's not here.'

'Where is she?'

'She doesn't live here now.'

'I can see that. It's on the gate. Is she in Cape Town?'

A tiny hesitation. 'No.'

So, she was lying. 'I could find out where she lives.' This was not a threat, but a reminder to himself that he was not dependent on her for information.

She was agitated now, she actually raised those brown thin forearms, pressing the long dry hands to her chest. James,' she said, urgent, appealing, afraid. 'You mustn't do this. Why are you doing this? Do you want to ruin her life? Do you want to break up her marriage? She has three children now.'

'One of them is mine.'

She did not seem inclined to dispute it. 'You just turn up like this, turn up, as if it's nothing, you just *arrive* and . . .'

'I want to see my son. He's going to have a birthday, his twelfth birthday.' And he recited his son's exact age, years, months, days.

She closed her eyes. Her lids were white against the tan of her face. She was breathing deep: she was shocked. He waited until she opened them. Betty had deep brown eyes, he remembered, brown kind eyes in a smiling lightly tanned face: he had thought of her as 'a nutbrown maid'. Well, there were the eyes, and there were tears in them. Not unkind, no, they were still kind.

'James, do you want to ruin Daphne's life?'

'No. I love her.'

'That's what you'll do if you go on with this.'

'I want my son.'

'But you *must* see . . .' She stopped. That sigh again, almost a gasp. Oh, yes, she was frightened all right. But she was on guard, fighting: she was protecting her friend.

'Do you still see her?'

'Of course. She's my best pal.'

He produced his great lump of parcel: the

letters. He held it out.

'What is that?'

'My letters. I've written to her, you see. I've always written to her. In the war there was the censorship. Then I didn't want to—cause trouble. So I brought them.'

She didn't take them from him.

He stood obdurately there, holding out the parcel: the force of his demand caused her hand to come towards it. She hesitated, then took it. 'Will you give them to her?'

'I suppose so.'

'Do you promise?'

They stared at each other, then her gaze lowered to the parcel.

'Yes, I promise.'

'My son,' he urged. 'It's my son. I think of him . . . yes, all the time. Perhaps he will come and visit us in England?'

'You're mad. Yes, you're mad. Yes, you are.'

But she held the parcel against her chest.

'You've promised,' he said.

She backed a couple of steps, then turned and ran for it, but over her shoulder she said, 'Wait, just wait there.'

He waited. He did not look at all at the verandah where the old woman now read her book, the dark glasses pushed up to her forehead.

After a good twenty minutes, the maid emerged from inside the house, white apron, white headscarf, a worried face. She stopped in front of him and held out a large envelope. There she stood while he tore open the envelope. She was peering to see what she could. From inside the house came a voice from the invisible Betty. 'Evelyn, Evelyn, I want you.'

Taking her time, her eyes never leaving the envelope, the maid turned and went off, sending back slow thoughtful looks over her shoulder.

Inside the envelope was a sheet of writing paper and scrawled on it, 'Please, please, go away. Go away *now*. Please. Don't hurt her. This is your boy.'

A photograph, a decent size for a casual snap, of a boy of about eight, standing by himself, legs apart, smiling. This picture was like one of himself, James, at about the same age. Black and white of course, so you couldn't see what colour his eyes were. But if the rest was like James, then why not the eyes? And Daphne had blue eyes.

He took his time putting the photograph back, and then the sheet of paper. He stood smartly to attention and saluted the invisible Betty, who was watching him, he knew. He went off down the street, slowly, keeping in the shadows from the trees, as he had learned to do in India where the heat struck and burned, was not kindly, as it was here.

It was late morning, a fine Cape day, and over the famous mountain thin loose cloud lay, white and shiny. The famous tablecloth. Down he went, sending distracted looks to the sea shimmering peaceably there. He walked clumsily, people were staring. He sat on a bench in some public place but then got up and walked on, found another, sat down, pulled out the photograph and looked at it, for a long time.

He could not stay still. He began aimless fast walking, and found himself in some kind of market, where under trees long trestles were laden with every kind of dried fruit: peaches, apricots, pears, plums, apples, yards and yards of them, every trestle with its attendant woman, who was black or brown, at least, not white. Fruit pale yellow, burnt umber, purple, black; fruit red and pale brown and gold and rosy and green. Some was crystallised, colours glowing though a frosty white crust. A vision of plenty. He picked up a greengage, put it in his mouth, heard a shout from the vendor, realised he had to buy, and bought a couple of pounds of mixed crystallised fruit. 'Helen will like this,' he thought.

Off he walked, went up streets and down them. They were full of people, but he did not see them. He sat on benches and looked at the photograph of the boy who might just as well be himself, at that age, put back the photograph, walked on. His feet had the devil in them, he could not keep still. Dusk came.

He was in streets that smelled spicy and hot: it was the Malay quarter, but Cape Town in his mind did not define itself in areas, it was a spreading smiling city, a Cape of Good Hope, radiating welcome, like the stamps he had as a child. He saw a stall, bought a sticky bun, ate it, standing up, while the Coloured man told him he had to pay for it. Oh, yes, that must be Afrikaans, he supposed, and gave the man a fistful of money. Then it was dark and he was in a public garden and he saw a bench and at once fell on it and bent sideways in a tight clench of his whole body. Pain had finally overcome him. He was afraid of crying out, and of people coming, so he stayed not moving, aching all over because of the tension of his position.

He was thinking of Betty, in her unlikable smart matron's dress. That scene was already in the past, gone, and if he did not choose to remember it, it was non-existent. Why was that realer than the one he loved to see in his mind's eye, the two beautiful women under the tree? Because it was more recent? Both were bright scenes, whose every detail he could recall: one of them, to him, was the truth. And he was thinking of Daphne, somewhere in this city, perhaps not more than five minutes' walk away. Yet nothing and no one could be more distant. Nearer to him were his memories of her.

He became aware that someone else was on

the bench. He did not look up.

She, however, was looking at him: Annette Rogers, who had finished her shift at the Fairview Hotel, a good hotel, and was interrupting her progress home as she did every evening on this bench. Her situation at home was to say the least unsatisfactory, and before she could face it, she needed to strengthen herself. This man here, was he ill? His face was white, his lips pale, from compression, his eyes were closed, and everything about him was tense and awkward. 'He must be stiff in that position,' she thought, and leaned forward and said, 'Hey, excuse me, I don't want to butt in, but are you ill?'

He shook his head, not opening his eyes.

She moved closer and lifted his tense hand which went limp in hers. It was cold. It was a fine warm evening. She continued to hold his hand, trying to take his pulse without his noticing. But he did notice and said, 'I'm all right.'

All right he evidently was not.

Unhappiness was something she was used to: you could say she had a talent for it. She began examining him for clues. His clothes were good: now, that was a really smart jacket, it must have cost a bit. His trousers were of fine cloth. His shirt—no, he wasn't short of enough for a meal. But his face, it was simply awful, perhaps it was a death, if it wasn't money . . . she moved closer and put her hand on his shoulder. Then something about him licensed her to put her other arm under his head. She was cradling him, hardly knowing how it happened. She was now getting anxious on her own account. Her jealous husband—suppose he chanced to come by and see her holding another man: she could count on a few bruises to pay for that. But she continued to cuddle this unknown man, and said, 'Hey, listen, don't let yourself go like this, it only makes it worse.'

He opened his eyes: blue, a strong blue even in this dusking light. He said, 'You see, I'm not living my own life. It's not my real life. I shouldn't be living the way I do.'

This complaint may be made, or thought, by all kinds of people; demands on Fate, or on God, that are everything from the reasonable to the preposterous; ('Oh, I wish I'd never been born!' 'I wish I'd been an aristocrat in the eighteenth century.' 'I wish I hadn't been born a cripple!) but the most frequently heard is the one instantly recognised by Annette Rogers. It made perfect sense to her. *Her* life certainly wouldn't include a violent husband, a senile mother, and two out-of-control teenage children. *Her* life—but she had several variants of her dream—her favourite life was a little house right on the edge of the sea, like those you could see if you took a trip out of Cape Town, and she would live there with a man whose features she did not specify, though she knew he was kind. A kind man, and they would live there quietly, in good humour, and eat fish, grow vegetables and have fruit trees.

'To know you're living the wrong life, not your own life, that is a terrible thing.' And now he began to weep, dry sobs, while she sat holding him together. She had to get herself back home, she had to, otherwise she was going to catch it, oh, yes, she could count on that. But she did not desert her post.

Annette was a tall stout woman, with dry fair hair in a roll on her neck—Betty Grable; her husband ordered her to keep it like that. She wore sensible shoes, which she needed for work, managing a whole floor of the Fairview, which kept her on her feet all day.

Now she hauled up this man, using strength, because he was stiff from sitting in that twisted pose. She put her hand into his arm and steered him through bright cheerful streets to his hotel. The Seaview. Surely he could do better than that, with those clothes!

He had left his parcel of fruits behind on the bench, which would be found later by a tramp.

She stood with him while he composed himself, and pushed the door open and stepped into a poorly lit and dingy lobby. She approved of his self-command, which was taking him to the desk for his key, and up iron stairs which would not have been out of place in a warehouse. She knew he would not turn and smile, or indicate he knew she was there:

he was too deep inside, dealing with whatever it was that was eating him. 'I'd give a good bit to know what's eating him, but I never will!' She caught a last glimpse of a wretched face.

And she went home, two hours late.

As for him he had no picture in his mind of the kind unknown who had, so he felt, held him together. His memory of Annette Rogers was of arms holding him: the haven of an embrace.

James and Helen continued their exemplary life. He was now in charge of a department at the Town Hall, and the wellbeing of a good many of his fellow citizens depended on him. She was prominent in all kinds of local charities. He played cricket. She taught gym and modern dance. They were members of a Ramblers Club and went for long hikes with their daughter, who was doing well at school.

James's father died. His mother at once turned off the radio, put her knitting and crochet into a drawer and let her house. She took trips all over the British Isles and then to Europe. With a group of merry widows, she went on long sea cruises or to exotic isles, by plane, sending postcards back to James and Helen. He had a carton full of them.

Not a letter came to their house without his quick glance at it. Helen knew what he was waiting for. She let him know she understood. He tried to be first at any telephone call. He had shown her the photograph of the boy who was as real to her as the ones she had seen of her husband, as a boy.

There was another trip to Cape Town and she said she would go with him. He did not demur.

Deirdre had changed, it seemed overnight, from a friendly and sensible girl into a vindictive, spiteful, cruel creature they did not recognise. 'Hormones,' murmured Helen. 'Oh, dear!' Deirdre was invited to go with them to Cape Town and said she would rather die. 'I want you *out* of my life,' she shouted, in one of the formulas of 1960s' teenage rebellion. 'I'm going to live with my friend Mary.' Judging that this stage might have passed by the time they returned, James and Helen set off without her, relieved.

By now the planes flew to Salisbury, then Johannesburg; the two glamorous stops in between had gone.

In Cape Town they were in a good hotel: James insisted on one high enough for a view of the sea.

Helen was enchanted by the Cape, for who is not? They drove up the coast, the incomparable coast, they visited gardens, and climbed Table Mountain and drove about through vineyards. James took her where he was pretty sure he remembered trestles full of fruit of all kinds, of all colours, but could not find it: stern hygiene had intervened.

She saw how he looked carefully at every

face, in gardens, in the hotel, in streets; and she did too, she was looking for a younger version of James. He would be a young man now, a very young man, like the photographs of James, in uniform.

Day after day: and then James said they should go to the university. It was term time. And they walked about everywhere, looking at every youngster who passed: Jimmy Reid, James the younger, walking towards them, or in a group, or with a girl. That was one day and then James wanted to go again, for another. After that, it would be time to leave Cape Town.

Helen said to him, 'Look, James, you mustn't give up. One day there'll be a letter, or a telephone call, or we'll open the door and there he'll be.'

He smiled. She didn't know of that thick pack of letters. He was certain Betty would have kept her promise: she *had* promised. Daphne would have read those letters to her which contained the best of himself, his essence, his reality, 'what I really am'. She must have read them. But if she had told her son, *their* son, then by now there would have arrived that letter, been that phone call, the ring at the door. He was twenty. Twenty and so many months and days. If he knew, he was old enough to make up his own mind.

'You'll see,' said Helen. 'It'll happen one of these days.'

They were lying in bed, and she knew what he was thinking, because he was staring, as he so often did, into the empty dark.

He put his arm around her and drew her to him, in gratitude for her kindness, her loyalty to him, her love. But he was thinking, a deep, secret, cruel thought: 'If you want to call *that* love.'

We hope you have enjoyed this Large Print book. Other Chivers Press or Thorndike Press Large Print books are available at your library or directly from the publishers.

For more information about current and forthcoming titles, please call or write, without obligation, to:

Chivers Large Print
published by BBC Audiobooks Ltd
St James House, The Square
Lower Bristol Road
Bath BA2 3BH
UK
email: bbcaudiobooks@bbc.co.uk
www.bbcaudiobooks.co.uk

OR

Thorndike Press
295 Kennedy Memorial Drive
Waterville
Maine 04901
USA
www.gale.com/thorndike
www.gale.com/wheeler

All our Large Print titles are designed for easy reading, and all our books are made to last.